THE NEWEST CALAMITY

"Why are you here, Tressa?" Townsend asked.

I shook my head and water flew from the tangled mass. "What do you mean? I came to retrieve my property from a demented little toadstool," I said, squeezing more water out of my hair.

"But what brought you to the hotel in the middle of the night?" Townsend asked, and I knew what he wanted to hear. And the sexually frustrated part of me wanted to tell him what he wanted to hear.

"*You* did," I found myself saying. It was, after all, the truth.

"I did?"

I nodded. "I was...concerned," I said, picking my words carefully. But then what had seemed like a certainty when I was lying in bed now seemed fanciful at best. I took a deep breath. "I think someone is after Kookamunga."

CALAMITY JAYNE
HEADS WEST

KATHLEEN BACUS

LOVE SPELL NEW YORK CITY

LOVE SPELL®

October 2007

Published by

Dorchester Publishing Co., Inc.
200 Madison Avenue
New York, NY 10016

ISBN-10: 0-505-52733-2
ISBN-13: 978-0-505-52733-2

The name "Love Spell" and its logo are trademarks of Dorchester Publishing Co., Inc.

Printed in the United States of America.

Visit us on the web at www.dorchesterpub.com.

For my dad, Buck, who bequeathed me his love of horses and John Wayne movies, a penchant for practical jokes, and—no trifle here—a tall, lanky frame that made it so much easier to walk like a trooper.

Thanks, Daddy Buck, for everything.

Love you lots.
'Parnelli'

CALAMITY JAYNE
HEADS WEST

CHAPTER ONE

A plane is on its way to Phoenix when a blonde in economy gets up, moves to the first-class section and sits down. The flight attendant watches her do this and asks to see her ticket. She then tells the blonde that she paid for economy and that she will have to sit in the back. The blonde replies, "I'm blonde, I'm beautiful, I'm going to Phoenix, and I'm staying right here!" The flight attendant goes into the cockpit and tells the pilot and copilot that there's some blonde bimbo sitting in first class who belongs in economy and won't move back to her seat. The copilot goes to the blonde and tries to explain that because she only paid for economy she will have to leave and return to her seat. The blonde replies, "I'm blonde, I'm beautiful, I'm going to Phoenix, and I'm staying right here!" The copilot tells the pilot that he probably should have the police waiting when they land to arrest this woman. The pilot says, "You say she's a blonde? I'll handle her. I'm married to a blonde—I *speak* blonde!" He goes back to the blonde, takes off his hat, bends over and whispers in her ear. She abruptly stands and says, "Oh . . . I'm sorry," passes her hand through her hair and moves back to her seat in economy. The flight attendant and copilot are amazed and ask the pilot what he said to make her move. The pilot just grins. "I told her first class isn't going to Phoenix."

I know what you're thinking. Everybody loves a good dumb blonde joke, right? Uh, think again, pilgrim. I hear them so often I see them acted out in my dreams at night. There's the one about the poor, dumb blonde tied to the railroad tracks. Her biggest concern? That the oncoming train will change the part in her hair. Or the blonde who tripped over the cordless phone and sprang a leak in her silicone implant. Or the blonde who spent twenty minutes staring at the orange juice can because it said "concentrate." What a laugh riot. I'm doubling over here, folks. You?

My grandma—a blonde before her hair turned the color of toilet-bowl cleaner—swears blonde jokes are part of a vast brunette conspiracy. You know. It's a by-product of the Blondes Have More Fun ad campaign that fueled the fires of discontent of envious brunettes everywhere and put blondes forever in their mahogany-colored crosshairs. Yikes!

Blonde jokes are the bane of my existence—along with my hair, which could do double duty as a scouring pad. They're like bunions are to my gramma. Come to think of it, blonde jokes seem to have been around just as long as my gammy's bunions. Hmmm. I wonder if there's a connection.

Some folks swear I'm living-and-breathing inspiration for my own cockeyed collection of dumb blonde jokes—an assertion I downright dispute. My official position on the matter? Prove it. I will ante up being somewhat notorious in my little hunk of heartland heaven, though. My name is Tressa Turner. Tressa Jayne Turner.

But thanks to a drop-dead gorgeous ranger named Rick, who is the only guy I know who can make my heart go pitter-patter one minute and give me indigestion the next, to my hometown homeys in Grandville, Iowa, USA, I'm better known as *Calamity*.

No, not *that* Calamity Jane—although I do like to think she and I have a few things in common. For one, we're both cool cowgirls with a bit of a rebellious streak thrown in to keep things interesting. Two, we're devastatingly attractive to men. Well . . . okay, you caught me. I admit I'm not your traditional beauty queen material—although I was State Fair Rodeo Queen runner-up one year. But for all I know, the original Calamity Jane was so homely that even horseflies wouldn't look at her twice. With her sidearm skills plus that harmless little ol' rebellious streak I mentioned earlier, I doubt anyone was foolhardy enough to suggest she was any less purty than a newborn filly with four white stockings and a matching blaze on its head. Unless they had visions of suicide by a Wild West sharpshooter, that is.

I'm your basic twenty-first-century, cute cowgirl type. Born and raised in small-town Iowa, I grew up loving horses, dogs, John Wayne movies, and beef—sadly for my hips and thighs, not always in that order. Growing up I always thought I'd have made a kick-ass Mattie Ross in the film version of *True Grit*. Well, except for that hideous bowl cut the actress had going. And that scene in the rattlesnake den? Big-time deal breaker.

Iowans worship John Wayne. Maybe because he was born in Winterset we feel like Duke was one of us. Simply say the word "grit," and John Wayne with an eyepatch pops into our heads.

Being from rural Iowa is both a blessing and a curse. In a town as small as Grandville—population: seven thousand—you have a sense of community and kin-ship pretty much impossible to replicate in larger cities. Someone dies in Grandville, the family gets enough casseroles, pies, and mac and cheese to feed the Carlisle Septuplets for a month.

That close-knit connection, however, comes with a cost. It's almost impossible to get by with much of anything that the entire population doesn't know all about. That's not a bad thing when you've made the dean's list or the state basketball tournament, but it's not exactly ideal when you have a history of misadventures that in-volve murder, malicious mischief, moldering mansions and matrimonial madness. (Not my matrimonial mad-ness, thank goodness. Just in case you're wondering.) In the last twelve months I've played hide and seek with a dead body, tag with a felonious dunk-tank clown, cat-and-mouse with a chiller-thriller author, and college-edition Clue with a campus criminal.

Uh, no. Funny you should ask. I'm not a cop by pro-fession, although I have spent a respectable amount of time in various law enforcement interrogation and in-terview rooms lately. I'm a journalist. Kind of. Sort of. Of the aspiring variety. A jill-of-all-trades—that pretty much describes my colorful and varied job history. I've worked my way through enough different voca-tions that I finally feel somewhat confident I've discov-ered what I want to be when I grow up. I'm just finding it a wee bit of a challenge to be taken seriously as a professional print journalist when folks still recall the time my horse crapped in the mayor's open con-vertible at the Fourth of July parade. Or when I made the front page of my employer's biggest competitor's newspaper dressed as the Wicked Witch of the West and doing the tango with a geriatric Van Helsing. It would be fair to say my nickname's been harder for me to live down than *Gigli* for Ben and Jen.

In between working as a cub reporter at the *Grandville Gazette* and as assistant chief cook and bottle washer at my Uncle Frank's Dairee Freeze, taking (and passing) college courses and getting my best friend married off, I'm also posing as fiancée to one very large and very mysterious felon—I mean fellow—much to the dismay of one certain ranger-type. To further complicate matters, I'm still attempting to decide if Ranger Rick Townsend, an Iowa Division of Natural Resources officer who would set a sales record for *Midwest Outdoors* if they stuck him on their cover, is the man for me—and if I'm the conflicted cowgirl for him. Sometimes I'm convinced that I could never settle for any other guy. Other times, I'm equally certain the studly ranger could never settle for just one gal. Sounds like something from my grandma's daytime TV shows, no? *The Days of Our Celibate Lives. The Carp Cop Casanova and the Confused. Ranger Romeo Meets Calamity Jayne.* Sigh.

While we're on the subject of relationships, it appears my seventy-year-old gammy is about to sample the joys of sex on a rather more frequent basis than her twenty-four-year-old granddaughter. How sad and pathetic is that? (Uh, no need to respond. That question was your basic rhetorical one.)

Things get even better. Gram's fixin' to hitch her wagon to a long-in-the-tooth *Townsend,* no less. My Grandma Turner recently became engaged to Joe Townsend—Ranger Rick Townsend's grandfather! Now, don't get me wrong. I think the world of ol' Joe. He was the Van Helsing I was tangoing with last Halloween in that photo. It's just that some even scarier mental images pop into my head when I think of Joltin' Joe, a senior citizen with a James Bond complex housed in a Pee-Wee Herman physique, getting it on with my gammy, who, in her younger days, was known as Hellion Hannah. My grandma collects anatomically-enhanced fertility statues—think Priapus on Viagra—never skips those hot, steamy sex scenes in romance novels—okay, she even highlights them for quick and easy reference later, and reads them out loud to me in the evenings—and I probably have her to thank for bequeathing me her predilection for getting into pickles. And we're not talking the kosher kind here, folks.

As a result, I'm just a teensy bit tense. Okay, so I've actually developed this rather unbecoming nervous twitch that has on occasion been confused with a grand mal seizure whenever I ponder these nuptials. Especially considering a good chunk of the Turner/Townsend clans were headed to points west to formally celebrate the auspicious union.

Considering the dynamic duo's history of doing their own thing—which usually spells trouble for Tressa—I'd initially supported a long engagement. "Take your time," I'd encouraged, reminding them that the glow of true love can often diminish when confronted with whiskers on the sink (Joe's, not Gammy's . . . I hope), and panty hose on the curtain rod (Gammy's, not Joe's . . . I hope), and toenail clippings on the nightstand. (Gotta level with you, folks. This one here's a toss-up.)

With my gramma taking up residence with me last fall, however, I must confess the idea of her moving out of our shared double-wide trailer outside Grandville and into Joe's residence morphed into a dangling carrot this little blond bunny was finding very hard to resist. Coupled with the thought of helping Gram pack up the phallic statues in the living room, and an opportunity to have intimate encounters of my own without worrying my gramma would wander in wearing nothin' but her dentures and wooly socks, said dangling carrot was now dipped in chocolate and coated with colorful candy sprinkles.

Wedding plans were hastily made, but I was having none of attendant duties. I'd just finished a stint as maid of honor for my friend, Kari, and that hadn't gone real well. Trust me on this one, folks. When you can use the words "strip club," "raid," and "attempted murder" as matrimonial scrapbook moments . . . well, you don't want to go there. Or, I didn't.

As a result, Gram insisted her daughter—my Aunt Kay—must perform that role. My dad's twin sister lives in northern Arizona. Aunt Kay is a media specialist at the Flagstaff Public Library. Her husband, my Uncle Ben (yeah, like the rice) is an art professor turned artist. His work is regularly sold in a pricey little art gallery in nearby Sedona, an elite tourist community with upscale souvenir shops and an eclectic collection of yummy eateries.

(I suppose this is as good a time as any to mention that I enjoy food. I manage to avoid rampant obesity only by virtue of the fact that I usually hold down a minimum of two jobs, feed and care for a small herd of horseflesh, and look out for two hairy golden labs big as miniature horses that, unfortunately, leave the watchdog duties to me. And living with a senior citizen who loves a walk on the wild side even if she has to use a walker to get her there, and who is about to hook up with a fellow AARP member with a gift for sticking his nose where it doesn't belong, I burn calories more efficiently than my Uncle Frank's new ninety-three percent energy efficient Dairee Freeze furnace burns heating fuel.)

So, Gram and Joe agreed to a short civil ceremony at our local courthouse to "make it legal," after which the entire family was fixing to fly out to Phoenix for a small but tasteful exchanging of vows that would take place in Flagstaff. As an added incentive, Gram and Joe had insisted the entire family join them to celebrate on their weeklong honeymoon cruise and, as Gram put it, "help the new blended family bond." I'd begged off, citing one how-low-can-you-go bank balance, two bosses, five critters and ten post-Easter pounds, compliments of a serious, long-term Cadbury Crème Egg addiction that made the idea of squeezing into a swimsuit and showing off what spills out around the edges about as appealing as helping my gammy wax her mustache . . . or any other part of her body for that matter.

I finally caved when Gram and Joe went ahead and purchased my nonrefundable passage—my birthday and Christmas presents from them for the next five years—and I found out a certain ranger with a certain booty that a certain cowgirl fantasizes about seeing in a bright red Speedo . . . or on a nudes-only beach somewhere—was to be a fellow passenger. I've said it before and I'll say it again: Contrary to what you may have heard, Tressa's momma didn't raise no dummy.

"So. You packed yet?"

I was in my bedroom at the open door of my closet, staring at hangers that held too many khakis from too many days employed at Bargain City, a local discount chain store; assorted T-shirts with cute cowgirl slogans for leisure time; hoodies, jeans, and low-rise slacks for the newspaper. I turned to discover my gramma in the doorway. With white beauty cream slathered on her face and her hair in a shower cap, she looked like something from *Scary Movie*'s 60th Reunion.

"Does underwear count?" I asked.

"Underwear?" My gammy's eyebrows met above her nose.

"You know, the garments we wear under our clothing to protect our modesty—and the sensibilities of the seeing public. You did pack underwear, didn't you?" I asked.

"Guess I'm not done packin', after all," she said. I winced. "You better get a move on. We leave Saturday," she reminded me.

"I'm not sure what to take," I replied, frowning at my closet contents again.

The last time I'd packed for an extended trip I'd been about fifteen. It was our last family vacation. My brother, Craig, had just graduated and was about to head off to college, so the folks thought we needed a final family fling. Paw Paw Will had died the previous winter, and the folks thought the trip would do my grandma some good. Me being . . . well, me, I'd packed a nice assortment of chocolate bars in my suitcase. (You know: Have chocolate, will travel.) Outside Wichita, the AC in our car went out. By the time we hit our hotel that night, my sister Taylor had gotten carsick four times and Gramma had to stop six more times for calls of nature. And my suitcase? Well, let's just say if I'd dressed in any of the clothing I'd packed, Willy Wonka would've been all over me. Not a pleasant mental image. Unless, of course, Johnny Depp was Wonka.

The next day we blew a tire in Amarillo, lost the hubcap along I-40 somewhere near U.S. Highway 38, and at a rest area just outside Albuquerque my dad got stung by a swarm of killer bees in the men's restroom. At that point he was ready to nuke our little farewell road trip and turn around and head right back to good ol' Grandville. There, if you lose your hubcap within the city limits, you'll generally find it propped against the stoplight pole at the intersection of Highways 18 and 6, waiting for you to retrieve it.

"What do you mean you don't know what to take?" My gammy stepped into the room and a glob of face cream dropped from her chin to the rug. "You take clothes. Makeup. Sanitary supplies."

I made a face. Considering her box of bladder control briefs presently taking up space under my bathroom sink, I didn't exactly want to discuss toiletries.

"Clothes? What clothes exactly?" I asked, motioning at my closet. "I have khaki slacks, blue jeans, T-shirts, and no time to shop." No money either, for that matter. Even working two-plus jobs, I always seemed to be borderline broke. I often dream of the day when I won't have to view my bank statement through slits between my fingers like I do horror movies at the theater.

"What about dresses? You got any dresses in there?"

I gave my grandma a one-eyebrow-raised look. Since my gammy took up residence with me, she's had her head stuck in my closet more often than I have. She knows exactly how many cowboy boots I own, how many of those she can wear without breaking an ankle, becoming lame, or suffering a flare-up of her plantar fasciitis, how many pairs of religious underpants I possess, (the *holey* ones—amen!) and how many pairs of too-tight designer jeans I'm holding on to for the day I finally lose ten pounds and am able to slide them up over my hips and zip them without snagging little tummy rolls with the mechanism in the process or resulting in that excess skin-spillage-over at the waistline commonly referred to as "muffin top." As much as I adore muffins, that is not a cool look.

"Why ask me? You know my wardrobe better than I do," I told Gram. "And, dresses?" I waved a hand in her face when she joined me at the closet and performed a little bow. "Uh, you do recognize your oldest granddaughter, don't you? The girl who wore the same dress to her best friend's rehearsal dinner she wore to her grandfather's funeral. Who popped out of her maid of honor gown when the preacher was asking the bride and bridegroom to exchange tokens of their affection. Who spends what little spare time she has hay-baling or on the back of a horse. Besides, I don't even know what kind of weather I'm packing for," I added. "It's bound to be warm in Phoenix, but seven thousand feet up in elevation, it could get nippy. Plus, there are those pleasant little monsoons to think about."

Iowans like to think they coined the phrase, "If you don't like the weather, wait ten minutes," but believe me, the sharp contrasts in weather you could encounter in a two-hour drive north on Interstate 17 from the valley into the Arizona mountains could really mess with your head, Fred. And your packing, too.

I also found myself uneasily thinking that weather was the least of what could jump up and bite us in our little westward-ho wedding wagon train.

"Well, you can't come to my wedding in blue jeans or those baggy gray sweatpants you wear around the house," Gram told me, sliding hangers across the pole in my closet with a shake of her head. "You need help, Tressa," she finally said. "You need to go on *Oprah* and have one of them makeovers. You know. When they stick gals up there with no makeup and ratty clothes and wearing the wrong bra size, then they hand 'em over to that fine Nate What's-his-name to work his magic."

"Uh, newsflash here, Gram. Nate's a home decorator," I told her.

"He is?" she asked.

I nodded. " 'Fraid so. He does bedrooms and baths, not bad hair and baggy boobs."

She shook her head and returned to her perusal of my wardrobe.

"All I know is that by the end of the show the gals have gone from looking like bag ladies to bitchin'. And their nipples aren't rubbin' their waistlines anymore." She looked down at her own bosom. "Think I could use one of them lifts?" she asked. She started to unbutton her blouse.

"No!" I shook my head and pulled her hand away. Gram had a proclivity for sleeping in the buff, so I'd already gotten enough glimpses of wrinkled, sagging flesh to almost scare me off junk food. Almost. Either way, I'd seen quite enough to render judgment in the matter.

"No, no. You don't need a thing, Gram," I assured her. "You've got a lovely figure for a woman of your . . . er, stature," I finished. "Just lovely."

Osteoporosis had robbed my gammy of several inches, and her brittle bones had snapped at the wrist and ankle in the past. She'd moved in with my folks several years ago after the fall, but had improved though weight training and calcium supplements. It was then she'd decided she'd done her time under the watchful eye of my mother and moved back to her home—the double-wide trailer she'd given to me. It was right around Halloween. I know. Scary.

"Besides," I added. "Remember what you said about Helene Dixon when she had breast surgery? You said if she tried to run, she'd blacken her own eyes."

"The ol' fool. She oughta known better," Gram muttered, rebuttoning her blouse while I took a deep breath of relief.

I continued surveying my clothing. Shorts and tank tops for the cruise were no problem. It was the wedding and related functions, and pool-side apparel that had me stymied.

"Maybe Taylor has something you could borrow," Gram suggested, not for the first time. I had the unladylike uncouthness to snort.

"Taylor the twig?" I said. "Yeah. Right. I might be able to get one-half of one leg in a pair of her slacks—and I'd have to grease up with petroleum jelly to stand a fighting chance," I told her. "And you know our taste in clothes is worlds apart." Sadly, as my sister and I often were ourselves.

Two years younger than me, Taylor looks kind of like a younger version of Catherine Zeta Jones. On the dean's list at the University of Iowa for two years studying psychology, she up and quit at the end of her second year. Now she works at my Uncle Frank's Dairee Freeze and lives at home while she decides for sure what direction she wants to take with her life. Okay, okay. I know that sounds an awful lot like a personal history I'd be up close and personal with, but I swear to you Taylor and I are nothing alike. The gulf in our relationship is like a little chasm you might know as the Grand Canyon.

"I wish I could figger out why you and your sister don't get along," my gramma said with a disgusted look at me. Or maybe it was at my closet. "Why, my sister was my best friend when we were girls. Still is," she added.

This one got my attention. Growing up, my grandma and her older sister's bickering had made for some interesting family reunions.

"What about the time when you were ten and Great Aunt Eunice chased you around the town square with a pair of pinking shears trying to give you a haircut?" I said. "And there was that time she said you took after her with a ball bat." At Gram's expression I added, "It *was* a plastic wiffleball bat like you said, right?"

"Schoolgirl high jinks," Gram said, turning her back on my closet, apparently coming to the conclusion that my wardrobe was a lost cause. Like I hadn't warned her.

"What about the time you got into a deviled egg fight at the church potluck?" I asked.

"More youthful shenanigans," she said.

"It was last spring."

"Eunice knows I've got her back," Gram said. "Any time she needs me, all she has to do is pick up the phone and call. You know. Like that song says."

"Which song?" I asked.

"That one about a bridge over water," she said, heading toward the door and the way she'd come in.

"I thought that song was about drugs," I said.

"Exactly." Gram shuffled out of the room.

I shook my head.

Go west, young woman! Go west!

I wondered if I could exchange my airline ticket for a less dangerous destination. You know, like the Bermuda Triangle.

CHAPTER TWO

An hour later I'd given up on packing for the moment, showered and headed to the newspaper office to finish up a few things before I left for my very first vacation in way too long. I parked my ol' not-so-reliable Reliant in the small lot behind the office, and headed for the back door.

I generally like to conduct a quick sweep of the building upon entering—you know, like the Secret Service does when a bigwig is coming to town—unless or until I get the green flag from Smitty, the *Gazette* sports and graphics guru and all-around good guy. Stan Rodgers—publisher, editor in chief, and the big boss man—is known for his mercurial moods. Unfairly, most of the time I'm the one who gets credit for triggering his little episodes.

I suppose I should tell you that my employment at the *Gazette* has been a little like my gramma's cholesterol numbers: up and down, up and down. I've actually been fired by Stan twice. But both times were so not my fault. You tell me: Is it my fault the boss's wife's dear Aunt Deanie's obit pic looked more like a Mr. Stubby Burkholder? And that typo in the Quik Lube ad with the picture of the local mechanics, arms crossed and grinning, that read: *We're here to service you* instead of *serve you?* Like that wouldn't have gotten past you, too.

Thankfully, Stan is first and foremost a man of business. When I came to him with my dead-shyster-in-the-trunk story last year, he was eager to give me a second—uh, third—chance. Okay, so I sort of blackmailed him into taking me back. Still, it worked out for everyone in the long run. As it happens, I have a certain nose for news that comes in handy when you're a reporter type. And Stan just wants to sell newspapers. It's win-win.

I'm also learning to exploit Stan's little idiosyncrasies to my advantage. This knowledge recently nabbed me some tuition assistance, a raise in salary, and office equipment that didn't qualify for *The Antiques Roadshow.* After I'd successfully completed two college journalism courses, Stan the man made good on his promise to replace a bow-legged card table he'd had the chutzpah to call my desk, a chair that could serve double duty as an interrogation tool at Guantanamo, and a computer that froze up so often it should be sitting alongside the ice cream cakes at Uncle Frank's.

I crept in the back door of the newspaper office, silencing with one hand the stupid little bell Stan had stuck on it last week to alert him of comings and goings. I spotted Smitty bent over ad copy in the layout room.

"Red, green, or amber?" I whispered.

"Amber," he replied. "Proceed with caution."

"Roger that," I told him with a crisp salute, then scurried over to my little corner near the back. I ran a hand across the top of my "new" desk—in reality, a cast-off from one of the local schools—and sank into my brand-new, black leather, ergonomically approved desk chair. And dropped so fast I almost smacked my chin.

"What the heck—?" I focused on my computer monitor, but had to lift my chin so high to see it that the back of my head touched my shoulder blades and my wrists bent at unnatural angles to access the keyboard. Hello, carpal tunnel!

"Who's been sitting in my chair?" I roared, feeling like a character from "Goldilocks and the Three Bears" but looking like one of the seven dwarves. "Okay, who's the smartass with too much time on their hands?"

A shadow fell over the top of me. Searing hot breath warmed the part in my hair.

"You rang?"

I found my new chair suddenly twirled merry-go-round style, stopping just this side of Vomitville so I could confront the culprit. I gulped when I discovered Goldilocks in this vignette stood over six feet tall, had flaming red hair and hands the size of Papa Bear's paws.

"Oh. Hey, Shelby Lynn." She was the high school homecoming queen I'd teamed up with last fall to get the goods on a reclusive best-selling author. And I'd just solved the *who's been sitting in my chair* whodunit in record time. How do I do it?

"Long time, no see," I said.

"You were at my graduation party two weeks ago," Shelby Lynn reminded me.

I nodded. "Which reminds me, I never got a thank you for my gift," I told her.

Shelby Lynn frowned. "You didn't give me a gift," she said. "Oh, wait. That's right. I remember now. The Dairee Freeze 'Buy One Slurpee, Get One Free' coupons that expire at the end of June. Gee. Thanks. You shouldn't have."

I winced. Between the local cops threatening to write an inspection order for my Plymouth unless I replaced two tires they claimed were bald as my boss's shiny head (okay, so I'm paraphrasing) and an unexpected veterinary bill for one of my pooches, May had been a lean month.

"Still, I suppose I do owe you for recommending me to Stan as your replacement," Shelby Lynn went on.

I blinked. Whoa, Nellie. Replacement? What replacement?

"Come again?" I managed.

"You did recommend I fill in for you, didn't you?" Shelby Lynn said, a glint in her eye that wasn't there before. "Knowing how much it would mean to me to have this kind of job experience to put on a résumé, and knowing how much I would give for such an opportunity, and how badly I want to be published someday. Considering I gave you a hell of a story last fall, I just know you thought of me as soon as you found out you'd be on vacation for two weeks. Right, Turner?"

If possible, I felt my body sink even lower into the chair. The truth was, I hadn't even stopped to consider that they'd need someone to cover for me. It wasn't as if Grandville was a journalistic utopia, a hub of never-ending news. Last June's hometown murder mystery had been an exception. At this point in the year—too early for state fair features and too late for school news—Stan generally relied on people to either kick the bucket or pop out a kid, the baseball and softball teams to at least be competitive, and an occasional weather event—either flood or drought; Stan wasn't picky—in order to fill his pages.

"About that recommendation—" Shelby Lynn loomed over me.

"Happy to do it!" I said, jumping up and motioning toward the chair with a flourish. "My pleasure! You just have a seat there and make yourself right at home on my new ergonomically designed chair with easy-lift feature. Go ahead!" I shoved the girl referred to as Sasquatch by people far braver than me into my chair. "Be my guest! Try out my customized computer, nineteen-inch flat panel monitor and executive keyboard pad!"

Shelby turned a wary eye on me, a puzzled look on her freckly face. I get that look a lot.

"Oh, and don't be afraid to put your feet up on the tiny little footstool I handpicked and keep under the desk there," I continued. "Enjoy. Enjoy my hard-earned perks while I just touch base with our boss for a second." I stopped, took a step back and cocked my head to one side, surveying Shelby's length in my chair. "Bless your heart. Don't you just look all . . . all Monica Lewinsky there."

"Huh?" Shelby Lynn said.

"Oh, you know what I mean, Little Miss Intern. Be right back," I said, and reached out and pinched one of Shelby Lynn's cheeks. "Oooh. Just look at that face," I said, and moved off before my own face cracked from the brittle smile I'd plastered on it.

I found Stan in the break room, his back to me, sticking coins in the pop machine, about to make his selection.

"You wouldn't be thinking about getting ready to push a button for 'the real thing,' now would you, Stan?" I asked, propping a shoulder against the doorjamb. "I could swear you promised your loving wife you'd switch to diet soda after your recent physical," I said, raising an eyebrow in challenge. "And what's that in your hand—a candy bar?" I clicked my tongue against the roof of my mouth a couple times. "Stan, Stan. What would the little woman say?"

The *Gazette* publisher's neck turned dark red, so it

was a safe bet his face was the same brilliant color. Stan turned, spotted me in the doorway, and frowned as he doubled his fist and smacked the diet cola button with the side of his hand. The soda dropped with the same velocity as would the good stuff that's not so good for you. With a snarl, Stan retrieved it.

"For your information, I actually like the diet pop better," he said, popping the top and taking a long swig. Unfortunately, he couldn't quite hide the gag reflex that followed. He made the face I imagined I made whenever I bit into a piece of gristle. Or my gammy's soy meatloaf.

"Such obvious enjoyment is truly a sight to behold," I said. "And now I know just what to give you for your birthday this year. So, do you prefer can or bottle?"

"What the hell do you want, Turner? To heckle me about my diet?"

Diet? What diet? I shook my head.

"I only heckle on Tuesdays. And every other Thursday on karaoke night at the East End Lounge," I assured him. "No, this is Wednesday, and Wednesdays are Twenty Questions days."

Stan blinked. I noticed he hadn't taken a second drink of his cola.

"Twenty questions? What do you mean?"

"Wow. You catch on quick."

"I do?" he asked.

"You're a natural, Stan," I exclaimed.

"I am?"

"You've played this before, haven't you?" I asked, narrowing my eyes and giving him a closer look.

"Played what?"

"Now, stop that! It's my turn," I said. "Okay. Ready? One, why did I almost slice my chin open on the edge of my desk just now? Two, why did you tell Shelby Lynn I recommended she fill in for me? And three—

why didn't I know about this arrangement before now? Okay, now it's your turn. Answer."

"One, you're a klutz. Two, Shelby Lynn assumed, so I gave you the credit. And, three, I'm the boss. That's why. I like this game," Stan said.

I moved out of the doorway and over to him. "I didn't know you planned to replace me," I said, feeling a lump in my throat that hadn't been there earlier.

"Shelby Lynn isn't a replacement, Turner. She's a substitute. You know, like one of those office temps they tout on the radio all the time," Stan explained.

Yeah. Right. And on the radio commercials, those temps always did a way better job than the person they were temping for. I felt so much better.

"But why Shelby Lynn?" I asked, recalling her fierce drive to nail down the scoop on acclaimed author Elizabeth Courtney Howard last fall. And at over six feet tall and built like a brick crap house, she'd be a hard reporter to say *no comment* to. I swallowed another esophageal lump.

"I thought she was your friend," Stan said.

"She was. She *is,*" I assured my boss. "That's why I'm a little concerned that, uh, with my recent impressive string of journalistic successes, she might find my shoes a little big to fill."

Stan frowned at me. "Are you kidding? Have you seen the size of her clodhoppers?" he asked.

"Shelby Lynn so badly wants to be a writer someday," I reminded Stan, the funny, funny man, "I'd hate for her to have a painful experience so young. It could scar her for life if she wasn't up to the task."

"Up to the task? She's a foot and a half taller than me!"

"Just know that if that young girl's spirit is diminished by disappointment, her hopes for the future dashed by defeat because she couldn't live up to the

impossibly high standards of excellence set by her pre-
decessor, then it will be on your head," I told Stan,
thinking I sounded pretty damned . . . what's the word?
Altruistic. In a self-serving kind of way.

Stan laughed. "Impossibly high standards? Have you
seen the length of those arms?"

I crossed my own arms and stared at him. Neither
one of us blinked.

"I think we both know what's going on here,
Turner," Stan finally said. "And the question you have
to ask yourself is, can you handle a little competition?"

I thought about it for a second, deciding the question my employer had to ask himself was whether he
could handle the fallout if a certain disgruntled, un-
predictable employee returned to find Shelby Lynn's
butt cheeks stuck for good to her brand-new ergonomically designed desk chair.

How about it? Do you feel lucky, Stan?

I managed to extricate Shelby Lynn from my chair by
appointing her the dubious honor of going to the
courthouse to pick up the traffic court dispositions
and the county sheriff's trip log for the previous week.
It was actually kind of nice to hand this task off to
someone else for a change. I didn't have the best relationship with county law enforcement. Uh, or with the
city cops, for that matter. And a state agent or two
probably has my name written down in some official
watch list somewhere, too.

I took time to readjust my chair to within human
range, typed up some general instructions for Shelby
Lynn, and grabbed my backpack that served as purse,
organizer, and makeup kit, then headed out the front
door and down the street to Hazel's Hometown Café
in search of a hot cup of coffee and one of Hazel's famous plate-sized cinnamon rolls.

Hazel's is legendary for the quality, quantity, and value of its home-cooked meals. Served in a circa 1950s décor that's a cross between June Cleaver's kitchen and Sam Drucker's General Store in *Green Acres* (minus the occasional visits from Arnold the pig—although the Todd Twins did let loose a good half-dozen Easter chicks there last April), Hazel's is also known as the place to go if you're lookin' for the latest dish on your neighbor. (Well, so I've heard. What? Me? Nah. I go strictly for the vittles. Any gossip is a cherry on top.)

I raised a hand in greeting to Reverend Browning of the Open Bible Church as I entered the café and tried to avoid prolonged eye contact. Things have been a little awkward between us since Kari's wedding ceremony. Plus, I wasn't in the mood for his "We haven't seen you at services lately, Tressa." Head down, I aimed straight for the counter.

I always sit at the counter. As a child, I got in trouble regularly for spinning around 'til I got dizzy and fell off the stool. Then, I'd climb back up and do it again. Yep. I was the kind of kid you see at your favorite eating establishment who causes you to shake your head and mutter, "If that was my kid, I'd . . ." and fill in the blank with something like, "blister her hind end," "yank her butt off that stool," "take her home and make her eat gruel"—what is gruel, by the way?—or the ever-popular, "If that was my kid, I'd blow my brains out." It wasn't that I was a bad seed or anything. I simply had boundless energy and, even at an early age, going out to eat made me giddy.

"Good morning, Tressa." Donita Smith greeted me with a coffee cup in one hand and a coffeepot in the other. She had a full steaming cup of java in front of me before my butt hit the cushioned stool top. You just don't get that kind of service in the big city. She cocked her head and looked at me. "I'm thinking cinnamon roll today," she said. "Right?"

"How do you do it?" I asked. "You missed your calling, Donnie. You should be forecasting the weather or betting on the ponies. You're way better than Psychic Sonya, the State Fair Seer." Although Psychic Sonya had predicted powerful sexual tension and long-term sexual frustration for me last summer (ya think?) her promised worth-waiting-for resolution hadn't materialized. What a shocker.

"I don't just sling hash back here, you know. I'm a keen observer of human nature," Donnie said. "You have that cinnamon roll look in your eyes. I've seen it before."

I brought my coffee cup to my lips and took a careful sip. "What makes my cinnamon roll look different from, say, my hot beef sandwich with 'taters and gravy look?" I asked, curious.

"A bubble of drool in the corner of your mouth," Donita said.

"Good to know," I said. "Good to know."

She laughed. "I'll just grab your cinnamon roll. Nuked, right?"

I nodded. "If it isn't too much trouble. And don't forget the little cup of butter on the side," I reminded her. "Or does that show on my face, too?"

"Cute," Donnie said, and headed for the kitchen.

I sat and sipped my coffee, and, unzipping my backpack, reached in to pull out a small notepad to jot down the number of days I needed to pack for and the type of clothing I needed for each of those days. Jeans, T-shirts and hoodies would work for most days, but I'd have to find something for the wedding ceremony that wouldn't put everyone's nose out of joint.

I smiled. The Navajo in northern Arizona produced some incredibly beautiful garments. I had purchased several woven saddle blankets, but they were so gorgeous I'd never had the heart to use them. They currently hang on the walls of my bedroom, colorful tapestries of authentic Americana. Maybe I'd dress in traditional Native American attire for the wedding. I shook my head. Taylor, with her dark hair and eyes, could pull it off. Me? I'd look like She Who Has Hair Like Sagebrush and Walks with Saddlebags Barbie. Without Barbie's hooters. Sigh.

The bell over Hazel's door jingled as the door opened.

"Tressa Turner! Where you at? I know you're in here!"

I'd just taken another drink of my coffee when I recognized the person belonging to that voice. My throat completely closed and I began to cough and choke, spewing coffee across Donita's shiny white counter. My gaze darted to the kitchen and I grabbed my backpack from the back of the stool.

"You stay put. Hear me, girl?"

Hear? Mrs. Corder, a block down at the B-Clean Dry Cleaners, who depended on closed captions for television viewing enjoyment, could hear. I got to my feet, prepared to creep around the counter and hightail it out the back.

"Don't you go tryin' to sneak out through the kitchen, 'cause I got Mick posted out back. And I told him to sit on you if need be so you wouldn't get away. We need to talk, Miss Tressa."

"Son of a—" I caught the good reverend's eye on me before I let loose with a naughty word that was sure to inspire a sermon in the near future on the importance of being pure of heart, mind and mouth. You see, I'd spent the last two months trying to elude the persistent pit bull that now appeared to have me cornered.

Marguerite Dishman, better known as Aunt Mo,

was a very nice lady who had a very devoted nephew who, when he thought his beloved "Ahnt Mo" was on her deathbed, wanted her last hours on earth to be contented ones. So the nephew, Manny Dishman/De-marco/da biggest guy I've ever seen (Manny has used several surnames I'm aware of—and probably many others I'm not.) had wanted to give his aunt a very special send off—give her something she'd wanted very badly: A mate for Manny. (Sounds like the title of a romance novel, doesn't it?) Being the giving, caring person I am, I'd agreed to pose as Manny's girl-friend/fiancée for a one-time, one-act performance, to put a smile on an old lady's face as she drifted off into the glorious hereafter. But neither Manny nor I had banked on Aunt Mo's miraculous recovery, and I sure as heck hadn't banked on having to perpetuate the *aren't they the cutest couple?* charade to keep Aunt Mo from relapsing.

Aunt Mo wintered in Arizona, so I'd managed to successfully avoid situations that required stealth, sub-terfuge and messy explanations. That was, until Aunt Mo returned to Iowa in early spring and began a per-sistent campaign to pin me down on a wedding date. Things had gotten a little hairy.

I'd pretty much kept news of my faux fiancé on the down low, with my sister Taylor and my boss Stan be-ing the only people besides Manny, Mo, and me (now that sounds like the name of a TV sitcom) who knew of the little coil in which I found myself. Unfortunately, Aunt Mo had crashed my friend Kari's wedding recep-tion two months earlier, and discovered me swapping spit with Ranger Rick Townsend. When I'd threatened to pull the plug (no pun intended) on the whole farce, Manny had promised to break the news of our breakup to his aunt, explaining that we'd mutually agreed to call off our engagement but remained friends. Unfortunately, having given his promise, Manny had left town unexpectedly, leaving me in limbo. Not sure how Aunt Mo would react to being scammed by her nephew, the boy she'd raised from a pup, there was no way this cowgirl was gonna spill any beans. Not unless it involved digging into a chili dog.

I sank back onto my stool and found myself wishing Reverend Browning knew of the charitable act I'd performed out of the goodness of my heart that now put my butt on the line—and in Aunt Mo's line of fire. I really could have used a few brownie points with the big guy upstairs.

Aunt Mo joined me at the counter. She didn't bother to try and maneuver her girth onto a stool top the size of a medium pizza from the Thunder Rolls Bowling Alley. Aunt Mo was a large, sturdy woman.

"Booth!" she barked. "Now!" She pointed to a corner booth where an older couple stood to leave.

I picked up my coffee cup and backpack and followed in Aunt Mo's wake like a well-trained pet. (Okay, so I don't actually know any well-trained pets. This is pure speculation on my part.)

Aunt Mo took the far booth against the wall, and I looked on as she slid along the bench, shoving the table away to make extra room for her midsection, just the way her nephew did to assure adequate clearance for his own bulk. In his case, it was all muscle.

"Sit!" Mo said, nodding at the bench across from her.

I planted my fanny without spilling a drop of coffee, saying, "It's good to see you again, Aunt Mo."

"Don't you bullshit me," Aunt Mo warned. "You've been avoiding me like I do them young men dressed in suits that come knockin' on your door and want to sit on your couch and talk about God."

I winced, praying Reverend Browning hadn't overheard.

"I've been busy," I said.

"Busy showing your boobies to that randy ranger," she said.

I could sense the pastor's posture shift perceptibly in our direction. "Can't we just get past that?" I asked, leaning across the table. "I made a mistake. A little too much celebratory bubbly," I said. "It could happen to anyone."

"You should know better than to let some sweet-talker ply you with alcohol and grope you. Lord knows where that dirty dancin' display would've led if ol' Aunt Mo here hadn't crashed the festivities."

I bit my lip and tried hard not to feel bitter toward the woman. I'd often wondered that very same thing myself. Ranger Rick had been about to give me the mother of all birthday kisses, and I'd been primed and puckered. In my sex-starved, lusty little mind's eye, what followed involved champagne, birthday suits and lots of cake and frosting. And maybe a noisemaker or two—but that's way more information than you need.

I shook my head Etch-a-Sketch style to erase the erotic images. Restless movement from the nearby table told me the pastor was getting an earful.

"I think it's about time Aunt Mo, Manny and Tressa had a heart-to-heart," I said, then winced, remembering the cardiac issues that had instigated the fake fi-ancée scenario in the first place. "I'm leaving for a wedding in Arizona in a few days, but when I get back, we all need to talk," I told her.

Aunt Mo got a big, broad smile on her face. Like I do when I walk into Calhoun's Steakhouse so hungry my navel's rubbing my backbone and I learn someone else is picking up the tab. Mo clapped her beefy hands together in front of her and held them to her ample chest. Like I do when I open my bank statement and discover I'm not overdrawn.

Donnie appeared tableside as Aunt Mo raised her hands toward the heavens. "Hallelujah!" Aunt Mo yelled, and I looked over at Reverend Browning. He stared at Aunt Mo. "Praise the Lord! Hand over a hunk of that cinnamon roll! Aunt Mo's gonna celebrate! Celebrate good times! Come on!" she sang.

I frowned, getting an ohmigawd-what-now feeling.

"What are we celebrating?" Donnie asked, setting my cinnamon roll on the table and shooting me a questioning look as the front door opened and the bell greeted Hazel's next hungry customer.

I blinked a couple of times—my personal sign language for "I'm clueless."

"Why, we're celebratin' the fact that Tressa here is finally ready to set the date!" Aunt Mo said in a loud, booming, praise-the-Lord-and-pass-the-sweet-roll voice. I stared at her in horror, and not just because she was consuming my cinnamon roll at an alarming rate. I felt my lower intestine twist and knot. The coffee I'd swilled turned bitter in my gut.

"Date? What date?" Donnie had to ask.

"Why, her wedding date, of course!" Aunt Mo shouted to the rafters. "To my nephew Manny. As soon as she's back from vacation, we're gonna be plannin' ourselves a wedding!"

"Uh, excuse me, ladies, but may I be among the first to congratulate the bride?"

I turned to find Ranger Rick occupying the booth bench behind me, his facial expression one with which I had become quite familiar. I was *so* screwed—and without even a kiss.

I let loose with a very naughty word guaranteed to earn me a visit from the good reverend before next Sunday's service. Good luck, preacher man. Arizona, here I come!

CHAPTER THREE

"Good afternoon, and welcome to Northwest Airlines Flight 111 Minneapolis-St. Paul to Phoenix. We hope you enjoy your flight with us."

I cast a sidelong look to my left, at my sister Taylor who was busy adjusting the vent above her to direct the air flow right at her face as we got ready for takeoff.

"Guess the gingersnaps aren't workin' for you, huh?" I said, noting the pallor of her face and the tiny beads of perspiration collecting above her upper lip. "You should've gone with the Dramamine," I added, shaking my head at my sister's stubborn insistence on using a natural remedy to combat her airsickness.

With no nonstop flights to Phoenix available, we'd flown out of Des Moines heading north to Minneapolis-St. Paul for the flight west. With the Townsend side of the aisle represented by Joe, Ranger Rick, Rick's parents Don and Charlotte Townsend, Rick's older brother Mike, and Mike's wife Heather, and their two kids Nicholas, aged ten, and Kelsey, eight, plus the Turner contingent numbering seven including Gram, my folks,

Taylor, me and my brother Craig and sister-in-law Kimmie, I felt like I was on one of those Hawkeye charters to a bowl game. Or the airplane from *Lost*.

As luck would have it—luck in the form of two manipulative matchmakers with a penchant for mischief-making, that is—Ranger Rick Townsend's seat assignment was smack dab between Taylor and yours truly. I'd been given an aisle seat on both flights, but following Taylor's third time crawling over my legs to go ralph in the john on the earlier flight, we'd mutually agreed to swap seats on this one.

"I'll live," Taylor snapped, still fiddling with the air control. "Is this thing even working?" she asked, moving the doohickey around some more. "I can't feel anything coming out."

"Here, let me see if I can help," Townsend offered, and I found myself watching his long, tanned fingers as they reached up to twist the knob this way and that to turn on the air—imagining those fingers reaching over to turn on Tressa.

I shut my eyes. Oooh. Baby. Oh. Right there. Oh. Yes! Yesss!

"Yesss!"

I opened my eyes to find Taylor and Townsend looking at me.

"—terday, all my troubles seemed so far away," I warbled, thinking it was probably a very good thing I was taking a vacation. I was in serious danger of cracking up.

Townsend raised an eyebrow and went back to adjusting Taylor's air flow.

I shook my head. I was so in a world of hurt here. Just sitting next to Townsend, thighs touching now and then, arms brushing occasionally, made every nerve ending in my body snap to overload status. Observing the strong cords of his tanned neck tense and

the way his shirt tightened across broad shoulders as
he reached overhead made my temperature head up,
up, up and away! I started to fan myself.

"You okay, Tressa?" Townsend asked, settling back in
his seat after he'd finished aiming Taylor's blast of recirculated air back at her face.

I shrugged, always somewhat insecure when it came
to Rick—especially when Taylor was within the same
field of vision.

"Me? I'm what you call your low-maintenance trav-
eler, Townsend," I told him. "Strictly no frills. Why?
Don't I look all right?" I asked, thinking the pink and
white T-shirt that read "Barn Diva," blue jeans, and
slouch boots made the perfect traveling ensemble. Taylor, on the other hand, had opted to wear a denim skirt
with a lightweight black blouse and matching black flip
flops. Despite the deathly pallor of her face, she looked
stunning. In an anemic, I-need-a-transfusion sort of way.

"You look a little flushed is all," Townsend said, settling his long, manly body back in his seat and easing
his dark head of hair against the seatback as his gaze
roamed my feverish face. "Tell me, T. Is it my close
proximity that has you all hot and bothered?" he asked
with a grin that sent my mercury into the danger zone.

"Actually, it's the hot sauce I drizzled all over my
Mexican sampler from Taco Time at lunch," I told
him, and heard a short intake of breath from the occupant of the aisle seat. Apparently, Taylor wasn't up
to thinking of belly burners and nachos with jalapeño
cheese sauce. "*Muy caliente*," I added.

"Right," Townsend said with a nod. "Right."

"What? You don't believe me? Check my breath," I
offered before I realized just what liberties that invitation included.

"Don't mind if I do," Townsend said, turning my face
in his direction, his fingers on my chin. I blinked twice,

fixed my gaze on lips that promised a hot time on the old silver bird today, ran my tongue across my lips before parting them slightly, closed my eyes and waited.

The fingers at my chin moved to my heated cheek and gave it a tender tap.

"Nope," Townsend said. "Nope."

I opened my eyes, shooting Townsend a what's-the-deal-Lucille look.

Townsend smiled and shook his head.

"Nope. I can't do it," he said, and dropped his hand to our shared armrest. "It wouldn't be right."

I looked at him.

"Can't do what?" I asked. "What wouldn't be right?"

Townsend sighed. "It wouldn't be right to fool around with an engaged woman," he said. "I'd feel . . . dirty," he added with a little shake of his broad shoulders.

I raised an eyebrow.

"Funny," I said. "But aren't you on the wrong plane? This plane goes to Phoenix. The bird to Vegas and your stand-up gig in the Carp Cop Casino was scheduled to depart from the go-straight-to-you-know-where gate."

"What? No layover?" Townsend said, and winked at me. "Sweet."

I shook my head.

"You know something, Townsend?" I snapped. "You're more like your grandfather than I realized."

"I'll take that as a compliment," he said. "And, by the way, you've got more than a token dose of my future step-grandmother in you."

Step-grandmother? I shuddered and closed my eyes. This was not happening. It was just a bad, bad dream, I assured myself. A product of too much red meat. Not enough fiber in my diet. A psychotic break. How else could I explain the fact that in a mere matter of days Ranger Rick Townsend, my childhood archenemy and bestower of nicknames harder to get rid of than denture cream on the bathroom faucet, and I would be . . . gulp. Stepcousins?

"Just think, Tressa. You and I will be cousins," Townsend said, parroting my thoughts. "Kissin' cousins," he amended, with several Groucho Marx lifts of his eyebrows. "Naughty, naughty," he said. "But, also intriguing as hell. In a let's-keep-it-in-the-family sort of way."

"That's just sick, Townsend," I told him, all the while Sinner Tressa on my loony left shoulder reminding me that forbidden passion, like Romeo and Juliet and Antony and Cleopatra, was the hottest of 'em all. Saint Tressa on my radical right cautioned me to remember that those relationships didn't exactly end up in happily-ever-afters. Party pooper.

"What? Don't tell me you've never considered how this marriage alters the family dynamics," Townsend remarked. "How it changes the status quo."

I turned to look at him. "Have you been reading back issues of Taylor's *Psychology Today*?" I asked. "Or has *Field and Stream* strayed way far afield?"

He smiled. "You can't avoid the inevitable for much longer, Tressa," he told me. "We're gonna be family. Just think of all the birthdays, reunions, graduations—"

"Funerals," I interjected.

He gave me another wicked grin. "You can run but you can't hide," he warned.

"Speaking of hide-and-seek and other children's games, your nephew is a rather, uh, interesting child," I said, deciding to change the subject to something safer. Marginally so. Townsend's ten-year-old nephew was a terror on Nike's treads. A carbon copy of his Uncle Rick at that age, Nicholas Townsend gave me flashbacks to a childhood filled with Townsend trickery, prepubescent pranks, and an adolescent array of one-upmanship. And that was just grade school. "He definitely exhibits Townsend-specific traits," I said, eyeballing the little twerp who had lifted my backpack at the airport and pilfered from my candy stash, replacing the chocolate with a pack of sugar-free Sen-Sens breath fresheners he'd begged from his great granddad Joe.

"Hmmm. Let's see. The Townsend charm?" Rick suggested. "Athletic prowess? The outstanding good looks? Sex appeal?"

"Humility," I noted. "Seriously, the lad seems a little hyperactive. Did he skip his meds this morning?" I joked. On the flight to Minneapolis-St. Paul, the pintsized poster child for birth control had peppered me with questions about the ordeal of a year ago when I'd been out to earn my merit badge for discovering dead bodies.

What did they look like? Was there a lot of blood? Did they stink? Were you scared? Did you puke? The kid was relentless. I'd finally stuck earphones on to tune him out.

Townsend shook his head. "When's the last time you were around kids, Tressa?" he asked. "They're all like that. Full of spit and vinegar."

Full of Townsend genetic material was more like it. The little urchin should be wearing a warning sign around his neck: *Danger! Frequent exposure likely to cause intense irritation.*

"Well, whatever it's due to, *Uncle Rick*, it's extremely annoying," I told him. "You're his uncle. You should talk to him. Tell him he's being an obnoxious little ass—uh—nine adolescent. It's your duty as his uncle to steer him in the right direction."

It occurred to me that this amounted to the blind leading the blind. Knowing Townsend, he'd probably tutored his nephew on the finer points of ticking Tressa Turner off before we even boarded the aircraft.

After all, Townsend was "da man" when it came to messing with my head.

"Oh? So, you think I'd be a good role model for kids now, huh?" he asked. "That's a new one."

I gave him a fake smile.

"Maybe I'm just curious to see what kind of father material you'd make," I said, batting my eyelashes. "That's important to women, you know. All the magazine surveys cite that as a major consideration when women select a mate," I told him. Personally, that requirement would be further down my list, behind great kisser, great body, great in bed and great sense of humor. Oh, and lover of dogs and horses, holder of a good job, and possessor of his own teeth—not in a container on the nightstand. Same went for the hair.

Okay, so maybe I sound a tad shallow here. It's a Mr. Right wish list, for crying out loud. Tell me yours says *Wanted: Flabby fellow with Trump's hair, healthy gums and scalp, who is not allergic to dogs or horses, and whose idea of heavy reading is the comic section of the paper.* Get my drift?

"Since when is Calamity Jayne concerned with the proper care and rearing of children?" Rick asked.

"Since I'm hoping to be Auntie Tressa soon," I told him.

My sister-in-law, Kimmie, had been trying for well over a year to convince my obstinate oaf of a brother, Craig, that he was ready for fatherhood. He was dragging his feet more than I do when it's time to clean out the gutters. Or time to try on last year's swimwear. I was becoming frustrated. Uh, I mean Kimmie was becoming frustrated. She refused to get pregnant until Craig was onboard with their joint life plan, so she'd undertaken a campaign of enforced celibacy several months back to give the couple some clarity on the issue. I hadn't inquired how that was working for them, but last I'd heard Craig was spending a lot of time working out at the Rec Center. Followed by long, cold showers.

"You could help out there, too, you know," I told the ranger.

He looked at me.

"I can help you become an aunt? Uh, that's not what I meant by keeping it in the family, Turner," Rick said.

"And that's not what I meant by helping out, you daft, daft man," I told him. "You're Craig's best friend. You can talk to him. Encourage him. Tell him how cool it would be for me to become an aunt—I mean, for him to become a father. Convince him what an absolutely awesome experience fatherhood could be." I looked across the aisle at Townsend's nephew, finger disappearing up one nostril. "And whatever you do, Townsend, whatever it takes, don't let Nick near Craig," I warned. "That'll set us back a good twelve months."

"You worry too much, Tressa," Townsend said. "Relax and let nature take its course," he advised.

Relax. Right. With all men's compasses set for fun and games? Booze and belching? Fat chance, bucko.

"Did I hear my name?"

Nick Townsend, finger now removed from nose, looked down at us.

"Tressa was just commenting on how much you remind her of me when I was your age," Townsend, ever the diplomat, explained.

"Cool," Nick, the miniature space cadet, said, obviously mistaking his uncle's words as a compliment. "Dad wants to talk to you," he told Rick. "Something about a deer party," he added, sneaking a quick peek at Taylor, who had her head back and her eyes closed. The kid forced his gaze away from my sister and over to me, realized I'd caught him making goo-goo eyes at Taylor, and flushed crimson.

Townsend men.

Rick looked at me.

"Stag party," he translated for my benefit. "We thought we'd better do something to commemorate Granddad's final days as a free man," he explained. "By the way, what are you doing for your grandma?" he asked.

"Running away. Far, far away," I told him. "I'm leaving it up to Aunt Kay," I elaborated. And me? I planned to be unexpectedly stranded at the top of the Snow Bowl at the appointed hour of the fun and frivolity. Snow or no snow.

Townsend stood and slid his long length past Taylor's legs, and his nephew took his seat. I groaned and focused my attention out the aircraft window, savoring several seconds of silence before the mouth-o-matic next to me started up and took off.

"What's wrong with your sister? Doesn't she like to fly? Is she afraid? How old is she? Does she have a boyfriend?"

I sighed and bowed to the inevitable.

"Taylor suffers from motion sickness. Planes, trains, automobiles." We'd see how she fared on a seafaring vessel. "She'll be twenty-two on her next birthday, and nope, she doesn't have *a* boyfriend," I said.

"Sweet!" the pint-sized Casanova reacted.

"Nope," I continued. "Not *a* boyfriend, runt. Taylor has two, or is it three guys she's seeing now? I lose track," I said, purely to needle the kid. "Let's see, there's the hunky veterinarian with the Hummer," I said, ticking the beaus off as I went. "Then there's that good-looking grad student with the gorgeous blue eyes. And who was that other guy she sort of fancies? Oh, yeah. The back-up quarterback for the Hawkeyes," I finished, spinning my little yarn.

"Oh," the Townsend twerp responded with a hang-dog look eerily like the one my cousin Frankie wore when he almost drowned in the water hazard at the Public Safety Academy obstacle course last fall.

I felt the teensiest twinge of regret for my exaggeration. Taylor *had* dated all of the aforementioned hotties. Just not all at the same time. But the smitten sixth grader next to me didn't know that.

Taylor stirred and opened her eyes briefly, moving her head carefully to the side and downward toward the dwarf who had taken Townsend's seat.

"Hello," Nick Townsend said. "Are you really dating three guys at the same time? 'Cause that's what *she* said," he told Taylor, jabbing an elbow in my ribs.

Taylor gave me a put-out-but-too-pukey-to-do-anything-about-it look and moved her head back and forth as if in slow motion.

"Not dating now," she said slowly, and closed her eyes again.

Nick Townsend shot me a dark glare that boded ill for me. Still, what could the munchkin do on an airplane at thirty thousand feet with a hundred passengers as witnesses?

"I like snakes. Do you like snakes? My uncle Rick collects snakes. He has lots of them. He lets me hold them. The ones that aren't poisonous, that is. Does Uncle Rick let you play with his snakes?"

Given another context, the mental imagery associated with playing with a snake that belonged to Ranger Rick Townsend might hold some appeal. However, given my very real—and completely rational—fear of all things slithery, this topic was unquestionably off limits. And totally taboo.

"Sorry, kid. I'm not into creatures of the cold-blooded variety," I told him.

"I think snakes are cool. Don't you think snakes are

cool? The way they wind around your arm when you hold them, all cold and dry against your skin. Snakes rule."

"They also bite," I told him. And pop out of hay bales when you least expect it. And take refuge on top of propane tanks where you can't shoot 'em. Diabolically clever creatures.

"You want to talk about movies? I saw a cool movie."

I nodded, thankful to get the subject off legless reptiles and onto less creepy topics of conversation.

"Oh, yeah? What was it about?" I asked.

"It was about this airplane and a bunch of poisonous snakes got loose and started coming out from everywhere and attacking and biting the passengers. It was, like, so whacked!"

I stared at Satan's spawn, wondering how the little sadist knew I was terrified of snakes, and simultaneously realizing who the sneaky snitch was. The kid smiled up at me with a big, wide, *gotcha* grin on his totally too Townsend face. My lips felt dry and I tried to wet them with my tongue only to discover I'd developed a serious case of cottonmouth myself.

"Have you seen the movie?" he asked, and I managed to shake my head. " 'Cause if you haven't, you can watch it now. I brought the movie with me, and I've got my portable DVD player. You can borrow them if you like."

I found myself all of a sudden examining the structure of the aircraft around me: the carry-on compartments, the seams that held the ceiling together above, the specter of a snake dropping down in front of me instead of an oxygen mask—the stuff my nightmares are made of. Rarely, if ever, afflicted by motion sickness, I felt my stomach rebel at the ghastly images in my head of row after row of writhing, squirming snakes hanging in the faces of air passengers and slithering up the center aisle.

"How about it?" Nick asked, holding out the DVD player.

" 'scuse me," I said, bringing a hand to my mouth. "I need out."

The four-foot fiend sat and looked at me.

"Now!" I ordered.

He simply smiled.

"I'm warning you—," I managed, just before the runt's facial expression informed me he'd received the message to move or suffer the consequences.

Unfortunately, time had run out. Before I could yell "barf bag," the little troll next to me was treated to an interactive, 3-D view of Taco Time's South of the Border fare. Rerun variety. How do you say, "Play it again, Sam" in Spanish?

We landed at Sky Harbor Airport in Phoenix ninety minutes later, a decidedly unpopular delegation from the nation's heartland, and hurried out of the gate and into the terminal. The sight and smell of hurl in a cabin that recycled and recirculated air had had epidemic implications. By the time we landed, thirteen passengers had performed the ol' heave-ho, and I was pretty sure the airline crew had taken down our names for future reference.

A glass-half-full kind of gal, I searched for the one positive to come out of any given unpleasant experience.

"Uh, sorry about that, bud," I said to Townsend's nephew as we waited for my aunt and uncle to arrive.

The smelly squirt gave me the bird and walked away without a word.

See? What did I tell you, folks? A silver lining.

CHAPTER FOUR

Aunt Kay and Uncle Ben arrived a few minutes later, squabbling between themselves about who had caused them to be late. It was Aunt Kay, according to Uncle Ben, because it took her too long to slap on war paint. (Uncle Ben had obviously lived out west too long, pardner.) It was Uncle Ben, claimed Aunt Kay, because he'd driven like a "half-blind, senile old woman" all the way from the hotel to the airport—and she'd been forced to follow at a snail's pace, so she should know.

Ah, love, southwestern-style.

I hadn't seen Aunt Kay and Uncle Ben since their last visit to Iowa three years earlier. Neither had changed very much. Aunt Kay still looked like my dad in drag. Naturally, I suppose, given they're twins. And Uncle Ben, with his salt and pepper hair and ruddy complexion, resembled Grissom from that CSI show, complete with cute little paunch.

I hugged them both, feeling that awkward hesitation and momentary discomfort reserved for those occasions when families reunite after a long separation.

Or when you have to use a public restroom and just know you're gonna make a heckuva lot of noise in the process. I just hate that, don't you?

"Welcome to the Grand Canyon State," Uncle Ben said, including the entire entourage in his statement. "Glad to see everyone made it here ship-shape." He must've sucked in a deep enough breath to get a whiff of little Nick's shirt, because his smile faltered. He put a hand on Nick's shoulder. "Ah, poor lad. Airsick, were we?"

The lad in question gave me the evil eye.

"Not 'we.' Her!" The stinky squealer pointed in my direction. "She threw up all over me!"

I folded my arms and tapped my foot.

"Really, Nick. It isn't nice to fib," I said. "There's no shame in an inability to control your bodily functions," I told him. "And I know my sister, Taylor, here agrees. Right, Taylor?" I bent to give the kid's cheek a tweak. "Silly boy," I said, with a Grinch-like smile. "And you thought the two of you had nothing in common. Imagine that."

The Townsend tot seared me with the intensity of his gaze. And not in the typically Townsend *you're one hot tamale* way.

Face it, kid, I thought. Time to take your plastic shield and fake lightsaber and go spar with someone your own size. Like Yoda.

"Tressa Jayne! Good to see you!" Uncle Ben gave me a tight bear hug. "Found any more dead bodies lately?" he asked with a broad smile and another hard squeeze.

I shook my head. "They're getting harder to come by, Uncle Ben," I replied. "But I'm always on the lookout."

He laughed. "Same ol' Tressa," he said.

Aunt Kay put an arm around Taylor and one around me. "Just look at you two girls. All grown up. Your cousin Sophie is so excited to see you. She would have come, but she had classes."

Sophie, my aunt and uncle's only child had recently turned twenty-one, and was in her second year at Northern Arizona University studying business. Three years ago Sophie had been—how to put this—on the robust side, taking after Uncle Ben's side of the family. Quiet and shy, Sophie had been easy to overlook. Well, apart from her size, that is. Sophie held the distinction of being only the second person ever to best me in a roasting-ear eating contest. She was more efficient at removing the kernels on those cobs than a brand-new John Deere combine.

"I'm anxious to see Sophie again, too," I said, wondering if she'd finally won the battle of the bulge and, if so, whether she would let her favorite cousin, Tressa, in on her little weight-loss secret.

We collected our baggage and decided on seat assignments for the two-hour climb from the valley to Flagstaff. Rick's father, Don, had made arrangements to rent a Suburban for the trip up the mountain. It held nine, but with luggage that dropped to seven. Gram wanted to ride with her daughter so they could discuss wedding plans. Twin sister or not, my dad wanted no part of a two-hour wedding chat, so he decided to reserve a seat in Uncle Ben's vehicle, slow-going or not. Craig concurred, so the group split along gender lines. My grandma, mother, sister, and sister-in-law were with Aunt Kay; my dad and brother were with Uncle Ben. I opted for a quiet, peaceful ride and snagged a seat with Uncle Ben. One of the Townsends would have to ride in our vehicle as well. Glutton for punishment that I was, I volunteered Ranger Rick. When given the opportunity, I always opt for the scenic route.

I grabbed Townsend's hand to haul him toward Uncle Ben's vehicle. "You're with us," I told him. "It will give you the perfect opportunity to put into motion what we talked about earlier," I added, for fear he would get the idea that I wanted him along purely for his purty face. What an ego.

Townsend got a confused look. "Come again?" he said.

"*Craig,*" I hissed, pulling Rick along. "You know. El bambino. La niña. The baby. Fatherhood. Baseball. Apple pie. Chevrolet."

I could tell I'd lost him.

"I'll draw you a picture in the car," I said, thinking it was maybe a good idea to also write a script for him. Sometimes men were so uninspired.

We were about to pile into our respective cars when I heard, "I want to ride with Tressa." I looked down to see Nick Townsend standing by our car.

"Don't you mean Taylor?" I asked. He shook his head.

"No. I want to ride with *you,*" he said.

A whiff of the smelly middle-schooler hit the ol' olfactory, and I fought to keep from gagging.

"That's so sweet, Nicky," I said, "but your Uncle Rick is riding with us and there won't be room. Maybe on the way back," I promised, deciding that my Uncle Frank's Slurpees would be served in Hades before that happened.

"That's okay," Townsend said, backing away from his ripe nephew. "You go ahead, Nick. I'll ride with Grandpa."

I shot Townsend an *I'll get you for this* look.

"Fine," I said. "You'll want to change that shirt first, though. Right, dude?" I added.

"Naw. I'm good," Pepe Le Pew said, and piled into the back of Uncle Ben's SUV. He patted the seat beside him. "All aboard, Tressa!" he said, and I muttered a few not-intended-for-younger-audiences words under my breath and climbed in.

Just my luck, the kid was a chip off the ol' Townsend blockhead. Good grief.

"Better fasten your seatbelt, Tressa," he instructed once I'd taken a seat.

I buckled up. I had a feeling it was gonna be a bumpy ride.

It's a one hundred forty-five mile drive on Interstate 17 from Phoenix to Flagstaff. Roughly two hours. But between my uncle Ben operating his vehicle like he was driving Miss Daisy or the hearse in a funeral procession and Rick Townsend's nephew auditioning for a role as an inflamed hemorrhoid, the trip felt longer than the Easter sunrise service when you know a free hot cakes and sausage breakfast featuring Abigail Winegardner's sticky buns (yeast variety) follow.

Aunt Kay had two spare bedrooms with full-sized beds, and my cousin Sophie had room to host one. My folks had dibs on one of Kay's spare rooms, and Craig and Kimmie on the other. Initially Gram was going to bunk with Sophie for two nights (so not Sophie's choice) before moving with the wedding party to The Titan Hotel, a legendary log hotel built in the early 1900s and within walking distance of the south rim of the Grand Canyon. Later it was decided that since we were "guests," Sophie would share the sofa bed in the rec room with Taylor or me.

Taylor and I duked it out for a spot with either Sophie or Gram for the duration. After a rock, paper, scissors marathon, I won. Sophie and the sofa bed was my choice. Like you didn't see that coming. I'd been housemates with Hellion Hannah for over six months now, and no way was I going to spend four nights with someone who is "underpants optional" in sleeping attire, or listening to my grandma's graphic prognostications on how her wedding night would play out. One for the ol' fast-forward button here, folks. Bleah.

The short ceremony would take place in the impressive hotel lobby with the massive stone fireplace as backdrop, the odd moose or buck head on the wall as a witness. Ranger Rick would feel right at home.

The Townsends had reserved rooms at a nearby resort hotel near the south rim for the first few days of their stay so they could spend some time exploring the canyon and local tourist spots before moving to The Titan. The Web site tour of the hotel spotlighted a humongous heated pool and gorgeous terrace, views to die for, several classy restaurants, plus amenities like a Jacuzzi hot tub—not to mention room service—and had me drooling like Butch and Sundance when a stray bitch wandered by. (Uh, yoo hoo! I'm talking about my two hairy Labradors here. Straighten up, y'-hear?)

Always one to look for the upside, I consoled myself by the fact that a certain relentless ring bearer with a forte for getting under my skin—talk about your inherited traits—would be miles away from Flagstaff and yours truly.

We all met up at Aunt Kay and Uncle Ben's house to unload the vehicles, use the restrooms, and grab a bite to eat before the Townsends took off to check in at their luxury accommodations. My aunt and uncle live in a northeastern section of Flagstaff with a country club golf course visible from their front windows and a spectacular view of Mount Eldon from their bedroom. The couple had relocated to Arizona more than twenty years earlier when Uncle Ben decided his muse was calling him west to the land of sharp, evocative contrasts and ever-changing beauty. Here in a state with red rocks, towering green pines, and flowering cacti, Uncle Ben found a connection to the land and people that filled the well of his creativity. See? Only here a day and I'm already waxing poetic.

Meanwhile, the professorial position at the college filled his wallet and paid the bills until he'd established enough success with his paintings and sculptures to quit and devote his time to his art. Aunt Kay, a marketing coordinator for the Flagstaff Public Library and an avid reader, thrived at her job, which included bringing popular authors in for book talks and workshops. So the westward migration had paid off for the Stemples, not unlike the California gold rush did for some lucky "there's gold in them thar hills" prospectors way back when.

The Stemple home was a three-level structure with kitchen, dining, living room and large great room on the walk-in level, three bedrooms and two baths up, and one bedroom downstairs off a long rec room. A collection of haunting yet compelling Native American kachina dolls and masks were displayed throughout the home.

I wheeled my suitcase to the short set of stairs leading to the lower level and looked at the sleeper sofa with a frown, bummed that Ranger Rick and Naughty Nick would be enjoying all the perks of a full-service hotel while I'd be fighting for blankets and bed space with a cousin so not of the kissin' variety. Inanely I wondered if my future stepcousin had his own room with a queen or was stuck rooming with the groom. And I wondered if I had the courage to ask.

I got a whiff of something very bad and winced. Eau de Ralph—and I don't mean Lauren. The Townsend twerp. When he wasn't shoving his DVD player in my face yelling "you gotta see this!"—"this" involving slithering serpents and flashing fangs—or purposefully wafting his odorous shirt front in my face, the kid chattered nonstop.

"Uncle Rick says your nickname is 'Calamity Jayne.' He says you're always in some calamity or another. What does that mean? How did you get that nickname? Do you like it? How come you don't look like your sister? Your sister's hair is shiny and straight. Why does yours have all those kinks? Were you adopted? How did it feel to find all those bodies? Did you get really scared? Did you pee in your pants? Do you like my Uncle Rick? Lots of girls do. He's had tons of girlfriends. Dad says the state should start making him buy doe tags to help the state coughers. What does that mean, anyway? Coughers? Are there like people who are paid to cough for the state? I could do that job. My mom says I'm a mucous factory."

That I could believe. By the time we drove into Uncle Ben's driveway, I was ready to do a Thelma and Louise.

I took my hoodie off, unzipped my suitcase, and rummaged around for a clean T-shirt. I grabbed a white T-shirt trimmed in turquoise that read, *It's all about the boots* with a pair of silhouetted cowboy boots. I love novelty shirts, don't you?

I had pulled my contaminated T-shirt over my head and tossed it aside when I heard a mucousy clearing of the throat and turned to find Nick Townsend, who should be known out west as "he who has a large oral cavity," staring at me, the telltale flush of embarrassment on his cheeks. A Townsend who blushes? Who'd-a thunk it?

"Uh, your aunt told me to come down here to use the restroom," the youngster explained, averting his eyes from the area of my sports bra.

"In there." I nodded toward the john and the kid bolted.

"Scared another one off with your striptease, huh, Calamity?" I caught sight of Rick Townsend at the bottom of the stairway. He took a couple steps in my direction. "Maybe your routine needs some practice. I'm willing to offer my services. You know. Observe and critique."

I shook my head. "I just bet you would," I said, recalling his nephew's comment about the collection of doe tags and thinking Townsend had probably already been treated to a private show a time or two. "But I'm very selective about who I perform for. Besides, I'm an engaged woman, remember? I wouldn't want you to feel dirty," I added.

"About that," Townsend said, taking a few more steps in my direction. "I get why you agreed to pretend to be Manny DeMarco's girlfriend. It was a sweet gesture. But what I don't get is why it's taking so long for you to break it off with him."

"It's complicated," I said. "His aunt was away all winter and the timing just didn't seem right. Now Manny is off somewhere and no way am I gonna break the breakup news to a woman with a history of near-death cardiac episodes," I added. "No freakin' way. Not with my history."

Townsend moved in closer and put a hand on my bare arm, my clean T-shirt clutched to my chest.

"You know what I think?" he asked, close enough for me to smell his aftershave and his musky, manly scent.

"What?" I managed, looking up into eyes more deliciously brown than Cadbury chocolate.

"You're flirting with danger, Tressa," he said, and I sensed he wasn't just being melodramatic. "The longer you let this fiancée fantasy play out, the harder it will be to cut yourself loose when the time comes. And anything connected to Manny Demarco, no matter how innocent or well-intentioned, holds a certain element of risk," he said. "It's just the nature of the beast."

I winced. Having someone refer to your faux fiancé as a beast is hardly the stuff fairy tales are made of.

And let's face it. I sure as heck wasn't the belle of anyone's ball.

"I really don't think there's anything to be concerned about," I said. "Like I told Aunt Mo, when I get back home the three of us are going to have a nice long chat and we'll explain things to her in a calm, loving, non-stress-inducing manner." I thought about it for a second. "Can a person rent a heart defibrillator, do you think?"

Townsend's lips twitched, and I was ready to declare myself a free and unattached woman right then and there and cover his sensational sexy lips with mine when Mr. Mucous Mouth exited the bathroom.

"Do you two want to be alone?" he asked.

I was about to yell, "You're damned right! Now get the hell out!" (being nookie-deprived has manifested in some rather unpleasant side effects) when Townsend turned to block me from his nephew's view and I slipped my shirt on over my head.

"I was just asking Tressa here if she wanted to tag along with you, me and your sister to Sedona tomorrow," Rick said by way of explanation. He turned back to me. "We're looking for souvenirs and the obligatory wedding present for the happy couple," he added. "But I imagine you've already got that covered. Right?"

"Of course," I said, lying. To be honest, buying a wedding gift hadn't even occurred to me.

"What did you get them?" Nick asked, coming over.

"Why, the gift of my presence at this auspicious occasion in their lives, of course," I replied.

"Huh?" the kid said.

"Me! I'm their gift! My being here is gift alone," I told the preteen.

"Didn't you, like, have to come?" he asked. "Like me? So how is that like a present?"

I gritted my teeth. I wondered if it was true that all kids went to Heaven. This one was close to finding out.

"You'll understand when you grow up," I told him. "And realize that sometimes the most valuable gifts cost nothing," I said, and patted his head when I wanted to paddle his behind.

"Sounds to me like something a cheapskate would say," he said, sloughing my hand off his head. "Why don't you ask Taylor to come with us again, Uncle Rick?" he said, looking up at Townsend. "I bet she'd come if you asked her real nice. I bet she's gonna buy a real gift for Grandma Hannah and Grandpa Joe," he said. "Let's ask her."

Townsend gave him a wobbly smile and then extended it to include me.

"You already asked Taylor to go?" I said, as the warm glow I'd gotten over Townsend's invite cooled like hot fudge drizzled over hard-packed ice cream.

Townsend swallowed. Once. Twice. I kept count by the up and down of his Adam's apple.

"I planned on asking you, Taylor, and your cousin Sophie to go along," he explained. "But your Aunt Kay said Sophie has classes tomorrow morning and Taylor isn't feeling up to another car ride so soon. So, what do you say, T? You up for a day of sightseeing in Sedona with a trio of Townsends? Lunch is on me," he added with a wink, trying to cinch the deal.

I thought about it. I shouldn't. I really shouldn't. My track record with Townsend men on my home turf wasn't good. Taking a road trip with two of them over a thousand miles from home down winding switchback roads and off the beaten path smacked of lunacy. Still, there *was* the issue of a wedding gift. Maybe I'd be able to talk Townsend into buying one from the both of us—and reimburse him for it later, of course. Hey. I hear that snickering. You all know I'm good for it.

Plus there was that free lunch and all those fabulous restaurants to consider.

I sniffed. "Thank you for your offer and, although I was apparently third on the list, it's still nice to be asked," I said with a miffed-but-would-live-with-it-tilt to my nose. "I accept your invitation to Sedona—and to lunch. You realize, of course, that I was joking about not getting the geezers a gift," I went on. "As a matter of fact, that was first on my list of things to do for tomorrow," I said. "Right after my five-mile jog and bran cereal breakfast but before my full-body wax."

"Eeeoww! Gross!" Townsend the smaller said, covering his ears while Townsend the taller grinned and reached out and tweaked my cheek. (Face, not butt. Dang it anyway.)

"We should be back in time for your wax job," he said with a lusty leer. "And if you need help buffing, just let me know. Come on, dude," he said, putting a hand on his nephew's shoulder. "See you at eight sharp, Tressa."

"Bye, Tressa," Eddie Munster said as he climbed the stairs. "Oh. I forgot to tell you. I left that DVD we talked about so you can watch it late tonight. When it's dark. Before you go to bed. Sweet dreams," he added with a grin only a mother who had spent ten years and twenty thousand bucks on fertility treatment to have kids could love, and hightailed it upstairs before I could think of some pithy comeback. And no, I don't have a lithp.

How the hell did Townsend stand that nuisance of a nephew? Even more puzzling was that he actually seemed to be fond of the adolescent.

I dropped to the sofa and pondered that for a second. Hmm. Now that I thought about it, maybe Craig wasn't ready for fatherhood just yet after all. It was certainly something to think about.

CHAPTER FIVE

I awoke late the next morning, my sleep fitful and episodic thanks to a diabolical ten-year-old whose reptilian repertoire had led to a long, restless night for me. Every time I closed my eyes and slipped off to sleep, I ended up dreaming of something crawling into the bed with me and getting into my pants (and not in an "ooh, baby" sort of way) and I'd awoken to find the sheet twisted around my legs.

I squinted and rolled over, expecting to find a lump next to me that represented my cousin, Sophie, but the bed was lumpless. Well, except for the considerable ones in the pull-out mattress, that is. I frowned, wondering how I'd slept through Sophie crawling in and out of bed with me and, for a fleeting minute of temporary insanity—blame this on the munchkin, folks—wondered if my dreams had some basis in reality and Cousin Sophie had . . . issues.

I had yet to even see Sophie since we'd arrived. She hadn't been home by the time the weary travelers had wandered off to bed. I could tell my grandma was none too happy with her granddaughter's no-show routine by the set of her shoulders and the pout of her lips. Oh, and by the fact that she crossed Sophie's name off her wedding guest list.

It had been three years since I'd seen my cousin Sophie. Shy and rather reserved, Sophie obviously took after Paw Paw Will's side of the family like her mother and my father. My dad is so unobtrusive, half the time you don't realize he's in the room. As a result, he's scared the bejeebers out of me a time or two. Dad likes to sit back and fade into the woodwork and observe the chaos around him.

The evening before, I'd watched my dad and my Aunt Kay visit, Dad on the end of the couch, Aunt Kay on a nearby glider. It was obvious the twins not only shared similar features, but they also shared a special bond. I'd stared, noticing the same shiny sparkle to my dad's eyes he wore when I caught him looking at my mom and he wasn't aware I was watching. Or when the Hawkeyes were about to play and he had the big-screen TV all to himself.

My gaze had shifted over to Taylor, who was still sipping lemon lime soda and nibbling on crackers to settle her stomach. Not for the first time, I wished we got along like my dad and Aunt Kay. Or my mom and her sister, Aunt Reggie. Or Gram and Great Aunt . . . Well, two out of three ain't bad.

I sighed. Maybe someday.

I checked the time. With two hours difference due to daylight savings time, it would be around nine o'clock back home. I reached for the phone. Time to check on my replacement who wasn't really a replacement at all. Or so Stan the man claimed. I punched in the number for my cell phone—well, the cell phone that was assigned to me that Stan had made double-dog sure I relinquished to Shelby Lynn before I left.

It rang several times before it went to voice mail.

"You've reached the voice mail of Shelby Lynn Sawyer, *Grandville Gazette*. Press one if you wish to leave a message."

I stared at the phone. I'd been gone less than twenty four hours and already the opportunist had switched my voice mail message. I punched *one* and waited for the tone.

"Hey, Shelby Lynn. Tressa here. I'm sure you probably have tons of questions by now. Don't hesitate to give me a call at my aunt and uncle's house. The number is on my desk pad. Along with my folks' number, Craig and Kimmie's number, the groom's number and the number for The Titan Hotel where we'll be staying later this week. And remember, there's no shame in reaching out for help. I'm here for you, girl."

I hung up and immediately dialed Stan's number at the *Gazette*.

"*Gazette*. Rodgers."

"I wondered if you had a reporter available to cover a breaking news story," I said, altering my voice.

"What story?" Stan asked.

"Read all about it! Hazel's Hometown Café is eliminating trans fat from their menu, and Thunder Rolls Bowling Alley and Bar is going smoke-free," I said. "Read all about it!"

"Turner. Even long-distance you manage to be a pain in the ass," Stan said.

"It's a gift," I told him.

"Well, I haven't got time to chit-chat. We're up to our ears in real news," he said. I sat up.

"Oh? Is Shelby Lynn not carrying her weight?" I said, trying to keep the hopefulness in my voice to a minimum.

"Carrying her weight? She's a regular pack mule," Stan said. I frowned.

"Uh, so what's the problem?" I asked.

"Let's see. The Farm Supply store burned to the ground last night. A city clerk was arrested on embezzlement charges. And we've got a parade of presidential hopefuls heading to the county park for the Historical Village Celebration Saturday."

"All that has happened since I left yesterday?" I said.

"And more," Stan said. "But with Shelby Lynn's help, we're on top of things," he added.

At six feet two, she's bound to be on top of things, I thought.

"Are you sure you don't need me to come back early?" I said. "I could skip the cruise and fly back home," I offered.

"Hell, no," Stan said. "Take your time. Enjoy that cruise. We're ship-shape here. Thanks to Shelby Lynn, we're operating at peak efficiency. She even got Smitty to organize his work space."

Uh-oh. This was bad. Very bad. Smitty thrived on clutter. He still had last year's calendar on his desk and candy from Christmas in his drawer. His filing system consisted of file folders made of oversized construction paper with masking tape labels he stuffed in plastic milk crates.

"I really don't mind missing out on the cruise—"

"Wouldn't hear of it, Turner. You just have a good time on the high seas. With Shelby Lynn on board, it'll be smooth sailing back here, too."

"If you're sure—"

"With Shelby Lynn signing on as first mate, we'll weather any storm back here," Stan said. "Bon voyage, Turner!" Stan added and hung up.

I shook my head. Who the heck did Stan think he was, anyway? Commodore Rodgers? The skipper on *Gilligan's Island* was more like it.

I rolled out of the sofa bed and tugged the sheets off

and folded them, stuffing the sleeper mattress back in the frame and replacing the cushions. I checked the time again, cursed, and grabbed a pair of black jeans, a tailored white shirt and underwear, and hurried to the bathroom. I'd showered and was getting ready to step out of the shower to dry off when a distinctly cold draft hit my "nekkid" (my gammy's pronunciation) bod. I stood shivering in the shower, somewhat alarmed to see the cloudy outline of a figure on the other side of the shower curtain.

The shower scene in *Psycho* entered my head. Okay, so I admit the possibility that the figure behind curtain number one belonged to Rick Townsend also got me thinking of a steamy shower scene from one of those highlighted passages in one of my gammy's romance novels. Either scenario gave me a birthday suit made of gooseflesh.

I held my breath and stood stone-cold frozen in place—like the statue of David but even more exposed—hoping to avoid any movement that would draw attention to the shower. And bare little ol' me.

A hand suddenly reached past me to grip the shower faucet handle and turn it on. A blast of cold water struck me at chest level and I couldn't hold back a shocked yelp. Outside the shower a surprised gasp prompted me to grab the opaque shower curtain and drape it around my wet body. I gathered my courage (I'm a cadaver collector, remember?) and peeked outside the shower.

"Sophie?"

"Tressa?"

"Who else were you expecting?" I asked. "Janet Leigh?"

"Sorry. I thought you'd left already."

"Left?" For the first time, I looked at her. Heavier than the last time I saw her, the Sophie I remembered rarely, if ever, wore makeup. This Sophie had on more mascara than Captain Jack Sparrow. A nonsmoker—or so I thought—Sophie reeked of cigarette smoke. "Sophie? Are you just getting home?" I asked, grabbing my towel off the towel bar and wrapping it around me as I stepped from the shower.

The twenty-one-year-old avoided eye contact.

"And if I am?" she said, with a challenging tilt of one eyebrow.

"Where were you?" I asked.

"I was at work," Sophie said, grabbing a tissue and beginning to wipe the gunk off her eyes.

"Work? I thought you worked at a restaurant," I pressed.

"I do."

"And it's open all night?"

"I went out afterwards."

"Alone?"

Sophie finally met my gaze in the mirror.

"Who are you? My mother?"

I blinked. Ouch. Definitely a new attitude to go along with the new Sophie.

"No, I'm not your mother. I can go and get her if you like, though," I offered, heading for the bathroom door.

"Like that?" Sophie motioned to the towel barely concealing strategic places.

I shrugged.

"Everyone has probably already seen Gram in similar *dishabille*"—this a new word also from one of Gram's highlighted romance excerpts—"so I'll seem ho hum by comparison," I told her, preparing to leave.

"Wait!" Sophie reached out a hand to stop me. "Please! Don't tell Mom."

I stopped and turned back.

"What's going on, Sophie?" I asked.

"It's nothing. Not really. I just don't want to worry my folks," she said.

"Worry them?" Now *I* was worried.

"They wouldn't understand."

They wouldn't understand? I was clueless cubed.

"Tressa!" Aunt Kay called down for me, and Sophie tensed. "Your ranger is here."

Sophie looked at me, a pleading look in her eyes.

"You and I are so gonna talk!" I whispered. Then, "Tell my gentlemen caller his ladyship will be with him momentarily," I yahooed up the stairs and then turned back to Sophie. "Later," I said. "You, me, and a whole lot of catchin' up to do."

I scurried to finish dressing and put on a face—with a much lighter hand than Sophie—grabbed my backpack and headed upstairs wondering if there wasn't more to Cousin Sophie than met the eye.

Metaphorically speaking, of course.

"Could we stop here? Can we go there? I'm thirsty. This art stuff is booooring! Can I have ice cream? When can we go see the Grand Canyon? Why do we have to look at stupid jewelry? Why do the Navajo have their own nation? Does that mean they're not Americans? I hate shopping. I thought we were gonna sightsee. I want to see Oak Creek Canyon. Can we leave the dopey girls here and come back for them later?"

We'd been hitting the Sedona shops for the last two hours, oohing and aahing over turquoise jewelry, hand-woven tapestries, and sterling silver belt buckles. Okay, so I was the one making noise over the belt buckles. The workmanship was superlative. And so, unfortunately, were the prices.

Townsend's niece, eight-year-old Kelsey, sighed. She and I exchanged knowing looks reserved for those

young girls who suffered with royal pains in the behind as brothers.

"Yes. Please, please leave us here, Uncle Rick,"
Kelsey begged. "And take Nick to the top of that stupid Coffee Pot Rock and play Blind Man's Bluff. He's
spoiling everything."

Rick smiled, seemingly used to the siblings squabbling. I, on the other hand, was more than ready to
supply said kerchief as a blindfold for yon youngster.

"We haven't found a gift yet," Rick reminded his
niece.

"And your uncle Rick hasn't taken us to lunch yet,"
I chimed in, not-so-subtly reminding Townsend of his
offer to buy.

"The reason we haven't found a gift yet is because
she's too cheap to spend any money," Nick said, pointing a nose-picking finger at yours truly.

I looked at Townsend.

"Are you gonna let him talk about me that way?" I
asked.

Rick Townsend shrugged. "If the tight—uh, wad
fits . . ." he said with a wave of his hands.

"Hey, I'm only doing what they tell me to in school,"
he-who-wouldn't-be-recognized-with-his-mouth-closed
stated. "I'm taking what I observe, applying it to what I
know, and then drawing a conclusion," he parroted,
sounding just like my schoolteacher best friend, Kari.
"Our teachers talk about it all the time. They call it
making an inference using critical thinking," he said
with a smirk.

"Oh yeah? You sure that isn't critical stinking?" I
asked with a snort. " 'Cause you were sure doing
enough of that on the plane ride here to get an
A-plus," I said. Kelsey and I high-fived each other.
"Yes!"

The squirt gave me a dirty look. "Uncle Rick?"

"Yeah, Nick?"

"Could we go back to that store that had the stuffed rattlesnake doorstop? I think I have enough money to buy it."

"I'm not sure Grandpa Joe and Grandma Hannah would have a use for something like that, kid," Townsend responded.

Nasty Nick's eyes narrowed on me. "I know," he said.

I gave him a "you want a piece of me?" look. After all, the snake was dead. Taxidermy-style dead, but dead nevertheless. What was so scary about that?

Still, the runt did have a point. Everything I looked at I thought Joe and Gram might like—okay everything that *I* might like when they passed gently into that good night and we divided their earthly possessions, and tell me this hasn't crossed your mind on occasion when gift buying—was way beyond this lowly cowgirl's bankroll. A turquoise bracelet for my gammy. A big, shiny belt buckle for me, uh, I mean Joe. An oil painting of Red Rock Crossing. A sculpture of an Indian pony. Perfect, but pricey.

We'd just entered another art shop and I stopped in my tracks. There it was: an absolutely striking statue of Kokopelli, the hunch-backed, flute-playing, Johnny Appleseed of Native American fertility gods. I'd recognize him anywhere—with certain embellishments, that is. Gram had a small knockoff in her collection but I'd accidentally knocked off a certain part of his anatomy that was—shall we say—disproportionately represented. I'd tried to glue the—uh, appendage—back on with the rather unfortunate result that my gammy's knockoff looked like he'd discovered performance enhancing pharmaceuticals.

I've always thought Kokopelli a particularly colorful historical figure. When Gram added the art piece to her collection, it came with an equally colorful biography—one guaranteed to appeal to art aficionados and hopeless romantics who love stories of randy Romeos who roam the countryside in search of fair maidens to plunder and pleasure. And in Kokopelli's case, impregnate.

"Eeow! Gross! Look at the ding dong on that dude!" Townsend's nephew exclaimed and I shot him a dark look.

"Hey! Have a little respect there, young man," I said with a harshness that rarely escaped me. "Kokopelli is very much revered by the Native American culture. He was featured in cave drawings thousands of years ago. It was believed his arrival in a village and the lyrical tones of his flute chased away winter and heralded the coming of spring and warmth and rain."

Ranger Rick gave me a surprised look.

"How do you know this stuff?" he asked.

"Wikipedia, of course," I replied with a dark look. "How do you think I know it? I learned it. Kokopelli's cool. And as I understand it, quite the Casanova."

"How come he's got such a huge, gigantic—?"

Townsend shoved a hand over his nephew's mouth, beating me to it.

"Kokopelli is the Elvis of Native American fertility gods," I explained. "He's in charge of reproduction—be it crops or kids. Therefore, he is represented in a certain anatomically enhanced way."

"How come he's all hunched over?" Kelsey asked.

"If you had to carry that much weight between your legs, you'd be hunched over, too," Nick said, once Townsend removed his hand.

"Eeow! Make him stop, Uncle Rick!" Kelsey yelled, putting her hands over her ears. "Make him stop!"

"For your information, he's depicted hunched over because one legend says he carries a bag of seeds and songs with him," I told the trio. "The Hopi legend has him carrying unborn babies on his back to distribute to women." I decided not to mention the myth that rendered Kokopelli's penis detachable so he could leave it in the river to mate with the young women bathing there. I so didn't want to explain that one.

"And you think Grandpa Joe and Grandma Hannah would like *that* as a wedding gift?" Nick pointed to the figurine with an unbelieving look on his face.

"For reasons known only to me and, maybe an additional person or two, yes. Absolutely. I believe this would make the perfect gift for the happy couple." I reverently picked the figurine up and turned it over. And about dropped it when I saw the price.

"Holy bags of babies!" I yelled. "Three hundred and eighty eight smackaroos!" I gently placed Kokopelli back on the glass shelf and ever so carefully backed away, my hands out at my sides to motion everyone to remove themselves to a safe distance. No way was I gonna risk a *you-break-it-you-bought-it* scenario. Not when I had first-hand knowledge of how fragile certain body parts were.

Once out on the sidewalk I breathed a sigh of relief.

"Dang it," I said. "And that would have been the perfect gift." A bona fide Native American Kokopelli for my gammy with the sweet, sweet added satisfaction of Joe Townsend having to greet the legendary lover of epic proportions each and every day thrown in.

Perfect. I sniffed. Just perfect.

In a noble attempt to cheer me up, Townsend treated the four of us to dinner at Oak Creek Grill in Tlaquepaque Arts and Crafts Village. I must've looked forlorn because Townsend ordered appetizers of wings and beer-battered onion rings. The two kids split a cheese pizza while Townsend opted for the steak sandwich. I debated over the menu until I sensed the natives were getting restless and then promptly decided on the Triple Decker Brew Pub Club, a sandwich guaranteed to challenge even my bite radius. Having ordered the Pub Club, it was a given I'd have to order an ice-cold draw of the pub's best light beer brewed to be the perfect complement to any appetizer or meal. Hey, I wasn't driving.

By the time I'd consumed my sandwich, I was too full to eat the three-layer dark chocolate cake that was their specialty, so I ordered a honking slice to go. I figured given my metabolism, I'd be hungry again in an hour.

"I've never seen a girl eat so much," Nick Townsend remarked as we left the restaurant. "Most of Uncle Rick's girlfriends eat like birds, picking at their food and moving it around on their plates."

"Oh, really?" I said, stifling a beer belch. "Good thing I'm not your uncle's girlfriend then, as I'm not a big fan of starving myself to conform to society's unhealthy appetite for women who, if you stuck a sesame seed on their heads, they'd look like straight pins."

Next to me, Kelsey giggled. "That's a good one, Tressa," she said, and reached out to take my hand.

I stared down at our joined hands, both uncomfortable with the contact and touched by it. Most of my experience with kids came from the snotty, demanding little bozos who came into the Dairee Freeze looking for ice cream and to screw around with their friends until Uncle Frank or I kicked their sorry butts out. This type of closeness I wasn't accustomed to. To be frank, I'm not a touchy-feely person. Expressing affection is as hard for me as giving up M & Ms. Well, as hard as I think that would be since I've never actually given them up before. And don't anticipate doing so.

"Stay tuned, kid. I got a million of 'em," I told Kelsey, an attempt at levity to get me back on safe, wise-cracking-Tressa turf.

We piled into the Suburban that Townsend's dad had rented and set out on our sightseeing trip through Oak Creek Canyon. On the way to Sedona, we had taken I-17 and cut across Old Schnebly Hill Road, but on the return trip we planned to take the series of switchbacks via Route 89A and stop along the way to explore various trails and overlooks, and appreciate the crimson-colored cliffs and crystal-clear pools.

We decided to head south on 89A for a ways and then double back so we wouldn't miss any of the spectacular scenery. We'd driven ten miles or so when I noticed a dull, faded van sitting down a side road, a pull-up awning erected for shade. As we drove by, I noticed a collection of figurines on a long table beneath the awning.

"Stop!" I yelled. "Stop the car!"

Townsend looked over at me.

"What's wrong?" he asked.

"Back there. The vendor. He had some cool statues," I said. "He might have a Kokopelli. Or a reasonable facsimile thereof. I'm thinking maybe his price could be right," I added.

Townsend took a look in his rearview mirror.

"I don't know, T," he said. "An old beater van. Way outside Sedona. I'm thinking unlicensed."

"And I'm thinking cheaper," I said. "Turn around! Please!"

"Yes! Please, Uncle Rick!" Kelsey chimed in.

Townsend took another look in his rearview mirror, sighed and pulled onto the shoulder, performing a U-turn.

"The things I do to please the women in my life," he said, and I felt my tummy do a belly button flip like you get when you crest a hill too fast. I looked over at Townsend, my eyes feeling as big as Sacajawea silver dollars.

The women in his life? Hello. When had I blinked and missed earning that notable distinction? And was I even ready to deal with everything that role implied? Like getting "nekkid" in front of Rick Townsend with my post-Easter pounds still clinging to my hips and thighs like a city slicker clings to the saddle horn on a dude ranch trail ride.

I continued to stare at Townsend.

"What?" he said, catching my scrutiny. "What? Are you all right?" he added, probably catching my pallor, as well.

"Yeah. Sure. 'Course I'm all right. Why wouldn't I be all right? Full stomach. Beautiful scenery. Great weather. Chocolate cake for later. Who wouldn't be all right?" I replied, running out of breath toward the end. I tend to babble when I'm nervous.

Townsend grinned, and I suspected he figured out the reason for my fluster.

"Don't forget to add perfect companions to that list," Townsend reminded me. "Good company in a journey makes the way seem shorter, you know," he recited as he pulled the Suburban onto the shoulder. "Izaak Walton," he added for my edification.

I nodded. "I'll file that bit of wisdom away for future reference, Mr. Ranger, sir," I told him. "Right alongside the mating habits of the common bull snake and the manual on defusing a C-4 explosive device."

We carefully crawled out of the vehicle and walked back to the sky-blue van. It looked like the kind of setup that should have Elvis tapestries and puppy dog wall rugs on display and blowing in the Arizona breezes. No Elvis sightings—thank you, thank you very much—however my hero, John Wayne, was more than adequately represented with his distinctive persona pasted on rugs, mugs, posters and coasters. He was on canvas and velvet, bookends and blankets. Even a

Duke Wayne bobble head. I picked it up and jiggled it. Sweet.

"Who is that?" Nick said, pointing to the bobble in my hand. "He looks weird."

I gave the infant a shocked look and put a hand to my heart.

"You live in Iowa and you don't recognize John Wayne? Sacrilege!" I said. "Uncle Rick has been most remiss in your education," I scolded.

"What's wrong with his eyes?" the youngun asked. "They're all squinty."

"That's his 'don't mess with this cowpoke' look. He's famous for it," I replied.

Nick shook his head. "He looks like Grandpa Joe does when he's taking a nap and we suddenly turn on the light," Nick told me. I grinned. I'd have to remember to razz Joltin' Joe about that.

I approached a woman sitting in a lawn chair reading an issue of *People* magazine that featured stars who'd packed on the pounds. The vendor wore a so-faux suede vest and denim skirt. With her bleached hair and red roots, she didn't look like any Native American I'd ever seen.

"Hello there," I greeted the dour-faced woman. "How much for the John Wayne bobble head?" I asked, thinking J.W. would make a nifty addition to my bobble head family. I could stick Duke between William Jefferson and George Dubya to keep the two in line.

"Twelve-fifty," the woman answered. "It's a good deal."

"I thought we were looking for a wedding gift," Townsend said, joining me at the table.

"We are," I said. "But this would make a rootin' tootin' addition to the bobble bunch, and an affordable souvenir of our trip to Sedona for me. So I can look back and remember our good time. You know, Like the time dishy Trooper Dawkins insisted on winning that giant Nemo for me on the midway at the fair last summer," I added.

Townsend shook his head and heaved a quantum sigh. "Give it here," he said, and I handed it over.

"Oh, Townsend, you spoil me so," I gushed, batting my eyes in as coy a manner as I could manage.

"Lots of John Wayne stuff," the clerk said, sensing maybe some gullible tourists. "John Wayne filmed many movies here in the Red Rock and Oak Creek Canyon area. The Duke loved it here. He even owned a couple ranches in Arizona." She picked up a bronze statue of John Wayne sitting on a rather disproportionately crafted horse. "The Duke was a real horseman, that one."

I snorted. Obviously this woman didn't know Duke like I knew Duke.

I snapped my fingers at the whippersnappers. "Listen up, you two," I said. "This is Lesson One in John Wayne Trivia." I turned back to the woman seated in the lawn chair. "Actually, Wayne was known as 'Duke' not 'the Duke,' as is often mistakenly expressed. You see, as a child in Glendale, California, he'd visit the local fire station with his Airedale terrier, 'Little Duke,' and the firemen started calling him 'Big Duke' and since he preferred Duke to Marion—and who wouldn't?—the nickname stuck. Trust me. I know about nicknames. Secondly, despite his brilliant portrayals of tough-as-nails soldiers, cowpokes, and lawmen, Marion Michael Morrison didn't really care for horses all that much. He much preferred the deck of a boat to the back of a horse."

The saleswoman stared up at me.

"Marion who?"

"Marion Michael Morrison—better known as John

Wayne. You see, a director figured 'Marion' was too sissified a name for a big, tough hero type, so they changed it to John Wayne. And the rest," I said with a wink, "is history."

"Is that a fact?" the clerk said, clearly not impressed with my demonstrated knowledge in this area.

I nodded.

"And I'll bet you didn't know Duke was born in Iowa either," I went on. "Just a couple counties over from where I live, as a matter of fact. They even have a museum at his birthplace site in Winterset," I told her.

"Fascinating," she said, not bothering to cover her yawn. "So, you're from Iowa?" she asked, taking in our little party with her query.

I nodded. "Yep. The 'if you build it, they will come' state.'"

"Huh?"

"*Field of Dreams.* Kevin Costner. Academy Award. Any of these ring a bell?"

The woman shrugged. "I know Iowa. I buy potatoes."

My ears began to burn. I hated it when folks got the corn state confused with the russet one. And I suspected this woman had done it on purpose.

"Actually that's not Iowa, that's Idaho. And nothing infuriates a Hawkeye more than—"

Townsend grabbed my hand.

"We need to get moving, Tressa," Townsend said. "Wasn't there something else you came for?" he urged as he led me over to the figurines.

I gave the woman an *I'm from Iowa and I'm proud* look and let myself be led away. I looked through the figurines, disappointed that none of them was quite right when I spotted a statue set apart from the others on the top shelf of a rickety old wire stand sitting behind the clerk. Approximately eight inches in height and, judging from certain anatomical attributes that could not be overlooked, it was obviously a fertility god of some kind. However, it certainly was not my friend, Kokopelli. This image was cruder. Rougher. With a phallus of phenomenal proportions. And totally, without a doubt, the butt ugliest statue I'd ever laid eyes on. Well, except for the gross outdoor one on the campus at Carson College back home that someone with a college education and smart enough to know better had slapped down six figures for, that is.

"That's it!" I yelled. "That's the perfect gift for the happy couple! I'm sure of it!" If the price was right, as Bob Barker would say. I pointed to the statue. "Could I see that please?" I asked. "The statue there. The 'no guess as to how happy I am to see you' one."

Townsend shook his head.

"That's not for sale," the woman snapped, obviously annoyed with me for my biographical moment earlier. "It's on hold for another customer."

I frowned. On hold? From a rolling flea market?

"Another customer asked you to hold this item for them?" I asked.

"That's right," she said.

"Well, then, do you have another one I could see?" I asked, my patience becoming as strained as the Gerber baby plums I used to snitch from time to time when I babysat the Parker twins. Trust me, it's good stuff. Uh, but let's keep it between the two of us, okay?

The woman shook her head. "It's one of a kind. Very rare. Unique piece."

Right. And just about now I should be hearing about some prime ocean-front real estate. Or a terrific time-share opportunity.

I put my woe-is-me face on and tried again.

"Please? It's a wedding gift for two dear old seniors who have finally found each other after fifty years apart," I said, trying to convince her. "Pretty please?"

"You want to give *that* as a wedding present? What'd the ol' couple do to you?" the woman asked.

Just my luck. Another Rosie O'Donnell wannabe.

"Well, you see, my grandmother and *his* grandfather have recently been reunited," I said, jabbing a finger at Townsend. "After many years of being married to other people, they are now both free, and they recently became engaged and made plans to marry. Since my Aunt Kay and my Uncle Ben live in Flagstaff—Aunt Kay is a librarian and Uncle Ben is a fairly well-known artist hereabouts—maybe you've heard of him? Ben Stemple? Well, anyway, my gammy decided on a Grand Canyon wedding and the whole family is here to celebrate the tying of the knot at The Grand Titan Hotel in three days time. The wedding party and entourage will then fly off for a week-long celebratory cruise with Carousel Cruises. Olé!" I said, finishing and putting my fingers up like castanets.

It took a bit for the woman to process my narrative. Once she did, she shook her head again.

"Sorry, it's sold," she said.

"But there's no sold sign on it!" I insisted. "And are you sure there's not another one just lying around in that van of yours? Could you take a look for me?"

"I'm sorry. I told you. That's the only one."

"Better get packed up. Looks like rain."

A tall, big-boned, slightly balding man with what hair he had pulled back into a ponytail stepped under the overhang from around the side of the van and addressed the woman.

"Please. Could you check for me?" I tried one last time before the perfect gift rode out of my life like Rooster Cogburn rode away from Mattie Ross of Dardanelle in Yell County at the end of *True Grit.* And what a tearjerker that was!

"Check for what?" the guy asked the woman.

"She wants to see that figurine," the woman told the newcomer, pointing to the let's-do-it statue.

"So, show it to her," he said.

"It's sold," the woman replied. "Remember the guy that stopped by a couple days ago and told us to hold it for him? Told us under no circumstances were we to sell it to anyone, that he'd be back to get it."

The man started to box up his wares. "He said he'd be back yesterday. Have you seen him? Show her the statue."

"But that guy was pretty insistent about us not selling it," she said. "Almost like he was warning us not to sell it."

"We're merchants. We sell stuff. That's what we do." The fellow walked over and picked up the bizarre-looking figurine and slapped it into my hands. "Sixty bucks and it's yours, blondie," he said as I examined the homely and horny collectible that Hellion Hannah would absolutely, positively adore. Still, sixty bucks was a little pricey for this cowgirl—unless she planned to live on beans and weenies for the next couple months.

"Sixty bucks? For this? How much was the other guy paying?" I asked.

"Okay. Fifty bucks," the merchant said.

"But was he also purchasing a John Wayne commemorative bobble head?" I asked, with a let's-make-a-deal smile.

The guy grunted. "Fine. Fifty bucks and I'll throw in the bobble head," he said. I smiled.

"Sold!" I said, clutching my find to my chest. "Now pay the man, Townsend," I ordered. "We're burnin' daylight, Mr. Ranger, sir."

Townsend pulled out his wallet.

"Low maintenance, my ass," he said with a snort.

"Don't worry, Mr. Ranger, sir," I said. "We'll settle up

later. And I'm sooo good for it," I told him with a couple come-up-and-see-me-some-time lifts of waxed brows.

"That remains to be seen, Calamity," he said. "That remains to be seen."

Oooo-weee! Apparently the little trinket in my hands wasn't the only male in these here parts who had a hankerin' to sow a few wild oats.

Yippee-kai-yay, Ranger Rick!

CHAPTER SIX

"So, are we through with the history lessons?" Nick whined as we piled back into the SUV. "Can we finally go look at some cool stuff now?"

I carefully placed the wedding gift in my backpack (I'd officially dubbed the statue Kookamunga) along with the John Wayne bobble, sticking my chocolate cake in the bag the roadside clerk had given me. I patted my backpack. I didn't want Gram getting a look at her gift until she and Joe unwrapped it together. And I wanted my digital camera handy to catch the exact moment Joe laid his cataract-clear peepers on it. It would be one heckuva snapshot for the wedding scrapbook. Just bee-yoo-tee-ful.

We continued our drive along Oak Creek Canyon, stopping at several overlooks to let Nick see Steamboat Rock, Courthouse Butte and Bell Rock, and to admire the incredible beauty of the area from different vantage points. I snapped a bunch of photos, thinking I could maybe make a picture album or scrapbook for

Gram and Joe. Hey, I can stick photos in an album as well as the next person.

Oak Creek Canyon Vista was our last stop before we headed back to Flag. The vista featured even more shopping opportunities, with various souvenir stands lining the paths, a fact that delighted young Nick to no end. Naturally Kelsey and I were drawn to the jewelry and trinkets. Uh, okay and the food, too.

The menfolk moved on ahead, deciding to explore a pathway that didn't feature anything that could be used as a fashion accessory or consumed. Or both. Kelsey and I left a stand hawking dream catchers and Snowbowl snow globes when I decided my stomach was empty enough to accommodate my dessert and we took a seat at a nearby table. I opened my bag and took Duke out and set him on the table. The bobble head bounced like my gammy before she put on her forty-eight-hour steel-reinforced support bra.

"And I say that's bull-talk for a one-eyed fat man," I told the bobble head, quoting a favorite *True Grit* line, pulling out the bag that held a little bit of chocolate heaven.

Kelsey gave me a puzzled look and I winked at her. I was going through my backpack for a handy wipe or tissue to clean up with when Kelsey nudged my elbow.

"That guy's been staring at you for, like, ever, Tressa," she said.

Okay. I have to admit initially I didn't pay all that much attention. I'm used to being stared at. Okay, so it's usually because I've got something gross and green stuck in my teeth after I've eaten, or something long and white plastered to the sole of a shoe after I've used a public restroom. Or—well, enough about me.

When I finally cast a casual look in the direction Kelsey motioned, I almost wet my pants. (I'm chalking this up to the beer.) Kelsey was right! A very good-

looking guy had his dark, brooding gaze locked on little ol' me. A much younger, black-haired version of
Fabio, my admirer had shiny dark hair, parted in the
middle, falling to rest on a set of broad, muscular
shoulders that shouted lots of sweaty hours in a gym. I
sighed. The Arizona Department of Tourism wasn't
wrong about the scenic splendor of the Oak Creek
Canyon area. Talk about your breathtaking natural
beauty. Hubba hubba.

I decided to respond with my coy cowgirl look,
which included a crooked little half smile and fleeting eye contact. The corners of my ardent admirer's
mouth turned slightly upward in response, so I let my
smile have its head and displayed the full power of my
pearly whites in all their ever-so-slightly prominent
glory.

I sucked my breath in when the Oak Creek Canyon
hunk started our way.

"Ohmigosh, he's coming over, Tressa!" Kelsey said.
"And he's so hot! Take a picture! Take a picture!"

I looked over at her. "He is pretty hunkariffic, but I
can't take a picture, I'd look like a hick," I said. Yet I
was thinking what a spectacular addition to my
gammy's scrapbook this southwestern hunk would
make. Centerfold placement, for sure. "I can't, but
you can!" I said, pushing my camera across the table
toward Kelsey.

"Me? Why me?"

"Nobody is going to pay attention to a young girl
taking photos. Just snap a couple and 'accidentally'
get him in one—or ten—of them."

"He is really cute," she agreed. "But I get a copy to
show my friends."

"Done," I said, shaking.

By this time our scrapbook pin-up protégé had
crossed the path and was almost within arm's reach—

just a figure of speech here, folks—of our table. He smiled and I bit down just to make sure my tongue was still safely within my mouth and not hanging out like my dogs' at Mighty Mutt mealtime. My breath hitched in my throat.

"Man, they grow 'em gorgeous out here," I muttered under my breath.

"Hello," he said.

Click. Click. Click. Kelsey finally emerged from her catatonia to snap several pictures.

My Oak Creek Canyon Casanova's smile vanished quicker than gift-card credit after Christmas. A scary-looking scowl took its place at about the same time our cover model reached out and tried to snatch my camera from around Kelsey's neck. Stunned, I looked wildly around for something to smack him with and spotted Duke on the table. I grabbed the novelty item and brought it down hard on the guy's arm, smacking his wrist hard. Once. Twice.

Kelsey began to scream. The scrapbook centerfold looked around, apparently noticed we were attracting some attention and let go of the camera. He looked at me, then at the bag on the table in front of me and his eyes got big.

His hand shot by me and grabbed the bag with my cake and took off running with it.

"Stop! Thief!" I yelled. "Stop! Stop that man! He has my cake!" I jumped to my feet, prepared to run after him when I looked over and saw Kelsey crying and shaking like I do when my car's thermostat gets stuck in the winter and the heater blows cold air. "Dammit," I said, and sat down beside her and put an arm around her shoulders. "Are you all right, Kelsey?" I asked, drying her tears with a napkin, and so not wanting to have to explain to Townsend why his niece was tearstained and semi-hysterical. "Did he hurt you?"

"I'm okay," she replied, obliging by blowing her nose when I stuck the napkin in front of it. "Why did he try to grab the camera?" Kelsey said. I shrugged.

"I guess some people are just really camera shy," I said, making it up as I went along. "And there are some folks who believe every time you have your picture taken, you lose some of your life force," I told her. "There are lots of superstitions out here."

"Okay. But why'd he take your cake?" she asked.

Hmm. That one would require some thought.

I looked over at my John Wayne bobble head. Poor Duke. He looked like he'd just defended the Alamo for the last time—or maybe how the real Wayne looked after his movie *The Alamo* bombed big-time at the box office.

"Oh, Tressa! His head's all twisted around and sideways!" Kelsey wailed, tears coming to her eyes again.

I took the camera from Kelsey and hit the review button. I felt my brows lower and my teeth clench when the Oak Creek Canyon Vista Villain's face appeared on the tiny screen.

"Who the devil is that?" I heard from behind, and turned to find Ranger Rick breathing hot air down my neck.

"That devil," I announced, "is the low-down, dirty, rotten, no-good polecat who broke my bobble!"

And there wasn't room enough in Oak Creek Canyon for the both of us.

We spent about thirty minutes combing the nearby area for the devil's food fiend who'd absconded with my slice of Tlaquepaque Chocolate Fantasy. Zero success. The Cocoa Casanova had vanished along with my dark chocolate dessert. I insisted a reluctant Ranger Rick escort me to the nearest ranger station so I could report the incident. Initially Townsend balked at the

idea. I really couldn't blame him. Somehow I didn't
think these official Forest Service rangers would at-
tach the importance to a snatched three-layer chocolate confection with inch-thick frosting that Ranger
Smith did to Yogi-Bear pilfered pickanic baskets in
Jellystone Park. But Uncle Rick did care about his
niece—very much—and the idea that some goon
(great-looking or not) tried to strong-arm her and
make off with her camera put a dark, angry look on
his face I'd never seen before. Dangerous. Disturbing.
And sexy as all get-out. As long as it wasn't directed at
me, that is.

We headed over to the visitors center and requested
to speak to an officer. Fifteen minutes later I spotted
an honest-to-goodness ranger enter the building and
walk over to the information specialist we'd visited
with earlier. She looked over at us, nodded to the employee, and headed in our direction.

"Hello, folks," the Forest Service officer said, stopping a few feet from our little group and giving us the
once-over. Or, in Townsend's case, the second-, third-,
and fourth-over. Her eyes widened and her nostrils
flared just ever so slightly when her gaze rested on
Ranger Rick. Beautifully shaped mocha eyes outlined
with black eyeliner flared perfectly at the edges, her
bronze coloring striking against the whites of her eyes
as those peepers fixated on Townsend's manly mug.
She touched her Smokey Bear hat with two fingers,
keeping dark eyes on Townsend.

"I'm Officer Whitehead. I hear you had a little run-
in with a scofflaw," the attractive Oak Creek Canyon
cop said. I blinked.

"What's a scofflaw, Tressa?" Kelsey said, pulling on
my hoodie.

"I'll tell you later, kid," I replied. Just as soon as I
Googled it myself to make sure.

"It's someone who ignores or disregards the law," Whitehead told Kelsey with a smile. "A lawbreaker."

"Thanks!" Kelsey said with a big smile for the female officer. I shrugged. I knew that.

"How long ago did the incident occur?" she asked, drawing a small notebook from a breast pocket.

"Fifty minutes," I said, and she finally looked at me. "Give or take a couple."

"And this was where?"

I pulled my camera out of my bag, turned it on and hit the review button.

"Right there," I said, shoving the camera in her face to show her the pictures we'd taken just before we spotted the Canyon Casanova with camera issues.

She frowned. "What is that?" she asked, and I looked at the photo to see what she meant.

"Oh. That's my John Wayne bobble head," I told her. "A before picture, of course. Poor Duke's in need of Percocet and a cervical collar now, I'm afraid," I said, shaking my head.

She stared at me. "Bobble head?"

I nodded, pulling J.W. from my bag and displaying his sad little lopsided neck, twisted head and sideways Stetson.

"I bought him at a souvenir stand down the road a piece. I collect them. Isn't he adorable? I'd planned to put Duke here between William Jefferson and George Dubya, but now that I think about it, maybe I'd better stick him between Mr. Clinton and Marilyn Monroe."

More staring.

"Tressa and my niece were sitting at a picnic table just down one of the hiking paths, taking photos, when they were approached by an individual who attempted to take the camera from my niece," Townsend told the confused canyon copper.

"Niece?" She looked at Kelsey and then over at Nick. "And I suppose you are the nephew," she said. I noted the young boy began to redden as he had when I'd caught him staring at Taylor.

"Yeah. I'm Nick Townsend, and that's my Uncle Rick," Nick explained. "He's a DNR officer back home."

Whitehead frowned.

"DNR?" she said.

"As in 'Ducks Need Rescuing,'" I quipped, and Townsend shot me an exasperated look.

"Iowa Department of Natural Resources," he said. "Enforcement Division."

"The Corn State, not the Baked with Sour Cream and Chives State," I clarified, just in case.

She nodded and put out a hand to shake Townsend's. "Nice to meet you," she said, her broad smile signaling we'd reached a new level of understatement in these here parts. "And this must be your aunt," she said to Nick, throwing a quick nod in my direction.

"Oh, no, she's not our aunt," Nick disputed—way quicker than necessary, I thought. "She's gonna kinda be our cousin soon, when our great-grandpa marries her grandma. She's just a reporter for a dopey newspaper back home who finds dead bodies," he told her.

Officer Whitehead frowned.

"What Nick means is that I'm an investigative journalist who specializes in crime reporting," I said, resisting the urge to goose the little twerp. "I have a history of going deep undercover to get the story," I added, "and I've had some success."

"I see," Whitehead said, her expression contradicting her words. "And this man who accosted you just came up out of the blue and tried to snatch your camera?" she asked.

"Well, we'd noticed him before," Kelsey said.

Whitehead turned to her.

"You had?"

Kelsey nodded. "He was staring at Tressa with this really weird look on his face," Kelsey went on. "I told Tressa and pointed him out to her."

"You did?"

Kelsey nodded. "Tressa thought he was hot," Kelsey said before I could shush her.

"She did?" Townsend said, and I felt my face warm.

"I don't recall that part," I said.

"Don't you remember, Tressa? You said 'Man, they sure grow 'em gorgeous out here,'" Kelsey responded.

Hello. What in criminy were they teaching kids in school these days? Total Recall 101?

"I think you may have misheard—"

"Then why did you want me to take his picture?" Kelsey asked, a totally sincere, thoroughly inquisitive look on her angelic but tattletaling little face.

"I think you may have misunderstood—"

"You have a picture of the man?" Whitehead interrupted, her eyebrows lifting a half an inch.

I nodded.

"Purely by chance, not by design, you understand," I assured her. "We're tourists, after all. Tourists take pictures. It's what they do," I said, suffering a sudden episode of runaway mouth. It's what I do when I'm nervous. And when I'm trying to stay out of trouble.

Townsend looked over at me and shook his head. He'd noticed the arrival of maniac mouth, too. Damn.

"May I see the photo?" Whitehead asked, and I hit the review button.

"There he is," I said, sensing stiffening in the posture of the forest service official at my side. I hit the review button again. "And there. And there. And there." I looked down at Kelsey. "For crying out loud, how many did you take?" I asked.

She shrugged. "I wanted to make sure we got a good one for your centerfold," she said, and I cringed. Ye gods! Had I said that aloud?

I reached over and patted her head. "Good one, Kels," I said, giving Townsend a sickly smile. "Good one."

She looked up at me, her eyes glazed with confusion. "Huh?"

"So you took these pictures?" Whitehead asked Kelsey, and she nodded.

"Tressa was right, too, wasn't she? He is hot, isn't he?" Kelsey asked.

"He is at that," Whitehead said, finally turning to give me the benefit of her full attention—and hard, searching gaze. "He is at that," she repeated. It occurred to me that something about the photo had captured this Oak Creek officer's attention. Something beyond the pretty face, that is.

"And what did this individual take, exactly?" she asked. "You still have your camera."

"He took her cake," Nick said, an impertinent smile spreading across his face.

"Cake?" she said, looking to Ranger Rick for help.

He nodded. "Cake," he said.

"Oh, but not just any cake," I told her. "It was a slice of triple chocolate fantasy cake from the Oak Creek Grill in Tlaquepaque. The fiend made off with it before I even had a chance to take one bite! He needs to pay, I tell you!"

"Why would someone want to steal a piece of cake?" she asked.

"Hello. Did you miss the 'triple chocolate' part?" I said, although now that I thought on it, the guy didn't look much like a chocoholic. "Still, now that you mention it, it does seem kind of strange." Strange, yes, but not out of the realm of possibility when it came to a serious chocolate addiction. Annually, beginning around February 15th, I started haunting the local stores, hounding them to unpack their Easter candy and put the Cadbury Creme Eggs out already. I'd been tempted to camp out in front of Bargain City until they got sick of seeing me there and obliged.

"And you're very sure that's all he took?" Whitehead asked again.

"That's it," I said. "But thanks to bobble head Duke, Kelsey the kid, and Terrible Tressa, that varmint will think twice about coming between a gal and her chocolate again."

"Don't you mean Kelsey the kid and *Calamity Jayne*?" Nick Townsend asked with a smirk. "That's Tressa's nickname," he told Whitehead. "Calamity Jayne. 'Cause she's always getting into trouble. Last summer at the fair she got chased up a giant slide by a dunk-tank clown, and when she slid back down she got this humongous burn on her—"

Townsend slapped a hand over his nephew's mouth, saving me the trouble.

Whitehead looked at each of us. "Never been to Iowa," she said. "But it sounds like an interesting place to visit someday," she added with a look at Ranger Rick that settled on his lips.

"Y'all come up and see us sometime," I told her. "I'll put on a chicken."

"And I'm telling you, she knew that guy!" I said, not for the first time as we drove along, still about ten miles outside Flagstaff. "I could tell by her reaction when she saw his photo."

"Maybe she just thought he was hot like you did," Townsend suggested with a peeved sidelong look at me. "Maybe she thought he'd make a good pin-up."

"Oh, puh-leaze! I saw the way you looked at Ranger

Service Barbie back there," I countered. "Tell me you didn't think she was attractive. And as frequently and for as long as you stared at her chest, I'm surprised you didn't memorize the service year from her name tag," I added with a sneer.

"'Serving since 2004,'" Uncle Rick and Nephew Nick recited together in unison. Like a choral reading but not. I stared at both of them in turn.

"Nice, Townsend," I said. "Real nice. Teach the kid to ogle women," I said, folding my arms across my own inadequacies.

"What's ogle?" Nick asked, leaning from the backseat to shove between us.

"It's rudely staring at a person's . . . person with the intent to objectify that individual in a negative or demeaning way," I said, quoting from something I'd read about some women's group attacking porn.

"What does 'objectify' mean?"

I turned around in my seat.

"Do I look like I have 'thesaurus' printed on my forehead?" I asked.

"Why would you have a dinosaur on your forehead?" Nick the twit asked, and I gave him what I hoped was a reasonable representation of a *did your mother have any children who lived?* look and turned back around to the front.

"Why did that officer lady give you her card, Uncle Rick?" Nick suddenly asked, snaring my attention once again.

"She gave it to me in case we need to contact her," Townsend said.

"But why did you give her your card, Uncle Rick?" Nick asked.

"I wrote down our contact information so she could reach us, squirt," Rick said, flashing me a smile that was long on teeth and short on truth.

"But why did she write down her home phone number?" Nick said. "And why did she write down the word 'Numbers' with an address, Uncle Rick?"

Uncle Rick hesitated a second too long.

"Yes, Uncle Rick. Do tell. Why did Officer Whitehead give you her home phone number, and what special significance does 'Numbers' have relating to our official investigation?" I asked.

"Sit back and buckle up, Nick," Rick barked, and his nephew quickly complied. I blinked at Townsend's uncharacteristic shortness with his nephew. The pipsqueak had obviously struck a nerve.

"So?" I said.

"So?" Townsend looked over at me. "She invited us for drinks," he said, with a shrug that looked a tad bit tense.

"Us?" I frowned. "Oh, really. When were you going to tell me about this little invite?"

He shrugged again. "What's the big deal? It wasn't as if I—we—were going to go."

"Oh? Why wouldn't *we* go?"

Townsend gave me another quick look. "Aw, hell. All right. She asked me. From what Nick told her, she gathered you and I weren't together."

"I see." Only, I didn't. Obviously Townsend hadn't corrected Whitehead's assumption. This left me wondering if I'd mistaken Townsend's ardent interest in me for something more than a natural inclination to explore new, unfamiliar—and challenging—territory. The possibility hurt me more than I cared to own up to.

"Look, Tressa, I never intended to go," he said. "She just mentioned that a group of her friends were meeting there this evening and said if I liked I could stop by for a drink," he said.

"You don't have to explain anything to me," I said, with a toss of my head. "Like you said, we aren't together. And it's your vacation, after all. You should go. Explore the possibilities."

Townsend gave me a long look. "Do you really want me to do that, Tressa?" he asked. "Explore the possibilities?"

"Hey, it worked for Lewis and Clark," I said, trying to defuse a situation with levity yet knowing I was only prolonging the inevitable showdown. I shook my head.

Coward. Calamity Jane would so not approve.

A muscle in Townsend's cheek twitched and I could tell from long acquaintance that his teeth were clenched. "Maybe you're right, Tressa," he finally said. "Maybe you're right. There's still the little matter of your inconvenient engagement," he added. "After all, you're not even available. So maybe I will check out Numbers tonight. Who knows? Maybe I'll strike gold exploring those possibilities you mentioned."

"It's a free country," I shot back, and turned my attention to the world passing by the car window. For the next few miles Townsend refused to look at me or talk to me, and reserved his short, terse remarks for his niece and nephew. My eyes begin to water as stupid tears pooled. I avoided blinking so as not to send any of the drops trickling down my cheeks, and pinched my nose to keep from sniffling.

I'm usually not a crier. By circumstance and design. In fact, I'm generally the first one to poke fun at women who get all teary-eyed and watery at the drop of a hat. My family refuses to watch sad, sappy movies with me because I sit there and crack jokes at those touching, somber moments. Little do they know that later I'll watch the same movie in the privacy of my own little domicile and bawl my way through a box of tissues.

I'm not a neat, petite crier. I'm messy as hell. And

when I'm done I look like I've just survived a serious allergic reaction. My eyes are puffy and red and my lips are swollen and huge. My nose rivals Rudolph's in the crimson department.

Even as a child I had issues with crying in front of people. Maybe because it didn't fit the persona I'd fashioned for myself. Maybe because I equated crying with vulnerability, with letting my guard down and letting my mushy insides show with weakness. All of which were big no-nos, as far as I was concerned.

Unfortunately, this firm control over my emotions over a long period of time occasionally results in a major meltdown. My grandpa's funeral is a great case in point. I loved my Paw Paw Will. His sudden death was a shock to the entire family. At the funeral home viewing when Taylor went up to pay her last respects, she broke out in this high-pitched, shrill, cat-in-heat caterwauling that I so didn't expect to hear. Nor did I expect the strain of keeping a tight rein on my own emotions would result in the sudden, uncontrollable onset of a fit of hysteria so potent and explosive I started to laugh. Effusively. Infectiously. Unforgivably.

I ended up having to conjure up this chest-crushing cough to cover up the giggles, and clapped a hand to my mouth and ran out of the funeral home, mortified.

I still remembered Townsend's reaction. He'd followed me out and chased me down the block and heckled me so effectively that my fit of laughter dissolved like Alka-Seltzer in water and I'd returned to the funeral home with tears of anger in my eyes. Later, in the privacy of my room, I cried into my pillow— long, silent, sloppy sobs of grief.

For the first time I wondered if it was possible that Rick Townsend had been such a jerk to me that day to jolt me out of my manic mirth so I wouldn't make a total ass of myself. I looked over at him, hoping he would look my way, but he kept his eyes on the road.

Damned men. Who needed them, anyway? Nowadays women did very nicely on their own, thank you very much. Modern women brought home their own bacon, fried it, and cleaned up afterwards with no help from men. Modern women made home repairs and serviced their own automobiles—among other things—without a man. Women got pregnant and gave birth and raised children, and all without a man in their lives.

I stopped. I sounded like an infomercial for *Lesbian Lifestyles*.

I glanced in the outside rearview mirror and through moisture-blurred eyes noticed a black Toyota following us. I frowned and squinted at the car's reflection. I could've sworn I'd seen a car just like that pull out behind us as we left Oak Creek Canyon Vista. The car in question had sported a dream catcher on the inside mirror. I squinted harder to see if I could make out the decoration in the mirror, but the distance was too great.

"What are you doing now?" Townsend asked. "Spot another hot guy? Isn't one engagement ring enough? You want me to stop so you can add another to your collection?"

I shook my head, watching the car as it kept two lengths distance between us.

"I think that car is following us," I told Townsend.

"That's because it is," he said.

"What?"

"It's behind us—i.e., it's following us."

I shook my head.

"No. I mean, I think it has been following us since we left Oak Creek Canyon," I told him. "I'm almost certain it's the same car."

Townsend's gaze shifted to the inside mirror. "So? It's pretty hard to pass on those switchbacks. If he's heading back to Flag, he's pretty much stuck behind us."

"I guess," I said, peering back at the driver but only making out distorted facial features, feeling unsettled but not sure whether it was due to the earlier incident or my disagreement with Townsend. Or both.

We rode along in silence until Townsend pulled into my aunt and uncle's driveway to drop me off. I opened the door to get out.

"Uh, thanks for lunch and for the sightseeing," I said, suddenly nervous as my mom when my gammy asks to use her computer, credit card in hand. "And thanks for stopping so I could get my bobble head and Gram's gift—not to mention treating me to a scenic southwestern snatch-and-grab. Gram'll love Kookamunga, by the way," I told him, avoiding eye contact. I shifted my attention to the back seat. "And remember, guys, it's our little secret," I said. "So mum's the word."

"Who's mum?" Nick asked.

I took a deep breath.

"See you, kids," I bade adieu to the tired younguns in the backseat. "Enjoy that luxury hotel, would you, and don't you worry your little heads one itty bitty second about Tressa here bedding down on a lumpy ol' sofa bed in a dark, ol' basement," I said. "I'll be just fine."

"Tressa, about Whitehead and Numbers," Townsend said, leaning across the front seat toward the passenger side.

"Hey, don't sweat it, Townsend," I said, grabbing my backpack and pulling it on over one shoulder. "I've got your number, you know," I said.

He looked at me for a long time and I knew just when his gaze shifted to my lips. Lips that I bit to keep from quivering. And I suspected he knew it.

"I wonder," was all he said, and he slid behind the wheel again, put the SUV in gear, backed out and drove away, leaving Duke, Kookamunga, and me behind in his rearview mirror.

I walked slowly up the steps to the front door, opened it and was about to close it when I noticed a car drive slowly past the house. I watched as the black Toyota passed by slowly, a dream catcher hanging from the mirror. A face turned to look at me. A haunting face. A lifeless face.

I stepped in, shut the door and locked it behind me, turning and coming face-to-face with the kachina mask that hung on the wall just inside Uncle Ben's door.

I shivered.

Who was that masked man?

CHAPTER SEVEN

The house was empty so I slipped down to the basement, shucked my clothes and took a quick shower to remove the trail dust, and thought about my yo-yo relationship with Rick Townsend. The guy had tormented me through much of grade school, junior high and high school. Best buddies to my brother Craig, Rick had enjoyed more access to our house than the family pets. And while he'd treated Taylor like a little princess, pampering her and complimenting everything she did, he'd generally treated me like a joke. The court jester. An object of amusement. Someone to be teased and trifled with. Someone good for a laugh.

Me? I became a jester in fact, playing one outrageous practical joke after another. Giving as good as I got. Until it stopped being fun. Or funny. Once I reached high school and realized the cartoonish caricature I'd created had pretty much taken over my life—and damaged my future prospects to boot—it was too late. Too late to convince those who had witnessed my blonde maturation since kindergarten that I was more than just a ditz with an attitude and a talent for finding trouble. Okay. Yeah. And sometimes for making it.

I sighed as I wiped the steam from the bathroom mirror and looked at myself, seeing what other people see when they look at me. And what they didn't see: a vulnerable young woman who wanted the same things other gals wanted—a husband, a home, a family, security, a weight-loss program that included mocha lattes (not lowfat) and DoubleStuf Oreos, and waxing made painless. And not to lose who I was in the bargain.

"Is that asking too much?" I asked my reflection. "Well, is it? You're normally not at a loss for words. Come on. Say something! Anything!"

"Tressa? Is that you? Who are you talking to?"

I recognized my cousin Sophie's voice and opened the door. "Oh. Hi."

She looked past my shoulder. "Do you have someone in there with you?" she asked.

I shook my head. "I was just giving myself a pep talk," I told her.

"Pep talk?" She looked at me. "It sounded like you were tearing yourself a new one," she said.

"Tough love," I explained, and she nodded.

"I hear you," she said, and moved to take a seat on the sofa sleeper. I noticed she had on considerably less makeup than the night before. She wore a pair of blue jeans and an NAU sweatshirt. I pulled on a pair of black jeans and slipped on a long-sleeved tailored white shirt with black stripes.

"So, have you spoken to Gram yet?" I asked as I buttoned my blouse.

"You mean, am I back in her will?" she responded. I nodded.

"Something like that."

"Yeah. We had lunch together. Mom brought Joe along so I could meet him."

"And?"

"Scary," she said. I nodded.

"You have no idea," I told her, taking a seat on the sofa to pull on a pair of socks and my black Calfy boots.

"That grandson of his is quite the looker," she said, and I looked up.

"When did you meet Rick Townsend?" I asked.

She smiled. "Chill out," she said. "I haven't met him. His grandfather showed me his picture. Nice. Very nice." She winked. "I gather you two are an item."

"Says who?" I asked. "That ol' coot of a granddad of his and our gammy who weaves more yarn than the locals who sell their wares to tourists hereabouts?"

She shook her head. "You just did," Sophie said with a grin. "With your reaction when I mentioned his name. Your eyes got big and sparkly all of a sudden, like you'd touched a live wire. Or I'd touched a nerve." She sobered. "The rocky road to romance," she said. I nodded.

"And we're talkin' some major construction, hellishly long detours, with movement down to a crawl at times," I said, reminding myself to keep my eye on the road and make sure I didn't get distracted by some good-lookin' flagman somewhere along the line, take a wrong turn, and end up at a dead end.

I love analogies, don't you?

"You're lucky," Sophie said. "Try slapping a 'wide load' sign on your bumper in the process," she said, and I winced. With my chassis, I'd never make center circle at the Detroit Auto Show, but I didn't think I was at the point I'd be mistaken for an oversized load just yet. Although, if I didn't cut out the chocolate . . . which naturally reminded me of the Oak Creek

Canyon shenanigans and chocolate delight that was never devoured. At least not by me.

I gave Sophie a quick show-and-tell of the incident, showing her the battered but still bobbling Duke, the perfect wedding present of Mr. Kookamunga (gaining Sophie's oath of silence not to let on to anyone about the hand-selected gift) and finally the digitals Kelsey had taken.

"You know, now that I really look at him, he's not all that good-looking," I told Sophie, looking over her shoulder at the photos. "His nose is too big. His hair too long. His teeth too . . . white," I added lamely.

"I think I've seen this guy somewhere before," Sophie said. I stared at her.

"You have?"

She nodded. "Yes. But I can't remember where."

"Think!" I told her. "Think!"

Sophie closed her eyes for a few seconds and shook her head. "I don't know. NAU maybe," she said. "I'm not sure."

"Damn," I said. "And we were so close."

"Why are you so bent on finding this guy?" Sophie said, taking one more look at the photos before she passed the camera back to me. "Why not just forget it?"

It was a good question. Why couldn't I ever leave well enough alone? Why did I insist on knowing everything that happened and why? Duh. I was a reporter. That's why. And I hated loose ends almost as much as I hated the latest legging trend.

"I just want to find out who the guy is and find out his story, that's all," I said. "Something's up."

"We all are. Seven thousand feet worth," she said. "By the way, what's on tap for tonight? Obligatory family dinner, I imagine."

I set the camera down, picked up my backpack from

the coffee table, saw one of my *Gazette* business cards and thought for a moment.

"Have you heard of a place called Numbers?" I asked Sophie.

"Uh, why do you ask?" she hedged, and I looked over at her.

"Because I want to know?" I said.

"Why?"

I frowned. "Is there a problem?"

"Why should there be?"

Gee. Another game of Twenty Questions and it wasn't even Wednesday yet.

"There shouldn't. Unless there is," I said.

"Huh?"

"Do you know the place?"

"I know of it."

"Could you maybe take me there? Tonight?"

Sophie gave me an assessing look. "How did you hear about Numbers?" she asked.

I told her.

"I thought you weren't invited," she said.

"I wasn't. That's why I want to go," I explained.

"And do what? Spy on your boyfriend?"

I shook my head. "He's not my boyfriend. So it's not spying. I'm just . . . gathering information before I make a very crucial decision," I explained. "A decision that could very well change my life forever."

Sophie looked at me. "You've got it bad," she said, and I felt tears well up in my eyes again.

"Probably fatal," I admitted.

Sophie sighed. "In that case—"

I grabbed her. "Thank you! Thank you! Thank you!" I said, hugging her. I released her and picked up the camera to shut it off.

"Oh . . . my . . . gosh!" Sophie said, and I stared at her.

"What?" I said.

"I just remembered where I've seen that guy," she said. My mouth flew open.

"Where?" I said.

"At Numbers!" Sophie said.

Holy smoke signals, Kemo Sabe!

"I'm not sure this was such a good idea after all," Sophie said several hours later as we sat in her red Pontiac across the street from the upscale hotspot located near a new—and high-end—shopping plaza on the east side of the city. "I've heard stories about what happens when people team up with you," she said. "Stories with bad endings."

"Oh, good grief," I said. "It's a public place, for heaven's sake. There are people all over. What could possibly happen?"

Okay, so I'd said that very thing to folks before with outcomes ranging from harmless fracases (is that even a word?) to ones that ended with white lies, red lights and sirens, and black body bags. Frankly, my life is pretty much a crapshoot. Sometimes heavy on the crap.

"I suppose you're right," Sophie said, still rubbing her chin and staring at the bright lights of the nightclub. "There are a few things you should know about this particular establishment before we go in," she said slowly, and I got one of those uh-oh feelings. Like when you agree to pick up DVDs your gammy reserved, only to find out they're from the eighteen-and-older section in the back room. Or you agree to be maid of honor without securing veto authority over the dress.

I swallowed.

"Things? What things?" I asked, my voice a tad high.

"The guy who owns Numbers has a couple other nightclubs like this in California. He opened one in

Phoenix several years back and it did so well, he opened this one about a year ago. His nightclubs are theme-oriented," she said.

"Theme-oriented?" I looked at her. "Is this a gay bar?" I asked. "Are you, like . . . gay?"

Sophie did one of those head moves where you look up to Heaven as if seeking divine guidance. Or maybe she just had a neck kink.

"No! This is not a gay bar, and no, I am not gay!"

"Because I want you to know I'm perfectly fine with it, Sophie," I blathered along. "Perfectly fine. Live and let live," I proclaimed, all the while recalling that disturbing little sofa bed snake dream.

"I am not gay," Sophie said.

"Cool," I said. "But cool, too, if you were. With me, that is. I mean cool with me if you were gay, not cool being gay with me," I said, thinking my Native American name by rights should be She Who Runs Off at the Mouth. "Cool," I said.

Sophie shook her head.

"Numbers is a bar that caters to people who are looking to meet other new people, but don't necessarily want the total anonymity and isolation of, say, an online dating service," she said. "Numbers provides a fun, nonthreatening environment where singles can get together, mix, mingle and hang out, but in a safe and organized fashion."

I snorted. "Isn't that illegal in some states?" I said.

"Funny lady," Sophie replied.

"So, where does the name 'Numbers' come in?" I asked.

"Glad you asked. Every seat in the bar has an assigned number. The numbers on the chairs light up. At various times during the evening, a computer randomly selects numbers and those numbers are called out. The folks sitting at those numbered seats have to leave their seats and do whatever the computer selects them to do. Sometimes it's a karaoke duet. Sometimes they have to entertain the audience with a skit. Harmless fun," she said. "They also have a time for interested folks to participate in speed dating," she said. I blinked, drawing a blank.

"What the heck is speed dating?" I asked.

Sophie shook her head. "You country folks need to get to town more often," she said. "It's a way of meeting people you might want to date. Women sit at one side of a long table and men at the other. A timer is set and the couples visit for five to ten minutes or so. When the timer goes off, the guy gets up and moves to the next seat and the whole thing starts all over again."

"How much can you learn about some guy in five minutes?" I asked. I'd known Ranger Rick all my life and was still in the dark about what went on inside that carp-cop cranium of his.

Sophie shrugged. "I can pick up a book and read the first page and know whether it's worth reading or not. I figure the same thing is true about guys to some extent. It doesn't take long to weed out the creeps or knuckle-draggers."

"How do you know all this?" I thought to ask. "You just turned twenty-one a few weeks ago," I said.

Sophie looked momentarily flustered but made a smooth recovery. "I'm sure even back in Iowa they've heard of fake IDs," she said.

My eyes grew big.

"I don't know nuthin' 'bout that, gel," I said in my nasally, Midwestern hillbilly best. "I git my hooch from a still in that there back forty. Put hair on yer chest, it will. Er take it off if'n you perfer, little lady," I twanged.

"You aren't going to embarrass me, are you?" Sophie asked. "I have to live here, you know."

I did a cross-my-heart-and-hope-to-die-stick-a-needle-in-the-eye move, followed by the chill sign. "I swear I will be on my best behavior," I told her, hoping she wouldn't inquire as to just what my personal best was.

"And if we see Rick Townsend?"

"I'm, like, so totally cool with it."

"And if he's with Ranger Whitehead?"

"I'm solid as red rock," I told her.

"And if we spot the cake bandit?"

"Piece of cake." Triple chocolate to be exact. I slapped Sophie on the shoulder. "I feel good about our little adventure," I said. "What about you?"

"I feel sick," Sophie said. "And like I'm going to regret this in the morning."

I shook my head. Sweet, naive Sophie. If things went south at the speed-dating Mecca, she was bound to regret it long before then.

CHAPTER EIGHT

Sophie reached into the backseat and grabbed her handbag. I stared at it.

"Is that what I think it is?" I asked, unable to take my eyes off the white calfskin leather shopper with the oversized brown leather buckle and tan trim.

"That depends," Sophie said. "What do you think it is?"

I ran my fingertips over the cool, smooth leather, and closed my eyes in ecstasy. "I think it's a pricey little Dolce & Gabbana," I told her.

"Then you'd be wrong," she said.

I traced the embossed D&G with a fingertip. "What about this monogram?" I asked.

"Ever heard of Dollar General?" she said. I shook my head.

"I may be a country girl, and the closest I'll get to leather this fine is one of my saddles, but I know a quality handbag when I see it—and sniff it," I added, bringing the bag to my nostrils and closing my eyes for a whiff. "And if my nose doesn't deceive me"—I sucked in the smell—"this little number goes for around five hundred smackaroos." I opened my eyes. "Where the heck did you get that much money to spend on a handbag?"

She took the bag and made a big deal of searching around in it. "I have a job. I earn money," she said. "Plus tips, of course."

I raised an eyebrow. Her waitressing job obviously brought in better tips than my gig at the Dairee Freeze. The best tip I'd gotten was from a grade-school customer who left a wad of bubble gum under the front counter.

"Is that so?" I said, noting the color in her cheeks. "Apparently pigs-in-a-blanket go for more out here than back home," I observed. "You've given me a serious case of purse envy. The bag rocks."

"Thanks," she said, and stuck her keys in the side pocket and closed the bag.

We approached the bar and I couldn't decide if I was tickled or ticked when the big, bulky, no-necked guy at the door with absolutely nothing in common with a Wal-mart greeter merely nodded at Sophie but requested photo identification from me. He took so long examining my driver's license I started to get nervous.

"Iowa, huh?" he said. I nodded, hoping to God he didn't say something about taters. Or my driver's license photo that could be used in photo line-ups. Or the weight listed on my driver's license. "Vacation?" he inquired.

I shook my head. "Wedding," I answered. "Not mine," I qualified. "Our gammy," I said, motioning in Sophie's direction.

He stared. "Right. Well, have a nice visit, Tressa," he said.

I stared back. "How—"

"Your license," he said, handing the plastic card back to me with a smile.

"Oh, uh, thanks," I said, thinking maybe there was something in the air up here that was making me paranoid. I hurried over to Sophie.

"You have been here before," I accused as we made our way over to the long shiny bar. "Did you see that? The guy didn't give you a second look but he detained me longer than the guy at Sky Harbor did after I set off the metal detector three times. And so what if it was my license photo that got his attention? I had a particularly nasty flu bug that day, and it was really windy outside and I'd jogged to the courthouse after just finishing a shift at the Dairee Freeze where the ice cream machine exploded on me. Other than that, I'd say it was a good likeness. And everyone lies about their weight on those things. I bet even Hillary Clinton fudges her weight on her driver's license. I'd say 'have you seen the ankles on that woman?' but I'm not sure she has any. No wonder she wears pantsuits."

Sophie gave me a look.

"So, what's good?" I asked as we bellied up to the bar.

She shrugged. "How should I know? I don't drink."

I looked at her. "You don't drink? Why the fake ID then?"

She cast an eye in the long mirror behind the bar. "I wanted to get in but I never drank."

"So, what did you do?" I asked, spotting the long tables set up for this evening's entertainment and the ol' generator finally kicked on. "Ah, you feel the need for speed," I said, nodding. "Speed dating, that is. How's that worked out for you?"

"I've met a few nice guys," she said. "But no one to write home about. It's more of a pastime than anything," she added. "I don't have time for a relationship."

"I'll drink to that!" I said with "hear, hear!" verve, at

the same time swallowing a sudden thickness in my throat. No time for dating. That was my own oft-used excuse for a lackluster love life of late. It was right up there with "I need to focus on my career," "I'll start dating seriously again once I lose these last ten pounds" and "all the good ones are married or gay." Whatever gets us through the night, eh, ladies?

I ordered a light beer while Sophie nursed a Diet Coke as the place filled up. I picked up my backpack and rifled through it.

"Why'd you bring what's-his-name, anyway?" she asked, motioning to the bag where Kookamunga presently resided.

"You know Gram and gift-giving," I reminded Sophie. "Remember the Christmas she unwrapped all the gifts under the tree to see who was getting what—and then wrapped them back up but in the process got them mixed up?" Imagine my dad's surprise when he opened a Lady Remington shaver and a gift certificate to the I'm Every Woman Salon and Day Spa. I knew something was afoot when I opened my gift expecting to find a Megamall gift card only to discover a six-month membership to the Rec Center. Okay, so my gammy's not the only one in the family to do a little pre-Christmas snooping. It's in the genes, folks. She's even been known to take back what she doesn't care for, replace it with an item she wants, and wrap it back up. One year when someone mentioned something to Gram, she pointed out that it saved her from a flare-up of her sciatica from standing in line after Christmas to take them back. After that, no one had the heart to say anything.

I shook my head. "Trust me, Sophie. Kookamunga is safer right here with us," I said, patting my bag.

I sipped my beer, keeping an eagle eye open for Ranger Rick, Officer Whitehead, or my new friend from Oak Creek Canyon—but trying not to look like I was looking.

"Numbers is pleased to welcome you folks this evening, and we thank you for coming out to party with us tonight," came over the sound system. "We'll be starting our first round of speed dating at eight o'clock sharp. That gives you just about five minutes, ladies and gentlemen, five minutes to take your places at the long tables and perhaps meet your match!"

Dancing lights raced around approximately twenty tables or so that were moved together to form one very long one. Two chairs facing one another at each table invited optimistic occupants looking for love in five minutes or less to sit down and try their luck.

"As always, Numbers accepts no responsibility for what occurs between consenting speed daters."

I took a sip of my beer. What do you know? A speed-dating disclaimer. Who knew?

I reached out to grab a handful of pretzels and was about to make some smart-mouthed remark to Sophie about the impossibly dire circumstances that would compel me to plant my carcass in one of those speed dating seats when my Ranger-Rick radar started humming and pulsing and pinging for all it was worth. My eyes darted to the long, broad mirror behind the bar, and my lip curled as I fixed Mr. I-never-planned-to-go firmly in my sights, locked and loaded.

Strike gold, huh? Explore the possibilities, huh? Who the hell did he think he was? Christopher Columbus? Suddenly the idea that he might discover me there spying on him no longer held the appeal it had. Maybe because I was afraid my being here might be interpreted as an admission of feelings for the sneaky ranger. Maybe because that could be right and I just wasn't ready to accept that terrifying little truth. Or even worse, broadcast it.

Or it could be I just didn't want to be such a piss-poor spy that I got made so early in the night.

Whatever the reason, the heart or the ego (sounds like something from a Dr. Seuss poem, doesn't it?), I wasn't about to let Ranger Rick discover me there until I was good and ready. I watched Townsend look around, then slowly make his way in the direction of the bar.

"Crap!"

I looked around for the exits—saw I'd have to go right past Townsend to use them—when I spotted several empty spots on the far end of the speed dating table. I reached out, grabbed Sophie's hand and yanked her down off her bar stool.

"Let's go," I said, leading her toward the empty seats.

"What are you doing?" Sophie asked as I shoved her into a chair opposite me. "This is for the speed dating and this side is for the guys."

I shrugged. "It's fine," I said. "It shouldn't be a problem. I'm sure no one will think anything."

"I am not gay!" Sophie said, and I sighed.

"Oh, for heaven's sake, are we back to that again?"

"This is nuts," she said. "What am I going to do when they start the timers?"

"We'll be out of here before then. I'm just waiting for the coast to clear," I told her.

Sophie frowned. "Coast? What coast?"

"Can you believe that rat of a ranger actually showed his Yogi-like face here tonight?" I asked.

"He's here? Where?" Sophie's head moved back and forth more than my Duke bobble head.

"Down, Sophie! Down!" I said, putting my hand on top of hers. "We don't want to attract attention."

The woman next to me looked at our hands on the table and cleared her throat.

"Too late for that, sweetie," she said with a lift of one painted-on eyebrow.

Sophie yanked her hand out from under mine. "We're cousins," she advised the woman.

"Right," she said. "Right."

Sophie shot to her feet. "That's it. You are on your own, cous'," she said. "I'm strictly an observer. I'll be at the bar when you come to your senses."

My partner stalked off.

"Sophie! Sophie, you forgot your bag!" I shrugged. If she wanted her money, she'd have to come back. Then I'd make her suffer for deserting a family member in her time of need. I set the large handbag at my feet. Sophie's seat hadn't gotten cold when another warm bod dropped into it.

"Well, hello there."

I looked over to see a guy who appeared almost old enough to be my pappy occupying Sophie's chair. A peachy-colored comb-over that trumped Trump's, ruddy cheeks that suggested he'd started the party early, and a string of silver chains, which drew attention to a furry upper torso that brought back memories of a Pomeranian my gammy used to own, super-charged my creepometer to alert status.

"I haven't seen you here before. Where have you been all my life?" he asked. The needle on my creepometer jumped.

"I'm visiting from out of town," I said, trying to be polite but not wanting to encourage anything beyond civilities.

"Okay, ladies and gentlemen, it's time to begin our first round of speed dating this evening. And it looks like the tables are full of adventurous folks eager to see if they can establish that special love connection, or make a match with the help of our Numbers Dating Game. So, start the timer. And good luck!"

I shrank down in my seat, hoping the announcer hadn't succeeded in drawing the ranger's attention to the speed dating tables—and little ol' creep-magnet me.

"I'm Ken," he said, looking nothing like a Ken any Barbie in her right mind would be seen with. "I keep a summer home here in Flagstaff. I usually work out of Phoenix."

"I'm Barbie," I said with a teasing smile. "So, what do you do, Ken?" I asked—*other than try to hit on girls who weren't even gleams in their daddies' eyes when you graduated from high school*? I kept one eye on Ken and the other trying to locate Townsend, receiving for my efforts a strange look from Ken and double vision for me.

"I'm in real estate," he said. "You said you're from out of town. Where does a great-looking gal like you hail from, and what does she do for a living?"

"I'm from Sheboygan," I said. "And I sell shoes."

Ken leaned across the table. "You know, Barbie, ever since I sat down, I've felt this force, this pulsating, throbbing, surge of explosive energy between us," he said and, squirming ever so slightly in his chair, he reached out and grabbed my hand. "Tell me you feel it, too?" he asked, stroking my palm with his thumb. By sheer force of will I barely managed to avoid a reflexive retching action when my creepometer gauge shot into the perv range. I yanked my hand away.

"Ken?" I put my elbows on the table and parked my chin in my hands. "I have a confession to make."

"Yes?" He leaned closer.

"I'm not really in shoe sales, and I've never been to Sheboygan," I told him.

"Oh? A woman of mystery, huh? How intriguing," he said.

I shook my head. "No big mystery, I'm afraid. Just a teensy little secret. You see that guy over by the door?

The one absent a neck." I motioned to the door and Ken's gaze followed. I made eye contact with the supersized fellow who'd carded me earlier and gave him a little wave and a "hey, big boy" smile. He obliged by smiling and winking right back.

"I see him." Ken said. "And?"

"And he's actually my boyfriend, and I'm doing this speed dating as a sort of favor to him. You see, Ken, the management has been receiving complaints concerning highly inappropriate behavior from some gentlemen who are, shall we say, old enough to know better, and I volunteered to sit through a speed dating session or two to see if I could nail the letch for my sweetie. All he's waiting for is the signal from me and he'll be on the guy like stink on, well, you know."

"Signal?" Ken's Adam's apple jumped up and down like a bobber with a teaser fish on the line.

I nodded. "Shhh! It's a secret signal," I said. "Now, where were we again, Ken? Oh, yes. You were talking about something pulsating . . . throbbing . . ." I stopped and tapped the table with Madly Mauve-painted nails and waited.

Ken put a finger behind the rows of chains around his neck that seemed suddenly a wee bit on the snug side.

"I really don't recall . . . I'm not sure . . . Sprinkler systems! That's it! I was talking about sprinkler systems!" Ken almost yelled. "In real estate, I find a lot of the pulsating variety on homes I list," he added, wiping his shiny forehead with a napkin from the table.

"Oh, that's right. We were taking about sprinkler systems, weren't we?" I said with a huge grin just as the timer sounded to end our little tête-à-tête. "Good talking with you, Ken," I told him as he got up to leave. "And remember," I said, putting a finger to my lips, "it's our little secret."

Ken grabbed a handful of napkins and skedaddled. I chuckled. This speed-dating thing was a hoot.

I stopped hooting when I noticed the seat across me was once again occupied, this time by a pale, dark-haired young man who looked like a younger version of the comic-strip dad in Dennis the Menace, complete with black cat's-eye framed glasses and long, pointed nose. Great. Just my luck. From creep to geek.

The timer signaled round two.

"Did I hear you say you sold shoes?"

I blinked.

"I may have said that. Why?"

"What are you wearing now?" he asked. What was it with this place? Pervs on parade or something?

"Just a minute," I said. "How dare you—"

"On your feet!" The guy's face turned red. "What are you wearing on your feet?"

I sat back, somewhat mollified. But only somewhat.

I shoved out my foot to reveal my black Justin Calfy boot.

"Nice," he said, but I could tell he was disappointed.

"What's wrong? Did you have something else in mind?" I asked.

"Have you ever considered wearing black Choo stilettos with those black jeans? I bet they would look sensational."

"Oooh, I love Choo!" I said. Unfortunately, my budget didn't. "And I'm bonkers for Blahnik!" I announced.

He took my foot in his hand. "With these puppies, you'd have to go with a wide size, and something's always sacrificed in the line of the shoe when you go with a wide. Now, with flip flops, width isn't as apparent," he said.

For the next four minutes Ozzy and I conversed

over footwear. And bags. (I might've implied Sophie's designer bag was mine, solely to impress.) Plus, we covered the odd accessory.

It was the best speed date of the evening.

I lost track of Townsend, and found myself getting into the whole speed-dating scene. Five minutes left you with zero time to shoot the bull. You had to cut right to the chase—ask the questions you wanted to ask—and move on to the next partner. There was a certain comfortable simplicity about the process. And it was sure to appeal to the drive-up mentality of our society. I could see it now:

"Can I take your order, please?"

"Yes, today I want a six-foot, two-inch cowpoke with a full head of hair under his Stetson, a six pack under his shirt (nonalcoholic) and buns made for squeezing beneath his Levi's. And hold the onions, please."

I speed-dated Brad the bookkeeper, Phil the pharmacist, Antonio the tattoo artist and Mel who was studying mortuary science. I have to confess, I felt more than a little naughty in your basic bad-girl kind of way, chatting up each guy then dropping him like yesterday's blue plate special and proceeding to the next new face. A nasty girl, yet kind of sweet.

I readjusted a backpack strap on the back of my chair and turned back to greet the next contestant on Tressa's Geeks and Freaks—and almost fell out of my chair. Sitting right across from me was none other than my Oak Creek Canyon Mystery Man. "He Who Scares Young Girls and Steals Cake" himself! For a tiny second I was once again sucked in by the beauty of his face. The long, noble nose and prominent cheekbones. The dark bedroom eyes complete with long, thick eyelashes even Maybelline's finest brush couldn't improve upon. The sleek, shiny hair I'd give up Cadbury chocolate to have. Well, maybe Hershey.

"You!" I hissed. "You . . . you . . . bobble-busting, cake-snatching, camera klepto!" I shrieked. "Of all the nerve. Well? What do you have to say for yourself?"

"If I may, I would like to humbly ask your forgiveness for that unfortunate incident the other day and, if you would be so kind, to permit me an opportunity to explain," he said, his voice slow, deep, and seductive, so soothing to auditory nerves on overload.

I folded my arms. "I'm listening," I said.

"You are very kind," he replied. "I knew that from the first moment I saw you at the canyon. Your kind, gentle spirit reached out to me that day."

I blinked. Kind, gentle spirit? Me? I sighed. They not only grew 'em gorgeous out here, but crazy as rabid coons. I should've known.

"Go on, Mr.—" I stopped, realizing I didn't even know his name.

"Raphael," he supplied, and I raised my eyebrows. Trust him to have a beautiful name, too.

"Raphael," I repeated, getting a bit of a jolly from hearing his name on my lips.

"I felt something when I saw you that day that I never felt before," Raphael said, and I hoped that *something* wasn't associated with the Three Stooges, milk of magnesia or Gas-X. I unfolded my arms and put my hands within grabbing distance of the glass votive, just in case he started using flowery words like throbbing and pulsating and I had to bust a cap or two.

"Yes?"

"Yes. You see, in my culture we believe you can feel the essence of a person—their soul, if you will—and connect with it. I felt drawn to you. For a reason, I believe."

Something other than my svelte figure and beautiful face? Something like . . . chocolate, maybe?

"I just wanted to get closer to you, maybe to exchange a word or two. See if the feeling was real. But when the young girl took my picture, I panicked. You see, I do not like having my picture taken. In fact, I studiously avoid it. I somehow got the idea your picture-taking was a joke—that you were making fun of me—and I became upset and tried to grab the camera. Silly, but there you have it. I am sorry if I frightened the girl."

I frowned. "Okay, so how do you explain taking off with my bag of cake?" I asked.

He shrugged. "I really don't know. Temporary insanity, maybe. Haven't you ever done something incredibly rash and stupid and had no idea why you did it?"

I gave him a beady-eyed look. He'd recited my standard operating procedure almost verbatim. Someone had obviously gotten to this guy.

"I did come back to try to return the bag and its contents, but by that time you had left," Raphael went on. "I'd like to make it up to you. Replace the item."

"Hmmm. And I suppose you just happen to have a nice, big slice of Tlaquepaque Chocolate Delight on you," I said. Then I frowned. I definitely needed to go cold turkey on the chocolate for a while. Somewhere along the line it had become my own personal Turkish delight.

"If I had known you would be here, I would have brought an entire cake," he said with a smile that was much, much sweeter than the cocoa-based confection I so didn't need cementing itself to my hips and thighs.

"Talk is cheap, buster," I responded.

"If you would permit me, I know of a place nearby that features many fine desserts," he said. "I'm sure you could find one to please your palate."

Talk about Code Talkers! This guy was one smooth-talking native. The invitation—as well as the inviter—was tempting as the chocolate itself, but I couldn't quite shake the memory of the slightly desperate look in his eyes the last time we'd met.

"I'm here with a friend," I said.

"Not a boyfriend, I gather," Raphael said. "For you would not be sitting at this table if that were the case."

I shrugged. "Maybe I like to live dangerously," I challenged with a tilt to my chin.

"That I can believe," he said. "I sense a spirit of adventure."

Misadventure was more like it.

"So, what do you say? Miss . . . ?"

"Jayne," I responded. "Calamity Jayne."

He hesitated for a moment and then smiled at me.

"Miss Jayne. How about that coffee and dessert?"

The timer signaled an end to our date and I shook my head. Living dangerously had lost some of its allure after I started collecting cadavers and attracting a certain criminal element.

"I'll accept your apology and we'll call it good," I said. I sighed. Besides, it never would've worked out. I could never be with anyone who had longer hair but fewer split ends than me.

Raphael smiled and nodded. "As you wish," he said, stood, put fingers to an imaginary hat brim and walked away.

I gave myself a good hard head slap. Figuratively, that is.

"Fool! Coward! Yellow-belly. And you call yourself a cowgirl!"

"Well, if it isn't the infamous Calamity Jayne!" Hot breath seared the back of my neck like a branding iron. "What brings the crime-fighting cowgirl to these parts? Cattle rustling? Snake oil salesman? Baked goods bandit?"

"How about the report of a certain ranger lookin' for love in all the wrong places?" I replied as Ranger

Rick Townsend took a seat across from me, gaining a dirty look from the rotund person next in line for that chair.

"What's love got to do with it?" Townsend asked with a smile so incredibly certain of his own appeal he made me want to slap it right off his handsome face. Or kiss it away. "I'm waiting for an answer, you know," he said.

Fat chance. Like I was gonna get into a discussion about love when Townsend had the *cojones* to show up here to meet another woman.

"I'm here following up on a lead from this afternoon's mugging," I said. "I'd ask why you're here, but we both already know the answer to that. Where is Officer Whitebreast anyway?" I asked.

Townsend grinned. "Carena is in the ladies' room," he said. I stared at him.

"Carena? Is that her name?"

Townsend nodded.

"Pretty name for a pretty woman," I observed, thinking Raphael and Carena should really get together. They could name their children things like Dmitri and Desdemona, Anastasia and Alejandro.

"So, you're here following a lead, huh?" Townsend said. "Funny. I could've sworn you were here to spy on me."

I made a *who, me?* face and straightened my spine in indignation.

"Really, Townsend. Give that ego of yours a vacation, too, will you? I'm here strictly on a fact-finding mission. To get some straight answers. To satisfy my curiosity."

"Isn't that what I just said?" Townsend asked. He sat forward in his chair, resting his arms on the table between us. "I knew you'd be here," he said, surveying me. "And I knew the minute you walked in."

"Oh, really? How?"

I raised an eyebrow, intrigued. Could Townsend have actually felt for me what Raphael had spoken of earlier? Of souls reaching out and locking on to each other? A connection that drew one to another? My kind, gentle spirit?

He nodded.

"By the grumbling and complaining of patrons in line behind you waiting to get into the joint," he said. "What'd that guy at the door do anyway? Take down your life story? What was his reaction when you got to the part about the stiff in the trunk? Did you mention your recent stage debut that almost turned out to be your last performance?"

My idiotic idyll disappeared like caramels out of a box of chocolates.

"As a matter of fact, we did share some meaningful repartee," I said. "And for the record, Sophie recognized this afternoon's mugger's photo as someone who frequented this particular establishment, and that's what brought us out. Not some morbid fascination with the mating rituals of a puffed up, egocentric booby on the 'in no danger of being mistaken as humble now or ever' list."

Townsend sat back and crossed his arms over his broad chest. His biceps bulged against the white sleeves of his polo. His arms looked incredibly tan. And manly.

"So, you expect me to believe you came here to track down a guy who snatched a slice of cake?" he asked. "Just admit it, Tressa. You're here because you were jealous. And I think we both know why."

Townsend's heated look locked on me, the fire in his gaze like a flaming arrow to the heart. I couldn't breathe. Couldn't think. Couldn't look away. Dammit. I couldn't even crack a blasted joke. All I could do was stare back at him.

I'd just opened my mouth to finally admit that he was right, that I was jealous, that I thought I knew why but wasn't sure, when the timer went off again.

"Oh my gosh, Tressa! Do you know who is here?" Sophie, breathless, appeared at the table.

I kept watching Townsend.

"Tressa, you're not gonna believe this! I spotted your Oak Creek Canyon Casanova over by the dance floor! He's here!" Sophie squealed.

I saw, rather than felt, Rick Townsend react. The light in his eyes dimmed perceptibly and he exhaled a long, drawn-out breath that took forever to end. He stood and held out his hand.

"Hi, Sophie. I'm Rick Townsend," he said, and Sophie's eyes got big like she was looking down the barrel of a loaded six-gun. "It's nice to finally meet you," he told her.

Sophie managed a weak smile and equally weak nod of her head. "Uh, nice meeting you, too, Rick," she said. "Tressa's told me a lot about you," Sophie added.

"I'm sure she has," he said. "What was that you were saying about yesterday? Something about the Oak Creek Casanova being here this evening?" Townsend pressed. "Tressa mentioned something along those lines, but I guess I didn't think I was hearing right." He looked down at me. "Guess I was way off base," he said. "Again."

I found myself battling a case of the weepies once more. This was getting ridiculous. And so not me.

"It's the reason we're here," Sophie said, and while I knew she was just trying to assist me in keeping the cocky ranger from figuring out I was there for more than payback for yesterday, that didn't keep me from wanting to reach up and pinch her to prevent her from helping me out any more. "I recognized the guy in the photo and finally remembered it was here that

I'd seen him. Tressa talked me into coming out to see if he would show. Plus, the speed dating concept intrigued her. Right, Tressa?"

I shook my head at Sophie, but she didn't pick up on the gesture. Apparently she was going all out to make very sure Townsend didn't get the idea that I was there because of him. Well, that was what I wanted, after all. Wasn't it? My pride demanded that I not be seen as obsessed or smitten. Didn't it?

"I see," Townsend said, and I knew Sophie had succeeded. "And this man is here tonight? That's why you're here?" Townsend was looking at me now, and from the set of his jaw I knew there'd be hell for me to pay no matter how I responded.

I hate that *damned if you do, damned if you don't* crap, don't you?

"If you'll excuse me," Townsend said, his face a study in self-control. "I see Carena over yonder so I'll leave you ladies to enjoy your five-minute mixers. For one of you, and I won't name names, I suspect these little interludes represent the longest relationships you've had in quite some time." Townsend turned and walked away.

"Well, how do you like that?" I said. "I have never been so insulted in my entire life!"

"You mean he wasn't talking about me?" Sophie asked, sinking into the chair across from me. I looked at her.

"He doesn't even know you," I said.

"People talk," she said. "And there's e-mail and phone calls, and letters."

And our gammy, who loves to gossip.

"You know, maybe I shouldn't say this, Tressa," Sophie said, continuing just the same, "but I got the impression that Rick Townsend really wanted you to be here tonight just because of him," Sophie said. "I think he felt let down and disappointed when he found out you weren't."

"But I *am* here because of him!" I said. "You know that! It's just that *he* can't know that. Trust me. There'd be no living with the man if he knew he had that kind of hold on me," I told her.

"Are you planning to live with him?" she asked.

Was I?

Of course not. Still, he did have that room at the luxury hotel. And face it; I was so hot for the guy my silver belt buckle was in serious danger of melting. Or was that smelting? Either way, "burn, baby, burn" didn't begin to cover how feverish Townsend made me. And, frankly, I wasn't sure how long I could hold out before I burst into flames. I'd seen photos of people who had self-combusted. It wasn't pretty. And frankly, I had no desire to be featured on Wikipedia or some medical Web site in a photo array of crispy critters.

On the other hand, I didn't want my aorta immortalized in a similar fashion if I finally gave in to my body's ravenous craving for the too-tempting ranger, and I ended up with a broken heart even the best cardiac surgeons would be shaking their heads and checking the latest medical journals over.

"I was using 'live with' as a figure of speech, Sophie," I told her. "After all, with our grandparents getting married, I'm bound to be around Townsend a lot more. I don't want things to be awkward and uncomfortable for Joe and Gram."

"Uncomfortable? Gram? Not likely," she said. "And I didn't get the impression her groom was one to stew and fret either. Sometimes, Tressa, you just have to take a leap of faith," she said, and I felt like the younger sister here instead of the older cousin.

"That sounds good in theory," I said, "but my track

record doesn't exactly inspire confidence. Usually when I take a leap of faith, I end up flat on my face." Or knee deep in shite. Or blood and guts. Or both.

"You need to have more faith in yourself, Tressa," Sophie said. "Don't be afraid to be who you are. Believe me. It's much, much harder to be someone you aren't. Or, rather, pretend you're something you're not."

I nodded. Hadn't I realized just that after playing the fool for way too long? And years later I was still paying for it. And that, I supposed, was what was at the heart of my reluctance to hop into the sack with Ranger Rick. While I had succeeded in getting others to see beyond the Calamity Jayne caricature—well, to some extent—it was glaringly apparent that I hadn't yet convinced myself that I was worthy of the attention—and affection— of someone like Rick Townsend. A guy who could make Johnny Depp insecure about his sexuality.

Well, what do you know? I was a complicated individual, after all. Who knew?

"You're pretty sharp, Sophie. You know that?" I said. "And I'm ready to split this pop shack and head for the barn. What about you?"

"You don't want to hang around and see what happens with Townsend?" she asked.

I shook my head.

"And the Oak Creek Canyon maniac?

"His name is Raphael and I've, shall we say, smoked the peace pipe with him. I'll fill you in on the way home."

She nodded. "And you didn't meet any nice guys during the speed dating you'd like to stay and get to know? None at all?"

"The guy with the shoe fetish admired my taste in boots," I told her.

"It's a start," she said.

I stood and pulled my backpack from my chair and

Sophie reached down to collect her bag from beneath the table. "Uh, where's my purse?" she said, as I slipped an arm through the strap of my backpack.

"It's under the table there," I told her.

"No. It's not!" she said, and I watched her drop to all fours.

"What do you mean?" I asked, joining her on the floor. "It's been there since you went off in a tiff," I told her.

"I wasn't in a tiff, and it's not here," she said. I scooted under the table to check for myself. "Maybe it got kicked down the tables," I said, and crawled under the next one.

"Do you see it?" Sophie asked.

"Nothing yet," I said, reaching out to pull a long denim skirt aside so I could see, and accidentally grabbing hold of an ankle. I heard a shriek, followed by a slap.

"Why, you pervert!" I heard above me. "How dare you play footsie with me!"

"I did no such thing!" a man's voice yelled.

"Are you telling me I don't know when someone's playing footsie with me?"

Another slap sounded.

"Now just a damnable minute!"

A flurry of activity erupted above me. Grunts, curses, more slaps, and what sounded an awful lot like beverages being flung escalated into a cacophony I suspected would soon be a free-for-all.

I crawled back to the safe end of the table, climbed out and stood up, looking down the rows that once upon a time had been in a straight line. Now they were helter-skelter, and across their linen-covered tops fingers pointed, folks shouted, and ice cubes flew.

In the midst of the chaos, Sophie hauled herself out from under the tables and directly into the path of the

woman who had speculated about our sexual orienta-
tion earlier in the evening. She spotted Sophie on the
floor beneath her and her face turned the color of
mine when I tried to run a mile around the track back
home without stopping. (Okay. A half a mile. You guys
don't let me get away with a thing.)

"You again!" the woman hissed, her finger pointed
at poor Sophie, who made the mistake of looking up
at the woman—and as it happened, directly up her
skirt. "Of all the disgusting, vile—"

She dove for Sophie, fingers curled like crimson
talons, her red-tipped claws designed for ripping and
tearing. I stood for a second in total shock at the
melee before me. However, once I saw the woman go
for a handful of Sophie's hair, I dove into action. I
grabbed the woman around the waist and attempted
to yank her off my cousin.

"You're . . . making . . . a . . . terrible . . . mistake," I
said, grunting with exertion as I tried to dislodge the
frenzied woman's hold on my cousin's brown locks.
"My cousin lost her purse. Her *Dolce & Gabbana* purse!
We thought it might have been kicked under the
table. That's what she was doing under there! For
God's sake, woman, are you listening? It was a five-
hundred-dollar white calf leather Dolce & Gabbana!"

"Seven hundred twenty-five dollars!" Sophie howled.

The fight went out of the woman like she'd suddenly been unplugged. She looked up at me.

"She lost her Dolce & Gabbana?" she asked. I nodded.

The woman let go of Sophie's hair and began to
stroke it. "Oh, you poor, poor thing!" she cried. "Here,
I'll help you look. Everyone! We're looking for a white
calf leather Dolce & Gabbana handbag."

I looked on as the woman maneuvered herself underneath the tables in search of Sophie's designer
purse.

"Oh . . . my . . . gawd!" I heard Sophie's attacker-turned-comrade yell from under the tables. "Quick! Call the police! Sound the alarm! Close off all the exits!"

"What! What's wrong?" I asked, squatting down and thinking no way could a body find its way under the table without somebody seeing. "What is it?"

The woman popped her head out from beneath the table, the maroon tablecloth fanning out from the top of her head and around her shoulders making her look way too much like a disembodied head for my peace of mind.

"Her Dolce & Gabbana!" the head shrieked. "It's been stolen!"

I stuck my head underneath the table to see for myself and shook my head in disbelief.

You don't tug on Superman's cape. You don't spit into the wind. And you sure as hell don't come between a woman and her designer handbag. That was considered a hangin' offense in these here parts.

I was about to scoot back out butt first when I felt pressure on the bottom of one foot. "Turner, what the hell are you doing down there?" came from above and behind me. I winced.

"Excuse me, but you've mistaken me for someone else," I said, lowering my voice a handful of notes. "I don't know any Turners."

"Well, I'd know that backside anywhere," came the response, and I clenched my teeth. Dammit. And so not my good side.

I thought about crawling all the way under the table, but figured I'd been coward enough for one night, so I backed out butt first and stood, brushing off the knees of my black jeans.

I smiled at Rick and Carena.

"You have got to try the speed dating!" I said. "What

an utterly fantastic way to meet, mingle, and interact with new people. Why, just look at Sophie!"

Townsend followed my nod to where Sophie and her new friend ripped tables apart and yanked linen coverings off like out-of-control illusionists, searching in vain for the lost bag.

Another "Hell!" reached me and my smile shriveled.

This was so not gonna be a keepsake moment for Gammy's Southwestern Scrapbook. My number was up—and so was the jig, pardner.

CHAPTER NINE

"It had to be him!" I said for like the twentieth time, but received much the same response as I had the first time I said it. "Raphael, cakeophile and con artist," I said. "I know it was him."

"How the devil do you know that?" Rick Townsend asked, running a hand through his thick head of dark brown hair, as was oft his habit when we were having a conversation.

"He distracted me," I said.

"Oh, yeah? How'd he do that?" Townsend asked.

I thought about it for a second.

"He was . . . nice," I told him. "And sincere and apologetic and . . . and . . . and poetic," I said, trying to explain how he'd gotten me off my guard. Which, I suppose when you think about it, isn't all that difficult when you're great-looking and come bearing promises of chocolate.

Townsend snorted. "Poetic? He was poetic? Since when do you give a shit about poetry?" he said. I bristled. I was not entirely without culture and sophistication. After all, Dr. Seuss was one of my all-time favorite poets when I was a kid. And that poem about stopping off by the woods on a snowy evening? That, like, totally rocked.

"Contrary to what you believe, I enjoy well-crafted iambic pentameter as much as the next person," I said. "And I've always been a huge fan of limericks," I added. "You know. Like: There was once a ranger named Rick. Who sometimes could be such a—"

Sophie chose that fortuitous moment to join us, clamping a heavy hand over my mouth before I could finish my little ditty.

"For the record, I'd be interested in how this guy managed to distract you so much that you didn't see him walking off with a huge handbag," Sophie said, apparently figuring it was safe to uncover my oral cavity, and removing her hand so I could respond.

I shrugged. "I don't know. Like I said, he was disarming. Lyrical, even," I said, trying to explain how I'd been duped a second time. "And charming. And sensitive. And sweet. He said if he'd known I was going to be here, he'd have brought me an entire cake," I said, my mind's eye conjuring up that image in my head. And the cute con man serving me up a slice in nothing but a Chef Boyardee hat, apron and a "Let-her-eat-cake" grin. I sighed.

Townsend shot me a disgusted look.

"If you're right about this guy, he's probably purchasing more than cake with your cousin's plastic right about now," Townsend pointed out. I slapped a hand to my mouth.

"Ohmigawd, Sophie! I am so sorry! I swear, if I thought for a minute that fast-talking rogue was going to pinch your purse, I never would have let him sit down in the first place, and I most certainly would not have accepted his apology."

Townsend's look grew even more disgusted. "Apology? He tried to grab a camera out of my niece's hands, scared the hell out of her, took off with your dessert, and you accepted his apology? Are you nuts?" Townsend rubbed the back of his neck. "Why the devil didn't you come get me so I could have a word with your newfound friend?"

"Because I didn't want to disturb you and *your* new friend!" I said, glaring right back at him.

Townsend's new friend Ranger Whitehead finally spoke up. "You know, Rick, I think I'm going to be taking off. I have to work in the morning and it looks like you'll be tied up here for a while. You've got my number," she said. "Give me a call if you free up sometime before you leave town."

I rolled my eyes so far up beneath my lids I blinded myself. Boy, did I ever have her number!

She looked at me. "Miss Turner. I hope you are able to enjoy the remainder of your stay in Flagstaff. Goodnight."

"I'll see you out, Carena," Townsend said, and gave me another dark look. "And you? You stay right here. Don't move," he ordered. "I'll be right back."

I shook my head as he walked off with Carena. "Who does he think he is? God Almighty? I'll go wherever I darn well please whenever I please, thank you very much," I proclaimed. "I answer to no man."

"So? Where do you want to go?" Sophie asked.

I gave her a sheepish look. "Nowhere," I admitted. "But he doesn't know that."

"I've got to tell you, cous, I'm having a hard time getting a bead on you two," Sophie said, giving me the once-over. "You have this thing between you. It's so super-charged a bystander wants to back slowly away and keep a safe distance. You're attracted to each other. That's apparent. But, and this may sound really weird, I'm not sure if you like each other," she said. I looked at her, surprised. I'd never thought of the relationship with Rick Townsend quite in those terms, but what Sophie said made perfect sense.

I was undeniably in lust with Ranger Rick Townsend—and had been for some time. But did I like him? Could I love him? Be *in* love with him? After all, this was the guy who took the Polaroid of me in the porta-potty at the third-grade field day and posted it on the bulletin board at the public swimming pool. Who brought a duck call and tooted it as I walked in to prom with Tony Goosman my junior year. Who kept a menagerie of reptiles as pets when he knew I was petrified of all things scaly and slithery.

The question was, did I even care about all that anymore? Maybe Sophie was right. Maybe it was time to throw caution to the wind, to take that leap of faith and into the sack with Townsend and damn the consequences. After all, wasn't it Townsend who'd said, "What's love got to do with it?"

I felt my entire body tingle at the mere possibility of sleeping with Rick Townsend. I shivered again, experiencing a feeling I generally got before I did something really, really foolhardy. Or naughty.

I watched Townsend make his way back over to us and couldn't take my eyes off him. The way he moved so fluidly yet so casually. The way he commanded attention—and yet seemed oblivious to it. The way he scowled when he was cranky (i.e. at present) and grinned when he was in the mood to tease. The way he made my innards knot and my breath hitch whenever I was near him.

I turned to Sophie. "Maybe you're right, cous," I said. "Maybe it's time for a good old-fashioned, cowgirl leap of faith."

And meanwhile? I'd be hopin' and prayin' that if I

did throw caution to the wind, it didn't boomerang on me and end up coming back to bite me on the arse.

A very efficient Flagstaff officer came to take the police report and said he'd follow up with Sophie the next day. We were getting ready to leave when a nice-looking guy around Sophie's age hurried over to us as we walked to the door.

"Sophie! I thought that was you. What are you doing here?" he asked, casting a curious look at Townsend and me.

"Oh, hi, Tristan," she greeted the chap.

What was it with the names out here? Raphael. Tristan. Antonio. Carena. This was the southwest. Land of hot, dry deserts, red river crossings, Old Tucson. Come on. Give me Buck or a Clint or even a Billy for good-ness' sake. But Tristan?

"I'm here with my cousin, Tressa, and her . . ." Sophie faltered. "Our cousin-to-be, Rick. Our grandparents are tying the knot this coming weekend. We were just on our way out."

Tristan looked like he was trying to picture this little family tree but had come up a few branches bare.

"I see," he said, my go-to line when I don't have a clue and really don't even suspect anything. "So, I caught the tail end of you at Babes the other night," he said. "Pun intended," he added with a wink. "By the way, Tristan likes," he said with a smile that looked shy but somehow wasn't.

I watched Sophie for a reaction and I could have sworn her eyeballs began moving back and forth in a shut-your-pie-hole-now way.

"Cool," Sophie said. "Uh, we have to be going. Lots to do before the big day, you know."

"Okay. Yeah. Sure. See you at—"

"Yeah. Uh-huh. I'll see you, too," Sophie inter-rupted, cutting him off like Simon Cowell does those

American Idol wannabes who are tone deaf and apparently no one has broken the news to them before. Yikes! Send in the hook!

"Oh, crap! I just forgot, my car key was in my bag!" Sophie explained, putting a hand to her neck. "We'll have to call my folks and have them bring my spare key out."

"What's wrong? Where's your bag?" Tristan asked. Sophie explained.

"Was it the Dolce or the Vuitton?" he asked.

I blinked.

"I can give you a lift home," Tristan offered. "And bring you back to get your car, if you like," he offered.

"That's okay. I can give my cousins-to-be a—," Rick started to volunteer, and I reached out and poked him in the side, grabbed his arm and stuck it through mine.

"Why, that would be lovely, Tristan," I trilled. "And I bet Sophie wouldn't say no to a cold drink before she packs it in. It's been a stressful night for her. You two just run along and visit, and I'll catch a ride with our cousin Rick here," I said, pulling Ranger Rick to the door. "See you later, Soph," I said, and waved back to her as we walked outside.

"What the hell was that all about?" he said, and I did one of those eye rolls that always earned me a lecture on insubordination from teachers. And people thought *I* was one tent pole short of a teepee.

"Hello! That guy is obviously interested in Sophie," I pointed out.

"So? How do you know Sophie feels the same way?" Townsend asked. I stopped and looked at him.

"I just know. That's all," I said. "Women know these things."

"Right. Women's intuition," Townsend said, steering me to the Suburban.

"That's right," I said, as Rick handed me up into the

front seat. He walked around and jumped in behind the wheel. "Women are intuitive creatures. We notice things that men simply do not." I turned a skeptical look on Townsend and added, "Or claim they don't."

Townsend nodded. "And how'd that women's intuition work for you when Raphael walked off with Sophie's bag right under his arm and your nose?" He started the car. "Face it, Tressa. Women can be as dense as men when it comes to matters of the heart." He looked over at me. "Some more than others."

"What is that supposed to mean?" I asked as he pulled out and sped down the road.

He looked at me for about a minute, suddenly veered off the road and pulled into a parking lot at a nearby strip mall. He parked the car and shut off the engine, and sat silent behind the wheel for several minutes, his face a slide show of so many emotions that I began to get dizzy. Uncertainty. Anger. Frustration. Fear.

Fear?

When he finally turned to me, his expression was unreadable.

"What is that supposed to mean?" he said, repeating my earlier query. "Just that if I'd known all it took to make you swoon was a few lines of romantic rhyme, a Betty Crocker mix, and a goddamned container of frosting, I'd have had pen in hand and ass in apron long before now. Jeezus, I would've become the freakin' Pillsbury doughboy if I'd known that's what it took."

I stared at him.

"If that's what it took to what?" I asked, my lips suddenly dry as the sands of the Sonoran desert.

He hesitated for a very long second. And another. Finally, he took a long, noisy breath and looked into my eyes and said those words every woman yearns to

hear from the drop-dead beautiful man she's fantasized about since puberty.

"If that's what it took to get you naked and into my
bed," he said.

I almost soiled the rented Suburban's upholstery.

Red-hot searing heat flooded my cheeks. My chest
felt tighter than when I tried on the miracle body re-
ducer in the dressing room at Victoria's Secret. The
miracle then was that I could breathe at all. But I
couldn't breathe now. Couldn't speak. (Yes, it does
happen on occasion.) I couldn't think. Couldn't begin
to know what to do, how to respond, how to act.

Okay, you tell me, smarty pants. What would you do
if a guy who'd needled you since you were nine, with a
perfect body and who knows how to use it, suddenly
confessed he wanted you naked in his bed? Come on.
Huh? What? Oh, a little tongue-tied there, I see.
You're a big help.

I ended up doing what I'd vowed never to do in front
of Rick Townsend. I put my face in my hands and began
to bawl. Not dainty little delicate whimpers, but big,
monstrous, shoulder-heaving mucous-manufacturing
blubbers.

I could hear Townsend rummage about for a tissue,
so I unzipped my bag and pulled out the napkins I'd
stuck in for the cake I'd never tasted. I covered my
nose and blew long and loud, mopping my eyes with a
dry napkin.

"Jeezus, Tressa, I'm sorry if I upset or offended you,"
Townsend said, and I could tell from his tone he was
extremely distressed. "I never meant . . . I didn't
think . . . Oh, shit, I should've kept my goddamned
mouth shut," he said.

I blinked the rest of the tears out of my eyes and
Townsend took the damp wad of napkins and began
to dry my cheeks.

"Dammit, Tressa, I didn't mean that the way it sounded," he said. I looked up at him.

"You didn't?" I said with a sniffle. "You didn't mean it?" Tears once again began to collect and pool in my eyes, along with that painful pressure you get in your throat when you're trying really hard not to cry anymore. "You didn't mean it?" I repeated, beginning to sob and snot like there was no tomorrow.

"Hell, Tressa, what are you crying about now?" he asked, patting my shoulder like a kindly uncle. Or a dad. "I said I was sorry."

My crying was now at that stage of silent sobs where the top half of your body moves up and down but no sound comes out your mouth 'cause you're all sobbed out.

"I'm crying," I said between sniffles and tiny little whimpers, "because it was the nicest thing anyone has ever said to me—and you didn't even mean it!"

Townsend retreated for a moment, sitting behind the wheel of the Suburban and staring out the windshield. One minute he was a still-life, a silhouette in stone, a study in repose, and the next? The next he was an action figure come to life, a flesh and blood man, a hunter claiming his prey. Okay, okay, so I'm getting a little carried away here. Would you rather I say, "he was all over me like hot butter on a roasting ear"? Kinda kills the mood, don't you think?

I went from whimpering like a little girl who'd lost her lollipop to whimpering like a big girl being soundly—thoroughly—and expertly kissed. Townsend drew me to his feverish body, flattening my breasts against his hard, hot chest, and I wound my arms around his neck and plastered myself to as much of him as I could, returning his kisses with all the passion I'd been saving for just such an occasion.

"God, you're gonna drive me to an early grave,"

GET UP TO
4 FREE BOOKS!

You can have the best romance delivered to your door for less than what you'd pay in a bookstore or online. Sign up for one of our book clubs today, and we'll send you **FREE* BOOKS** just for trying it out...**with no obligation to buy, ever!**

HISTORICAL ROMANCE BOOK CLUB

Travel from the Scottish Highlands to the American West, the decadent ballrooms of Regency England to Viking ships. Your shipments will include authors such as CONNIE MASON, CASSIE EDWARDS, LYNSAY SANDS, LEIGH GREENWOOD, and many, many more.

LOVE SPELL BOOK CLUB

Bring a little magic into your life with the romances of Love Spell—fun contemporaries, paranormals, time-travels, futuristics, and more. Your shipments will include authors such as KATIE MACALISTER, SUSAN GRANT, NINA BANGS, SANDRA HILL, and more.

As a book club member you also receive the following special benefits:

- **30% OFF all orders through our website & telecenter!**
  (Plus, you still get 1 book FREE for every 5 books you buy!)
- **Exclusive access to special discounts!**
- **Convenient home delivery and 10 days to return any books you don't want to keep.**

There is no minimum number of books to buy, and you may cancel membership at any time. See back to sign up!

*Please include $2.00 for shipping and handling.

YES! ☐

Sign me up for the **Historical Romance Book Club** and send my TWO FREE BOOKS! If I choose to stay in the club, I will pay only $8.50* each month, a savings of $5.48!

YES! ☐

Sign me up for the **Love Spell Book Club** and send my TWO FREE BOOKS! If I choose to stay in the club, I will pay only $8.50* each month, a savings of $5.48!

NAME: _____

ADDRESS: _____

_____

TELEPHONE: _____

E-MAIL: _____

☐ **I WANT TO PAY BY CREDIT CARD.**

☐ VISA ☐ MasterCard ☐ DISCOVER

ACCOUNT #: _____

EXPIRATION DATE: _____

SIGNATURE: _____

Send this card along with $2.00 shipping & handling for each club you wish to join, to:

**Romance Book Clubs
1 Mechanic Street
Norwalk, CT 06850-3431**

Or fax (must include credit card information!) to: 610.995.9274. You can also sign up online at www.dorchesterpub.com.

*Plus $2.00 for shipping. Offer open to residents of the U.S. and Canada only. Canadian residents please call 1.800.481.9191 for pricing information.

If under 18, a parent or guardian must sign. Terms, prices and conditions subject to change. Subscription subject to acceptance. Dorchester Publishing reserves the right to reject any order or cancel any subscription.

JOIN NOW!

Townsend said, stopping to catch his breath. "But what a way to go," he added, lowering his head to take my lips once again in a kiss so hot and wet the interior of the Suburban felt like a sauna. I opened my eyes briefly and couldn't see beyond the steam on the windows.

"Uh, we're fogging the place up," I said against Townsend's lips.

"Who the hell cares?" he growled.

"It's hot in here," I said, my lips tracing a path to his ear and nipping at his lobe.

"Take some clothes off," he suggested, nuzzling my neck and pulling my white shirt out of my waistband, letting his hand crawl under my blouse and up over my breasts.

"You first," I said, and I heard him chuckle against my neck.

He touched the tip of one aching breast then removed his hand, and giving me one last quick kiss, he moved away.

"I wonder what you would do if I did shuck my clothing," he asked, looking at me with a fire, only slightly banked, still glowing in his eyes. "You'd probably take off running like you did that day a year ago when I showed you my tattoo," he said with a wicked grin.

"Duh. You were supposed to chase me, fool," I growled, still breathless from his kisses and feeling a need inside me so deep and urgent that it was almost a physical pain. I shook my head. "And I'm supposed to be the half-wit."

His eyes widened. "What are you saying, Tressa?" he asked, and I could swear he wiped a moist palm on his pants. My god. Was it possible? Was Townsend as scared as I was? As nervous at the prospect of making love?

I frowned. Oh boy. This wasn't good. I'd been relying on Townsend to make the first move. Uh, and the second and third and so on.

"Tressa?" he asked again, his body turned slightly in my direction. "What are you saying?"

What *was* I saying? Was I ready for this? I hadn't lost that ten pounds I'd sworn to shed before I shucked my clothes for any man—and most certainly for a man with a body like Rick Townsend. My hair was still . . . well, my hair, in all its untamable, unruly, unmanageable glory. And this early in the season I still sported a pretty bad case of farmer tan to boot. Not quite the package I'd hoped to deliver.

So, what was I saying? That I was okay with lower marks for presentation if I snared high ones for performance?

I thought about my mom and dad. Craig and Kimmie. Even Gram and Joe. I thought about leaps of faith, runs for the roses, and reaching for the stars. But most of all, I thought of Ranger Rick Townsend. And in that moment I knew with crystal-clear clarity what I was saying. What I'd wanted to say for a very long time, but just hadn't let myself admit.

I turned to Townsend, my feverish back pressed against the cool glass of the car window.

"You got room under that hotel bed for a pair of boots, pilgrim?" I said, feeling my lips quiver as I attempted to keep my teeth from chattering in my head.

Even in the limited light of the parking lot, I could see Townsend's Adam's apple yo-yo up and down. And again.

After what seemed like an eternity, he nodded.

"I think something could be arranged," he said, and I was gratified to hear that his voice sounded as husky and tentative as mine. "If you don't mind my granddad in the next bed, that is," he said, and I winced at that mental picture. He couldn't be serious. "On second thought, I'm thinkin' a room with a king-sized bed, a great big tub with a Jacuzzi . . . ," he went on.

"Yeah, I think I'm up for that," he added with a crooked smile.

I grinned back at him.

"There's one more thing to consider, buckaroo," I said.

"Oh? What's that?" Townsend asked with a wary look.

"A cowgirl wants more than an eight-second ride," I said with a slow wink I prayed didn't come across as a nervous tic.

Townsend grinned and reached out to pull me next to him, kissing me hard on the mouth. "That definitely won't be a problem," he said. "Not a problem at all."

We headed for my aunt and uncle's house so I could pick up a few things. On the way I sat next to Townsend, his hand resting on my knee, and I felt very out-of-body sitting so close to him in this intimate way. We'd been adversaries for so long that the transition to . . . whatever we were or whoever we were to become to each other was hard to adjust to. I didn't know how to act. Where to put my hands. Where not to put my hands. What to say. What not to say. God in Heaven—what had I just agreed to?

As we pulled onto the street where Aunt Kay and Uncle Ben lived, I contemplated jumping out of the vehicle and hauling ass down the street like the girl in that runaway bride movie. Panic welled up in my throat. At any moment I was going to let out this go-dawful bloodcurdling scream.

I opened my mouth.

"What the hell is going on?" Townsend said, and I turned to explain that I was about to have a panic attack and expected to be hyperventilating at any moment and did he have a paper sack handy, when I realized he was talking about the flashing lights down the block. He slowed the Suburban and parked across the street from my aunt's house. "What the—?"

Two police cars were parked in my aunt's driveway, their top lights reflecting off windows down the block. Townsend opened the driver side door, got out, and helped me out.

I spotted my aunt and uncle and my folks in the front yard and I began to run, fear causing my heart to pound in my chest like an out of control dinner gong.

I ran up, breathless and scared.

"What's going on? What's happened?" I looked around for my grandma. "Is Gram all right?" I asked, not seeing her.

"No. I am not all right!"

I let out a relieved breath when I recognized my gammy's voice. I ran over to her and put an arm on her shoulder. "What's wrong? What happened?" I asked.

"Some asshole broke into the house while we were out and trashed the place. Bastard destroyed the wedding dress your Aunt Kay bought me. And you should see what he did to that John Wayne bobble head of yours. Snapped his head clean off."

I looked at her. What kind of burglar took time to destroy an old lady's dress and behead a deceased western actor?

Townsend walked up and put an arm around my gammy. "It'll be okay, Hannah," he said. "Granddad won't care if you don't wear a stitch as long as you marry him." Rick winked at her. "In fact, he'd probably prefer you did wear nothing—except a smile, of course," he said.

I stared at Townsend, my heart doing little flip-flops in my chest at the soft, comforting manner he'd used with my gammy. I felt a sudden yearning to cuddle up to that softer side of the ranger, to lose myself in his embrace and regret it in the morning.

"Bless your heart," Gram said, patting Rick's cheek.

"To tell you the truth, I didn't much care for that dress anyway. Kay has such old fuddy-duddy taste. I'll have to go shopping tomorrow and pick out something new. You interested in coming, Tressa? You need a dress, too, you know. Don't want you coming wearing nothing but a smile or nobody will notice the bride."

I looked at Townsend, smiling my regret. "I'm in," I told Gram.

"You tell Joe not to worry, that I'll find something that'll knock his socks off," Gram promised, and went back to make sure the officers did their jobs.

"I guess this means I'll have to take a rain check," Townsend said, reaching out to touch my lower lip with his thumb. "And a long, cold shower," he added with a grimace.

"Sorry," I said, thinking maybe this was Someone's way of telling Tressa to proceed with caution. If so, I wanted to punch them and their amber lights out. "Maybe we can get together tomorrow?" I suggested, and he tucked a strand of wayward hair behind my ear.

"Count on it," he said. "Maybe this will give me time to pen some poignant poems especially for you. Now that I know you like poetry, that is." He smiled. "Let's see. There once was a cowgirl named Jayne. Who put a ranger in oh, so much pain."

I giggled and he started to bend down to give me a kiss, but must've sensed prying eyes, as he straightened and settled for tweaking my nose.

"I've got to go diddle with my ditty," he said. "Unless you've changed your mind? I could use your help, you know. Ditties can be . . . difficult to diddle with, you know."

"They can also be dangerous to diddle with," I replied.

He shook his head. "Goodnight, Tressa," he said. "Enjoy dress-shopping with your granny there." He handed my backpack over, crossed the street and climbed behind the wheel of the SUV, and he started to pull out.

A thought occurred to me, and I chased after him, unzipping my bag as I sprinted across the yard. "Wait! Townsend!"

He stopped the Suburban immediately and rolled down his window, and from his look, I knew he was hoping I'd changed my mind and was going along for the "ride" after all.

I jogged up to the car window and, after checking that Gram was safely indoors, I pulled Kookamunga from my bag and handed it to Townsend through the open window.

"Could you keep this?" I asked, slightly out of breath and not all due to my trot across the avenue. "If I keep it here, Gram will be sure to discover it and I don't want to spoil the surprise," I said, meaning I wanted to see Joe's face when they opened it together—and he had to pretend to like it for his new bride's sake.

Townsend took the figurine, looked at it and shook his head. "If I keep this in my room tonight, it will give me nightmares," he said. "That or major inadequacy issues," he added with a grimace. "You sure you don't want to come hold my . . . hand and stroke my, uh, brow while I sleep?" he asked. "Last chance."

"I can't," I said, shaking my head. "Not with the whole household in an uproar."

"And that's the only reason?" Townsend asked.

I couldn't bring myself to fib. Not to him. Not about this. "There is a certain level of *trepidation* on my part," I admitted. "No doubt related to a jockstrap juvenile delinquent who turned my formative milestones into a minefield," I said. "Not to mention a battle of wills. I guess I'm still trying to get a handle on this new dynamic we've got going. It's like going from an English saddle to a western pleasure saddle. It takes a little time to adapt, but the ride is so worth it."

Townsend sighed. "I guess it's just you and me Kookamunga," he said, talking to the statuette. "But I'm first in line for the cold shower, hear? And T, I'll look into a room of my own. Just in case you change your mind," he said with a crooked smile and drove off. I watched his taillights fade until they disappeared, resisting the temptation to run after him like a car-chasing pet.

I headed for the house, wondering just how critical Duke's condition was and if there was any hope for the cowpoke at all. Once inside, I surveyed the damage, stunned at the amount of senseless destruction inflicted on my aunt and uncle's home. Drawers were dumped. Mattresses flipped. Closets ransacked and cupboards cleared. Taylor's and my suitcases had been emptied and pawed through, our unmentionables strewn around the rooms for all the world to see, and my novelty T-shirts tossed. It creeped me out to think some lowlife thugs knew what kind of panties my sister and I wore. (Taylor prefers thongs while I go for the hipsters. Horseback riding while wearing a thong can be . . . tricky.)

Surprisingly, apart from some odds and ends and a small amount of cash, nothing had been taken.

Uncle Ben's art studio—a large add-on behind the garage that featured great big windows, a huge sink, and a work area that ran the length of one wall—had also been hit hard. Paint tubes had been opened and squeezed all over the walls and windows, a disturbing abstract. Canvasses had been slashed and sculptures dropped and crushed beneath a heartless, unfeeling heel. It broke my heart to see Uncle Ben bent over, picking up the ruined remnants of hours of painstaking work and inspiration and depositing them in the trash.

I bent down to help him. "I'm so sorry this happened, Uncle Ben," I said, carefully cradling an oil painting that featured red rock cliffs and wild ponies—and a large footprint where someone had tracked neon green paint on the oil painting. I hung it where it had always hung. It had been the first painting he had finished and framed when he came west. "This one is my very favorite," I told him, touching the frame with a fingertip.

Uncle Ben got up and joined me, and together we studied it. "I know," he said. "It's not my best, though. Not by a long shot. Still, I'm kind of partial to it, too."

"Can you fix it?" I asked. He nodded.

"It'll take a little doing, but yes, I can restore it." He winked at me. "Maybe I'll even make some improvements," he said, putting an arm around my shoulders. "I always thought that black rogue stallion there was slightly disproportionate. You're the horse expert. What do you think?"

I put my head on his shoulder. "I wouldn't change a thing," I told him truthfully.

Later, in the sofa bed, as I waited for Sophie to return home, I pondered the events of the last twenty-four hours, amazed at all that happened in the span of one day. It had started off fairly normal. Our sightseeing trip to Tlaquepaque. Lunch at the Grill. The beer. The roadside vendor. Bobble head Duke and Kookamunga. Then things suddenly went south. Raphael at Oak Creek Vista. Whitehead. Numbers. Speed-dating at Numbers. Raphael at Numbers. Designer bag snatch. Hot kisses. Steamy clenches. Dangerous admissions. Close calls. Break-ins. More thefts.

I scrolled through the day's highlights once again, this time in how-slow-can-you-go motion. How was it possible that, in the span of a single day, one person could be involved in three separate incidents that included theft or attempted theft and have them be happenstance and coincidence? Even for me, a person whose biggest talent is finding trouble, the odds of this occurring purely by chance were roughly the same as my gammy settling for a wedding dress that was age-appropriate.

So, what was the explanation? A full moon? Bad karma? Bad timing? Business as usual for Calamity Jayne?

The day had held such promise. The night, I reminded myself, even more. I groaned and grabbed my pillow and put it over my face. I thought of poor Duke who had made the ultimate sacrifice, and Kookamunga who'd luckily escaped unharmed and was, at this very moment, where I by rights should be: in Ranger Rick's nicely appointed luxury hotel room.

I pulled the pillow off my face and hit it a couple times. Wretched statue. I'd had nothing but grief from the moment I purchased the infernal thing. I should have let the poor unfortunate soul who'd originally wanted it have it. My luck had been for spit since Kookamunga became part of our little southwestern wedding wagon train. Gram was lucky I'd taken the fertile fellow along this evening or he'd have been laid out alongside Big John—and likely missing something other than his head. Close call, Kooky. Hard to sow seed without the right tool there, bud.

I closed my eyes and thought about it some more. The term "jinx" flashed in my subconscious. My luck *had* headed south after Kookamunga signed on. He'd been with me at Oak Creek Canyon and again at Numbers. And both times I'd been robbed. The first time, my cake. The next time, Sophie's purse. But how did I explain the break-in at my aunt's house? Was it just a coincidence that their house was hit the very same night, and unrelated?

It hit me then. Sophie's purse had her wallet in it. Her wallet had her driver's license. Her license had her home address. Her home address could have led the criminals straight to Aunt Kay and Uncle Ben's door. Her keys could have let them walk right in. But why? What were they looking for? And why here? Why now?

I mulled those questions over in my head. Why here? Why now? Why me? I'd performed this kind of deliberation before.

Why me?

"No way!"

I shot up in my sofa sleeper and clutched the pillow to my chest. I chewed my lip. Why me? Because I had something that someone wanted. And what *was* that something I had that someone wanted . . . ?

I shook my head. As kooky as it sounded even to my own imaginative brain, I was suddenly convinced I was right. They were after Kookamunga!

As quickly as that realization sank in, another one arrived hard on its tail.

Holy jalapeños! Ranger Rick was sharing a bedroll with a wanted character that, it now appeared, had a very determined posse on his tail, and he had no way of knowing an ambush was in the making.

Talk about your lone rangers.

CHAPTER TEN

"Sonofabitch!" I yelled. Tossing the covers off and vaulting from the sofa bed, I threw on the closest clothes I could find, wrinkled and mismatched, yanked on socks and my boots, grabbed my backpack and flew up the stairs and out to the garage, snaring the phonebook from a desk in the kitchen on the way.

I debated for a second which car to take, remembered what happened the last time I borrowed an uncle's automobile and climbed into Aunt Kay's Accord. I hit the garage door opener remote and as soon as I had clearance, backed into the street and peeled out. I turned the dome light on, flipped through the phonebook and found the phone number and address for the hotel the Townsends were staying at, and reached for my cell phone only to realize it was back home in the massive hands of an Amazonian with designs on my vocation. Damn.

With the aid of a phonebook map, three grouchy convenience store clerks, two slightly inebriated pedestrians and one bleary-eyed cab driver, I made my way to The Titan Hotel. It was after one A.M. when I wheeled into the parking lot, not sparing the brake pads in the process.

I hurried into the hotel and up to the registration desk. The uniformed clerk behind the desk eyed me with open curiosity. I wasn't surprised. I'd caught a reflection of myself in the mirror behind her. Jeepers creepers summed it up.

"May I help you?" the attractive female with the nametag *Tiffany* asked. I nodded.

"I need the room number of one of your guests," I told her. "It's an emergency."

"I'm sorry. It's against our policy to give out that kind of information," she said. "To protect our guests, you understand."

I nodded. "But this really is an emergency!" I assured her. "It could even be a matter of life and death. Then again, I could be totally wrong."

"Huh?"

"The name is Townsend. Rick Townsend." The clerk's eyes took on a familiar glint. I should've known. "The room number?" I prodded.

"And how do you know this individual again?" Tiffany asked, and I was tempted to peek over the counter to check for the tackle box and fly rod, because this girl was fishin' but good.

"Uh, he's my boyfriend," I told her.

"Your boyfriend," she repeated, so I nodded.

"That's right. He dropped me off at my aunt's house in Flagstaff a couple hours ago. We'd been out clubbing." In reality, the closest I'd ever gotten to clubbing was my best friend Kari's bachelorette party gone bad (the experience had ended with a police raid at a strip joint) and the time I used a Swiffer sweeper to club a big, ugly black snake who'd invaded my home turf.

"The room number, please," I said with a sugar-sweet smile.

"How do I know what you're saying is even true?" the clerk asked.

"Easy enough to verify, right, Tiffany? Why don't you ring his room and find out?" I told her. "My name is Tressa. Tressa Jayne Turner."

She hesitated and reached for the phone.

"Are you looking for Uncle Rick?" I turned to find the notorious Nick Townsend looking up at me. Dressed in baggy shorts and a T-shirt, his feet were bare.

"What are you doing down here at this hour, Nick?" I asked.

"That's funny. I was wondering that about you, too," he said with a lift of his eyebrow. "Isn't it kind of late to be visiting my uncle? Most people are asleep, you know."

I forced a smile. "You're not," I pointed out.

He shrugged. "I'm a kid. We don't count. Besides, I'm on vacation."

Right. "So what are you doing down here? Do your folks know you're sneaking around the hotel?"

He cocked his head to one side. "Do your folks know you're sneaking around the hotel?" he responded, and I glanced at Tiffany the receptionist and flashed a tight smile.

"I came to see your Uncle Rick," I told the runt. "Something happened tonight and I need to talk to him right away. Could you please tell this nice lady that I am a friend of your uncle's? Then you can show me to his room."

At first I didn't think the kid would comply, but after a long pause, he nodded to the girl behind the counter.

"It's okay. She knows my uncle," the twerp finally admitted. "Uncle Rick says they have a strange and wonderful relationship." I felt my insides get all soft and gooey until Nick went on. "He says she's strange"—he pointed a fat little finger at me—"and he's wonderful." I shook my head. Nice. "If you give me a keycard, I'll take her up to his room," he volunteered, and I shot a gloating departing look at Tiffany as we headed for the elevator.

"You know, it isn't really safe for you to be running around a strange hotel in the middle of the night, kid," I told him as we entered the elevator and he hit the button for the seventh floor. "You never know who could be lurking around a hotel lobby at that hour."

"You got that right," he said.

Man, this kid was a regular Howdy Doody.

"What do you want to see Uncle Rick for?" he asked. "Are you going to stay in his room with him? Are you going to sleep with him?"

I stared at the little voyeur. "Excuse me?"

"Is that why you're here? To have sex?"

My ears grew hot. "No! I am not!" I exclaimed. "As a matter of fact, I have something important to share with your uncle," I insisted.

"I thought so," he said with a disgusted look.

"Now just a minute!" I insisted as the elevator opened and the squirt stepped out. "I am not here to sleep with your uncle!" I hissed, as we made our way down the hallway. I caught the surprised look on the face of a hotel guest who was making his way to the vending area in search of ice, a plastic bucket in hand. "I just want to talk," I told Nick. "As if it's any of your business, little man. What room is he in, anyway?" I asked, thankful Rick had decided to get his own room.

"It's down here," he said, handing me the cardkey. He yawned. "I'm really tired. I think I'm gonna go to bed. Night, Tressa," he said. "Maybe I'll see you in the morning." He smiled at me, his expression warm and genuine, and for a moment I forgot he was a trying little turd muffin.

"Good night, Nick," I told him. "And thanks. I owe you one," I added.

"Sure," Nick said. "See you."

He turned and made his way down the hall. "Have a good night," he said just before he disappeared around a corner.

I stared down at the card in my hand and shook my head when my hand shook so much I had trouble inserting the card in the slot. Why did I feel as if I would experience a defining and life-altering moment with the opening of this particular door? That by stepping inside I would turn the page from a familiar, comfortable chapter in my life to a new and uncharted one?

And was I ready to open the door to those wondrous possibilities? You ain't just whistlin' Dixie.

I jammed the card in the slot and heard the click, and the light blinked. I opened the door, both elated and nervous, when I realized the security mechanism had been left off. It appeared the ranger really had thought I might change my mind and end up at his door tonight. The fact made my legs quiver and my heart race as I approached the bed. Or, rather, beds. Apparently, Townsend hadn't been able to secure a full-sized bed after all. I could detect dry, raspy snoring and made a mental note to razz Townsend about it in the morning.

I stopped. The morning? Was I really prepared to spend the night with Townsend? Sleep with him? All night long?

I took a deep, cleansing breath and fought the impulse to run out the way I came in. This was not the way I'd fantasized making love with Rick Townsend. In my dream world my hair was long, silky and shiny, not knotted and ratty. In my storybook imagination, I wore a black teddy with matching panties, not a wrinkled *Cowgirls Love Cuttin' Up* T-shirt and soiled black jeans. I sniffed myself. I smelled like cigarette smoke and turpentine.

Suck it up, Tressa, I scolded myself. You're thinking way too much. Stop the sniveling and second-guessing and haul your cowgirl cookies over to that bed and jump that man's bones. Those boots were made for walkin', Miz Calamity.

I had the means.

I had the opportunity.

God knew I had the motive.

I took a deep breath. It was time to commit the act. Before I expired from long-term sexual frustration and self-imposed self-denial.

Ready, boots? Start walkin'.

I made my way to the bed, shucking my hoodie and T-shirt on the way. I winced, feeling wanton and lusty. I unzipped my jeans and slid them down, sucking in my stomach as I slid a hand over my midsection. Good thing I'd passed on Raphael's dessert invite. It occurred to me to wonder if the eatery even existed, and whether I'd have ended up in a Dumpster somewhere, had I gone with the sweet-talker after all.

I kicked off my boots and nudged them under the bed with a grin.

I yanked my ponytail scrunchy out, and dragged my fingers through my freed head of hair—struggling to extract them once they were inside the tangled network of curls. Then I bent over and shook my head, allowing my hair its head. I straightened, feeling the tickle of my locks on my shoulders and down my back.

I leaned over the sleeping man.

"I heard tell a cowgirl could get a long, sweet ride

hereabouts," I whispered near the sleeping man's head. "How about it, stud?"

The figure stirred and groaned in his sleep, letting out a throaty snore.

I put a knee on the bed and slipped in beside the now lethargic Lothario. I shook like a bag of Mexican jumping beans. An antiseptic, medicinal smell reached me and I made a face. Nasty-smelling toothpaste. He'd have to switch.

"You ever heard 'save a horse—ride a cowboy'?" I whispered, tugging on an exposed ear lobe. "Heigh ho, Silver!" I purred. "Away!"

The figure next to me finally came to life. I felt a hand reach over and grab my backside, trying to squeeze, but completely muffing it.

I frowned. What the—?

"Hannah, Hannah, Hannah. You little hellion, you. I thought you wanted to wait for the next time 'til after the wedding vows."

Reality rolled over me in roiling waves with equal parts of nausea, horror and disbelief. My head snapped back. I threw my arms out to the side. I flew off the bed and landed in a heap on the floor.

I lay there stunned, my eyes tightly shut while I tried to come to terms with what had just transpired. A light suddenly clicked on and I slowly opened one eye. Then the other. Above me, peeking out over the side of the bed and breathing Polident breath down on me was Ranger Rick's grandpappy—and my step-grandfather-to-be—Joltin' Joe Townsend.

The horrified look in his eyes matched what I was feeling at the moment. We stared at each other.

"I can explain," I began. "It's not what you think. There really is a perfectly logical explanation for this." I stopped. "Are you gonna believe what you see or what I tell you?"

Joe shook his head. "Good God, girlie, get dressed! I'll pee. Then, we talk," Joe said. "And this better be good. I'll be up all night going to the pot now. I hope you're happy," he grumbled as he climbed out of bed and headed for the bathroom. I stared when I noticed he was wearing what looked like a silky kimono-type nightshirt.

I sat up and located the clothing from my demented striptease and dressed, unable to look at myself in the mirror.

I supposed there was something to be thankful for: At least Joe didn't sleep in the buff like my gammy did, thank God for small favors. No pun intended. Eeww.

A half hour later, when Joe finally finished in the bathroom and I'd retched in the sink, I filled him in on the high points of that evening while we sat in armchairs near the window, a safe, discreet distance from each other. Since I didn't want to spoil the wedding gift surprise, I merely told him that there had been a break-in at my aunt's house and I thought it might be related to the theft of Sophie's purse earlier that evening, and wanted to discuss a theory I had about the crime with his grandson. Assured that my grandma was unharmed and set to stun him with a new bridal dress, he relaxed.

"So, you see, I came here strictly to compare notes with Rick," I pointed out.

"And you shucked your threads because . . . ?" Joe asked.

I knew there was no way I could talk myself out of this escapade. Not even with Steven Spielberg putting the words in my mouth. Not with a fellow who belongs to the NRA, reads *True Crime* magazines as light-reading fare and visits Web sites like mercs_r_us regularly.

"I'm in lust with your grandson," I told Joe. "I'm pretty sure."

"I see. But are you in love with him, girlie?" Joe questioned, verbalizing what I'd been asking myself ad nauseum of late.

"I'm not sure," I told him, truthful. "I think maybe that's why I came here. You know. To find out."

Joe looked at me for a long time. "I think you're holdin' out on me, girlie," he said. "I think there's more to this little late-night rendezvous than a stolen purse, a residential break-in, and a cowgirl lookin' for a sweet ride."

My cheeks felt warm as a spanked baby's bottom. "I'd just as soon you'd forget I ever said that, Joe," I told him. "It was said in—shall we say—the heat of the moment."

"You think?" he responded.

"I would really appreciate it if you wouldn't mention this to . . . anyone," I said. "It's rather . . . embarrassing."

He looked at me and got a twinkle in his eye. "I'm not sure this is the kind of thing I should keep from my grandson," he said. "Familial duty, you know."

I raised an eyebrow. *Right.*

"I see," I said. "Duty, huh?" I looked at him. "I reckon then, it's my duty to let everyone back home know that macho Joe Townsend sleeps in a silk dress at night. Very chic and retro, by the way," I said, and his eyes got big and bulgy like those bug-eyed fish that live near the bottom of the ocean. "So bright and . . . *gay.*"

"You wouldn't," he said.

I raised an eyebrow. "Freedom of the press is a lovely thing," I remarked.

Joe considered me for a second. "So is family loyalty," he countered.

"You squeezed my butt," I pointed out. Or, rather, tried to. The poor guy couldn't get a grip. I didn't care to speculate on whether it was due to his lack of pincer power or too much posterior on my part.

"You stuck your tongue in my ear," he declared.

"I did no such thing!" I declared, jumping out of my chair.

"Gotcha!" he said with a grin. "I'll give you this much, Blondie," he continued. "If I do decide to tell my grandson what transpired here, I'll do you the courtesy of letting you know beforehand, just in case you decide you want to tell him first. Fair enough?" He offered his bony hand to me and I took it.

"I don't suppose I have a choice," I said. "But be warned, Mr. Geezer, if you spill the beans without warning me ahead of time, I'll make sure your dirty laundry, cold-water washables and all, is hung out to dry from the water tower back home!"

He grunted as we shook on it.

" 'Til then, old man, we speak of this to no one," I said.

"Ten-four, Gypsy Rose," he said with a grin. "Sweet, sweet Gypsy Rose."

From a lady outlaw to a stripper who was no lady. Some days it didn't pay to get out of bed. Unless you found yourself in that bed very nearly naked with a seventy-year-old man in silk, that is. My stomach roiled again.

"So, where is your grandson?" I finally thought to ask, taking a look at the time and thinking it strange Ranger Rick was still out and about.

"How should I know? I thought he was out with you," Joe commented.

"He was," I responded, "and wasn't."

Joe crossed his scrawny bird legs and tapped his knee. "What's that mean?"

"It means we didn't go together, but we ended up leaving together," I said.

Joe raised an eyebrow. "Sounds like a pick-up story if I ever heard one," he said.

I shook my head. "It wasn't like that," I told him.

Well, it hadn't started out that way. "My cousin Sophie met up with a friend who was going to see her home, so I caught a ride with Rick to give them a little time to themselves."

"I see. Pick-ups run in the family, huh? So, if you left with Rick, where is he?"

"I have no idea. He dropped me off at Aunt Kay's house and left. That was hours ago." I rubbed my gut. I was starting to get a bad case of nervous stomach. Where the devil was that man?

"You're sure he didn't come back to the room?" I asked. Joe shrugged.

"I'm a heavy sleeper," he said. "I expect that's why I didn't wake up when you crawled into bed with me." He must've seen the look on my face, because he self-corrected before I could object. "I mean, when you came into the room. How'd you get in here, anyway?" he asked, and I frowned, wondering why it hadn't registered before.

"Why, that conniving, treacherous, two-faced little toad!" I said, jumping to my feet again. "He tricked me into climbing into that bed with you, the demented little troll!"

"Who? Rick?" Joe asked.

"No!" I said, running to the door of the hotel room and yanking it open. "Him!" I pointed to the eaves-dropping urchin crouched in the hallway outside the door with a drinking glass against one ear and an *I'm-busted* look on his face.

"Nick? Nick's the demented little troll?" Joe asked. I nodded. Nick started to crawl away but I took hold of one ear.

"Oh, no, you don't," I said, pulling him into the hotel room. "We need to talk, buster."

"But it's late. It's past my bedtime!"

"You should've thought about that before you pulled

a stunt that resulted in an encounter I'll probably require extensive therapy to treat before I ever commit to an intimate relationship," I told him.

"Huh?"

"I heard that and I resent it!" Joe yelled from across the room.

I ignored him and focused on the kid at my feet. "You knew your Uncle Rick wasn't in here when you got me that key and brought me here. How?"

The kid hesitated, no doubt trying to make up another doozy.

"And don't even try to lie to me this time, mister," I said, crouching at his level to make eye contact. "Your Uncle Rick could be in trouble."

"What kind of trouble?" Joe asked.

I waited.

"Girl trouble," Nick finally said, and I sat. It was not what I expected to hear.

"What do you mean, 'girl trouble'?" I asked.

Nick paused again.

"Nick?" I prodded.

"He was with *her*," he said, lowering his gaze and looking away from me.

I frowned. "Her? Who, her?"

"The lady from Oak Creek Canyon. Whitebread," he said, and I almost smiled.

"Whitehead? He was with Officer Whitehead?"

"Who the devil is Whitebread?" Joe asked. "You two are keeping me out of the loop."

Nick nodded. "I saw them together. They were outside talking."

"What time was this?" I asked.

The kid bit his lip. "I dunno. An hour before you got here. Maybe more. He said he was gonna take a walk to clear his head. I thought it was awful cold, but

Uncle Rick said the colder the better—whatever that meant."

I winced. "So, you talked to your uncle after he got home?" I asked.

He got a crafty look in his eyes I didn't care for. "Yeah. He brought something to our room for safe-keeping," Nick said. "Something very special."

"What's he talking about? What's special? What did he bring for safekeeping?" Joe had stood and moved over to us. Standing with his arms akimbo and feet spread apart and in his silk robe, he looked like a geri-atric King of Siam.

"It's nothing," I said. "The kid's right. It's past his bedtime. And yours, too, Joe." I took Nick's hand and pulled him to his feet. "You don't want to get so worn out that you're unable to, uh, consummate the mar-riage," I pointed out to Joe. "Although from your ear-lier remarks, I take it that particular pony has left the starting gate," I added. He gave me an annoyed look.

"Come on, pardner," I said, leading the adolescent to the door. "Time for little cowpokes to bed down for the night," I told him. "See you tomorrow, Casanova," I said to Joe.

"Oh, and before I forget, little Miss Easy Rider. The black bra? It's, like, totally workin' for you, girl," Joe said with a wink. "Think you can talk your grandma into getting one, too?"

I yanked little T out into the hall and shut the door on Joe's dry cackles.

"You Townsend men should take your act on the road," I told Nick.

"You mean like Vegas or Branson?" the runt asked.

I shook my head. "I mean like Ringling Brothers," I replied.

"Can I go to bed now?" Nick asked. "I'm really tired."

I nodded. "Certainly. Just as soon as you hand over my property," I told him, marching him down the hall in the direction of his room.

He stopped. "I don't have it," he said, and I looked at him.

"What do you mean, you don't have it? You just said your uncle brought it up to your room for safekeeping," I pointed out.

"He did."

"So? Where it is? Where's Kookamunga?"

He looked at his feet again, and I knew I wasn't going to like the response.

"I got rid of it," he said, and I felt this almost uncontrollable urge to wrap my hands around his scrawny neck and lift him off the ground and shake him. Instead, I backed him up against the wall.

"You—got—rid—of—it?" I enunciated. "You got rid of it! Why? You knew that was a wedding gift for your great-grandpa and my grandma. Why would you do that?"

"Because it was a sucky gift, that's why!" he said. "Who gives an ugly statue with a hoo-hah bigger than the Oscar Mayer Wienermobile as a gift for a wedding?" he asked. "It's dumb! And you're dumb for buying it. So I got rid of it."

I put my hands on the wall on either side of his head.

"Where did you put it?" I asked.

"I'm not gonna tell. It's ugly and stupid and gross."

I bent down to eye level. "Listen very carefully, Nick. There is a chance—a slim chance, but a chance all the same—your uncle could be in trouble because I bought that statue. I need that statue. Do you understand?"

He stared at me. "Is this for real?" he asked, and I nodded.

"I wouldn't fib about something like this, Nick," I said.

"Uncle Rick could be in trouble?"

"I don't know. But it's possible."

He studied me for several seconds. "It's in the drink," he said, and I stared at him.

"What?"

"I dropped him in the swimming pool," he said. "The deep end. It was so cool. He sank to the bottom like an anchor."

I shook my head. When I'd contemplated taking the plunge tonight, this was *so* not what I had in mind.

Then again, on the bright side, maybe I'd luck out and find Nemo.

Most likely, I'd find heap big trouble.

Cowabunga.

CHAPTER ELEVEN

Since I needed someone to stand guard while I retrieved Kookamunga from the pool's depths and Ranger Rick was nowhere to be found—I'd stew over that once my rescue dive was completed—I had to enlist the dubious assistance of Nick the nephew. The pool area was dark but the doors were unlocked. I posted Nick just outside the door.

"You stay here and keep watch," I told him. "If someone comes by, stall them. It shouldn't take me long to locate Kooky and bring him up."

"I'm tired. I want to go to bed," Nick whined.

"You should've thought of that before you decided how fun it would be to play your pervy little joke on me," I told him. "Not so funny now, is it?" I taunted.

"What do I say if someone comes along? What if they ask what I'm doing here?"

"Do what you do best, boy. Jerk 'em around like you do me. That'll give me more than enough time to finish up. I need three minutes, tops. You've annoyed people much longer than that with your endless questions. You know. Like, 'Why don't they have the pool open at night? What if someone wants to swim? Do you have heated towels? Does swimming after you eat really cause cramps—' "

"Can guests skinny dip in the pool and take their clothes off in the hot tub?" the pipsqueak piped in.

I made a face. "You get the general idea," I said. "Let's go. Once I've collected Kooky, you can take your cunning little kiester off to bed where you can wreak all the havoc you like in your dreams," I told him.

He crossed his arms and gave me the silent treatment, which suited me fine. I slipped into the pool area and, for the second time that evening, stripped down to my underwear. This was getting to be a bad habit. I peered down at the dark water. I was a decent swimmer but the idea of diving to the pool's depths with only a kid who was about as trustworthy as my Plymouth Reliant in cold weather looking out for my welfare gave me more than a little cause for concern.

I moved to the deep end of the glistening pool, sucked in a heavy-duty breath and dove in. I swam to the bottom of the pool and groped around the bottom, searching for the ugly but defenseless fertility figurine who'd been no match for an adolescent with an attitude. Losing breath and finding nothing I surfaced, gasped for more air and did a return dive, all the time wishing I'd made the little twerp rescue Kooky himself. As Dr. Phil likes to say, *You choose the behavior, you choose the consequences.* Dr. Phil so rocks.

I did some more groping—non-lewd variety—and still no luck. I was just about to resurface for one more dive when I felt a tug on the waistband of my panties from behind. I turned, making out only a large shadow in the water. Instinctively, I reached out to shove the object away—and made contact with hot, wet, naked skin.

Air bubbles shot out my mouth as I pushed off from the bottom of the pool and headed for the surface. What the devil had that little turd sniffer done now?

Just as I was about to break the surface, I was hauled back under by a tug on my ankle. More bubbles escaped. Something grabbed me around the waist—my imagination immediately identified it as a villain: an octopus, maybe, or the bad guy here to collect Kooka-munga even if it meant drowning me—and I began to struggle. I flailed about, swinging my arms as I propelled myself upward. I hit pay dirt when my fist collided with what felt like a nose.

I broke free and thrust my body up and away, breaking the surface of the pool with a cough and a sputter before long strokes took me to the end of the pool and the ladder. I'd climbed two rungs and was about to pull myself out when I was hauled back into the water with a loud splash, getting a mouthful of chlorine in the process.

A long, dark shadow loomed out of the shimmering depths again and I was just about to start punching when I was grabbed by my upper arms and pulled in the shadow's direction. The next thing I knew lips were locked on mine in a hard, breathtaking—and breath-sharing—kiss.

I'd know that kisser anywhere.

The seconds ticked by. With each measure of breath I gave and received back, it felt like I was willing myself to give more and more of myself away. Strong arms hugged me, cradled me. As one we broke the water's surface, lips still sealed in a kiss.

We kissed, treading water for a long moment, ending the kiss when we were both good and breathless.

"Who'd have guessed I'd find a mermaid in northern Arizona?" Townsend said, pushing my hair back out of my face. I was so gonna pay for this when I combed my hair the next day. I'd probably go through at least two wide-toothed combs.

Who'd have guessed I'd go from jumping in bed with one Townsend to jumping in the pool with his nearly naked grandson in the same night, I thought, giving thanks for nondisclosure clauses.

"Are you naked?" I asked instead.

"Do you want me to be?" he asked.

Did I?

"Your nephew is just outside the door," I pointed out.

"Not anymore. I sent the kid to bed," he said. "After I chewed his ass, that is."

I shoved Townsend away, remembering what had brought me to the pool in the first place: Townsend trickery.

"Oooh. You talked to him. Wow. I bet he was scared," I said. "What that kid needs is a kick in the seat of the pants by someone who isn't afraid to do it," I told Rick. "Do you know what he did?"

"He told me," Townsend said.

I hesitated. "What exactly did he tell you?" I asked.

"About Kookamunga. What else? If it makes you feel any better, I think he's sorry."

"Sorry he got caught is more like it," I scoffed, relieved the practical jokester hadn't informed Ranger Rick of my troubling tryst with his grandpappy. "I almost drowned diving for a gift I personally hand-selected and spent my—er, your hard-earned money for and the damned thing was never there. Was it?"

Townsend shook his head.

"It was hidden behind a floral display in the lobby," he said.

"Of all the asinine things—"

"Why are you here, Tressa?" Townsend asked.

I shook my head and water flew from the tangled mass. "What do you mean? I came in here to retrieve my property from a demented little toadstool," I said, squeezing more water out of my hair.

"But what brought you to the hotel in the middle of the night?" Townsend asked, and I knew what he wanted to hear. And the sexually frustrated part of me wanted to tell him what he wanted to hear.

"You did," I found myself saying. It was, after all, the truth.

"I did?"

I nodded. "I was . . . concerned," I said, picking my words carefully.

"How so?"

"I know this may sound really Area 51, but I actually thought you might be in danger," I told him.

I could see him shake his head. "I'm not reading you," he said. "Why would I be in danger?"

What had seemed like a certainty when I was lying in bed miles away fretting now seemed fanciful at best. I took a deep breath. "I think someone is after Kookamunga," I said.

A long poignant pause filled the distance between us.

"Run that by me again," Townsend said.

"I think someone is trying to steal Kookamunga," I repeated. "I'm serious."

Townsend covered his face with a hand, wiping away the moisture. "That's what I'm afraid of," he said. He swam to the side of the pool and pulled himself out. I followed.

"What does that mean?"

He crossed the pool area to where a pile of clothes sat, and grabbed something, turned and walked back to me and slapped Kookamunga into my hands.

"You think someone is after that?" he asked, putting a hand through his hair. From the light streaming in from the patio area outdoors, his silhouette reminded me of a muscled, ripped romance cover model. Townsend's silhouette, not Kooky's, that is.

"Huh?" I said, my concentration centered on the ripped ranger across from me.

"Why would anyone in their right mind be after that thing?" he asked again, and I looked down at Kookamunga. Okay, so on a scale of one to ten he'd get about a .5 for attractiveness. But he'd be off the scale as a conversation piece.

I hurried over to Townsend as he grabbed his pants and pulled them on. I watched, way too fascinated for my own good.

"Don't you see? At the roadside stand someone told them to hold Kooky for him and not sell him, but they sold him to us anyway."

"Kooky?" Townsend paused, leaving his jeans open at the waist—and my tongue stuck to the roof of my mouth.

"His nickname," I said. "Then, at Oak Creek Canyon, we have the little run-in with Raphael."

"The poet," Townsend said. "How does he fit in? He took cake."

I'd thought about this on the drive up.

"Ah, but did he know it was cake?" I said. "It could easily have been Kookamunga in the bag. I'd switched the bags after we left the roadside stand. To avoid frosting fallout," I clarified. "And you can't forget what happened at Numbers."

Townsend picked up his shirt. "I'd like to give it a try," he muttered. "And . . . he took Sophie's bag. Not yours."

"Ah-ha. But did he know it was Sophie's bag? Sophie had left the table. I was the only one there. My backpack was on the back of my chair. He could easily have missed it. And being a Dolce & Gabbana bag, well, class shows, and he'd naturally assume the bag belonged to me."

Townsend pulled the shirt over his head. "Naturally," he said. "And I suppose these same bad guys used Sophie's identification to break into your aunt's house shortly thereafter," he said. "All that effort to get their hands on a fifty-dollar fake fertility idol with, as Nick pointed out, a pecker the size of a teepee pole. And pointing the same direction, I might add. I'm having a hard time with this one, T," he said.

He moved in my direction and stopped in front of me. I shivered, feeling uncomfortably vulnerable clad in only my wet black bra and panties with Townsend now fully dressed.

"I'd rather you tell me you came back to the hotel because you were tossing and turning in your bed thinking of me, instead of Mr. Erectus Enormous here," he said, moving closer and closer until Kookamunga threatened to jab him. He put a hand out to deflect the protruding protuberance. "Easy there, fella," he said. "Take it down a notch."

I smiled.

"Black looks good on you," Townsend said, shifting his attention away from Kooky to me. My smile faltered when I recalled Joe Townsend's earlier similarly approving assessment of my undergarments. "But I'm thinking it would look even better off," he said, looping a finger underneath a bra strap, pulling it down. His palm swept over the top of my breast and I felt my nipple grow and harden under his touch.

"I don't think this is exactly the time or the place," my lips protested while my body beckoned. "And you've got a roommate who assures me he'll be up visiting the privy the remainder of the night," I added.

"You spoke to Pops?" Townsend asked, his lips nuzzling my neck.

I nodded, bending my neck so he had easier access. "Just before your nephew, Nosy Nick, fell into the room with his ear to the keyhole."

"Hotel doors have keyholes?" He nuzzled an earlobe and I shivered.

"That kid doesn't need a keyhole. You better be careful, Townsend, he even spies on you." I stopped, replayed that in my head, and realized I'd totally spaced on the little twerp's earlier claim that Townsend had been with Officer Whitehead.

"Kids will be kids," Townsend said, drawing my other bra strap down. "And men . . . will be men," he added, shifting his lips to the other side of my neck.

"The kid's got an imagination, that's for sure," I said, trying to keep my voice at a conversational level. "He even said he saw you and Whitehead outside the hotel together tonight. About the same time I was fracturing more than a few traffic laws and waking senior citizens trying to locate you."

The nuzzling at my neck was placed on pause. Townsend's hot breath heated my skin. I waited for his response—well, for all of ten seconds, that is—and reached out and grabbed a hunk of his hair at the back of and pulled up so I could see his face. "That was all just a figment of the kid's imagination, right, Townsend?" I asked, trying to read the sparks of light in his dark eyes.

He straightened.

"Carena was here," he said. "She was still troubled about the incident at Oak Creek Canyon. When the guy showed up at Numbers and Sophie's purse was snatched, she was concerned. She wanted to see if I had any more information on the guy."

I stepped back. "Why didn't she contact me, then?" I asked. "Or Sophie? Why you?"

Townsend shook his head. "I don't know. I guess

since I'm in a similar profession she thought I might be more—I don't know—helpful."

"And were you?" I asked.

"Was I what?"

"Helpful."

He shrugged. "She seemed satisfied when she left," he said with a grin, and I felt my lip curl.

"I'm sure she was," I snapped, and stomped over to my pile of clothes. I put Kookamunga down and slammed my legs into my jeans, stuffing my arms into my T-shirt. I threw the hoodie over my head, leaving the hood on my wet mane.

"I'm leaving. See if I protect your arrogant ass again, Mr. Ranger, sir," I said.

"It was a joke, Tressa," Townsend said. "Just a joke."

I nodded, "Sometimes I wonder if everything is a joke to you where I'm concerned," I said, fatigue and disappointment adding a resigned tone to my words. "Calamity Jayne, sideshow attraction and comic cow-girl extraordinaire. Hurry, hurry. Step right up and get your ticket, folks! We promise one heckuva good time! Yeehaw!"

Townsend took a step in my direction. "You know, Miz Calamity, that kind of promotion usually ends with your basic guarantee of satisfaction," he told me, a suggestive huskiness to his voice.

I cocked a brow. With a head of hair that now resembled a tumbling tumbleweed, a body scent that made you think of industrial-strength cleaners, and an ass so waterlogged my butt cheeks probably resembled two rather large, wrinkly prunes, no way was I going to make good on any guarantees of satisfaction tonight.

"Sorry, bucko, but after the day I've had, any performance this little cow gal gave would be on a strictly 'As is—No warranty provided' basis," I said, quoting the paperwork on the used cars at the car dealership my brother worked at. "Besides, there's another thing that keeps popping up between us that kind of gets in the way," I told him.

"What are you talking about?" Townsend asked.

"Oh, just a little, ole, nagging double standard, that's all," I replied.

"What do you mean, double standard?" Townsend asked.

I looked at him for a long second. Did I really want to get into this tonight? I shrugged. "Just that for the last year I've listened to you lecture me on my 'trust' issues, on how I don't open up to you, how I keep you out of the loop, blah, blah, blah, blah, blah, but you don't seem to realize you do the same thing to me. Hello! You've kept me in the dark so much I'm considering training Butch and Sundance as seeing-eye dogs! I'm pretty sure that trust thing is supposed to work both ways," I told him. "At least, that's how it works with me," I said, and walked out of the pool area and headed for the front door.

"Where the hell are you going, Tressa? It's after two. Let me get you a room at least."

"No, thank you. Kooky and I have had more than enough of Townsend hospitality to last us for quite some time," I said. "We're going home to the sofa bed." I blew Rick a kiss. "Sleep well, Mr. Ranger, sir. I do hope Joe's prostate won't wake you every hour on the hour 'til morning and that phlegm factory from down the hall doesn't come banging on your door at dawn. Sweet dreams!" I said, preparing to make my escape.

"Oh, hello! I see your girlfriend found you." The hotel receptionist, Tiffany, hailed Ranger Rick from across the lobby. "She was really quite concerned, you know, when she came in looking for you. Said it could be a matter of life or death, so I gave her the key to your room. I hope that was all right." She looked at our saturated heads and the dampness seeping through our clothing. "Is it raining out?"

Townsend stared at me for a second and looked over at Tiffany. "My 'girlfriend' here told you she needed to find me because it was a matter of life and death?" Townsend asked.

Tiffany nodded. "Uh, it was, wasn't it? I didn't do anything wrong, did I? She is your girlfriend. Right? Your nephew confirmed it."

Townsend looked back at me. His gaze didn't waver. "Yeah," he said. "She's my girlfriend. The daft woman just doesn't realize it yet."

I gave myself a hard pinch and Kookamunga a big squeeze and ran like hell before I fell over the edge and into Townsend's arms.

CHAPTER TWELVE

I managed to replace Aunt Kay's car—if not the petrol I'd used—without anyone being the wiser. Well, except for Sophie, that is. It's kind of hard to crawl into one-half of a sofa bed without rousing the occupant of the other half.

"So? Did you take that leap of faith?" Sophie asked. "Or maybe I should say jump of faith, as in jumping the handsome ranger's bones," she added. "And I warn you, I want details."

I pulled the covers up to my neck and sighed. "You ever heard, the spirit is willing but the flesh is weak?" I asked. "Well, change that to 'the spirit was willing but the flesh was wrinkled' and that about sums up this night's romantic activities. And trust me on this one, Sophie, if you want to avoid disturbing images in your head for the rest of your days, you don't want the details."

She sniffed. "Do I smell chlorine?"

"Go to sleep, Sophie," I said. I closed my eyes and

dreamed of silk jammies, wet, naked chests, and phallus-shaped hat hooks.

It seemed like only minutes later when someone tugged on my arm. "You awake? You need to get out of this bed and get movin'."

I rolled over. "I swear I won't tell a soul, Joe," I mumbled. "It's our little secret."

"Secret? What secret? Is Joe keepin' secrets from me?"

The pulling on my arm became vigorous shaking. I opened one protesting eyeball. My grandma stood over me.

"Huh?"

"You said you and Joe were keeping secrets. Is he having a last fling before the wedding?" she asked.

That got my other eye open. I so didn't want the distinction of being Joltin' Joe's final fling.

"Of course not," I said, trying to figure out what little fib might pacify her.

"Then what's the secret?"

"It wouldn't be a secret if I told you, would it?" I said, putting the covers aside and swinging my feet over the side of the bed.

She got a gleam in her eye.

"It's a secret wedding gift, isn't it?" she said. "I knew it. The sweet, sweet man."

I managed a weak smile. Crap. I hoped Joe had thought about a wedding gift for his hellion bride.

I put a hand to my lips. "Shhh!" I said.

"You better get going. The rest of us are almost ready," she said.

"Ready for what?" I asked.

"Wedding dress shopping. I need a new one, re-member? We're going down to Sedona. Sophie says there are lots of fancy-shmancy boutiques down there. I'm thinkin' this may be the last wedding dress I'll buy, and I figure it's okay to splurge." She looked at me. "What do you think?"

I stood and gave her a hug. "Go for it, Gram," I said, squeezing her shoulders.

She patted my back. "You're a good girl, Tressa Jayne," she said. "Don't know diddly about men, but a good girl. Maybe too good."

"Thanks, Gram," I said. "I love you, too." I padded over to my suitcase, spotted my backpack, and turned to Gram. "You said you were going to Sedona."

She nodded. "We're taking Ben's car. It'll hold all of us."

"Us?"

"You, me, Taylor, Sophie, and Kimmie."

"Aunt Kay's not coming?" I asked.

Gram shook her head. "I'd end up with another old-lady dress if she did," she said.

Oak Creek Canyon was on the way to Sedona. As well as a certain souvenir stand, if I wasn't mistaken. Regardless of the skeptical ranger, I was still convinced there was a connection between the recent thefts and break-in and the statue I'd purchased roadside. The shopping expedition would give me an opportunity to question the vendors about how they acquired the fertility fellow in the first place, and to find out who had put the hold on Kookamunga. Then maybe I'd know once and for all if I was on to something here or blowing smoke. Either way, I'd know for sure. And knowledge, as I was so often reminded, was power.

I showered the chlorine out of my hair and scrubbed away all traces of my previous dead-of-the-night activities. I only wished I could wash off the memory of Townsend's lips on my neck as easily.

I stuck my face under the pulsating showerhead and sang off-key, "I'm gonna wash that man right outta my hair. I'm gonna wash that man right outta my hair." I groaned. If only all it took was salon shampoo and a detangler, I'd be home free.

I dressed in blue jeans, a pair of tan Skechers with maroon stripes, one of my trademark cowgirl T-shirts, this one with the slogan, *Rodeo Chicks Love Horsin' Around*, and grabbed my wardrobe-staple zippered sweatshirt and my backpack and headed upstairs.

Everyone was gathered in the family room off the back of the kitchen. I snared a cinnamon roll from a plate in the kitchen on my way through.

"Here she is," Gram said. "It's about time. What'd you do? Take time to shave? We're burnin' daylight here."

I colored, avoiding eye contact with my dad and uncle. "It took longer than I thought to get the chlorine out of my hair," I said before I thought. Something I do way too frequently, I'm afraid.

"Chlorine? How did you get chlorine in your hair?" my sister Taylor asked with an intrigued look on her face.

"Did I say chlorine? I meant conditioner. I did a five-minute conditioning treatment," I said. "Split ends, you know."

Taylor shook her head.

"Time's a-wastin'," Gram said. "I got me a wedding dress to buy."

Aunt Kay stood. "Now remember, Mother, a wedding is a solemn occasion," she said. "And you'll be making memories—not to mention a photographic record—of this day to cherish for years to come. So, select your attire accordingly." Aunt Kay's expression was reminiscent of mine when I got roped into attending a senior-citizen Halloween costume party.

"That's the idea," Gram said with a nod. "I want to make a statement for posterior," she stated.

"Uh, I think you mean posterity, Mother," Aunt Kay said.

"You make the kind of statement you want and I'll make the kind of statement I want," Gram responded.

I smiled. Oh, what a day it promised to be. I noticed Kimmie packing saltines for the trip.

"What's with the crackers, Kimmie?" I asked.

"They're just in case any of us experience the same bug Taylor had," Kimmie explained.

I blinked. "Bug? What bug? You mean Taylor's air-sickness?" I said.

"I'm not convinced it was due to air-sickness," Taylor said. "More likely, it was a bug. You know how unhealthy that recirculated air on those planes is."

"Are you kidding?" I looked at Kimmie. "Taylor has a history of chronic and virulent motion sickness that dates back to preschool. She used to puke on the merry-go-round. She couldn't even do the hokey-pokey without getting dizzy," I said.

"I think you exaggerate, Tressa," Taylor said.

"I think I don't. Remember how you always got to sit in the front seat on family trips because you'd get sick if you sat in back?" I countered.

"I grew out of that," Taylor insisted.

"Oh really? Then why'd Aunt Kay have to stop so often on the way to Flag from Phoenix? Or are you gonna blame it all on an old lady's bladder?" I said.

"What old lady?" Gram asked.

"Are we ready to go?" Sophie spoke up. When I nodded, she said, "Then let's load up. I'm driving. Who wants to ride up front with me?"

I raised my hand. "Since Taylor no longer suffers from her motion malady, I'd like to know what it feels like to ride up front for a change," I said. "Taylor can sit in back. That is, if you don't want to ride up front, Gram—so you can see better."

"See what better? I've got me a *People* magazine to look at. Saw some dresses from the Oscars that I want to take a closer look at. Don't need to be up front to do that. Besides, Sophie'll be concentrating on her driving, and I'll have to twist my head around to visit anyway, so I might as well be in back to begin with," she said.

"So, we're all good to go," I said, sending a bright smile in Taylor's direction and getting a glare for my effort as we piled into the SUV. "We're off on the road to Sedona," I sang.

"Sounds like a Bing Crosby/Bob Hope movie," Gram observed.

"Bing who?" I teased, and she gave me a cross look.

"Kids these days," she said.

Sophie took the quickest route to Sedona, via I-17 and Schnebly Hill Road, so I didn't have an opportunity to watch for the roadside souvenir stand. I figured I'd try to convince Sophie to let me borrow Uncle Ben's vehicle and I'd take a quick drive up Highway 89A and see if I could locate the traveling sales van. If all else failed, I'd ask Sophie to take the alternative route back and keep a sharp lookout as we drove.

We arrived in Sedona just as the shops were opening. Sophie, being familiar with the area, had made a list of boutiques for Gram to visit in her search for the knock-the-groom-dead dress. I figured now was a good time to take my own little mini-sightseeing side trip. If we stopped on the way home, Gram would most likely find out about Kookamunga and spoil the surprise. And I was determined this was one gift she wouldn't know about ahead of time.

"Uh, Sophie, you don't mind if I take Uncle Ben's truck just down the road a piece? I'd like to replace my John Wayne bobble head while I'm in the area," I said.

She frowned. "You want to drive my uncle's car?" she

asked. "Didn't you borrow your Uncle Frank's SUV a couple months back and wreck it?" The uneasy look in her eyes told me it was going to be a tough sale.

"Define 'wreck,'" I said. "Because I'm thinking technically you have to be behind the wheel of an automobile to be in a wreck. The vehicle in question was parked, and I was actually standing in front of the vehicle at the time and a pickup sideswiped the Suburban and took off, so it really wasn't a wreck per se," I explained.

"Hit and run then. I feel so much better," Sophie said. I winced.

"I'm just driving up the highway ten miles or so and right back," I said. "Jeesh. It's not like I'm taking it four-wheelin' cross-country."

"And a bobble head is that important to you?" she pressed.

"Duh. It's John Wayne," I said, as if that would explain my urgency.

Sophie bit her lip. "You can get your bobble head, but I'm driving," she said. "You forget. I've heard the stories. And last night I saw up close and personal how things have a tendency to get out of hand when you feel passionate about something," she told me.

"Are we talking about Rick Townsend again, because I'll have you know—"

Sophie shook her head. "Ever heard the phrase 'figure of speech'?" she asked. "Sheesh, you do have it bad. Come on."

We assigned Kimmie and Taylor the morning shift with Gram, and after promising we'd meet for lunch at the Oak Creek Grill at noon and relieve them so they could have the afternoon off, we set out.

"So, what really happened with you and Rick after you two left Numbers last night?" Sophie asked.

"History repeated itself," I grumbled. Staring out

the window I wasn't seeing the breathtaking scenery, but instead Rick Townsend as he'd appeared last night in the pool. Like a god from Atlantis. Sleek, hot and wet. Fan me.

"Tressa?"

"We kissed, real life intervened, we kissed some more, real life intervened, we disagreed, we called it a night."

"That sucks," Sophie said.

"How about you? How'd it go with Tristan?" I asked, and noted the color appear in the cheek nearest me. "He seemed very nice."

"He is," she said. "Very."

"Cute, too," I said.

"That, too," Sophie replied.

"Come on, Soph, give me something here!" I said, frustrated. "Is it serious? Where did you meet him? Do you love the guy?" I leaned across the seat. "Have you been *intimate*?"

She gave me a *good gawd* look and shook her head.

"I think we'd better change the subject," she said, and I shrugged.

"You brought it up," I pointed out.

"I did, didn't I?" she acknowledged, and gave her own cheek a soft slap. "Don't know what I was thinking," she said. "I guess I just got carried away. I've never had a sister to discuss personal girl stuff with. And apparently, I'm more comfortable eliciting that information from others than I am sharing my own. At least at present."

I nodded. "That's cool. I spent years filling my résumé as a ditzy blond bimbo and I'm trying to update now. Change hasn't come easy. Kicking and screaming is more like it," I told her. "But I figure eventually the upgrade will be complete. Having a job you love helps. You really want to be taken seriously—and try to take full advantage of all opportunities that come your way that aid in your personal metamorphosis."

Sophie nodded. "Like dead bodies, crazy clowns, reclusive writers and campus crooks?" she suggested.

I nodded. "I'm an equal opportunity opportunist," I said. She smiled.

"Journalists live for truth, then. Right?"

"The respectable ones do," I said.

"Then level with me. This little excursion is about more than a John Wayne bobble head, isn't it?" Sophie said. "So, what is it really about?"

I chewed my lip. Although Sophie knew all about the Kooky wedding gift, I didn't much relish receiving the same reaction from her I did from Ranger Rick Townsend when I'd laid out for him my suspicions regarding Kookamunga.

"If I tell you, you have to promise me one thing," I said.

She frowned. "What's that?"

"If you think I'm completely bonkers, don't let on. Just smile and nod and say something like, 'I see' or 'I understand.' That way there won't be any hard feelings," I pointed out.

She nodded. "I see," she said. "I understand."

"I haven't told you yet!" I said.

"I want to make sure I have it down. Okay. I'm ready," she said.

But was I? I shrugged. What did it matter? In a couple of days I'd be on a cruise ship on an ocean far, far away.

"Keep in mind, I'm a professional journalist and have had some success in following hunches," I told her, and proceeded to fill her in on my theory about how the incidents at Oak Creek Canyon, the nightclub, and the burglary at her own house were all related. She processed the information in silence.

Or make that shock and awe. Her eyes didn't leave the roadway. I finally reached over and poked her.

"Soph?"

"Give me a minute," she said, and I obliged.

"You think the bad guys are after that grotesque guy with the gargantuan gonads?" she asked, and I raised my shoulders slowly. "I don't know much about art or artifacts," Sophie finally continued, "but it didn't look like it was what you'd call a work of art, if you know what I mean."

"Agreed," I said, "but I can't think of any other explanation for this particular series of events," I told her. "And although I'm not what you'd call a great mathematician, the random acts of thievery alternative theory just doesn't add up. Too coincidental. Too convenient," I added.

Sophie seemed to be considering my words—and maybe the coincidental chronology. Or maybe she was just making sure she had her giggles under control before she opened her mouth again.

"I suppose we could have my dad take a look at it," she finally said. "He'd be able to tell you if it was worth anything."

"We?" I asked.

She nodded. "We."

I felt all warm and gooey inside.

"So, what do you hope to find out from the roadside vendors again?" she asked.

"I just want to know how they acquired the piece and who wanted them to save it for him and under what circumstances. Maybe this information will shed some light on why it may have become such a coveted commodity," I said.

"And all you're going to do is ask questions. Right?" Sophie replied. "That's it?"

I pointed to my mug. "Would this face lie?"

"I feel so much better," Sophie said.

"Hey! Look! Over there! There they are!" At a different location and on the opposite side of the highway, it was the same blue van with the same striped pull-up awning and the same wares displayed on the same tables. "That's the one!" I yelled. "Quick, pull over!"

Sophie complied. I grabbed my backpack and got out of the car, checking traffic before I jogged across the highway. A breathless Sophie joined me.

"Oh, look! They have more Duke bobbles!" I said, hurrying over to pick one up, tapping his Stetson with a finger. "Ah, Duke, it's good to see you've bounced back from your brush with those rude ruffians. High-fives!" I said, slapping a hand against Duke's gun hand.

Sophie cleared her throat.

"Uh, sorry," I apologized. "I'm cool. I'm cool."

By this time the woman who had waited on me the first time had vacated her lawn chair and was heading in our direction. She glanced at the John Wayne bobble head in my hands and her gaze flew up to my face. Her mouth flew open and her eyes grew larger than my pastor's when Gram presented him with massage certificates to the Sahara Spa for him and the wife on Pastor's Appreciation Day.

Her stride slowed and then faltered, as if she'd stubbed her toes. Her approach appeared wary rather than welcoming. Suspicious rather than sociable. Cautious rather than convivial. In a word: unwelcoming.

"May I help you?" she asked, her tone suggesting she looked forward to it about as much as being poked with a hot branding iron. Geez, had my Duke bio moment ticked her off that much?

"Yes, please," I said with an engaging smile. "You do remember me, don't you? From the other day?" At her blank expression I held the Duke bobble head out in front of me and couldn't resist jiggling it. The cowboy hat bounced up and down. "I bought one of these—and gave you a little thumbnail sketch on Duke. I tend to get a little—" I curled the fingers of one hand inward like claws—" 'rrreeeaaar' when folks get their facts wrong on Wayne," I said. "Uh, sorry about that, by the way."

"I don't understand," she said, her expression impassive.

I frowned. Like I haven't heard that a time or two. I shook it off.

"It doesn't matter," I said. "What I really need, besides another J.W. bobble, is some answers," I said.

"Answers?"

I nodded. "When I was here the other day I purchased a statue, a kind of fertility figurine, but not," I said. "You remember. You had it sitting back there." I pointed to the shelf that had held Kookamunga the previous day. "Someone had requested you hold the item for them, but the gentleman who works with you agreed to sell it to me. What I need to know is where you got the statue and who asked you to hold it for him." I opened the side pocket of my backpack and pulled my digital camera out and turned it on, hitting the review button. I thrust the picture of Raphael in front of her face. "Was it this gentleman?" I asked. "Did he ask you to hold the statue for me and tell you he'd be back for it? Was it him?"

The woman stared at the digitalized image, her nostrils widening and then narrowing. She shook her head.

"I've never seen this man. And I've never seen you. I have no idea what you're talking about," she said, and I stared at her.

"What are you talking about?" I said. "I was here just yesterday. I was with a very handsome man—who actually paid for the purchase and is nuts about me, a sweet young girl with big brown eyes, and a whiny little snot of a ten-year-old with behavior issues. You couldn't have forgotten. It was just yesterday."

She shook her head. "I have no recollection," she said.

"How could you not recall? How many of your customers buy John Wayne bobble heads, haggle over the price, and provide a personal lesson on how John Wayne got his nickname?" I demanded. "Huh? How many?"

"I don't know what you're talking about," she said. "I think you had better leave." She put a hand to her throat and took a step back. Like I somehow posed a threat.

"What is wrong with you?" I asked, totally puzzled. Yeah, I know. You're shocked by that admission, right? I rubbed a hand over my eyes. "Look, ma'am. You can't get all that many customers to your little traveling tradeshow here," I pointed out. "And let's face it, with our own little traveling sideshow from the other day, we're kind of hard to forget, so what gives? Why do you insist on pretending I was never here? Who are you protecting?"

I stopped, noticing the quiver of her lower lip. "Oh my gawd! You're protecting yourself, aren't you?" I said, the woman's reluctance to acknowledge me now making perfect—and disturbing—sense. "Someone else has been here, haven't they? Haven't they? Someone asking questions about that statue you sold me."

While the woman didn't confirm my revelation in so many words, it was clear from her expression I'd struck pay dirt.

"Who? Who was it? Was it the man in the photo I showed you? What did he want? What did you tell him? Why is that statue so important?"

A car drove by slowly, and the woman's eyes got large and frightened as she tracked its passing.

"I don't know! I don't know anything! I can't tell you anything! Please, please, just leave!" She thrust the bobble head into my hands. "Here, take this and just go! Please! I have a family. Children. Please, go!"

I felt Sophie tug on my elbow. "Come on, Tressa," she said. "It's time to leave."

I opened my mouth to protest, saw the fear in the saleswoman's eyes and stopped. I nodded. "You're right, Soph," I said. "It's time to go." I took my billfold, withdrew a twenty-dollar bill and handed it to the woman. "Thank you," I said.

She slowly took the bobble head and put it in a bag. She turned back to give me the sack. I reached to take it from her and she held on to it for a moment.

"Keep it secret. Keep it safe," she whispered, and released the bag.

I stepped away. A frisson of fear rippled the length of my spine. Wasn't that what Gandalf said to Frodo just before he was mercilessly hunted by a gang of ruthless dark riders and misshapen "orcses" in pursuit of a shiny ring?

Oops! I'd done it again, precious.

CHAPTER THIRTEEN

Sophie and I made the short trip back to Sedona in silence. Once Sophie parked the car and pocketed the key, she turned to me.

"So. Where is the horny little devil anyway?" she asked.

I patted my backpack.

"You brought him with you?" she said.

"I thought he'd be safer with me," I told her.

She made a couple quick blinks. "What about us? Are we safe with him?" she asked. "Because I'm getting the feeling we'd be a heckuva lot safer without him," she said. "What if someone comes looking for him and we have it with us?"

I did a few rapid blinks of my own. "What if they come looking and we don't?" I countered.

"A valid point," she said. "So, what do we do? Do we tell the others?"

I shook my head so hard my fillings were in danger of coming loose. "Absolutely not!" I said. "First of all, if we tell Gram it's like posting on MySpace," I said.

"Secondly, I'm really not in the mood to hear one of Taylor's 'I knew it' lectures. Not today."

Sophie nodded. "So, we act like nothing has happened? Like we're not in possession of God-only-knows-what that God-only-knows-who wants and we just go ahead and shop 'til we drop?"

"Whew, for a minute there I didn't think you'd understand, but you've so got it," I said. "That's perfect. And just what we're going to do."

She looked at me. "You're serious, aren't you?"

I nodded. "We stick with the plan: Help Gram get a dress. Have a nice meal. Do a little shopping. Then, once we get back we'll take your dad aside and have him check Mr. Kookamunga out. See if he has any idea why this little gentleman holds such a fascination for someone that they're willing to swipe from young children, steal from unsuspecting speed daters, and scare the suede off some poor souvenir-stand worker just to get hold of him. Agreed?"

Sophie nodded. "I suppose so. I wonder if we should bring law enforcement into this. You know. The professionals. The people who get paid to investigate things like this. Who have badges and bullet-proof vests and guns—and can legally carry them—and who do this kind of thing for a living."

"And what proof do I have that any of this is true?" I asked. "If Ranger Rick won't even believe me, how can I expect law enforcement officers will?"

Sophie looked at me. "Ah, so that's what you and Rick argued about, and why you came home all hot and bothered."

I shrugged. "So what? Big deal. It's not as if it's the first time the good ranger has doubted my credibility." Or sanity.

"I'm still waiting for an explanation of why you

smelled like a swimming pool," Sophie said, and I shook my head.

"Don't hold your breath," I responded.

She smiled and pulled out her cell phone, and called Kimmie's cell while I got out and stretched, pulling one backpack strap over my shoulder and holding on to it with a firm grip. Sophie exited the car a few minutes later.

"Kimmie and Taylor are about ready to pull their hair out," she said. "Gram wants to meet with a spiritual advisor."

I wasn't surprised. Every year Gram dragged me to the latest and greatest psychic on the midway at the Iowa State Fair. Last summer the psychic had come up with the startling revelation that I courted chaos and attracted trouble. Like Mr. Potato Head couldn't predict that after reading my press last year.

"Seems harmless enough," I said. "And you know Gram. If we don't take her, she'll stub 'til next June."

"You're right. And what could it hurt?"

I winced. I said that—or a variation on the same theme—regularly. And regularly discovered it could hurt like the very devil.

We met up in a courtyard outside a string of eateries. No one carried a garment bag, so I suspected the dress-shopping hadn't been a resounding success.

"Where'd you two hightail it off to?" Gram said, and gave Sophie and me one of those glares she usually reserved for my mother. Or for my happy hounds when they almost knock her off her feet. "You were supposed to help me pick out a dress."

I walked over and put an arm through hers. "Get real. You've seen my clothing. Do you really want me selecting apparel for your blessed nuptials?" I asked.

She harrumphed and turned to Sophie. "What

about you? I've seen the purses you carry. You got fashion sense. Why did you bolt?" she asked.

Sophie looked around, as if for guidance, and decided none was on the way. She finally threw her hands up. "I'm fat. I buy my dresses from Tent City," she said. "My waist hasn't seen a belt around it since I tried on Tressa's plastic cowgirl gun-belt and holster in the first grade. And I had to poke an extra hole in it to let it out enough to buckle."

I blinked. "So that's where that extra hole came from," I said. "I blamed it on Craig and his beast of a best friend, Townsend. As I recall, I filled their shoes with horse manure. Guess I owe someone an apology, huh?"

"I was telling Kimmie and Taylor that I'd like to see one of them spiritual advisors, get a reading, make sure all my auras and chakras are in the pink before I take my final vows," Gram said, making it sound like she planned on entering a convent.

If only she were Catholic. She already had the underwear thing down pat.

"So I've heard," I said.

"You got a problem with that?" Gram asked, giving a defiant lift of her wrinkled chin.

I shook my head. "Should I?"

"You remember what happened when we went to Psychic Sonya," she said.

I shrugged. Lightning didn't strike twice in one place. Besides, it was all a bunch of hooey. Almost a year later, and I was still in a romance rut that made Oak Creek Canyon look like a plowed corn row.

"Psychic Sonya sucked as a seer," I said. Try saying that three times fast.

"I dunno. She said she saw me on a shipload of people," Gram pointed out, "and here we are goin' on a cruise."

"So she was a good guesser. They've got sneaky methods they use to figure these things out. Besides, lots of people your age take cruises at some time in their lives, so it was a pretty safe guess," I told her.

She sniffed. "So young and already so cynical," she mourned. "Well, I'm fixin' to get my palm read or tarot cards turned over or my aura realigned or whatever, and don't nobody try to stop me. I'm a grown woman. I know my mind." She looked at each of us in turn. "Aren't one of you gonna try and stop me?" she asked, and we shook our heads.

"Nobody has an objection?"

None were raised.

She looked at us again and then made a great show of looking at her watch. "Would you look at the time!" she said. "I've got pills to take at noon but I need to take 'em with something. I'm thinkin' we should eat lunch and then go see the spiritual advisor. Besides, my aura could do with a shot of red meat before it gets its picture taken."

I looked over at Sophie and smiled. "You can't walk in wearing an anemic aura, that's for sure," I commented. "And I'm starving. That tiny little cinnamon roll I consumed this morning is down to my little toe," I said. "So what are we up for?" I asked.

"I hear they have a restaurant that's got 101 omelets," Gram said, and I shook my head.

"No way. You and I change our minds on what to order a dozen times when there's only a dozen items to choose from on the menu, Gram," I pointed out. "I don't think either one of us have the stamina—or our loved ones the patience—to take on 101 different omelet possibilities. I really don't. Besides, I thought you wanted red meat."

"Excuse me. I couldn't help over-hearing, but if

you're looking for something you can sink your teeth into with a little local flavor, I highly recommend The Wrangler Bar and Grille."

I turned to find a very attractive woman wearing a wide-brimmed hat, flowered mauve ties securing it beneath her chin, in the courtyard with us. Cream-colored sunglasses covered her eyes and freshly applied rosy lipstick covered her lips.

"The Wrangler? Is that the restaurant with the saloon-type décor that features such festive fare as rattlesnake skewers, cactus fries, and buffalo burgers?" Sophie asked. The woman nodded.

"There's not a bad meal on the menu. If you want a taste of the real West, the buffalo filet mignon is very good," the woman said. "Tender and flavorful. I recommend you have it prepared medium rare. If you're a dessert fan, they do a fabulous vanilla bean crème brulee, and their warm chocolate cake with homemade vanilla ice cream is worth the extra time on the treadmill."

My salivary glands kicked into high gear at the mere mention of chocolate cake and ice cream. "And where can we find this here Wrangler?" I asked.

The woman smiled and removed her sunglasses. "You go down to that corner," she said, pointing the way with a hand bedecked with rings and nails that shouted regular manicures, "hang a left, and it's a block and a half down on your left. But I'm actually on my way there myself, so I can show you."

"What do you say, ladies? Who's ready to wrangle?" I asked.

"You look familiar," Gram suddenly said, falling into step beside the woman. "Didn't you used to be somebody?" she asked. I winced.

"Gram!" Taylor exclaimed.

"What? What did I say?"

"It's okay. Really," the woman said. "Your grand-mother is right. I did used to be someone." She put out a skinny, long-fingered hand. "Gloria Grant." She took Gram's liver-spotted hand in hers.

"Gloria Grant! I knew it! You did used to be some-body," Gram said, pumping Grant's hand up and down like the handle on an outdoor spigot. "You used to be in motion pictures and on TV," she said. She stopped. "I thought you died," Gram said.

"Gram!" Taylor said again.

The woman laughed. "You're not the only one to think they've seen a ghost when they recognize me," she said. "But, alas, rumors of my demise have been greatly exaggerated. I'm still alive and kicking—if not with the same vigor of yesteryear." Her smile was sad.

"Didn't you star in that TV series about the Siamese twin aliens who took over a hospital to force a surgeon to separate them? And there was that sitcom set in the booby hatch. What was the name of that again?"

"*Cracker Factory*," Gloria supplied with a pained look. "It was canceled after three weeks. I never did recover from that."

"I thought you were good in the commercial for overactive bladder," Gram said. "Very realistic. I could swear you had to pee bad before you took that medi-cine," Gram told her.

"I think Ms. Grant has heard enough of your Siskel and Ebert routine, Gram," I said.

"Here we are," Gloria Grant announced. "The Wrangler."

"You meetin' someone?" Gram asked.

"Uh, Gram, that's none of our business," I said, try-ing to steer her into the restaurant so the actress could make her escape.

"Nobody likes to eat alone," Gram said. "So, you meetin' somebody?"

"Well, no," Grant said, and Gram took her elbow.

"Then you can eat with us. Mebbe we can put our heads together and see if we can come up with a new career plan," Gram said. "'Course, you'll have to take your hat off. A person can't get within two feet of you with that sombrero on," Gram observed.

I sighed. I was no spiritual advisor, but I felt confident in predicting two-thirds of our party would be reaching for the Tums—or a bottle from behind the bar—before this meal was over.

The Wrangler lived up to Gloria Grant's press. The Wild West décor appealed to the cowgirl in me. The cuisine appealed to the carnivore in me. Gram peppered Gloria with questions about her life story, Taylor fretted over what from the menu was least likely to cause her an upset stomach, Kimmie questioned whether the buffalo meat was really lower in cholesterol and healthier than beef, and Sophie and I kept one eye on the exits, one eye on my backpack and somehow still managed to make our lunch selections and wolf them down.

"You seem fairly familiar with the area, Gloria," I said, between shoveled bites of a cheese and sautéed onion–smothered half-pound grilled burger. "Do you vacation here a lot?" I asked.

"I actually live here," she said, and I raised an eyebrow. Real estate in the Sedona area was reserved for the rich and famous. "My aunt owned a home here long before it became the tourist and New Age Mecca it is now," Gloria explained. "She left the house to me several years ago, and I moved to Sedona after my career hit the skids. But I have every hope of walking the red carpets once again. My spiritual adviser, Cadence, assures me she sees such grand days ahead for me. I also draw strength and power from the energy that is all around us here in Sedona. Have you taken your vortex tour yet?" she asked.

"What's that? Some kind of factory tour?" Gram said. "Not interested. If I want to visit a plant, I can do that back home with the meatpacking plant. Or the tape factory where Tressa worked until she got herself stuck to the wall."

I resisted the temptation to hail a waiter and order a shot of whiskey with a beer chaser, reminding myself that in a matter of days the ol' gal would be married and residing a good ten miles away.

Sophie shook her head. "A vortex is a funnel of spiraling current—kind of like a tornado of whirling energy," she explained. "Sedona is said to have a number of these swirling centers of energy coming from the surface of the earth. People visit these vortex sites and try to connect to the energy of the vortex to achieve balance and direction in their lives. There are special ceremonies—drumming, meditation, channeling—to establish a deeper connection."

"Does it work?" Gram asked.

Sophie shrugged. "Sedona attracts three million visitors a year, and I imagine a good number of those folks visit the vortexes. So, who's to know?"

"Shouldn't that be vortices?" I said, thinking this sounded a little too Roswell even for me.

"In Sedona, they say 'vortexes,'" Sophie said.

"Good to know," I replied. "Good to know."

"Cadence has seen a miraculous reversal of fortunes for me," Gloria said. "I don't know what I would do without her. She has brought me from the brink of despair to a new awakening, a new enlightenment, and a new optimism. I have but to listen earnestly and follow faithfully the edicts of my spirit guide and all glory and fame and power and riches will be returned to me. Cadence has seen it."

I stared at the aging actress. She really did believe in this New Age stuff. Lock, stock and pocketbook.

"Wouldn't buying self-help books be a lot easier?" I asked. "And cheaper? And Dr. Phil's brand of 'the BS stops here' daily therapy is totally free of charge via the airwaves."

Gloria looked over at me and got this sad, tired look on her face. "The young are always looking for an easy fix," she commented. "I was like that when I was your age. When you get older, you realize that those Band-aid solutions never last. That healing has to come from the inside, not the outside. I know I'll be on top again one day. Cadence has seen it. I *feel* it. I have only to follow the path that is laid before me by the spirits and I'll reach that summit once more."

"You climb mountains?" Gram asked.

Gloria nodded. "I will," she said. "And I'll soar with the eagles. And swim with the dolphins. And maybe sleep with an actor young enough to be my son, too!" she added with a wink. "If I draw on the energy that is here around me and the power that is here"—she put a hand on her heart—"within me."

Gram wiped the raspberry plum barbeque sauce off her chin. "I'm fixin' to get me a reading from a spiritual adviser," Gram said, and explained about her upcoming nuptials. "I figured I'd better get everything aligned before I march down the aisle. Speaking metaphorically, you know."

"Uh, I'm thinking you mean metaphysically there, Gramma," I said. "And you make it sound like you need your back cracked by a chiropractor. Frankly, I think your aura and chakras and past lives and vortices"—I saw Sophie wince and self-corrected—"vortexes are in pretty good shape for a woman of seven. . . ." I stopped when Gram started making a slashing motion at her throat. "Uh, I'm thinkin' you're good to go," I told her.

"Well, I'm not so sure. You think I could get in to

see that adviser of yours, Gloria?" Gram asked, and I couldn't understand how Gloria failed to see a quartet of women performing various hand gestures, eye rolls, and body movements that screamed, "Hell no!" But she did.

"That shouldn't be a problem," Gloria said. "I'm sure if I call and explain the situation to Cadence, she'd be more than happy to squeeze you in. In fact, I was supposed to go in for my weekly appointment at two, but she can get me in anytime. Why don't you take my appointment?" Gloria reached into her purse and brought something out. "Here's her card. I'll call and tell her you'll be coming in my stead, and that should take care of that. Her shop is the last you come to down the next block over," she said.

"Oh, no, you shouldn't give up your appointment, Miss Grant," Taylor said. "Really, it's not necessary!"

"Please. It's not a problem," she assured us.

Maybe not for her.

"Tressa? You got one of your reporter cards?" Gram asked. I nodded.

"Why?"

"Give one to Gloria. And write down the hotel info on the back." She turned to Gloria. "I'm invitin' you to my wedding," Gram said. "You can meet Joe and the rest of the family and have cake and toast the newly-weds," Gram said.

I scribbled the hotel name and the date and time of the wedding, and handed it to Gloria.

"Well, I'll try," she said, standing to leave. "It's been very pleasant meeting you all. Good afternoon."

Gloria left, and we followed suit several minutes later.

"Let's get this over with," I heard Taylor comment. Spoilsport. It could be fun.

We took the directions Gloria had given and found

ourselves at the last shop on the left. "There it is,"
Gram said, and pointed to a shop with a great big illuminated blue sign that read, *The Spiritual Boutique.* A
sign in the window indicated that the boutique spe-
cialized in spiritual readings, spiritual advice, aura
photography, and vortex tours.

"The Spiritual Boutique? Sounds classy," I said.
"One-of-a-kind, designer auras."

We opened the door and, unlike the annoying little
bell Stan Rodgers installed to monitor his employees'
comings and goings, a voice announced "Blessings on
you" as we entered.

The outer area featured items we'd seen many times
already: crystals, jewelry, special lotions, books, CDs
and the usual tourist trinkets sold in the area. Background music of rushing water made me have to tin-
kle, and I looked at Gram, hoping it would have the
same effect on her so we could cut this reading short.

Long lengths of turquoise beads on a door off the
main room parted and a woman approached us. Clad
in a long flowing black and teal robe, red hair piled on
her head, her movements measured and slow, it almost looked like she was on a conveyor belt. Or one
heckuva moonwalker. Michael, eat your heart out.

"Welcome to The Spiritual Boutique," she said,
spreading her arms in a gesture of greeting and acceptance. "You must be Hannah," she said, moving straight
to Gram and taking both liver-spotted hands in her own
very white, pale ones. "I am Cadence. I'm a Clairsen-
tient, Clairvoyant, Clairaudient, and Empathic. I understand you wish a psychic health consultation," she said,
and Gram looked over at me.

"Do I?" she asked.

I nodded.

"I do," she said. "I want to make sure everything's in
tip-top shape for me and Joe to tie the knot. I'm not

much for surprises. I had that scope up the bunghole two years back, so I'm good to go there for another five, and I got a thumbs-up from my dentist last month."

Cadence lost her rhythm for a second but recovered nicely. "I do offer a package that includes a psychic checkup. You receive an activation and alignment of your seven basic chakras, a psychometric reading, and a channeling exercise," she said. "Is that something you might be interested in?" she asked.

Gram turned to me. "Would I?" she asked.

"What is the charge for this checkup?" Taylor chimed in.

"For a friend of Gloria's? One hundred and fifty dollars," Cadence said. I winced, wondering what the cost would be for an enemy.

Gram also seemed to be taken aback by the cost. She rummaged around in her purse. "I'm not sure I have enough cash on me," she said.

"We accept debit and all major credit cards," Cadence said.

"Not to worry, Gram," Sophie said, pulling out a wad of dough that made my eyes pop out of my head—and it wasn't even the chocolate chip variety. "It'll be my wedding gift to you," she said.

"Where *do* you get all your money?" I asked Sophie. "And don't you dare say tips again. Because the only gals I know who get that many tips are prancing on a stage somewhere in a G-string and pasties," I told her.

A telltale blush colored Sophie's cheeks. "Here." She handed Cadence the money.

"All right then. If you'll come with me, Hannah," she said, gesturing back to the beaded doorway. "We'll get started."

Gram hesitated. "Do I have to get undressed?" she asked. " 'Cause I just want to tell you that I don't usually wear white old-lady underwear. Today's the exception. I knew I'd be riding in the car and those bikinis can ride up on you, if you know what I mean." She followed Cadence to the beaded door and stopped. "So, who's comin' with me?" she said, and the phrase, *Don't everyone volunteer at once* popped into my head.

"I paid," Sophie pointed out. "I've done my part."

Kimmie fingered through her purse and pulled out a twenty. "Here." She slapped the twenty in Sophie's hand.

"Taylor?" I asked, and she put a hand to her mouth.

"I still have a bit of a queasy stomach," she said. "I'm not sure I'm up to it." She added her twenty to Taylor's. I shook my head.

"Cowards!" I said, and followed Gram and Madame Cadence.

We were taken to a nicely appointed room with a round table covered by a shimmery tan print cloth. I expected to see a crystal ball in the middle of the table; however, I spotted it on a nearby bookshelf beside a colorful, eye-catching tray. Cadence motioned to a couple of chairs.

"I like to begin with the psychic consultation," Cadence said. "Do a reading and in so doing enhance the aura before it is photographed, giving it more color and clarity. I can hang that up for you if you like," she said, reaching out to take hold of my backpack. I snatched it away, almost ripping her fingernails off in the process. She stared at me.

"Uh, no thanks. I'll just hold on to it," I said, setting it on my lap and flashing her a weak smile.

She gave me a wary look as she took her seat.

"So, you are about to embark on a new phase in your life, Hannah," Cadence said. "A new husband. Brand-new experiences."

Gram's eyes grew big. "See that, Tressa?" She jabbed

me in the ribs with her elbow. "See how she knew that? And you thought this was all hooey."

"Uh, Gram. You told her you were getting married, remember?"

"Oh," she said.

"May I?" Cadence reached out to take hold of Gram's hands at the same time I reached across to take Gram's bag and our hands collided. The spiritual advisor jumped. Like you do when you sit down on the toilet only to discover the seat is up. Lazy men. I stared as she suddenly grabbed my hands and clutched them in a finger-crushing grasp.

"Hey. You got the wrong hands!" Gram exclaimed, but the adviser ignored her. Instead, she closed her eyes, dropped her head back, and began to hum.

I looked over at my gammy and shrugged before focusing my attention back on the spiritual seer.

"What's that smell?" Gram asked, and I sniffed, a sweet fragrance reaching my nostrils.

"Flowers," I said, looking around. "Are you all right, Cadence?" I asked, my fingers beginning to cramp. "Hello? Cadence?"

The adviser's eyes snapped open and fixed directly on me. The humming stopped.

"Your spirit guide speaks," Cadence said, tugging my hands in her direction. "Beseeches me on your behalf. You are on a quest. A search for truth. Nay. For answers. Yet you protect a dark secret. A secret that threatens to end your quest. Nay. Even your life." Talk about your "nay" sayers!

"You really do have the wrong hands," I said, yanking those appendages back toward me. "Along with the wrong client," I said. "This is my gammy's reading, remember?"

"Shh!" Gram shushed me. "You hear that? Her voice is even different. Her lips are movin' but somebody else's voice is comin' out. Like that exorcist movie. The one with the pea soup."

Not what I wanted to hear when I was on the receiving end of an alleged message from beyond.

"I wonder who your spirit guide is," Gram said.

More information I didn't particularly care to know.

"I see a change of heart," Cadence went on. "Great pain. Sadness. Loss. Yet, a chance at redemption remains. Death. So much death."

Cadence's grip on my hands became a death grip— no pun intended—and her eyes closed once again. "I understand! Yes! Yes! I see! I see! Yes! Yes!"

She swayed about in her chair and seemed to be in the throes of something almost orgasmic. Gram and I exchanged uncomfortable glances as the adviser collapsed in her chair like a balloon suddenly deflated. Her head lolled on her chest to one side.

"Well, how do you like that?" Gram said. "I'm supposed to have the psychic encounter, you get a spirit guide looking out for you, and she tunes in to a dirty cosmic channel just in time for the climax."

I broke our clasp, jumped up and ran around to the other side of the table.

"Uh, Madame Cadence!" I shook her shoulder. "Hello! Are you all right? Hello?"

She finally stirred and looked up at me, shivering noticeably.

"You need to go," she said. "Leave. Now."

"What?" I frowned. This was the second time today I'd been asked to leave a business establishment.

She shoved her chair back, got to her feet, and slapped Sophie's cash into my hand.

"Go!" she said.

"Well, I never!" Gram got to her feet. "This is the worst reading I've ever had. I don't know what Gloria

Grant was thinking. Why, I'd have better results with a magic eight ball," she said. "Let's go, Tressa!"

I grabbed hold of my backpack and followed Gram to the door. "Are you sure you're all right?" I asked, hesitant to leave the medium alone. "Should I call someone?"

"No. No." Cadence reached out to take my hand again. "I'm so sorry," she said. "Truly sorry."

I shook my head. "No sweat. We all fall under the weather at inconvenient times. Feel better," I told her.

"I will," she said. "I will."

I nodded and left, steeling myself to listen to Gram bitch and moan all the way back to Flagstaff.

I had to hand it to the Cadence, the Spiritual Adviser. She'd added a whole new meaning to the phrase, When the spirit moves you. I knew I should've had firewater at lunch.

CHAPTER FOURTEEN

We returned to Flagstaff mid-afternoon, a ragged group of tourists. Gram was still steamed by the spiritual-advice snafu and wanted us to drop her by the Better Business Bureau so she could file a complaint. Kimmie was battling a headache. Taylor was crabby because there was still the matter of the wedding dress. Sophie was preoccupied, stuck in the middle of a perplexing puzzle. And me? I was split on the conundrum I currently found myself in: Part of me was totally ticked off that my vacation time in Arizona was being threatened, while another part of me—the part that loved saying "I told you so," despised victim status and wanted to jettison Shelby Lynn Sawyer out of my brand-new office chair—was determined to get to the bottom of the Kookamunga connection.

As we pulled up I noticed the Townsend rental SUV was parked on the street outside Aunt Kay's house.

"Oh, I bet Joe's here!" Gram said, and I wondered who had provided chauffeur services. My heart rate increased. From anger, I told myself. (Okay, so I fib on occasion. Even to myself. Okay, so sometimes especially to myself.)

"I wonder what he'll think when I tell him I still don't have no dress," Gram said.

"I don't imagine Rick will care much one way or the other," I said.

"Rick? I'm talking about Joe!" Gram said, and I felt my cheeks warm.

"That's who I meant," I said.

We piled out of the car and made our way into the house. I was anxious to get Uncle Ben aside and let him have a crack at Kookamunga, and motioned to Sophie that I was heading out to Uncle Ben's studio. She nodded and made her way over to where Uncle Ben sat conversing with my father. I barely gave Ranger Rick any notice at all as I marched by him. He sat in a nearby chair with one Nike-covered foot resting on a blue jean-clad knee, looking very southwestern in a turquoise three-button polo shirt, his black shades sitting on the top of his dark head. Honest, I hardly noticed him at all.

I said a quick "Hullo, how's it goin'?" to the other occupants of the room and escaped to Uncle Ben's room. He'd done a decent job of clearing away the debris, and I scolded myself for not helping out.

I hurried over to the long table in the middle of the room and pulled my bag off my shoulders, set it on the counter and unzipped it. I carefully removed Kookamunga and set him gently on the counter. I stood there for a long moment just looking at the fertility-enhancing fellow.

Less than a foot tall, the crude (in more ways than one) statue stood on a large base made to look like a rock or desert sand. Behind him was a large moon and a black silhouette cut out of not the prickly pear cactus that was indigenous to this area, but the taller, skinnier, more familiar saguaro cactus from Sonoran regions. I put a fingertip on the figurine, softly tracing a path from his head to his phallus.

I'd watched *The Antiques Roadshow.* I'd seen people bring in items that looked like rejects from the local thrift shop their Great-great-aunt Ernestine had given them—or a piece they picked up for five bucks at a garage sale—and walk away stunned when they learned their little impulse purchase was worth thousands of bucks. It could happen.

I cocked my head and continue to appraise the object before me. Could I be looking at a priceless work of art created by a master? A genuine artifact from prehistory that ended up somehow in a dusty little roadside stand—and, as luck would have it, in my hot little hands?

"Okay, Kooky." I tapped his Johnson. "Spill it. I want to know all your secrets," I said.

"What's this? A Tressa Turner testicular torture technique designed to extract the truth from the well-endowed males in her life?" I heard from behind my right shoulder. "I'm one part intrigued and one part fearful as hell."

"You forgot one part jackass," I added, wondering why my Ranger Rick radar hadn't picked him up.

Rick moved to stand beside me. He lifted the statue and turned him around, examining Kooky from various angles.

"And you're convinced this is the little prize everyone is after?" he asked. "Gotta tell you, Calamity, I'm not seeing the attraction."

I grabbed Kooky from Townsend and set him back on the table. "That's because you're not an expert in objects of art," I told him. "You're more of an authority on wet T-shirts, NCAA tournament brackets, and

ridiculous reptiles, so I'll leave the art appraisals to ex-
perts like Uncle Ben."

Townsend grinned. "The rice guy?" he asked.

"*My* Uncle Ben, you dorfwad," I told him.

He looked at me. "You're going to have your Uncle
Ben assess that thing's worth?" He pointed at Kookamunga. "Art expert or not, I can tell you exactly what
it's worth. Fifty hard-earned ranger bucks," he said.
"And that's with a bobble head thrown in," he added.

"I'll file your considered opinion where it belongs,"
I told Townsend. "In the cabinet right next to my
gammy's fleet enemas and glycerin suppositories."

Townsend winced. "Thanks for the visual," he said.
"I thought maybe in the light of day you'd reevaluate
your hasty conclusion of the other night."

I shook my head. "On the contrary. This day's events
have only served to reinforce my earlier theory," I told
him. "That's why I'm having Uncle Ben take a look at
this piece. Something about it has aroused a whole lot
of interest."

"Interesting choice of words, considering the fellow's obvious attributes," Townsend observed. I made
a face. "So, what happened today that makes you think
you're right about Special K here?" he asked.

I explained about the encounter with the roadside
vendor. Townsend stared at me once I'd finished.

"You went back to that roadside stand and grilled
the sales lady?" he asked.

I nodded. "And she freaked out, Townsend!" I told
him. He nodded. "She was scared to death!"

"I know the feeling," he said. "You can be pretty
frightening at times."

I frowned. "Not of me, you lunatic. The bad guys. She
clearly felt threatened if she disclosed any information."

"So, she didn't really tell you anything, right?" Townsend said. "And you're interpreting that refusal as the result of something with sinister overtones," he said.

"You didn't see the woman, Townsend," I pointed out. "Ask Sophie. She picked up on the vibes right away, too. We were both looking over our shoulders the rest of the time, I'll tell you that," I told him. "It almost spoiled my meal at The Wrangler. As it was, I couldn't do justice to my dessert."

Townsend shook his head and was about to add what I suspected was another typical rejoinder when Uncle Ben and Sophie joined us.

"Well, Tressa, Sophie here tells me you've got an art piece you'd like me to take a look at," Uncle Ben said, and I nodded, watching Townsend fold his arms and lean his hips against the edge of the table.

"As a matter of fact, yes I do, Uncle Ben," I responded. "For a number of reasons I think this object may be of some value," I told him. "I'm hoping you can confirm that."

"Well, let's have a look at this objet d'art," he said, and I moved aside so he could get a good look at Kookamunga.

Uncle Ben's steps faltered as he approached the table. His eyebrows came together above his nose. He pulled his eyeglasses from his pocket, stuck them on his nose and bent down in front of the figure. He got one of those *Who cut the cheese?* looks on his face and straightened. He looked at me and then at his daughter. He picked Kookamunga up as Townsend had done earlier, turning him this way and that as he inspected the idol.

I held my breath as he looked at my discovery for several long minutes.

"You paid how much for this?" he asked, and I felt my breath hitch in my throat.

"Fifty dollars," I said.

"*My* fifty dollars," Townsend elaborated.

"I see." Uncle Ben set Kookamunga down and bent over to take another long look at him. After several more anxious moments, he straightened and removed his eyeglasses.

"Then you've got a problem, Missy," he said, and I stared at him.

"I do?" I asked.

He nodded. "Because this little eyesore on a good day should only bring about half that," Uncle Ben announced. I blinked.

"Come again," I said. "You mean to say Kookamunga is basically worthless?"

"Kookamunga?" Uncle Ben frowned. "Who the devil is Kookamunga?"

I pointed to Kooky. "That's Kookamunga."

"Oh."

"He's not priceless?" I asked. "Not an authentic artifact? Not a one-of-a-kind find?"

Uncle Ben scratched his head. "He's certainly not priceless, but he may well be a one-of-a-kind item," he said, picking Kooky up again and looking at him. "I sure haven't seen anything quite like it—him," he said. "And I'd remember a piece like this," he said with a frown. "That I'm certain of."

"I don't understand," I said. "I was so sure, so convinced he was a valuable commodity—a hot property—and that's why all the theft attempts were occurring. I don't get it."

I avoided eye contact with Townsend, afraid I'd see the *Good ol' Calamity, she's always good for a laugh* look.

"Don't feel alone, Tressa." Sophie tried to comfort me. "The way that woman acted I was convinced we'd found ourselves in a *Da Vinci Code* remake. Well, maybe parody," she amended. "She sure acted weird enough."

"People have a habit of doing that after even limited exposure to the cub reporter here," Townsend observed. He started to twitch. "As a matter of fact, I was perfectly normal before I started hanging around the Turner household," he said. "Now look at me."

Sophie tried, unsuccessfully, to stifle a giggle. Nice.

"And you're sure the statue has no significant value, Uncle Ben?" I asked, just to make sure.

"Other than the obvious one as a conversation piece?" He shook his head.

"He could also make a nifty holder for your house keys," Townsend said, eliciting more giggles from Sophie.

"Single, easy on the eyes, and funny, too. What more could you want in a guy?" she observed rhetorically.

"Fair play, fidelity and unconditional faith in one's instincts, for starters," I suggested, picking up Kookamunga. "Or at the very least, a reasonable pretense of same."

Townsend unfolded his arms and moved away from the table. "If I were the kind to ignore my sense of fair play and hit below the belt, I'd probably say something like 'Give it up, Calamity, no one is that good of an actor,'" he commented, and Sophie barely managed to contain her mirth. Uncle Ben didn't even try. He slapped Townsend heartily on the shoulder and they headed back upstairs.

Sophie moved beside me. "I'm sorry your theory didn't pan out," she said.

"Thanks. Me, too," I said. "Do you think I'm flaky, Soph?" I asked as I stuck Kookamunga back in my bag.

She seemed surprised at my question. She looked at me. "Flaky? No," she said, shaking her head. "A free spirit? Gotta go with a big yes there."

I nodded. "I wouldn't tell just anyone this, Soph," I said, "but being a free spirit can get kind of lonely sometimes. Especially when everyone else thinks my compass is all out of whack," I told her.

"We all march to the beat of a different drummer at times," Sophie said, giving my shoulder a squeeze. "The secret is to not march too far afield."

I nodded.

"I'm glad I could confide in you, Sophie," I said, hugging her back. "It's good to have someone to share things with." I stepped back and looked at her for a second. "Suppose I return the favor. Care to tell me how a struggling college coed can afford a seven-hundred-dollar designer handbag?" I asked.

Sophie's smile faltered. "I told you before. Tips," she said, and took the stairs three at a time.

As I watched her flee, I shook my head. I'd cracked tougher nuts than Sophie. Before we set sail for a week at sea I'd find out just how my cousin made all her moolah. And maybe put in an application of my own.

I sulked for a few more minutes and decided this might be a good time to place a call back home to Stan—absence making the heart grow fonder and all. It was two hours later back in Iowa, so Stan should still be at his desk. I figured Aunt Kay wouldn't mind since it was a business call. I dialed Stan's direct number.

"*Grandville Gazette.* Stan Rodgers's desk. Shelby Lynn Sawyer speaking. How may I help you?"

I sank onto Uncle Ben's stool. "Shelby? What are you doing answering Stan's phone?" I asked. "Is everything okay?"

"Who is this?" Shelby Lynn asked, and I muted the naughty word that sprang to my lips before it could escape.

"It's Tressa, of course," I said. "What are you doing at Stan's desk? I forgot to warn you, he's pretty territorial about his work area. He's been known to use a

Web cam to catch people invading his turf," I warned the rookie.

"Oh, not to worry. Stan gave me permission to use his computer to scan and print some things," she said.

"He did?" The only thing in Stan's office he'd ever given me permission to use was the door. "Uh, could I talk to him for a minute?" I asked, getting ready to rip into him for the double standard.

"Oh, he's not here," Shelby Lynn said. "He took the afternoon off."

I felt my sphincters pucker.

"Stan took the afternoon off?" I repeated, incredulous. Stan the man Rodgers, who hadn't voluntarily missed a day in five years? Who refused to stay home the afternoon before his colonoscopy and stunk up the newspaper office with frequent trips to the john? Who was late for his own surprise birthday party getting quotes for an article on how many seats the new high school auditorium should hold? That Stan?

"Yep. He said something about going fishing. I told him we could hold down the fort," Shelby Lynn said.

"I'll just bet you did," I muttered.

"What's that? The connection went funky," Shelby Lynn said.

"I said, 'I'll just bet he's glad you're on the job,'" I said. "So, everything's cool at that end? No crises to handle? No fires to put out—well, apart from the three alarm one that made the newspaper there, of course," I added. "Everything cool?"

"Couldn't be better," Shelby Lynn said. "How about on your end? Are Joe and Hannah getting excited? The big leap is just days off."

"There have been a few minor glitches," I said, "but we're still on course to get the deed done," I told her.

"You keeping out of trouble?" Shelby Lynn asked.

"As a matter of fact, I may have stumbled onto a bit of a puzzle out here that could have some reader appeal," I confided. "A riddle or two begging to be solved, and you know how I love little whodunits," I said. "So make sure you tell Stan I might have a high-profile piece for him from the contrasting climes of northern Arizona."

"Uh, okay. I'll do that," Shelby Lynn said. "Oh, and I'm really glad you called, because there actually is something we need to talk about," she added, "while I have you on the phone."

"Anything, Shelby Lynn," I said. "I'm here to help you in whatever way I can. What's the problem? Having trouble with your headlines? Need a snappy, reader grabbing opener? Can't get my new chair to lower? Tell me. What is it?"

"Uh, it's about Marguerite Dishman," Shelby Lynn said, and I felt my throat begin to close up. "She came in today to place something in the paper."

I could feel my heartbeat pulse in my right eyeball. Bup. Bup. Bup.

"And? What did she want to run?" I asked, suspecting I wasn't going to like the answer.

"An engagement announcement," Shelby answered.

Good Lord, I was right.

"She had an announcement?" I asked.

"Well, not so you'd know, but she did have a picture of your groom-to-be and she had a picture of you. She wanted us to use the computer to put the two pictures together and make it look like it was a picture of the two of you together," Shelby Lynn explained.

I frowned into the phone. "How did she get a picture of me?" I asked.

A long pause.

"She had the Grandville yearbook for the year you

graduated," Shelby Lynn finally said. "She wanted us to scan your head shot and stick it with her nephew Manny's picture."

Good gawd in Heaven, it was worse than I thought! My senior picture could've been a before shot for Curls Gone Wild hair tamer. Coupled with the make-over I'd received at the mall compliments of my gammy, and I looked like something from Macabre Theater. Or a streetwalking mime on crack.

"For all that's holy, please tell me you're joking," I begged.

"It's not all bad news," Shelby Lynn said.

"It isn't?" I asked.

"The announcement indicated that a wedding date hadn't been set," Shelby Lynn said. "So you still have time to break it off. If you're so inclined."

"Break it off? Break what off? This engagement is a product of a well-intentioned but not well-thought-out favor for a friend. It's not real. It's just pretend! Under no circumstances are you to run that announcement!" I yelled.

"How are we going to get around it?" Shelby Lynn asked. "She's willing to pay good money to run it."

"Stall her!" I said. "Tell her you're having trouble with the picture! Tell her the next issue is full! Tell her anything, but don't run that announcement!" I yelled.

"Two thousand miles away and you can still create chaos," Shelby Lynn said. "I'll see what I can do. After all, I suppose I owe you for recommending me to Stan," she added.

"Uh, yeah, there is that," I said, and turned to find Townsend on the stairs watching me. "Hope you can follow up on the instructions I just gave you without too much difficulty," I said. "And don't hesitate to get in touch if you need further assistance. I'm here for you," I told her. "Bye-bye now."

"Good grief," Shelby Lynn said and hung up.

"Problems?" Townsend asked with a raised eyebrow.

"Oh, you know. Putting out fires long distance for the rookie reporter," I said. "It's rather trying being indispensable."

"I'm sure," he said, with a twitch of his lips. He held out his cell phone. "You're so popular I've got people calling for you on my cell phone," he added, and I stared at him.

"Huh?"

"It's Carena Whitehead," Townsend said.

"What?"

"She wants to speak to you," Townsend replied.

"Me?" I shook my head. "Why would Whitehead want to talk to me?"

Townsend shrugged. "Guess you'll find out," he said, and handed me the phone and left. I'd expected him to stay and eavesdrop—which is exactly what I would've done if he'd been speaking to the lovely Carena.

"Hello?" I answered.

"Miss Turner?"

"Speaking," I said, maintaining a cool, detached tone.

"This is Carena Whitehead."

"Yes, I know. What can I do for you, Officer Whitehead?" I asked.

"Maybe it's what I can do for you," Whitehead said, and I was instantly intrigued.

"Oh? How so?"

"It's about Raphael," she said. "I have some information I'd like to share with you. Could we meet somewhere?"

I considered my options. With my past history, you weren't about to find me in some dark, underground parking garage, taking shorthand notes from someone I barely knew. And had no reason to trust.

"We were getting ready to head to the mall to shop," I said. "I suppose I could meet you there."

"Will you be able to get away on your own?" Whitehead asked.

"I'm a professional," I reminded her.

"Oh, right. There's a bookstore at the west end of the Flag mall. Can you meet me in the coffee shop there at six?" Whitehead asked.

A bookstore? It was a safe bet my gammy wouldn't be shopping there for her wedding attire.

"I'll be there," I said.

"Come alone," Whitehead said, and hung up.

She just had to say that, didn't she?

Several hours and more than a few dress changes for Gram later, I checked my watch. A quarter to six. It would take me fifteen minutes to get to the other end of the mall—if I didn't stop to window shop at all.

"Has she found anything yet?" I asked, knowing the answer.

My sister-in-law, Kimmie, shook her head. "She's in the dressing room with your Aunt Kay, arguing about how much cleavage is appropriate for a woman of a certain age to show at her own wedding. Your aunt says a half inch, and Hannah says as much as you can get away with."

I shook my head. Thank goodness Aunt Kay was dealing with this crisis.

"Have you found a dress yet, Tressa?" Kimmie asked, and I shook my head.

"Still looking," I said.

"Kimmie! Tressa! Gram wants your opinion on her latest frock." Sophie motioned to us from the dressing area.

"You go on, Kimmie," I said. "I saw a cute little number over there I want to try on. I'll join you in a second," I said.

Once Kimmie was out of sight, I hurried from the high-end department store and made my way to the bookseller located at the other end of the mall. I located the coffee shop and spotted Whitehead at a table in the corner. I looked around. Lots of foot traffic. Lots of people. Seemed benign enough.

I dropped into the booth across from her. A waitress materialized in record time.

I wanted a chocolate milkshake but when I saw the price I settled for a Coke instead. I was happy with my choice until Whitehead indicated the food was on her. Talk about your opportunities lost. Dang.

"So, Officer Whitehead, how do you know Raphael?" I asked. Whitehead smiled.

"I knew I'd given myself away that day at the canyon," Whitehead said, "when I looked at the pictures. I was just so shocked to see him there. In your pictures. I suspected you picked up on my reaction."

"I'm a trained observer," I said, sipping my cola. "It's a requirement of the job. So, you were about to tell me how you know this Raphael," I reminded her.

Whitehead took a long swig of her Fiji water.

"He was my boyfriend. We were together two years."

"Were?" I asked.

She nodded. "We broke up about a year ago. He started getting very secretive about his activities. He'd up and disappear for days at a time with no explanation as to where he'd been, other than 'business.' Raphie had always traveled a lot in his job as a consultant, so I really didn't think much about it until he started getting angry and moody whenever I questioned him about his trips. I finally told him that he had to level with me and tell me what the hell was going on or we were through." She took another drink of her bottled water. "Guess you can see what his choice was," the ranger said with a sad smile.

"Why were you so shocked to see him in the picture?" I asked. "Apart from his actions, that is. I gather he still lives around here," I added.

Whitehead shook her head. "That's just it," she said. "I thought he had left the area. I hadn't seen or heard from him for well over a year until that day at Oak Creek when I found out that not only was he still around, but that he'd been right there in the same park as I was and he hadn't even cared enough to stop and say hi. I was crushed," she said.

"You sure hid it well," I told her, taking a drink of my Coke.

"I'm uncomfortable showing weakness, especially in uniform and in public, so I put my game face on and it was business as usual," she said.

"Uh, and that business included giving your number and an invite to a certain ranger from out of town?" I asked. Whitehead had the good grace to color.

"I was angry and hurt and I thought what the hell, Carena, go out, have a good time with a handsome man and forget all about Raphael Calderas," she said. "Turns out the good-looking ranger apparently had another woman on his mind."

"He did?" My gawd, was there no end to the line of females in Townsend's world? "Who?" I asked.

Whitehead looked confused. "I was going to say you," she said. "Would I be wrong?"

I shook my head. Would she? Who knew?

"After the incident at the club when you accused Raphael of stealing your cousin's handbag, I really started getting concerned. I've contacted every friend or acquaintance of Raphie's to try and get in touch with him, but without success," Whitehead went on. "I'm worried about him. I'm scared about what he's gotten into. I want to help him."

I looked at her. "I think you're still in love with him," I said.

"I care about him," Whitehead admitted. "That hasn't changed despite our differences."

I nodded. I knew just how Whitehead felt. No matter how ticked off Townsend made me, I still had feelings for him. I would risk much to help him if I thought he needed me.

"Do you have any idea what Raphael might be involved in? Why he's acting this way? What he could be up to?" I asked.

Whitehead chewed her bottom lip. "There are many possibilities," she said. "None are very pleasant to consider," she added.

"Did your boyfriend by any chance own any kachina masks?" I asked. Whitehead looked at me.

"Ex boyfriend," she corrected. "Many natives possess such items. Why?"

"Someone drove by my aunt's wearing one the night of the break-in at their house," I said. "And I thought someone wearing one followed us back from Sedona our first day here. Could it have been Raphael?"

Whitehead shook her head. "I wish I knew," she said. "I wish I knew."

Whitehead placed two of her business cards on the table.

"If you happen to see Raphael again, could you give me a call or give him this card and tell him Carena needs him to call her right away? I'd appreciate it."

I considered the cards. How did I know that any of what Carena Whitehead had just told me was on the level? She'd already lied by omission. By her own admission, she presented a fake face to the world. Who knew what else she could still be keeping close to her vest?

An awkward silence followed and Carena smiled. "I understand," she said. "Trust but verify? Am I right?"

I nodded. "A wise man once recommended something like that," I said. "Seems like pretty sound advice."

Whitehead smiled. "I suppose it does at that," she said.

Her cell phone began to ring and she excused herself from the table to take the call. I watched her from the table and something about her body language and the way she kept her back to me made me suspect a certain ranger was on the other end of the call. Whitehead returned to the table.

"I've got to run," she said, placing bills on the table.

"Give Ranger Townsend my best," I told her and she smiled.

"Those keen powers of observation again?" she asked.

I shook my head. "Playing a hunch," I told her.

"Goodbye, Miss Turner," she said, shaking my hand. "I hope you do manage to enjoy the remainder of your stay in the Grand Canyon State," she said and left.

I counted the bills Whitehead had thrown on the table.

"Miss! Oh, miss!" I said, raising my hand to hail the waitress. "I'd like to order a chocolate shake, please," I told her. "And don't skimp on the whipped cream."

Tomorrow we'd make the move to The Titan Hotel. In two days time my grandma would be hitched, Rick Townsend would be my stepcousin, and Kookamunga, along with a wide assortment of fellow phallic fellas, would have a new home with Mr. and Mrs. Joseph Townsend.

And me? I'd have my domicile to myself once again.

Funny. The prospect of coming home to an empty trailer each night didn't hold the same appeal as it once had. I shook my head. Who'd been smoking too much locoweed now?

CHAPTER FIFTEEN

The following morning I sat on a leather sofa in front of the mammoth-sized fireplace in the lobby of The Titan Hotel and debated if it was too early in the day to hit the hotel bar and start a tab. Here I was, just steps away from one of the seven natural wonders of the world and my sole companion was a bronze statue with a perpetual erection. On the brighter side, things couldn't get much worse. Unless Joe walked through the lobby in a Speedo. Or Townsend sauntered past with Whitehead.

"Hi. What are you doing here? Where's Uncle Rick? How come you're sittin' here all by yourself? Did you two fight again?"

Or his nephew Little Lord Fauntleroy showed up to interrogate me some more.

I sighed. "I'm on vacation," I said. "Can't you tell?"

He looked at my bag.

"Is that ugly dude still in there? Why do you carry him around? Are you really going to give it to Grandpa and Hannah? Are you still mad at my Uncle Rick? How come you don't like kids?"

That got my attention.

"Hey, I like kids all right," I said. "Nice ones. Who know their place. And who don't give me a lot of attitude."

"Like I do, you mean?" Nick asked, and I didn't deny it.

I shrugged. "I try to take into account that you can't help it. It's in your genes."

He looked down at his shorts. "But I'm not wearing jeans," he said.

I shot him a half smile. "Ah, the Townsend wit. I rest my case," I said.

"So, are you gonna give the statue as a wedding gift or not?" he asked. I nodded.

"Yeah. Sure. Why not?"

"It's a fertility god, isn't it?"

I nodded.

"And it's supposed to help things reproduce, right?"

I nodded again. "In theory," I said. "Why?"

"And you want to give it to our grandparents? That's, like, really sick, dude!" he said.

"Exactly," I said.

The little twerp reached out and grabbed my bag.

"Hey, knock it off, kid. I want to keep the surprise under wraps until the happy couple uncovers the token of my affection. Do you mind?" I reached out to grab the bag away.

"I just want another look," he said.

"No way. Last time he ended up in a freakin' fountain of foliage. Give him back." I yanked on the bag.

"And I think he's the ugliest thing I've ever seen and you're dumb for buying him!"

"That's where I've got you, kid," I stated, pulling on

my backpack, " 'cause your Uncle Rick bought him, so that must make *him* the dumb one."

"Then it's more mine than yours, 'cause he's my uncle!" the tiny troll yelled, tugging on the bag again.

"Well, he's my boyfriend!" I yelled back.

"Is not!"

"Is, too!"

"Is not!"

"Is, too!"

I heard a rip and the shoulder strap of my bag tore loose and the silly little goose yanking on the bag fell backwards, my backpack sailing through the air along with him. It hit the wood floor with a clunk.

"Now look what you've done!" I hissed, retrieving the bag. I opened it up and pulled Kookamunga out. "If you've damaged him, I swear I'll take that iPod of yours and toss it over the south rim!" I promised him.

"You wouldn't," he said.

He obviously didn't know me very well, did he?

I ran an eye over Kooky. He appeared to be unscathed. I turned him upside down and noticed the base was loose.

"Oh, great, you've knocked the bottom askew," I said. "Way to go, Poindexter."

"It's a piece of junk anyway. I heard Uncle Rick laughing with Dad. He said you were convinced it was worth a fortune and that everyone was after it because it was so valuable."

"Oh, really? Well, your uncle's idea of real art is some poor animal head stuffed and mounted on the wall and a molting wood duck filled with sawdust, sporting glass eyes, and perched on a piece of wood. Excuse me if I don't give too much credence to his opinion."

I surveyed the damaged base closer, surprised when

the bottom twisted to the side revealing a hollow compartment inside.

"What in the world?"

I examined the base more closely. Inside the three-by-four inch base appeared a small item, all rolled up. I pulled it out. It was a tiny scroll, held together by a small braided tie. My knees suddenly felt like they did after I finished walking in the Crazee Day parade, on stilts: all rubber bandy and Gumby-like. I dropped into the nearest seat, my hands shaking worse than my gammy's when she wants to get out of washing dishes.

"What's the matter? You look weird."

I ignored the insulting little snot whose bad behavior may have just unlocked the key to the mystery at Oak Creek Canyon. I slowly untied the ribbon from around the off-white paper and unfolded the scroll. I stared at the words and drawings on the page. My mouth flew open in stunned amazement.

"Holy Native American Idol!" I shouted. "Dan Brown, eat your heart out!" I said.

"Who's Dan Brown?" Nick asked.

I shook my head, keeping my attention focused on the tiny roll of paper in my hands.

"What's that paper?" the kid asked. "Did that come out of the statue? What is it? What does it say?"

I quickly rolled it up and stashed it in my pocket.

"Nothing. Nothing at all. Just a wad of paper. That's all. It's nothing."

Nick peered at me. "My Uncle Rick says he can always tell when you're hiding something 'cause you start to talk real fast and babble a lot," he said.

"Does your uncle have nothing better to do than talk about me?" I asked.

"I guess not. He talks about you a lot."

I felt my heart go pitter-patter. "He does?"

"He bitches a lot."

Terrific.

"So, are you going to tell me what was on that note you found in Kookamunga, or am I going to run to Uncle Rick and tell him all about it?" Nick blackmailed. I stared at him.

"You're pure evil. You know that, don't you?" I said.

He shrugged. "What's it gonna be, Calamity?"

I removed the note and read it to him. "It says, 'A bird's-eye view awaits you here. It will take the eye of an eagle and the heart of a warrior to succeed where others have failed in this quest for truth. He whose eye misses nothing is aware of all that has gone on before and has made a record.' There. Happy now?"

"That's it? What does it mean? What quest? Whose eye? Is it a clue of some kind, do you think? What do you think it leads to? Where do we start looking?"

I caught the *we* part right away. Hey, I'm a trained journalist. Well, a journalist-in-training, at least.

"Uh, what do you mean 'we', paleface?" I said, the punch line from a joke I'm rather fond of.

"You and me," he said.

I shook my head. "There is no you and me. No us. No we. Just me, myself, and I," I told him. "*My* quest for truth. *My* eagle eye. *My* warrior's heart."

"My Uncle Rick who's gonna know all about that note and who'll blab it to that hot lady ranger before you can say Kookamunga," Nick said, planting himself on the table in front of me. "So, am I in or what?"

I looked at him. "I'm not even sure I'm in," I said. "But I know if I let you tag along, I'm in for it," I added. "There are people after this note. Bad people. Dangerous people."

I stopped. Ohmigawd! I was right! About the idol. About its value. About the bad guys wanting it back. I gulped. Somehow being able to say I told you so didn't hold the same magic it had before I knew I was right—and I realized that being right meant I was, like, so screwed.

I looked at the note again.

Still, if this intrigue did pan out and I nailed down a newsworthy story with AP possibilities, I'd put the kibosh on any designs Shelby Lynn Sawyer had on my job back home—as well as on my new ergonomically designed chair. And prove once and for all to a certain reprimanding ranger that I was oh, so much more than a pretty face and nubile body.

Uh, just seeing if you were paying attention there, folks.

I studied the note, noticing a crude drawing in the bottom right-hand corner. I frowned and brought it up to my face.

"There's a picture here," I said, "but I'm not sure what it's supposed to be." I squinted at the paper. "It looks like a snowman with a pig's snout," I said, and Nick got up to stand behind me and peer over my shoulder and breathe down my neck. Like uncle, like nephew.

"That's not a pig's snout," Nick said. "It looks like a bowling ball. Why would someone draw a bowling ball for a snowman's head?" Nick asked. "That's whacked."

I thought about it. "It's a clue!" I said. "A clue to where we go next!"

Nick looked at me. "Where?"

"The Snowbowl!" I said. "We go to the Snowbowl!"

"Sweet!" Nick said. I heard a click behind me and turned to find Nick holding a camera phone. He turned it around and I caught an image of the back of my head and the clue in my hands. Geez. I really needed a deep conditioning treatment. And maybe I should have an inch or so trimmed off the bottom of my hair while I was at it.

"So, when do we go?" Nick said, and I stood.

I looked at him. "Oh, no. I said I'd show you the clue and I did. I can't take you with me on this scavenger hunt. It would be too risky. Too dangerous."

He flipped his cell phone open. "Let's see. Where's Uncle Rick on the directory?"

I snatched the phone from him. "You can't come!" I said. "You're just a kid!"

"Exactly," the kid said. "And no one would think anything about you taking a kid up the Snowbowl, right? You'd attract less attention than you would if you went alone. I'm thinking people would look at you a lot more if you were alone. Who goes to a place like that all by themselves? Only people without boyfriends who are lonely and miserable," he said. He put a hand to his forehead and made a letter L. "You know. Losers."

I shook my head. Genetics. "I suppose you might have a point," I told him. "But you will do exactly what I tell you to when I tell you to do it. Understand? And just so you know, this is a one-time partnership, pal, and one time only. Agreed? Or I'll spill the beans about your little shenanigans the other night—plus tell Taylor you have naughty little dreams about her. Got it? Pal?"

He blushed but nodded.

"Good. Now our first hurdle is how to convince your folks that I actually want to spend time with you," I said, and I could swear the brat boy got a hurt look on his face. "Hey, I was kidding," I said. "I do that."

He raised a supercilious brow.

"What about Kelsey? She'll want to go, too," I added. "She thinks I'm cool." I sighed. "It's hard to be a role model," I said, and Nick snorted.

"Kelsey went shopping again," he relayed with some disgust. "Girls shop all the time. I don't get it. All that walking just to try on stupid clothes. Booorrring."

"Okay, you go up and get ready and meet me back down here in fifteen minutes. And bring something warm. It can get nippy up at the top. I need to arrange our transportation."

Nick nodded. "Ten-four," he said, and ran to the elevators. "And you better be here when I come back down or I'll tell everyone you slept with Grandpa Joe! And liked it!"

Darn that little perv. And I was so close.

I got up, looking down at Kookamunga. I really didn't want to drag him up to the top of the Snowbowl and back down. "You've done well, my warrior," I said, tapping him on the head. "You deserve a rest for your labors, my well-endowed friend."

I hurried into the gift shop and came out with silver foil wrapping paper featuring adorable white bells and a roll of tape. I'd wrap Kooky up and stash him in the hotel room somewhere my gammy wouldn't think to look, and he'd be ready for his unveiling come the wedding day!

I hurried to the hotel room. Time to rustle a set of wheels, and let the vision quest begin.

May the best spirit guide win!

I lucked out and Sophie was out of the room, her spare car key on the TV table. I quickly wrapped Kooky and hid both him and the rest of the paper in a place Gram was almost guaranteed not to look: in the bedside drawer with the Gideon Bible.

I left a note on the bathroom mirror saying I'd taken Nick Townsend sightseeing and would be back soon, signing it with a big "T" and a happy face.

I met Nick in the parking lot.

"You did tell your folks you would be with me, right?" I asked.

"Sure. And they didn't even freak out. All that much."

"Good to hear," I said, moving to Sophie's car.

"Do you even know how to get to the Snowbowl?" Nick asked as we got in.

I shrugged. "I'm female and I'm blond. People expect me to ask directions," I said. "Frequently."

He nodded. "I had a blond teacher once."

"You did? Cool."

"She was really pretty. The kids liked her, but I don't think the parents did."

"Oh? What makes you say that?"

"My mom said she couldn't add one and one and get two, and my dad said 'Yeah, but with the two she does have, who cares?' "

Men.

This particular blonde—who eventually gets things to add up—only had to ask for directions three times before we found ourselves at the Snowbowl. I looked over at the kid beside me.

"You know, I really think the smartest thing would be for you to stay down here and guard the car so we can make a quick getaway if need be," I said. "If anyone messes with you, you can call nine-one-one on the cell."

He got a *Get real, blondie* look on his smug little kisser. "Let's cut to the chase," he said, sounding old beyond his years. "We both know the minute you're out of sight, I'm going to get my own ticket and follow you up anyway. So, think about it. A kid. On his own. In a strange state. A mysterious clue. Might be safer to take me."

I eyeballed the Townsend troublemaker, knowing he had me. Even the blond teacher lacking math skills couldn't argue with this logic.

"Fine," I spat. "But remember, you do exactly what I say when I say to do it. No exceptions. And I'm serious as a heart attack here," I added. "Meaning deadly serious."

He nodded.

We went to get our tickets. I paid for mine and stepped aside. The kid stared up at me.

"Is there a problem?" I asked, raising an eyebrow.

"What about my ticket?" he asked.

I looked at him.

"I never said I'd pay," I told him.

He gave me a Dark Lord Fauntleroy look and pulled a billfold out of his front pocket. My jaw dropped when I saw the wad of cash he had. Why did everyone have discretionary income except me?

He purchased his ticket.

"See, I was right. You are a cheapskate," the runt said.

"I'm just selective about who I spend my moolah on," I corrected. "I pamper my pooches and ponies."

"Yeah. And stick your grandma with some Viagra dude."

"How does a ten-year-old even know about Viagra?" I asked.

"Hello. TV."

We waited for our turn to take the shuttle. A skiing facility, the Snowbowl does double duty as a sightseeing excursion from May through Labor Day. The scenic skyride takes you to an elevation of 11,500 feet. It's an especially colorful ascent when the fall colors are turning. You can even spot the north rim of the Grand Canyon from that elevation.

"You're not afraid of heights or anything, are you?" I asked the kid as we plopped our bottoms on the lift. "Because I've had some experience with that sort of thing with a close relative, and it wasn't one of those mustn't-miss moments." Unless you were a fireman looking for some rescue experience or a good laugh.

He gave me a strange look. "I'm ten. I live for stuff like this," he said. "So, what exactly are we looking for once we get to the top?" he asked.

I took out the clue and read it again. "My guess is something to do with eagles," I said. "Or hearts maybe."

"And don't forget the pig snout," Nick said with a devilish grin.

"Like you'd let me," I told him as we headed up the mountain.

"You know, you might get further with my uncle if you kissed up to me a little bit," Nick observed. "Most of his other girlfriends do, you know. They pat my head and pinch my cheek and say how cute I am and buy me stuff. How come you don't do that?"

"My gag reflex is too strong," I responded.

He looked at me. "Huh?"

"And there's always the blind horse factor," I added.

"What does a blind horse have to do with sucking up?" he asked.

"You see, kid, when I buy horseflesh I like to know what I'm getting for my money," I told the youngster. "Nothing worse than thinking you bought one thing only to learn later you've been scammed into something else entirely. I expect that holds true when scouting for a boyfriend or girlfriend. I wouldn't want some guy clowning around with my hounds and giving them treats and pretending to like them just to get in good with me. That's dishonest. And not the way I operate. I'm way more Popeye than Calamity Jayne, truth be told," I said.

"Huh?"

"I yam what I yam and that's all that I yam," I clarified. I looked at him. "Don't you want people to like you for you—not for who you think they want you to be?" I asked. " 'Cause I'm thinking anything else is false advertising."

"Maybe," Nick conceded. "Still, Uncle Rick doesn't seem to mind, because he buys an awful lot of blind horses," the kid added.

And Rick probably got more than a little cheek pinching and head patting in the process, I thought to myself, feeling depressed yet determined not to lose my focus. Or my heart.

"When you're older you'll understand that, just like with Kookamunga, beauty is only skin deep," I told the lad.

"My dad says that's just what ugly girls say to give themselves hope," he pointed out. I shook my head. I had my work cut out with this one.

We kept our conversation limited to *ooh*s, *ah*s, and *look at that*s or *wow*s for the remainder of the twenty-five minute ride. It grew noticeably cooler the higher we went and I was glad for the warmth of my hoodie. I noted the kid had thrown on a heavy Iowa sweatshirt, as well.

At the top we jumped off and I looked around at the scenic vista before us. The peaks were breathtaking and the view spectacular, but there was no time to appreciate God's bounty. I was on a mission.

"Okay. Let's see." I read the scroll again. "Eagles. Warriors. Eyes. Hearts," I mumbled, half to myself.

"And bowling balls, snowmen, and pig snouts," Nick reminded me.

"Right." I noticed the Peakside Café attached to the ever-present souvenir store along with an information booth, and grabbed Nick's shirtsleeve.

"Let's start there first," I said.

"Why there?"

"Because it's a souvenir and gift shop. It's bound to have all of the aforementioned items."

"Even the pig snouts?" Nick asked.

"Absolutely. Piggy banks are very big with tourists," I told him. "Very big."

"Good. I thought maybe you were hungry again. Uncle Rick says he wonders where you put it all."

"Oh really? What else does Uncle Rick say?"

"That you drive him to Distraction sometimes. Where is Distraction? I've never heard of it."

"That's because it's a product of your uncle's troubled psyche," I said.

"Huh?"

"It's all in his head."

"Oh."

We entered the tourist buildings and I caught a whiff of deep-fried something or other, but I stoically ignored it. Despite what I'd let on, I wasn't sure what exactly we were looking for. I'd hoped it would turn out to be one of those *you know when you see it* kind of things.

"See?" I pointed at the collection of porkers promoting the Snowbowl and Arizona. "Pig snouts. Not to be confused with pork rinds, of course," I added. I did warn you food is frequently on my mind.

We moved through the building, checking out the gift shop. We checked all the books that looked like they might have eagles or Native American warrior types in them, with no success. We checked out the ceramic section and even went through the tedious task of picking up and examining each pot, but with no luck. We made our way to the informational portion of the indoor space. I stopped and stared. There it was. On the opposite wall: a huge picture of our national bird in living color, its large striking eyes alert and intent.

I whistled.

"Talk about your eagle eyes," I said. "I'm thinking that's where we need to look. What about you?" I asked the kid.

"I guess. But how?"

"Well, if I was going to hide something like a note, I'd slip it behind the painting—so I'll need to take it down or at least lift it enough so I can get a look behind it," I said. "See if there's maybe a hollow or cut-out place on the back of the frame."

"How are you gonna do that without people noticing?" he asked.

I looked around the place. Business was brisk. A big, burly man with hands the size of boxing gloves flipped through several magazines, while two women chaperoned a group of eight youngsters. While the lone clerk would probably keep her eyes glued to the kidlets, I didn't think I'd be able to yank the picture down, take a look at the back and then replace it without her noticing.

"You'll have to create a diversion," I told Nick, and he just looked at me.

"A what?"

"A diversion. A disturbance or ruckus of some kind. Something to put the focus on you long enough to give me time to yank the picture off the wall and take a quick look-see behind it."

"You're giving me permission to cause a commotion?" Nick said. "What exactly did you have in mind?"

"Well, nothing illegal," I said. "Maybe you could get sick and barf again like you did on the plane," I suggested. "That would sure draw some attention."

"Great. Only problem is, I wasn't the one who barfed. You were," he pointed out.

"Oh yeah." I was becoming such a good prevaricator

I even had me believing my whoppers. "You could pretend to choke on something," I said.

"Yeah. And have that ham-fisted dude over there perform the Heimlich on me and break a couple ribs. What else you got?"

I chewed my lip. "You're the annoying little brat here. You create chaos and pathos as a pastime. Surely you can come up with something that'll work."

"I could go put soap in my mouth and collapse and pretend I'm having an attack or fit or something and even foam at the mouth," he said.

I shook my head. "Too risky. You could end up with a comb pressing down your tongue or that same beef-fisted Good Samaritan doing chest compressions and blowing in your mouth."

He made a face. "Yuck. No way. Maybe I could trip and fall down and pretend to be hurt," he suggested.

I thought about this possibility. "Can you cry if necessary? Complete with tears and snot, that is."

"Piece of cake. I pull this one on my Grandma Clare and Grandpa Ed at least twice a year, once at Christmas and once during the two weeks during summer vacation I stay with them. It's usually good for ice cream, video game rentals, and a couple bucks."

What a manipulative little mooch.

"Okay, but make sure you do it around the corner and over by the door so everyone will move in that direction. That'll give me time to do my snooping."

"What happens if you're wrong?"

I shrugged. "We keep looking, I guess."

He nodded.

"So, are you ready for your acting debut?" I asked.

"I usually get compensated for this kind of thing," he reminded me. "What are you offering?"

"A Happy Meal on the way to the hotel," I told him.

He looked at me. "That's it?" he said.

I tipped an imaginary hat. "Miss Cheapskate here. Remember, pal?"

He frowned. "What if I want a Big Mac?" he asked. "And supersized fries?"

I looked at him. "I'll think about it."

He shook his head. "Scrooge," he mumbled and walked away.

I chuckled and moved over to the painting, waiting for the clerk behind the counter to gravitate in Nick's direction. I didn't have long to wait. I heard a big crash followed by the sound of things dropping. A few seconds later, tons of multicolored rubber balls with Snowbowl logos rolled across the floor in the direction of the counter. The clerk disappeared.

Ignoring the howls of pain from the other side of the store, I grabbed the picture and pulled it toward me, running a hand along its underside. My breath caught when my fingers ran over an item near the center. I leaned down and peered beneath the picture and discovered a small manila envelope taped to the back.

Beads of nervous sweat popped out above my upper lip as I used an unpolished fingernail to work the duct tape loose.

"Wouldn't you know? Duct tape," I swore as I tried to pull the tape off without ripping the envelope.

"It hurts! It hurts!" reached me, and I shook my head. The kid oughta be in movies.

I finally got the stubborn tape unfastened and I removed the package. I stared at it for a second. Hell's bells! I was right, after all!

I quickly replaced the picture, stuck the envelope in my backpack and zipped it up, then hurried to retrieve my child star. I came around the corner, slipped on a rubber ball and almost fell on my butt. I spotted Nick prone on the floor, his face red and tearstained.

He'd done it, the little phlegm wad, I marveled. He'd done it.

A man bent over him solicitously—thankfully not the big 'un with the king-sized mitts—and I started to step forward to claim my little man and assure everyone he would get proper medical care when the back of this Southwestern Samaritan got my attention: the long, dark, shiny silken locks that set off a familiar stab of envy that tame tresses inspire in me. The even length along the bottom that so didn't need a trim. The chiseled profile.

Raphael. Poet and purse snatcher. Lyricist and liar.

Holy wampum.

How the devil had he tracked us?

I wanted to beat my head against the nearest tom-tom. All he had to do was stop at one of the numerous businesses I'd requested directions from and ask where I was headed, bringing him straight to the Snowbowl. He would have beat us here. And to Nick.

I retreated out of sight. A few possibilities for escape flashed through my head—and I swear to you nice folks, hardly any of them included leaving the little twerp there and taking off. The pressing problem was how to handle this new wrinkle in my rapidly fraying tapestry.

I shook my head. I'd have to wing it. I took the envelope from my backpack and opened it, my mouth flying open as a necklace slid into my palm along with another scroll. I unfolded the note and read it hurriedly, realizing the chance of me memorizing it under pressure was roughly the same as me losing ten pounds on the upcoming cruise. I remembered the pictures the kid had taken of the earlier clue and grabbed my digital camera, spread the scroll out and snapped a couple close-ups. I pocketed the camera and replaced the clue in the envelope. The necklace I hurriedly fastened around my neck, concealing it beneath my shirt.

I thought of stuffing it in my bra, but sadly acknowledged that my cup size wasn't up to the task.

I resealed the envelope as best I could and stuck it
back in the backpack, removing my billfold and stuffing it in the pocket of my hoodie along with the kid's
cell phone.

I took a deep breath and rounded the corner.

Lights. Camera. Action!

"What are you doing?" I screamed. "What are you
doing to my nephew?"

I ran to Nick, still on the floor, and came up behind
Raphael before he could rise. Making eye contact with
Nick, I pointed to the top of Raphael's head and made
a long slashing motion across my neck and stuck my
tongue out, for good measure adding a gesture above
my own head as if pulling on a noose to tighten it.
Whether it was the slashing or the hanging that got the
message to the kid, I realized it had been received
when his eyes grew twice their normal size.

"Get away from him!" I screamed.

By this time Raphael had experienced his own
incandescent-light moment and he got slowly to his
feet and turned.

"You!"

I didn't much care for his smile, blasted white teeth
and all. His eyes roamed to my backpack and he took a
step in my direction.

"Help! That guy tripped me and knocked me down,
and while I was down he . . . he . . . he touched me!"

We all just looked at him.

"Down there!" Nick continued, pointing to the zipper area of his britches.

The tone of the room changed perceptively as I
helped Nick get to his feet.

"How could you?" I hissed at Raphael, cradling Nick
against me. "He's only a child!"

Raphael started shaking his head, his long hair flying back and forth.

"I did not!" he yelled. "I did not touch the kid! I swear. Not like that!"

"He did! He did! He groped me!" Nick wailed. "And he squeezed!"

I blinked. Wow, the kid had the instincts for improv.

"Have you no decency?" I said, doing my part, backing Nick and myself toward the door. "A poor, defenseless boy!"

Raphael took another step in my direction but the big, burly guy we'd commented on earlier stepped up behind Raphael and grabbed him in a *you ain't goin' nowhere, bub* armlock.

Seeing our chance to scram, I drew Nick out the door and we ran to the loading platform for our own shuttle take-off. I shoved several other couples waiting in line aside and moved to the front.

"Please, my ex is after our son! He's abusive and not allowed to see little Tobias, but he followed us here! Please, let us through!"

We bustled to the head of the line and planted our butts in the seats as the lift came by.

"Hey, aren't you a little young to have a kid that old?" one patron observed, and I smiled back at him as we went airborne.

"And aren't you a sweet man for noticing," I said. "Mmmwaa!" I blew him a kiss.

"Tobias?" Nick said, with a look up at me.

I shrugged. "I've always thought if I had a son I'd name him Tobias and call him Toby for short," I said, a bit choked up at the thought of having a child of my own—and not all due to sentimentality. "What do you think?"

"I think he'd get his butt kicked a lot," Nick said.

"Good to know," I replied. "Good to know."

The twenty-five minute ride down the mountain seemed to go a darned sight slower than it did on the way up. I kept twisting around in the seat to check behind me.

"Who was that guy? Do you think he followed us? Is he dangerous? Do you think he's good-looking? How come he has girl hair?" Nick's questions flew like flaming arrows.

I shook my head. "He's a bad man," I said. "A very, very bad man." Anyone who would spout poetic prose while pinching a designer purse was downright evil. Evil through and through. "But he does have a lovely head of hair," I conceded.

We finally touched down and I was more than ready to get the heck out of Dodge and back to the relative safety of a large, historic hotel with security and those lovely little devices on the room doors that kept housekeeping from walking in on you when you were showering, sleeping, or dressing.

The lift operator at the bottom lifted the bar that kept us from falling out and thanked us.

"Let's go!" I yelled as we jogged through the parking lot toward Sophie's car. A short burst of acceleration from behind me was the only warning I had before a car pulled alongside me and a hand whipped out, wrenching my backpack from my shoulder and almost pulling my arm out of its socket in the process.

The backpack strap caught on my wristwatch and I felt myself being dragged car-side along the parking lot, the toes of my new Skechers scuffing along the pavement and the legs of my jeans creating enough friction to burn at the contact with the cement.

"Let go!" I heard from inside the car. "Drop it!"

I looked frantically at the driver and was shocked and terrified when a frightening white kachina mask stared back at me.

I wanted to make some smart-mouthed remark, but found my breath taken up by a long series of terrified screams as I struggled to free myself from the bag before I found myself towed out into Flagstaff traffic.

The car dragged me for another twenty feet before I managed to unclasp my watch and free my arm. I tumbled to the pavement, the impact sending me rolling ass over appendages across the parking lot until I smacked into the bumper of a shiny new Prius.

I sat, stunned but relatively unhurt except for cuts and scrapes. Nick ran up and crouched beside me.

"Wow, that was awesome the way that guy dragged you along beside him. What did it feel like? Was it scary? Did you think you were gonna die? Wow! That was the schizz!"

The lengths one had to go to impress kids these days.

"We need to keep moving," I said. "That goon could come back and his partner, Slick, is probably on his way down as we speak." I took a deep breath and winced as I leaned on Nick to get to my feet.

"Are you all right, Tressa?" the squirt finally thought to ask. I nodded.

"The only thing hurt is my pride. And my Skechers will never be the same," I said, looking at the scraped and battered toes. "And I just bought them. The bastards."

I retrieved the key from my pants pocket and unlocked the car and we got in.

"He got the clue, didn't he?" Nick said. I nodded.

"The bastard," Nick said and I winced. I hoped Nick wouldn't tell anyone where he'd heard that little gem.

I started the car and burned an excessive amount of Sophie's tire rubber exiting the parking lot. I shrugged. From what I could see, she could afford new tires.

I looked over and noticed the dejected look on Nick's face at the realization that our little adventure

had come to an abrupt end. I wasn't about to en-
lighten him otherwise.

It seemed I'd landed smack dab in the middle of a
southwestern amazing race where my competitors
were playing for keeps. And me? I was stuck with a
mouthy munchkin with way too much Townsend 'tude
for my comfort.

Yep. This had all the earmarks of a notable event in
American history.

Custer's Last Stand.

CHAPTER SIXTEEN

I made good on the runt's Happy Meal on the way back to the hotels. Neither of us appeared to have much of an appetite, but I didn't want the tyke to dine by his lonesome, so I got a burger, fries and a shake to go. You know. Just to be a bud. We ate our meals in relative silence.

I dropped the kid off at the hotel, making sure he got delivered safely into the hands of his mother.

I wasn't looking forward to facing Sophie after taking off with her car, but I decided after she heard the latest update on just what Kookamunga had really kept under wraps, she'd be as hooked as I was by the latest development. And as eager to solve this prickly pear of a puzzle.

More than anything I wanted to hunt down a certain ranger and flaunt my *I told you sos* in his skeptical face.

Of course, that probably meant admitting that I had inadvertently put his nephew at risk. I chewed a fingernail. Hmmm. Let's see. Was lording my superior detecting skills over Ranger Rick Townsend really worth the butt chewing I'd get in return?

You bet your tomahawk it was.

I made my way to the gift shop to pick up a backpack to replace the one I'd lost. I shook my head when the only one they had was a youth-sized bag with a weird-looking, hairy midget pig on it that I learned was called a javelina. I made my purchase, voicing my concern with their limited selection of backpacks, and headed through the rustic lobby I'd moped around in just hours earlier, when I caught the sunlight reflecting off a familiar head of blue hair and spotted my grandma sitting on a red-cushioned couch in a corner of the expansive room. Seated next to her was none other than former stage and screen star and spiritual advisee, Gloria Grant.

Talk about being early for a wedding, I thought, amending my planned route and hurrying over to them. As I wandered closer, I recognized the balding head of Gram's fiancé, Joe Townsend, occupying a nearby chair, one leg swung over the other as he followed the exchange between the two women. I plopped down in the seat next to him.

"Hey Joe, whatdya know?" I greeted my step-grandpappy-to-be with one of my usual salutations.

"Tressa Jayne! Where have you been?" my gammy scolded me. "Rick's been looking all over for you." She looked at the state of my attire. "Glad he didn't find you," she said, shaking her head. "You remember Gloria here, don't you? She's come for the wedding," Gram added.

"Uh, isn't that auspicious event still a day or so off?" I asked.

Gloria nodded and picked up a glass of what looked like white wine from a nearby table and took a sip. "I decided I needed a change of scenery," she said. "And after I lunched with your entertaining group and Hannah here extended an invitation, I said, why not get away for a few days? I dug out your card, saw The Titan and knew this was the place to get away from it all and attend the wedding of a new friend. I just love this hotel. It brings back memories of some very good times," she said with a slight tilt of her eyebrow. "I love the sense of history here. And although I do love the amenities of a luxury hotel, there are times my soul yearns for a simpler existence." She sighed and took another sip from her glass.

I fought the urge to grin. Somehow I couldn't see Gloria Grant starring in *The Simple Life*. I looked over at Joltin' Joe Townsend, who'd been uncharacteristically quiet since I sat down, to find the same rapt expression on his face as he stared at Gloria that I get when I pull out a bag of DoubleStuf Oreos from the pantry and a quart of fresh white milk from my fridge and set them on my kitchen table. Or when I watch my horses mix it up on a frosty fall morning, their flared nostrils emitting white puffs, tails raised in high-spirited fun.

I took a quick peek to see if Gram had noticed Joe was majorly in need of a drool bib, but she seemed oblivious to his thrall. I shook his arm.

"Earth to Joe. Earth to Joe," I said in a low voice. "Please replace your peepers before a certain hellion we both know and love discovers yours have popped out and are rolling about on the floor at Gloria Grant's feet."

Joe pulled his attention away from the star and looked over at me. "Nice backpack," he said. "Is that supposed to be a pig? When'd you get here?"

I shook my head. "It's actually a peccary," I said. "And aren't we living a wee bit dangerously?" I asked.

"Whatdya mean?" he asked, and I reached over and removed his glasses and looked through the lenses.

"Just as I suspected," I said. "Fogging up."

He grabbed them back from me and put them on his nose. "Gee, guess we've got the wedding entertainment covered after all, since Ellen DeGeneres had to cancel on us," he commented, staring at me. "What in Hades happened to you? You look like you went a few rounds with a prickly pear. Or was it a prickly person?"

"Actually I'm onto a story out here that could just win me some national exposure. Of the literary kind," I elaborated.

"Oh, yeah? Let me guess. Extra, extra, read all about it. '*Granny gets more rolls in the hay than overly cautious cowgirl granddaughter.*' Some story. Bet that'll get picked up by the wire for sure."

"How about this headline? 'Groom Gutted For Making Goo-goo Eyes at Guest.'" I tapped a cheek. "By the way, does your fiancée know you sometimes call her 'Granny?'" I asked. "And does she know you have a thing for Ms. Grant there?" I added.

He shook his head and turned his attention to Gloria and my grandma. I smiled. I loved hassling Townsend men.

"So, Gloria, did Gram tell you about our sixty-second consultation with Cadence?" I asked. "I hate to break it to you, but the woman is a little screwy," I added.

Gloria nodded. "Hannah described your appointment. I am so sorry. I can't think what got into Cadence. I've never had a disappointing session with her. I swear by her advice."

"That's nice. You and Gram have something in common then," I said. "'Cause she was doin' some swearin' of her own when we left The Spiritual Boutique," I told Gloria.

"I just can't understand what happened. Cadence is usually dead-on in her counseling. She says I need to get outside my comfort zone in my own journey for self-fulfillment and renewal. She insists I need a mission. A cause. That's what I'm trying to do. Find a cause. She thinks if I can prove to myself I can take a stand and find the power from within, I can achieve anything I set out to do. Even the rebirth of a career. I'm sorry your experience with Cadence was a negative one. I hope she didn't charge you."

I shook my head. "No. In fact, I almost got the feeling she'd have paid us to leave the place," I said. "Still, that's not entirely without precedent," I added. "She acted . . . I don't know, scared. Definitely weirded me out."

"She might have been receiving negative energy from one of you," Gloria said. "Or saw something in your futures or lives disturbing to her. Sometimes when that happens, Cadence shuts down."

"It was Tressa!" my gramma shouted. "She had hold of Tressa when she went all 'woo-hooo' on us. Said all kinds of gibberish, too. Stuff about secrets and truth and death and redemption. Oh, and she had one of them orgasmic experiences at the end, too, I'm pretty sure," Gram said. "Don't you think so, Tressa?"

I shook my head. I wasn't touching that line with a ten-foot totem pole.

"That *is* strange," Gloria said, assessing me with an odd look of her own. "Very strange."

Remembering the necklace around my neck and a certain clue burning a hole in my pocket and waiting to be deciphered, I got to my feet.

"Well, it's been real," I said, "but I need to clean up. I'll see you up in the room, Gram," I said, bending down to give her a peck on an Oiled of Olay cheek. "Nice to see you again, Miss Grant," I said and took the hand she raised.

"Gloria," she said and smiled. "Call me Gloria."

I nodded. "Gloria, it is." I turned back to Joe. "Don't you take it into your head to have one last fling, there, big boy," I whispered in his ear, squeezing his shoulder. "Remember, my gammy's partial to pepper spray and has been known to pack heat."

"I'll keep that in mind, girlie," Joe said, and I headed for the showcase staircase that led to the rooms of the sprawling old lodge.

Meanwhile I had a heap big riddle to solve. Then it was on to the next leg of the race. And the clock—as in most good thrillers—was ticking.

I hurried to the hotel room and let myself in, stopping short when I saw Taylor stretched out on one of the beds, her laptop beside her.

"Oh hey, Taylor," I said. "I didn't expect you to be here," I said, wondering how I was going to decode my latest clue with my critical little sis looking on.

"Where did you expect me to be?" she asked.

I shrugged. "Jogging. Hiking. Sightseeing. Babysitting our gramma. You know. Something that burns calories," I told her.

She sat up. "I should be asking where you've been. You look like you're ready for the last roundup." She frowned. "What on earth happened to your shoes? Weren't those brand-new?"

It was my turn to frown. "You're damn right they were!" I said before I could stop myself. I have a serious, long-term attachment to my footwear. Could you tell?

Taylor got a suspicious look in her eyes. "So, why do they look like a Rottweiler took a fancy to them?" she asked. She bent over to take a closer look. "Are those rocks?" she said, pointing to the pebbles embedded into the toes of the sad little shoes.

"When I get tired, I drag my feet," I said. "I know where Gram is, but where is Sophie?" I asked, changing the subject.

"She said something about filing a police report on a stolen vehicle," Taylor said, and I blinked.

"Sophie knew I had her car," I said.

Taylor nodded. "No doubt accounting for the nervous tic accompanied by mild hysteria," she said, and I made a face.

"If you'll excuse me, I need to answer a call of nature," I said. "But we can bond more later." I flashed her a half smile and hurried to the bathroom. I locked the door behind me, put the seat of the toilet down, and sat. I pulled out my digital camera and punched up the pictures of the scroll I'd hurriedly taken. I frowned. My photographic skills made Kelsey's shots appear *Vogue*-quality in comparison. Of course, I wasn't dealing with a subject who loved the camera like Kelsey.

I adjusted the view, zooming in on the written note. I brought the phone eye-level. I read it out loud.

"'Sit back and prepare for a wild water ride. You won't get wet but you'll enjoy the thrill all the same. With plenty of company—up to 523 others can share the experience—snake eyes will hold the key to your next test.'"

I shook my head. Nothing. I read it again.

"Uh, who are you talking to, Tressa?" Taylor asked through the bathroom door.

"I'm reading the hotel literature," I said. "Did you know that the eclectic architecture of The Titan is a combination of the Swiss Chalet and Norway Villa?" I asked, setting the camera down and removing the necklace from underneath my blouse. I stood and moved to the mirror. A shell with a turquoise inlaid pendant, the necklace was simple yet striking. I cocked my head.

The turquoise set off the blue in my eyes. And brought out the dirt smudges on my face and chaos of my coiffure. Trés chic.

"Nice," I said. "Very nice."

"Tressa, what is going on in there?" Taylor rattled the doorknob.

"Duh. The process of elimination," I responded, flushing the toilet. "What do you think is going on?"

I admired myself for a few more minutes, washed away the facial reminders of my tug of war with a three-ton automobile, and wondered what significance the necklace held. I stared at it a few seconds longer.

What tale did it have to tell? What secrets was it meant to shed light on? I waited for a message to show up like on a Magic 8-Ball, but got nothing.

I sighed, tried to figure out a safe place to put it, and decided that place was still around my neck so I tucked it back underneath my shirt. I took several additional minutes to copy the clue down on a notepad and stick it back in my Harry Javelina bag.

I opened the door.

"If I told you I was going to take you on a wild water ride that you could share with five hundred and twenty-three other people but where you wouldn't get one bit wet, could you guess where I wanted to take you?" I asked Taylor, deciding I needed to call upon her admittedly higher intelligence.

She gave me a long look. "You want to take *me* somewhere?" she asked.

I nodded. "I told you I wanted some bonding time," I reminded her.

"So why the guessing game?"

"To make it fun and entertaining."

"I'm supposed to be entertained?"

"You will be if you go along. So what place in the area am I thinking of that takes you and five hundred twenty-three other people on the same wild ride without breaking a sweat?" I asked.

"You want to take me to the Grand Canyon IMAX Theater?" she asked.

I stared at her. "I do?" I asked.

Taylor blinked several times. Blink. Blink. In rapid succession.

"I mean, I do! I do!" I said, my brain taking some time to play catch up and realize that Taylor had cracked the clue without even knowing about it. Figures. Miss Overachiever. "That is exactly what I want to do with my favorite sister," I said.

"You mean only sister," she muttered. She gave me one of those I-wish-I-had-X-ray-vision-so-I-could-see-right-through-you looks and tilted her head to one side. "And you actually want the two of us—you and me—to go sightseeing together?" she asked.

I shrugged. "What can I say? Native American culture values and reveres familial connections and ties. And with all the talk about finding balance in one's life, what better place to try and establish that kindling warmth of kinship?" I asked, hoping I sounded whimsical and poetic.

From Taylor's expression, I hadn't succeeded.

Okay, so the competitive cowgirl in me mostly was looking for someone to ride shotgun just in case the bad guys figured out the clue and showed up at the visitors center to check out the same wild ride. But the big sis in me earnestly did want to reach out and connect with my sibling in some meaningful—and lasting—way. I bet you never realized what a complex individual I am. Did you?

"The last time we went anywhere together alone you took off and left me in the girls' restroom at the city park. I think I was in kindergarten at the time," Taylor observed.

I winced. "As I remember it, I was protecting you from a neighborhood bully at the time," I told her, recalling my version of events. Actually, Little Peter Patterson had snatched my baseball glove from a picnic bench and I'd taken off in hot pursuit after the brazen little thug. Even at eight I had spunk. Gotta give me that.

"But you never came back to get me," Taylor responded, providing her own recollection of the incident. "I waited in that park bathroom for three hours! No telling what would have happened if the ding-a-ling man hadn't come by."

Whoa, folks! Don't go getting any strange notions here. The ding-a-ling man was our name for the ice-cream truck driver who drove through the streets of Grandville during the hot summer months ringing a bell to announce the sale of cool dairy treats. My Uncle Frank, who was the ding-a-ling man's competitor, had a similar, not-so-nice name for him.

Anyway, by the time I caught up to Pee-pee Peter and thumped him a couple times with my ball glove, I'd drawn enough of a crowd that we decided to play a couple innings and I totally forgot about my sister left standing in the stinky bathroom at the park. Hey, I was eight! And it was baseball season!

"But if you'll also recall, I was grounded for a month and couldn't ride all that time, horse shows included, so I figure I paid for it in spades," I reminded my sister. "Not that I was able to ride for several days after the incident due to gluteus maximal soreness." It was one of the only times I could recall my laid-back, quiet father spanking me.

"And you're serious about this little outing to the IMAX?" she asked again.

"To the max!" I said, with a *cross my heart and hope not to die young* pledge.

She gave me that look again and slowly nodded.

"Okay. Sure. Why not? In the interest of 'familial

bonding' and 'sisterly sharing,'" Taylor said. She looked at me. "You do plan to do something with your hair, right?" she added. I nodded.

"You drive and I'll braid it on the way," I told her, tossing her Sophie's car keys.

"Shouldn't we ask Sophie if she wants to come, or at the very least get permission to use her car?" Taylor asked. I shook my head.

"No time!" I snapped. "Uh, what I mean is . . . not this time. We don't want to ask her along this time or we won't have our one-on-one time, and if we ask her to borrow the car, we're kind of obligated to invite her to come along," I explained. "Besides, we won't be gone all that long. You know, basically just in and out."

I watched Taylor deliberate: Should I or shouldn't I? I'm more of a spur of the moment kind of gal and rarely do this evaluative process myself, so it's fascinating to observe.

She expelled a long gust of air. "I suppose it couldn't hurt," she said.

"It won't hurt a bit!" I told Taylor. "Not one bit."

Taylor shook her head. "I'll just leave Sophie another little note and let her know where we are so she won't worry," Taylor said, writing a quick note and taping it to the mirror.

"Let's go!" I said, grabbing Taylor's arm. "Come on! I want to catch the next show!" I pulled Taylor out of the hotel and down to where I'd parked the car.

Taylor got behind the wheel, buckled up, and started the engine.

"Tell me there won't be any unexpected sisterly surprises on our little sibling sojourn," Taylor said. "I'm not much for surprises."

"You really need to loosen up a little, sis," I told Taylor. "Surprises keep life interesting. Spice things up."

"So you say," she said. "As for me, I'm content without constant scintillation and drama," she said. "It's safer that way."

I gave her an *oh brother, sister* look as she slowly backed out of the parking space, then stared at her.

"You're not going to drive this pokey all the way there, are you?" I asked.

"I'm not going to take a chance with Sophie's car," she said. "So I'll drive at the speed I'm comfortable with."

I wanted to give my cheek a smack. I should've left the driving to me.

We got there less than five minutes before the next on-the-half-hour showing of the thirty-four minute Grand Canyon movie. I hauled Taylor out of the car and literally dragged her up the sidewalk and into the visitors center, and up to the ticket booth.

"Two, please!" I wheezed.

"That will be twenty-five fifty-six," the woman in the booth said.

"Twenty-five bucks?" I said. "Are you kidding? For a thirty-minute movie?"

She stared at me. "Excuse me? This is the highest grossing IMAX film of all time," she said, and I nodded.

"At these prices, I can believe it," I said, rummaging around in my backpack for my billfold.

"Here you go." I looked up to see Taylor place a twenty and a ten on the counter.

"Thank you." The ticket lady nodded to Taylor, giving me short shrift. "I'm sure you'll find the film well worth the ticket price," she said.

At forty cents a minute, at the very least I expected to see a half-clothed Orlando Bloom white-water rafting down the Colorado River. Or Hugh Jackman leading a nature hike along the canyon trails au naturelle.

"Isn't there a law against price gouging?" I asked,

grabbing a couple visitors center brochures and hurrying Taylor along to the theater doors.

"Price gouging is inflating the price of necessary goods in a time of disaster or extreme need," Taylor said.

"My point exactly!" I said, pulling her over to the ticket taker and into the theater. Still early in the vacation season, the theater was only a quarter full at best.

I looked at my watch. Three minutes 'til showtime. I pulled out my notepad and tried to read my handwritten version of the clue before the houselights went down:

> Sit back and prepare for a wild water ride. You won't get wet but you'll enjoy the thrill all the same. With plenty of company—up to 523 others can share the experience—snake eyes will hold the key to your next test.

"Snake eyes will hold the key to your next test," I muttered. "Snake eyes. Snake eyes." I made a face. I sure as heck hoped the snake eyes in question weren't attached to an actual reptile or I'd be in deep voodoo. I rather hoped, instead, that the snake-eyes reference indicated a pair of ones.

"Onesies," I said. "Two ones."

"Tressa, are you okay?" Taylor asked, nudging my elbow.

I closed the notepad. "Absolutely. Lovin' every minute with my little sis," I said, staring around the sizable auditorium as the last few filmgoers straggled in. "Good times. Good times."

I looked at the three sections of seating. Okay. If "snake eyes" referred to the theater seating, then I probably needed to check out the first seat in the first row. I frowned. The way the auditorium was set up there were four different seats that could conceivably be the seat in question. Somehow I had to check out each one.

I pinpointed each seat. Two were unoccupied. One was occupied but the seat next to it was unoccupied, and the last was part of a group of elementary school-aged kids. I'd check out the unoccupied seats first and hope I struck pay dirt. If not, then I'd worry about how to check out the ones that were a bit more challenging.

"Would you excuse me for just a second?" I said to Taylor. "I'm going to check out a couple of the other seats to see if the view is better," I said. "BRB."

I slid to the end of the row before Taylor could object and did an X-Y axis number to make sure I'd targeted the correct seats. I hurried to the first seat and conducted a thorough examination, thankful that the lights had gone down and the film had started so I could do it without attracting a lot of attention—or shushes.

I crossed off that possibility and proceeded to the next one.

I scooted in beside a middle-aged couple.

"Excuse me. So sorry," I said as I bumped into the legs of the man sitting in seat two. "Pardon me." I finally made it to the seat next to him and dropped into it. I felt under the armrests and down into the cushion areas to see if I could find anything. I shoved a hand under my seat and ran it across the bottom of the chair. Unable to examine the entire seat while sitting in it, I moved to the seat behind it, thankfully unoccupied, and got down on my hands and knees on the narrow floor of the theater and stuck my head under the seat, sliding a hand over the entire bottom of the chair, feeling for the outline of an envelope.

"Did you lose something?" The woman who occupied seat three in the row ahead of me turned and directed the question to the fleshy portion of my anatomy pointing in her direction.

"I dropped my Juju Fruits," I said, bringing my head out from under the seat.

She gave me a stern look. "You're not supposed to bring food in the theater," she pointed out. "And certainly not sticky, messy candies," she scolded.

"Maybe they're Sweetarts, then," I said. "Those aren't sticky or messy. Unless you get 'em wet and then they're a real bummer to clean up 'cause the colors have a tendency to run," I said.

I made one final sweep of the seat to make sure I hadn't missed anything and stood up to move back to the aisle.

"Excuse me. So sorry. My apologies," I said as I yanked the couple's chair backs in my direction when I hauled myself to my feet and moved back into the aisle. I put my hands up, palms out. "And look! No mess! M & M's melt in your mouth! Not in your hands!" I exclaimed and grinned.

Two down, two to go.

After my dealings with Nick Townsend, I decided to appeal to the mercenary, materialistic side of youth these days and offered the juvie in the next seat a fiver for the opportunity to search the area for an earring I'd lost. The entrepreneurial spirit of the group would've made The Donald proud as they negotiated the access fee to twenty bucks for a permit to search.

By the time I'd finished, I was aware I'd generated some attention—some of the curious kind, but mostly of the "Sit down and shaddup, Blondie" variety. I could feel their pain. At twelve bucks a pop, no one wants a distraction akin to a howling baby at the Cinema-Plex.

Before the theater-goers turned on me like a vigilante mob, I decided to take my seat and simply keep my own eagle eye glued to that final chair and take a peak underneath once the film was over and folks filed out.

"What in God's name are you doing?" Taylor hissed as I sat down beside her. "You've been flitting all over the theater like Tinkerbell on meth," she said. "What is going on?"

"I wanted to get the full effect from different vantage points for the inflated price of my admission," I told her.

"You mean *my* admission price," Taylor said. "And while we're talking about getting our money's worth, what about *my* enjoyment of the exhilarating, not-to-be-missed experience I bought and paid for? It sure hasn't been entertaining for me to sit here and watch you play musical chairs and rile the other patrons up into a frenzy."

I winced. "Sorry, sis," I said. "I promise I'll be a perfect patron from here on in. Now sit back and enjoy the show."

Taylor looked at me, shook her head, and sat back in her seat, turning her attention to the megasized screen touted to be seven stories tall.

I shifted my attention between the screen, the snake-eyes seat I still needed to check out and the film-goers. I chuckled when the helicopter in the film took a sudden dive to the left and the audience followed suit. I hooted out loud during the white-water rafting portion of the film as people literally leaned from one side of their theater chairs to the other as they navigated their way along the treacherous, choppy waters of the Colorado River.

"Oh my gawd, this is so freaking cool!" I said, feeling my own body move back and forth and up and down with the swells of the river. "What about you, Taylor? Sweet, huh?"

I turned to look at my sister. The first thing I noticed was the grayish green tinge to her normally healthy complexion. The second was her fingernails embedded in the padding of our shared arm rest.

"Taylor?" I placed a hand on hers. "You okay?"

She shook her head back and forth slowly, leaning over in my direction sharply before positioning her body to the other side of the chair like she was on a funky roller coaster.

"I'm getting sick!" she managed.

"Turn away!" I told her. "Shut your eyes!"

"I can't!" she said. "It's like a train wreck. You want to look away but you can't! Oh, gawd, I'm going to throw up!"

"Shhh! Would you pipe down? You've been a constant distraction since you came in," someone behind us hissed.

I grabbed the back of Taylor's neck and stuck her head between her knees.

"Close your eyes and breathe. Breathe!" I ordered.

"Let go! I'm not hyperventilating! You're making it worse!"

"Shhh! Hold it down up there!"

"Do you mind?"

"I paid good money to watch this film so shut the hell up!"

Yikes! The natives were getting restless.

I started to glance around to see where the most vocal contingent was located, and found my gaze caught by a late arrival making his way down the aisle to my right.

It was Raphael. And he didn't look happy.

I made a headlong dive to the floor, praying he hadn't spotted me.

"Dammit!" I swore, trying to think of my next move and knowing it had to take me to the last remaining unexamined seat. Making like the reptiles I loathed, I slithered my way down the row and across the far aisle. I rolled to my back and began to slide underneath the chairs, face up, making my way to the seat.

"Eeow! Gross!" I said, sickened by wad after wad of gum stuck to various parts of the theater seats. What? Theater-goers can't wrap gum in tissue and use a waste receptacle like the rest of us?

I continued my backstroke and awkwardly made my way to the seat in question, avoiding the legs and feet of as many Canyon customers as possible. I finally found the top of my head even with the back of the second chair in the first row of the section. Slowly, slowly, I propelled myself upward—well, in the direction of my head, anyway—until my head was completely under the chair.

It was only when I shoved myself upward and spotted the crotch of a man's pants that I realized that the dude in the snake eyes seat had moved. The unfortunate occupant of the chair chose that moment to look down and our eyes met. I managed a weak wave and equally weak smile.

The man's eyes grew big as Joe Townsend's had been earlier as he sat across from Gloria Grant.

"Well, hullo there!" The owner of the crotch in question said. "I've had dreams of moments like this in a dark movie theater. Wet ones. Wicked ones."

I gulped. Great. Of all the seats in the place to pop my head out from under, I'd picked the one occupied by a dude with triple-X fantasies.

"Hello," I responded. "How are you today? I'm with the IMAX staff and I'm trolling for gum violations," I said, visibly wincing at how lame this cover story was, but going with it just the same. "You didn't, by any chance, leave this little memento of your visit to this fine establishment behind, did you? I asked, forcing myself to pick up a disgusting wad of pink chewing gum—cotton-candy flavor if I wasn't mistaken—and hold it up for him to see. "Here at the Grand Canyon IMAX theater we have tough rules prohibiting the damage of our fine facility and regulating the disposal of debris within the theater proper. Did you know you could be fined up to five hundred dollars for depositing this wad of gum under your seat?" I asked.

The dark dream weaver shook his head. "It's not mine. I swear!" he responded. "I only chew spearmint!"

I gave him a long look. "You do understand I'm only doing my job, right, sir?" I asked. He nodded. "I'm going to take your word for it that this isn't your gum. However, I'll need to clear the chairs of gum on either side of you. For your own benefit, you understand. I'd appreciate your discretion as I continue to perform my duties," I added. I handed him the pink wad of gum. "Thank you, sir. Enjoy the rest of the show."

I quickly slid to the next chair and began a hurried up search of the bottom. My heart rate picked up when my hand came across an envelope taped to the inside of one of the seat legs. My fingers shook as I peeled the tape away and freed the tiny package.

Sticking it in the front of my pants, I changed direction and started pulling myself toward the back of the theater, catching myself before I automatically reached out to dislodge hard wads of gum en route like a for-real wad terminator.

I maneuvered myself into the same row but across the aisle from Taylor, trying to get her attention, but her eyes were once again focused on the screen. The glutton for punishment.

I bit my lip, trying to figure out a subtle way to signal

her that it was time to go, remembered the hard, round missiles that were within my very grasp, and I reached out and pulled off a wad of dried gum. I lobbed it in Taylor's general direction. The gum missed her completely but hit a guy in the head two rows up. I winced and waited a moment before selecting another gum wad and letting fly.

It bounced off the Dumbo ear of the greedy little kid who'd profited from my generosity earlier.

That'll teach him, the little greedy Gus, I thought. But dang. My arm wasn't what it used to be. I so needed to sign up for a summer softball league.

Sensing the end of the film wasn't far off, I grabbed several wads of the disgusting cast-off cuds and combined them to make one super large, super-dooper, superwad. This time I took aim before I sent it sailing. It smacked Taylor in the side of the head. Yes! I still had it!

Taylor looked quickly in my direction, and from my prone position, I waved and smiled and pointed to my wrist where my watch should have been and then to the exit, nodding to see if she got the point.

She simply sat there.

I did my *Let's get the heck out of Dodge* routine again, punctuating it by slipping out into the aisle on my belly, making my way to the exit like a seriously messed-up sidewinder snake.

The climax of the film exploded onto the huge screen, featuring abrupt drops and twists and turns that left your belly in your throat, continuing with the stomach-wrenching, three-dimensional wild ride through the rapids. The audience screamed and oohed and ahed. One audience member moaned. I'd know that moan anywhere.

A gust of air hit the back of me as Taylor rushed by,

a hand to her mouth. I waited for her to vacate the theater before I resumed my crawl in her wake.

I'd made it to the door and was just about to crawl around the corner when something grabbed hold of my ankle and I felt my body being dragged for the second time that day. Instead of pavement burns, however, I felt my knees warm with the sting of rug burns.

I reached out and took hold of the door frame and started to kick my legs to dislodge the manacle around my ankle when the cell phone I'd copped from Nick Townsend began to play. The Iowa Fight Song rang out.

The pressure on my right foot continued and I found myself in a bizarre tug of war—with yours truly as the rope.

"Tressa?" I heard above me. I twisted around to see Kelsey Townsend staring down at me. "Uncle Rick! Uncle Rick! I found her! I found her!"

"I see that," I heard, and recognized the shoes that appeared in front of me. The hold on my foot disappeared and I was catapulted at Townsend's feet in a heap.

I groaned.

And thus this little Hawkeye's fight song ended on your basic sour note.

CHAPTER SEVENTEEN

I handed over the cell phone to Townsend, and I stood guard as the theater emptied several minutes later, ready to confront Raphael the Romeo Rat—now that I had ample backup in the form of Ranger Rick, Sophie, Taylor and the munchkins, that is. I waited. And waited. But Raphael never came out. I ran back into the theater. It was empty except for a maintenance man who was mumbling that he'd like to take varmints who drop huge wads of gum on the floor for others to step on and ground into the carpet and slow roast 'em over a spit. I hurried out of the theater.

"What's with taking off with my car?" Sophie asked.

I shrugged. "It was her idea," I said, pointing to Taylor. "She wrote the note and everything."

Taylor shot me a dark look. Her face was flushed now. Kneeling over a toilet bowl will do that to you.

"Tressa wanted to 'bond,'" Taylor said, wiping her upper lip with a tissue. "Just us two sisters."

I saw Rick Townsend raise an eyebrow. "You had to travel two thousand miles across the country to bond?"

he asked. His tone was liberally laced with disbelief—and suspicion. "Why here? Why now?"

I wrinkled a brow. Townsend had the knack for maneuvering through the BS and cutting right to the chase.

"Why not here? Why not now?" I responded, knowing it really irked the ranger when I answered his questions with questions of my own. It also gave me time to come up with some plausible explanations. Well, semi-plausible.

"For one thing, your sister here gets dizzy if she stands up too fast," Townsend pointed out, and I saw Taylor flinch.

"Now I wouldn't say that—," Taylor began.

"Secondly, considering the one-woman thug magnet you seem to have become, it probably isn't a good idea to go gallivanting all over northern Arizona without letting anyone know," Townsend continued.

"Especially in someone else's automobile," Sophie interjected.

I looked at the face of each of my jurors in turn. Seemed like someone was always weighing every action I took, and indicting me for one offense or another.

"Uh, we did let someone know," I said. "Taylor left a note, or you nice supportive folks wouldn't be here now." I paused. "Considering this reception, maybe next time I won't bother to leave a note."

Townsend took a step in my direction. "If you have a death wish, Tressa, that's one thing. You're an adult," Townsend said, and I couldn't help but notice the slightest hesitation when he got to the word *adult*. "But don't involve innocent children in your over-the-top escapades."

I staggered back a step and stared at Nick Townsend. Why, the no-good little snitch! He'd gone running straight to Uncle Rick as fast as his knobby little knees could carry him and blabbed everything. The Snow-bowl. Raphael. The clue. The foot chase. Tressa being towed.

And innocent? That kid was about as innocent as O.J.

"I'll have you know your 'innocent' nephew there blackmailed me into taking him along," I told Townsend with a sneer.

"Oh yeah. How'd he do that?"

"He threatened me."

"Threatened you? How could a ten-year-old threaten you?" Townsend asked, crossing his arms across his chest and waiting for my response.

"He said he'd narc me out to you and Whitehead," I said. "And while I knew what I was getting with you, frankly I didn't trust the ranger woman. Any gal brazen enough to slip some guy she just met her card, and to set up a date with him with the girl he'd brought to the party standing right there didn't inspire confidence. Or confidences."

"I see. You didn't trust me enough to let me know what was going on," Townsend said.

"I didn't trust Whitehead," I corrected him. "Plus, I wasn't even sure I wasn't chasing a phantom story," I said. "I wanted to be sure."

"Sure of this story? Or sure of me?" Townsend asked. "Or sure that I wasn't in a position to stop you from putting yourself at risk once again? There's a word for people like you, Tressa," Townsend said.

"Investigative journalist? Adventurer? Soldier of truth?" I suggested.

"Impulsive, sensation-seeking, neurotic risk-taker," Taylor, ex-psychology student turned short-order cook, supplied. I shot a quick *screw you* look at her.

"You don't get it, do you, Tressa?" Townsend said, running an agitated hand through his dark brown head of hair. "If you keep chasing off half-cocked on the latest misadventure that comes your way, you're going to have a sight more than shredded Skechers and ruined Riders to contend with. One of these days you're going to bite off more than even you can chew."

I blinked. "Excuse me. Is that a jab at my overbite?" I said. "Because I'll have you know I went through four years of orthodontic trauma to pull these babies back in place. It's not my fault my jaw kept growing. And as far as leaving you out of the loop, as I recall, Mr. Ranger, sir, I shared my theory about the thefts and Kooky with you early on and your response was to laugh in my face. Like I felt comfortable confiding in you after that! Still, I suppose I ought to be used to that kind of reception from you by now," I added. "Good ol' Calamity Jayne, always good fer a belly laugh. Hardy har har." I moved toe to toe with Ranger Rick. "The only time you aren't laughing at me, buster, is when you're trying to get in my drawers!" I said, poking him in the chest with my index finger. Townsend's mouth popped open. "But now that I think about it, maybe that's just another joke on me, too!" I stepped away. "Sophie. Taylor. I'll be at the car."

I tromped across the lobby of the visitors center with my nose in the air. Interestingly enough, there were no tears to swallow, no snot to suck up, no self-recriminations to recite this time.

I was too damned pee-ohed. It seemed the harder I tried to promote credibility and inspire confidence, the more people were bent on forcing me back into the blond bimbo caricature I'd fought so hard to shed. I frowned. It occurred to me for the first time to wonder whether that dumb blonde persona had not only been comfortable for me for so long, but also, in some bizarre way, equally as comfortable to those around me. After all, it was the yardstick, the known and unchanging constant by which I'd been observed and measured for so many years. I never considered it might take others some time to catch up and come to terms with a new and improved rubric for evaluating a new and improved Tressa Jayne.

But how much longer did I have to wait? At this rate I'd receive my due in credibility right about the same time as my first social security check. If I lived that long. According to Townsend, if I kept up my 'sensation-seeking risk-taking' I'd be pushing up daisies long before I reached retirement age. Nice.

I leaned on the car and fumed. Sophie and Taylor showed up a few minutes later.

"Where to?" Sophie asked, getting behind the wheel and buckling up, adjusting the rearview mirror so she could make eye contact with me in the back seat. I had let Taylor have the front so she wouldn't get pukey again.

I raised my eyebrows. "Why ask me?" I said. "I only still have to buy a dress for a wedding in two days and tame the wild beast I call a head of hair. Oh, and there's also the little matter of figuring out the significance of *this* little beauty," I said, holding up the turquoise necklace while Sophie did a double take. "Some people might say I discovered this here charm as the result of my neurotic need for impulsive sensation-seeking risk-taking misadventures. Then again, it could be that I discovered it as the result of Clue Numero Uno in an *Amazing Race* Arizona-style. Hmmm. And there's always the issue of the latest clue I just discovered taped to a seat in the IMAX theater that still needs to be decoded and followed up on. But I imagine you two ladies have other, more important things on your agenda for the day, so you know, whatever you two want to do is peachy keen with me." I sat back. "I'm just along for the ride."

Sophie's body did a one-eighty in her seat—not easy

considering her girth and the steering wheel. "Let me get this straight. You're telling me you were right about Kookamunga?" she asked.

"Kookamunga?" Taylor said.

"Someone *was* after him?"

"After whom?"

"He did hold a secret?"

"What secret? What are you two talking about?" Taylor didn't bother to hide her exasperation.

I looked at her. "I'm not sure I should share the details," I said. "I wouldn't want to put you innocent children at risk."

"Would someone please tell me what the hell is going on?" Taylor yelled, and I looked at her with wide eyes. Holy shat. Taylor never swore. Not ever.

"Maybe it would be safer if you just went back inside and waited for Ranger Rick to conquer the rapids and take you home, Taylor," I said, reaching up and patting her on the shoulder. "Like a good little girl."

"Screw you, Tressa!" Taylor shrieked, and I sat back stunned.

Hello, Sybil. This was a side of Taylor I'd never seen. Not certain if I should scold or applaud like crazy, I opted to let it go.

"Rick did say he wanted us to hang around until they got done so he could have a nice long talk with you, Tressa," Sophie said. I made a face. I'd been the guest of honor at more than a few of Townsend's nice long chats, and frankly, I failed to find anything remotely nice about them. Unless it was the way his nostrils flared and his pupils dilated and the way his dark hair fell over his forehead when he banged his head. Sigh.

"Tressa?"

I shook myself out of my trance and removed the latest clue from my pocket and opened it. A colorful piece of pottery fell into my palm.

"Well, would you look at this?" I said. "Hmm. Looks like it might've broken off a larger piece. Could be a pot."

"Let me see that!" Sophie snatched the pottery piece out of my hand.

"I'm no authority, but this looks real," she said.

I frowned. "Of course it's real. Did you think I imagined it?" I asked. "I admit I've got a pretty vivid imagination, but even I can't make other people see things that aren't there."

"Oh, for the love of—"

Taylor took the pottery from Sophie and looked at it. "I think what Sophie means is that this appears to be an actual artifact," Taylor said. "Not from a recent piece, but from a much more distant past."

I sat back up and leaned over the seat. "How distant?" I asked.

Taylor and Sophie shook their heads.

"Too distant to not be in a museum somewhere, I'm thinking," Sophie said. "Dad would know."

I put a hand to the turquoise necklace hanging between my boobs. "Do you mean that the pieces I've found are actual, honest to spirit-in-the-sky, bona fide artifacts made by the hands of the inhabitants of this area long, long ago?" I asked.

"Why else would they be of such urgency to someone?"

"But what are they doing taped in public places where only someone with these clues can find them?" I asked, still not on top of what we were dealing with.

Sophie shook her head. "I'm not sure why all the intrigue," she said. "But I know safeguarding Native American artifacts is a constant problem. Smuggling rare and valuable Hopi or Navajo artifacts is a lucrative business. People will pay a lot of money for authentic Native American artifacts."

"So, what are you saying? That we stumbled onto an illegal smuggling ring?" I asked.

"I don't know what I'm saying. We can't know what any of this means until we find out if these two pieces are true artifacts," she said. "But, one thing we do know: It all started with Kookamunga."

"Okay, that's it." Taylor reached over and yanked Sophie's keys out of the ignition. "You don't get these keys back until someone tells me what the hell you're talking about! Who is this Kookamunga? What is his secret? What clues are you yammering about? And why should we get involved? We're here for a wedding!"

Sophie and I looked at each other.

"I have all the time in the world," Taylor said. "And from the time, I'd say Rick and the kids should be finished in a couple minutes. So what's it going to be, ladies? The truth or the consequences?"

I stared at my sister. I'd never have believed she had it in her to be so underhanded. So tricky. So calculating. So much like . . . me!

"Oh, Taylor," I yelled. "You've made me so happy!" I patted the top of her head. "Now give the keys back to Sophie and I'll tell you everything you say you want to know—and will probably regret asking," I told her.

She gave me a long look and finally handed the keys to Sophie.

"Now, step on it, Soph!" I said.

"Where to?" she asked, starting the car.

I caught the Townsend trio exiting the visitors center in the passenger-side rearview mirror.

"Just drive! Drive!" I yelled. "And don't spare the rubber!"

Sophie peeled out of the parking lot, and I looked back just in time to read Rick Townsend's lips as he jogged in our direction. Tsk, tsk, Mr. Ranger, sir. It didn't take a code-talker to figure out it wasn't role-model language. Not even close.

I filled Taylor in on the events surrounding my acquisition of Kookamunga, the thefts, Raphael, Numbers, (she was so not believing this one) and my suspicions about the fertility figurine. I then took both Sophie and Taylor through finding the clue in the figurine, what the clue said, how the sneaky little backstabber, Nick Townsend, had forced my hand and convinced me to take him along, our encounter with Raphael at the Snowbowl, our inauspicious escape, the precautions I took to protect the newest clue and the necklace, and my tug of war with a masked man, and how that latest clue had brought Taylor and me to the IMAX.

"So that's what was behind all that 'bonding' baloney," Taylor said. "I knew there was more to it. And that ridiculous riddle."

"Hey, you figured it out, sis!" I said. "Bravo! Bravo!" She frowned at me and shook her head. "Well, with the exception of the snake eyes reference, of course, and that was all me."

"Snake eyes. First row. First chair. So that's what you were doing crawling around the IMAX theater like a maniac," Taylor said. "I thought you were going to get us thrown out of the place."

"Like you'd have minded, Miss Bilious," I said, and she shook her head again.

"So, any questions, class?" I asked, in summation.

"Just one," Taylor said, raising her hand as if in school.

"Miss Turner?"

"Why does this stuff keep happening to you?" she asked.

I shrugged. "Only the Good Lord knows and He ain't tellin'," I said. "Maybe it's a gift. You know. Like with Cadence, the spiritual advisor. Okay, so maybe that's not the best example. How about Psychic Sylvia? You can't deny she has a gift. She was on *Montel* a month ago and told this lady she was soon going to be abundantly blessed with the fruits of her labor and she just found out she's pregnant. With triplets! Pretty amazing, huh?"

Sophie and Taylor exchanged looks.

"So, what does the latest clue say?" Sophie asked. "Maybe between the three of us we can figure it out."

I carefully unrolled the latest scroll and read it out loud. " 'Brother, sister, man, wife. Home and hearth are intertwined. Twin sorrows. Twin joys. Mirror images connected by sport. Reflections and wishes. Your reward awaits you here.' " I reread it. "Okay, gotta confess. I got nothin'," I said. "You, Taylor?"

My sister shook her head. "But remember, if we're operating under the theory that these clues are for someone familiar with the area, then we probably wouldn't know some of them," Taylor said. "It was pure dumb luck we knew the first two. And let's face it, they were no-brainers."

Speak for yourself, Einstein.

"So, Soph, anything jump out at you?" I asked.

"Read it once more," Sophie said, and I complied. "There's a little drawing in the corner here, too," I said. "Like a stick figure of an animal or something," I added.

"Let me see," Sophie said, and I gave the clue to Taylor who held it out so Sophie could look at it.

"Crude drawing," she said. "Home and hearth intertwined. Mirror images connected by sport. Oh, my gosh! I think I know where it's talking about!" she screamed. "I think it's Riordan Mansion!"

Taylor and I looked at each other.

"Riordan what?"

"It's a huge old mansion built by two brothers just after the turn of the century," she said, her words matching her driving: fast and furious. "The two logging baron brothers married two sisters and built this spectacular mansion. The two halves of the house are almost mirror images. The two separate living spaces are connected to each other by this huge, magnificent billiard room the two families shared."

I stared at Sophie. "Brother, sister, man, wife. Home and hearth are intertwined. Sophie, I think you could be right!" I yelled, my voice getting high-pitched and squeaky like it does when I discover the Easter Bunny has left a basket of Cadbury Crème eggs on Easter morning. "But what's this about 'twin sorrows'?" I asked.

"I seem to recall something about both families tragically losing a child on the same day due to polio," Sophie said. "It's been a while since I've been to the mansion."

"Is it open now?" I asked. Sophie nodded.

"Should be. They have tours on the hour."

"Okay, so all we have to do is figure out where to look for the next clue once we get there," I said.

"That's the easy part," Sophie said. "Reflections and wishes. Your reward awaits you here. There's a stone fountain on the grounds. There are hidden animal drawings in the fountain, that's where that crudely drawn sketch comes in."

"So all we have to do is get to this Riordan Mansion and snoop around the fountain. Sounds simple enough."

"Doesn't it, though?" Taylor said. "There is one more thing we probably need to do before we hunt down that next clue," she added.

I frowned. "What's that?" I asked.

"Ditch the dark Toyota that's been tailing us since we left the IMAX," Taylor said, and I glanced back.

From what I could see, it looked like the same vehicle I'd hung on to for dear life at the Snowbowl that morning. And that meant the same masked marauder.

"Any ideas?" I asked.

"I could try to lose him," Sophie said, and I shook my head.

"I don't know, Soph. The guy kind of struck me as pretty determined. At least that's what it felt like when I was hanging on to his mirror and being pulled along like some human experiment in friction," I said.

I caught Sophie's expression in the mirror. From the lip biting, she seemed to be considering something carefully.

"There is a place we can go and leave my car," she said, very slowly. "And I know someone there who'll let me borrow theirs," she added.

"Is it a guy named Tristan?" I asked with a slight raise of one eyebrow.

"Oh, great. It's Tristan now," Taylor said. "Why am I always out of the loop?"

"It sounds like a good plan, Sophie," I said. "What do you think, Taylor?"

My little sis turned a cold shoulder on me. "Why ask me? I don't even know who Tristan is," she snapped.

Ouch! The Black Dahlia has thorns! "Let's see. It's daring, reckless, and rife with risk," I said. Which, according to Rick Townsend, exemplified my personality profile. "I say we do it. One for all and all for one, just like the Three Musketeers. Right, ladies?"

The response was underwhelming.

"So, just where are we planning to make this little switcharoo?" I asked Sophie.

She smiled. Or maybe it was a grimace. In the rearview mirror, who could tell?

"Bountiful Babes," Sophie said.

" 'Scuze me?"

"Bountiful Babes. It's a club for discriminating men who appreciate the . . . full-figured woman," Sophie explained.

"You're so gonna have to spoon-feed me on this one, Soph," I said, "because I'm just not quite there."

"Fat! All right?" Sophie hollered so loud I jumped. "Chubby. Plump. Hefty. Obese. Rotund. Stout. Chunky. Fat! You know. What you call 'porkers' back in Iowa! Okay?"

I sat back, my spine pressed against the car seat. "Oh," was all I could think of to say. Well, for all of twelve seconds. Then: "So, how do you know about this heavy-duty hot spot again?" I asked, my query followed by a long, silent pause.

"I know the place," Sophie finally said, "because I work there."

"Oh."

I processed that information. "Oh," I said again once I got the data to compute. And my programming told me this was one chubby, plump, hefty, obese, rotund, stout, chunky, porker of a mess I'd gotten myself into.

Again.

Note: Fat puns used solely for effect.

CHAPTER EIGHTEEN

Sophie drove us to a section of Flagstaff I was unfamiliar with. A handful of colorful nightspots and sports bars dotted the landscape, along with several restaurants and dance clubs. Sophie pulled into an alley behind one of the establishments and parked. I blinked. Long and low, the building resembled the Thunder Rolls Bowling Alley at home.

"This is it?" I asked.

Sophie nodded. "This is where we go in," she said. "Any sign of the Toyota?"

Taylor nodded. "It's still there. I saw him park on the street near the entrance to the alley."

"Good. Then he should get a bird's-eye view of us entering," she said, amazingly at ease with this cloak and dagger stuff. "Ready? Let's hit it, girls."

I shook my head. Bountiful and bitchin'. What a combo.

We entered at the end of a long hallway. In the background I detected your basic bump and grind music that signaled it was time for the late matinee.

Taylor and I followed Sophie down the hall like two trained pups. Taylor kept her eyes riveted on Sophie's back. Me? I cast a curious eye into each room as we passed—purely for professional purposes only, you understand. Hey, reporters observe and then report, guys. I was strictly honing my observational skills.

We walked through a thick door at the end of the hallway. Here the music bitch-slapped us like a cymbal clash in the face. There was a long bar to the left, but what appeared in my peripheral vision to the right snared my attention like the after-Christmas seventy-five-percent-off Christmas candy sales at Wally's World. On a stage approximately five feet off the ground, a dancer clung to a pole—well, what looked like a pole if said pole was the width of a wooden post. Not only was the pole supersized, the dancer was, too.

With long blond hair tumbling down over fleshy shoulders, the queen-sized performer wore a red and black jacquard bustier with a lace-up back that had to accommodate a cup size in the triple letter category, black garters, and a matching G-string. An abundance of white flesh spilled out over the garment's frame, resembling the "over-the-top" poppy seed muffins my gammy made several months back. Talk about your cups runneth over. Yikes!

Sophie headed straight for the bar and Taylor followed, leaving me behind to marvel at how fluid the dancer's moves were, despite the fact that she probably tipped the scale at two hundred-plus pounds. She grabbed the pole with two hands and vaulted onto it. Gripping it with both legs, she twisted and twirled around the pole to the blaring music, her ample thighs intimately hugging the pole. Suddenly she pulled herself up the pole, gripped it with her ankles and let go with her hands to descend ever so slowly upside down. I stared, impressed with the strength and skill required to not only perform the moves but to do them in perfect sync with the music.

"Holy dancing queen!" I said. "Would you look at that!"

I felt a tug at my elbow. "Come on, Tressa," Taylor whispered. "I think you've seen enough. Remember what happened the last time we were in a similar establishment."

I did. Still, Bountiful Babes seemed pretty tame compared to Big Burl's back home.

We watched the performance for several more minutes until Sophie joined us.

"That's Tiny Dancer," Sophie said, and I looked at her.

"Tiny Dancer?"

Sophie nodded. "That's her stage name. Pretty good, isn't she?"

This time I nodded. I'd be lucky if I could manage a quarter of the moves she'd just performed so fluidly. And that upside-down number? Even with rock-solid thighs honed from years on the back of a horse, I'd probably look more like an inebriated firefighter than an exotic dancer. And likely end up snapping my spine.

"She's awesome," I said. "How does she do that?"

"Tons of practice," Sophie said, and I remembered her earlier remark about working here.

"You don't meant to say . . . ," I stammered. "Can you really . . . ? Do you . . . ? Are you . . . ?"

"Don't get your knickers in a knot, cous," Sophie said. "I mainly serve drinks. But I have strutted my stuff a time or two on amateur night," she added. "It's great exercise, and it's nice to be ogled by men out of appreciation rather than revulsion for a change. And from what I hear, I'm not half bad."

Whoa. I looked at Sophie and then at the stage. This was so not what I was expecting to hear.

"So this is what you've been hiding," I said. "And how you can afford designer bags and shoes?"

She shrugged. "Our clientele is generous, so the tips are great. Our club is the only one that caters to men who truly believe big is beautiful and can express their appreciation without being ridiculed," she said.

I watched as Tiny Dancer finished her performance and the dozen or so patrons applauded and expressed their approval with lucre. I found myself thinking a G-string that size could hold a heck of a lot of greenbacks. Tiny Dancer accepted their tokens and exited stage left.

"Come on," Sophie said. "I'll introduce you to Ellie. She's a sweetheart."

We followed Sophie back the way we came in and stopped at a door to our left.

"Knock, knock," Sophie said with a tap on the door. "You decent, El?" she asked.

"I hope to hell not," I heard, followed by a chuckle. "Come on in, Sugar 'n' Spice Girl."

Taylor and I exchanged looks.

"My stage name," Sophie said with a shrug.

"Catchy," I said.

"I thought so, too," Sophie remarked. She motioned us into a long room that resembled a beauty salon with four stations, sans the sinks. Bright lights illuminated each makeup station. Tiny Dancer a.k.a. Ellie sat in front of a mirror blotting her face with a tissue. I admit it. I gawked. She seemed so comfortable with her body I felt ashamed that I wasn't more at ease with my own perceived physical shortcomings and imperfections.

"Hey, girlfriend, what you doing here today? I thought you took a week off," El said.

Sophie nodded. "I did but I need a favor," she said, introducing us and explaining that she needed to borrow Ellie's car to run an errand.

"Sure thing, Spice," Ellie said. "No sweat. I'm on 'til ten, anyway. It's parked out front. What's the deal?"

"You recall the fan that followed you around last summer?" Sophie asked, and Tiny Dancer nodded.

"Do I ever! Every time I looked in my rearview mirror I swear the little dick was there. He had it bad. Finally took my boyfriend hiding in the backseat while I drove around and then jumping out to threaten the wiener to get him to stop. Poor little guy peed in his pants," Ellie said. "My boyfriend's a third-round draft pick for the Arizona Cardinals," she explained for my benefit and Taylor's.

"Actually our guy is after Tressa here," Sophie said, pointing to me. Tiny Dancer raised a meticulously constructed eyebrow. "You're Tressa, right?" she said, addressing Taylor, who shook her head and pointed to me.

"She's Tressa."

Ellie looked at me. "You look like you got a set of sturdy thighs," she said. "You ever do any dancing?" she asked.

"Does around the truth count?" I said, with a you-gotta-be-joking snort.

Ellie smiled. "You got 'tude," she said. "You could go a long way in this business."

"I could?" I blinked, trying to picture me dressed in a black bustier, garters, and black boots, with a long, shiny pole between my legs. Calamity Jayne. Have love handles, will dance.

"You'd need to gain some l.b.'s," Tiny Dancer said. "And do something about that hair."

I put a hand to my head. "It's also got 'tude'," I said, with a long-suffering sigh.

Ellie and Sophie exchanged keys and hugs, and we hurried out the front door and over to a black Lexus. Automobile envy hit me hard. Shaking your groove thing, it seemed, was quite lucrative. Even if you had a Pillsbury doughgirl body type.

Sweet.

This time I hopped in front, giving Taylor the back-seat. We buckled up and Sophie pulled out. It was only about a fifteen-minute drive to the Riordan Mansion. My mouth flew open as I caught my first peek of the rambling, rustic log home. Talk about your Ponderosas. I expected to see Hoss or Little Joe rush out to greet me—Adam often being away from the ranch due to contract disputes, according to Gram.

"What a rocking ranch house!" I said, exiting the car and staring at the sprawling structure. "I could see me living in a place like this. Can't you, Taylor?" I asked my sister. "Can't you picture me as the lady of the manor?"

She walked over to me, holding her head as she moved. "Yeah. Sure. I see it now," she said, putting one hand up. "You standing out front of your country home in your bib overalls, a lasso above your head. A contemporary cowgirl. Grant Wood heads west. A real "American Gothic." Now, can we get this hunt under-way? I've got a killer headache."

"Well, excuse me for wanting to take in a little local color on the way," I complained. "Sheesh." I turned to Sophie. "So, where is this fountain?" I asked and Sophie's brows became one.

"It's been a while since I've been here, but I think it's around the corner of the house over there," Sophie pointed out.

"Good thing it's early in the season or we'd probably have tourists up the yin yang to contend with," I said, jogging down the path near the house. "If the clue culprit operates true to form, we should find some-thing taped to the fountain," I said. I turned to Sophie who huffed and puffed on one side of me and Taylor who flanked me on the other. "Isn't this fun? Three cousins tracking down clues in a puzzle worthy of Holmes," I said.

"Holmes? Who? Katie?" Taylor asked.

Reearr! Someone was crabby.

Sophie grabbed my arm. "Slow down! Slow down! We don't want to attract a lot of undue attention. If we come galloping up like a loco posse from Hicksville, USA, we might as well be wearing bandanas over our noses and mouths and holding six-guns yelling 'This is a stickup!'" she said. "Just take it nice and easy. Catch your breath. Get a grip. And remember, Calamity, I've got to live here long after you've left and gone back to raising hell in the Heartland."

"I feel so loved," I said, with a hand to my heart as I grudgingly slowed my pace to match Sophie's strides.

"There it is!" my cousin said. "There it is!"

I couldn't help but feel a certain amount of smugness at the excitement in her voice. I followed her pointing finger and frowned when I saw a couple gazing into each other's eyes like two lovesick pups.

"Sit rep. Two lovebirds. Stone birdbath. Six o'clock," I reported, feeling very: *Bond, Jane Bond.*

Sophie and Taylor looked at each other and shook their heads. I shrugged. Party poopers.

"Okay, so what's the plan?" Taylor asked. I frowned.

"Plan? Plan? We don't need no stinkin' plan!" I said.

Sophie and Taylor looked at me.

"Okay, okay, you want a plan. Fine. Why don't we just divide the fountain in thirds and each of us check out our respective sections for anything unusual, and we'll know we're done when we butt heads," I suggested.

"Okay. And what if we find something? What do we do about the lovers?" Sophie asked.

"Drown them in the fountain, of course," I said, thinking the situation was spiraling out of control if people were looking to me for strategy. "You take the female, I'll handle the gent."

Taylor started tapping one toe, which is never a good sign.

"Okay, okay, just injecting some humor into an otherwise stressful situation," I said. "And the answer is . . . first we run 'em off, then we search."

"How are we going to do that?" Sophie asked. "They seem content where they are."

And they did. It looked like they were trying to swallow each other's tongues.

"We could go over and get in a big argument. You know. A catfight," I suggested. "That would send them packing."

"And right to the security guy, as well," Sophie said.

I tried again: "How about one of us begins a conversation with them? You know. Spoil the mood."

"I vote you as the candidate most likely to succeed in the mood-spoiling category," Sophie said. "And you are also better at BS on the fly than Taylor or me. Besides, I have to—"

"I know. I know," I interrupted, waving a hand. "You have to live here. Fine. I'll do it. But while I have the amorous couple occupied, you two start nosing around."

We agreed that I should go first so it wouldn't be obvious that we were together. At least that's what I took Sophie's "not be seen together" comment to mean. I straightened my braid, squared my shoulders and once more into the breach I ventured.

I approached the fountain. The clinching couple continued to clasp. Ah, romance. Ain't it grand?

I motioned to Sophie and Taylor to begin their examination of the fountain while the lovers only had eyes for each other. Sophie took the higher points of the fountain while Taylor got down on her hands and knees to examine its base. I gave them high marks for their technique.

I watched the woo-some twosome exchange a couple more kisses. They must've picked up on my perusal, as the woman's eyes opened and her gaze fell on me. She broke off the kiss, put a hand to her mouth and took a step back from her boyfriend.

"Hey," I said, waving a hand and smiling. "Nice day."

The dark-haired woman's companion turned in my direction. "Oh, er, hullo," the fortyish fellow said.

"Hi. I'm Tressa," I said, putting out a hand, deciding to take a page out of Nick Townsend's *How to Irritate Without Breaking a Sweat* manual. "This is a fantastic place. Do you come here often? Have you seen Ben Cartwright around?" I asked, with a cute little guffaw. I shook my head. "Naw, he's probably off finding another beautiful young wife to bring home to the Ponderosa so she can up and die on him before they can celebrate their first anniversary." I snorted. "Arizona is awesome. Have you been to Oak Creek Canyon? It's really cool, too, even though I did get mugged there. Have you ever been to Numbers? It's a really hot night spot. They have five-minute speed dates. My cousin got her designer handbag lifted there. Have you been to the Grand Canyon yet? We just went to the IMAX theater. My sister got sick. She didn't actually hurl in the theater itself, but it was a close call."

I finally had to stop to catch my breath. Being irritating by running off at the mouth was harder work than I thought it would be. Even for a seasoned, trained, professional motormouth like me. There's always a first time for everything, huh, folks?

I continued to smile at the couple in the friendly, open way that I have when I realized their smiles resembled the one I got when I went to one of those home jewelry parties expecting your typical heartland spread (meaning not particularly heart-healthy), only to find the hostess was on a low-fat, no carbs, organic kick. Her sales were disappointing that night, let me tell you.

I glanced down at the left hand of the Riordan Ranch Romeo and noticed a gold wedding band—its corresponding mate conspicuously absent on the ring finger of the young lady with whom he'd just been swapping spit.

I frowned. Whoo, doggy! It appeared we'd stumbled on a illicit little afternoon encounter of the cheatin' kind. Hey, don't get me wrong, folks, I'm no Pollyanna, but where I come from you leave the dance with the one who brung ya. Marriage vows are taken as seriously as the markets. The way I figure it, you don't try out a new mount when you've got a perfectly good one waiting at home. And if said "stud" can't resist following through on those baser instincts, the honorable thing to do is cut your former filly loose before you toss a lasso around another little mare.

Sometimes horse sense is all you need.

"Hey, I have an idea," I told the misbehavin' man and little Ms. Mistress. "I'm a journalist, and I'm doing one of your basic travel pieces. I thought of calling it 'Arizona Ambience.'" I pulled my digital camera out of my javelina backpack. "You two southwestern sweethearts would add just the right romantic touch to the article. If you wouldn't mind, that is?" I added.

"You want to take a picture of us and include it in an article?" the philandering fellow asked, taking off his glasses to wipe his brow with the back of his hand. He shook his head. "I don't think so," he said, "but thanks for the offer."

"Oh, come on," I said. "Let's ask the better half here. I bet she'd love to have an opportunity to see a picture of you two splashed across the pages of the *Ari-*

zona Daily Sun and posted on the Internet for family and friends to see and enjoy. What do you say? The title heading could read, 'Lovebirds quench their thirst at historic fountain.' Okay, so maybe the headline needs work, but you see where I'm going with the piece," I added. "How about it?"

"Hmm. Maybe it's not such a bad idea, Donald dear," the woman said. "You know. Get *us* out there. As a couple. You keep saying you're just waiting for the right time and place to make it official. I say, that time and place is here and now."

I stared. The sound of the gauntlet being dropped in this little drama was deafening.

Mr. Married but Acting Single shook his head.

"My god, Marti, you can't be serious. The Daily Sun? The Internet? Trudy would have a field day with that. I'd never hear the end of it. She'd use it to pummel me for the next thirty years!"

Little Miss Lovebird took a step back.

"Thirty years? Thirty years! I thought you were going to divorce her as soon as she finished her master's," she said. "You said it was only fair, considering she put you through med school." The lady lovebird looked like she'd just happened onto a bad seed. "Why, you no good, lying bastard!" she hissed. "You never had any intention of divorcing your wife, did you? All that talk about us being together was all bullshit, wasn't it, Dr. Feelgood?" The distraught woman's face was red and blotchy, her hands poised like talons, ready to rip into the closest object. I took a discreet step back.

"Marti, please be reasonable! Let me explain!" the hypocritical—or is that hippocratical—physician pleaded.

Marti shot him a look that left little hope that reason would figure into her next move. "Here's a head-

line for you, sweetie," she said, turning to me. " 'Prominent plastic surgeon takes dip in historic fountain,' "
she said, and suddenly planted both hands against the
doc's chest and shoved him backwards off his feet and
into the water. He sputtered and floundered about in
the fountain while his now ex-lover looked on and
nodded. "Too bad you're in print media. That
would've made a hell of a YouTube video," she said,
clapping her hands together in a gesture signifying a
job well done. "So long, Dr. Dick!" she said to the man
trying to retrieve his floating spectacles from the pool
and stalked off.

I watched as the medical professional pulled himself
out of the fountain and shook like my pooches do
when they've been in the farm pond.

"Wait! Marti!" Dr. Dumped raised a hand and hurried off after the woman scorned. "Marti! We drove
your car!" he yelled. "Wait!"

I shook my head. Oh, what a tangled web we weave,
I thought, moving quickly to the fountain. "Mission ac-
complished, ladies!" I said with a tap of my heels and a
salute.

Taylor shook her head. "Only you could take a romantic interlude and turn it into a scene from *Ti-
tanic*," she said. "And I'm not talking the love scene,"
she said. "I'm talking 'we're going down, we're going
down!' "

"You may find fault with my methods, but you can't
argue with results," I told her.

"Shut up and hunt for the clue before someone else
comes by and Tressa has to get rid of them, too," Sophie urged. "Frankly, I don't want to see any more ex-
amples of Tressa securing the area. That one was
brutal enough."

"Wait! I found something!" Taylor yelled. "It's here
near the base of the fountain! It's a box!"

"Hurry up! Grab it! Someone's coming!" I warned, hearing voices on the path.

"I'm trying! The guy used duct tape! If I can just get a corner up . . ." Taylor said.

"Hurry!" I urged. "I'm not real thrilled with running interference again. Even though I do appear to have a natural gift for it," I added.

"Come on, Taylor, pull!" Sophie urged, and the next thing I knew Taylor was flat on her back, holding a small box about an inch thick and about the size of a single-serving pizza. Thick crust. "Let's go!" Sophie cried, holding out a hand and hauling my sister to her feet. "But hide that box before anyone sees it!"

Taylor looked around wildly and tried to stick it under her tight-fitting hoodie. I shook my head. Being a twig had some limitations.

"Give it to me," I ordered, taking it and shoving it inside my hoodie and pulling the zipper up over it.

"Can we go now?" Sophie asked. I shook my head.

"First we need a photographic record of our moment here at the Ponderosa," I said, pulling my camera out. "Now smile pretty for the camera and say *Bonanza!*" I ordered. After snapping the picture of my very reluctant models, I reviewed the photo and shook my head. "Dr. Dick would've made a more enthusiastic subject," I said, "and he was all wet. You know, Taylor, you're usually more photogenic," I pointed out. "You look like you caught a whiff of butt stink in this picture."

Taylor gave me a long, unpleasant look and set off on the path ahead of me with Sophie right behind. I followed in their wake.

Jeesh. Supermodels and pole dancers can be so touchy.

CHAPTER NINETEEN

"So long, Hoss!" I performed the queen's wave as we motored away from the Riordan ranch. "Keep an eye on Little Joe!" I carefully unwrapped the box Taylor had discovered. "It's a basket," I said. "Kind of. It's really pretty." I handed it to Taylor and she showed it to Sophie.

"It looks like a basket tray," Sophie said. "Made of grass and yucca leaves. I'm thinking Hopi. What does the clue say?"

"'Divining much but seeing little. Foretelling futures while raiding the past. A gift for gleaning corrupted. Sold to the highest bidder. Lost generations cry out. Defile us not!'" I shivered. "Talk about your somber turns," I said. "Hello, how do you say creep me out?"

"Is that it?" Sophie asked.

"There's more written at the bottom," I said. '"Your quest ends where it once began.'"

"That sure doesn't give us much to go on."

"It sounds like they're talking about some kind of

spiritualist," Taylor said. "That 'divining much' part along with the 'foretelling futures' and 'gleaning' bits. Could be we're talking about a psychic or spiritual adviser here," Taylor said.

"Oh, great. And we only have about one thousand and three of those in the greater northern Arizona area," Sophie grumbled.

"Ah-ha. But only one I know about who has a basket tray thingy almost identical to this one," I said, and Sophie reached up and adjusted the rearview mirror so she could make eye contact with me.

"You're kidding," she said. "Cadence of Spiritual Boutique fame?" she asked. I nodded.

"She had an item like this in her back room," I said. "I saw it when Gram and I went in for her thirty-second consult." I reread the clue. It gave me only slightly less chilly-willy chills than before. "Raiding the past. Raiding the past," I repeated. "I think maybe you were on the right track earlier when you were talking about the artifact smuggling, Soph," I said. " 'Lost generations crying out defile us not'? My take is that someone's screwing with some serious karmic shinola here where paybacks could be of the metaphysical kind."

"You know, a spiritual adviser's business would make a pretty effective front for a smuggling ring," Sophie said. "It would provide a place to traffic the stolen artifacts. Buyers could actually be posing as clients and could transact business under the guise of a spiritual checkup."

"And don't forget online business. Many of these advisers have Web sites and probably provide long-distance advice to their clients, as well. They could easily box up artifacts and send them out as client products along with their crystals, potions, books, and tapes," Taylor added.

"Potions?" I raised an eyebrow, and Taylor shrugged.

"Whatever," she said.

"So our theory is that someone had the goods on a gang of artifact smugglers, and for some reason put information they had in different areas of northern Arizona, beginning with a rather unattractive fertility figurine? That figurine is left at a roadside stand for someone else to pick up, perhaps when the heat is off. However, yours truly gets there first and I buy the figurine out from under the nose of that guy. So, is the guy who hid the clues and the artifacts one of the good guys or one of the bad guys?" I asked. "And if a good guy, wouldn't that also make the person who went to retrieve the figurine a good guy? And if that is the case, then, conceivably, couldn't Raphael actually be gorgeous and be one of the good guys, too? Huh. What are the odds of that? If that's what we're saying." I rubbed a throbbing temple. "Is that what we're saying?" I asked.

"Beats me," Sophie responded. "I'm still trying to figure out what the devil you just said."

"Ditto," said Taylor, who usually caught on much quicker.

"What I'm saying, ladies, is we need to pay a call on Cadence at The Spiritual Boutique," I told Sophie and Taylor. "Maybe lean on her a little bit to see if she caves. Do some nosing around. See if we can find anything to confirm our suspicions. Plus, that would give me an opportunity to finally have that wedge of Chocolate Fantasy Delight cake I've been denied. How about it, women? Shall we take up the battle cry for those poor unfortunate lost souls who cry out, 'defile us not'?" I blinked. "By the way, what exactly does 'defile' entail?" I asked. " 'Cause my 'eeww-gross' meter is registering some significant activity."

"In this case? Something along the lines of dishonoring something or someone. To desecrate, dishonor, despoil or debase," Taylor said by way of edification, and I winced. Too many d-words, which so wouldn't add up to your basic good time had by all.

"If we don't agree, you'll go anyway, won't you?" Taylor said, and I nodded vigorously, all the while thinking no way in hell would I go off on this little southwestern scavenger hunt by my lonesome when people in scary death masks were tracking me like hunters on the trail of a prized rack. Uh, I'm talking antlers here, for those of you who had something else in your heads. But thanks for the compliment just the same.

"You bet your sweet patooties I'll go on my own!" I claimed, lying my lily-white rear off. "We're on to something huge here. Something meaningful and worthy and deserving of our continued resolve to get to the truth. Something bigger than the three of us," I added.

"Another notch on your journalist coup stick?" Taylor asked, and I put a hand to my heart.

"You wound me, my sister," I said. "The jab of your distrust pierces me like a lance to the heart. Tell me, what have I done to foster such painful suspicion?" I asked.

"Hmm. How have you deceived me? Let me count the ways," Taylor said, putting up a finger to delineate point one.

I shook my head. "Good grief, can't you recognize your classic hypothetical question when you hear it, Taylor?" I asked. "Don't go all literal on me, for goodness' sake. Not when we're dealing with vortices——" I saw Sophie wince. "I mean 'vortexes' and auras and energy fields and spirit guides and afterlives and guys in scary masks. You need to suspend belief for the present."

Taylor gave me a sour look. "Lord knows I've had a lot of practice doing that whenever I'm around you."

I nodded. "Good deal. Then we're set." I said. "Old hat and all that."

Taylor shook her head.

We returned to Bountiful Babes. Sophie drove around and around the establishment to make sure the coast was clear before we parked and switched cars again.

"You know, I'm getting a not-great feeling about this little trip," Sophie said as we headed once more for Sedona.

"That's good," I said. "Most of the time when we expect the worst, things turn out just fine. So, keep thinking those bad thoughts, Soph," I told her.

And me? I'd been thinking how best to lord it over Ranger Rick Townsend and Officer Whitebreast when I—uh, I mean *we* cracked the case of the Kookamunga clues and stopped the unforgivable desecration, despoiling, debasing, and defiling of relics that belong to this land and its people, not in some rich, selfish, lowdown, dirty rotten son of a polecat's private collection.

I hear ya. That's bull talk for a cockeyed cowgirl. Right? Oh ye of little faith.

On the way back down the switchbacks, Sophie very nearly scared my black hipsters off me, taking those twists and turns at a speed I personally felt was way too fast. Taylor must've held a similar opinion, because by the time we got to Sedona and parked, we had to massage her fingers to loosen them from the upholstery.

"Sweet ride!" I told Sophie as we rubbed the circulation back into Taylor's fingers.

"You should've ridden up front," my sister said. "For the full effect," she added.

"Next time," I promised myself. "Next time."

Dusk found us back at the door of The Spiritual Boutique. A sign in the window—highly-charged neon green hands that gripped a glowing hot-coals orange orb meant to be the earth—added to the *we're not in Iowa anymore* ambience.

"I'd feel better if we had a plan set up going in," Taylor said. "I'm not a big fan of winging it," she added, giving me a grumpy look.

"I don't know. Winging it worked out pretty well with the lovebirds," I pointed out with a chuckle. "Pun, like, *so* intended." Gotta love me. In the midst of strategizing, I've still got it. "I say we go in and confront her with what we know."

"You mean with what we suspect," Sophie corrected. "It's all still conjecture at this point. We can't prove a thing."

"That's what we're here to do. Prove I'm right. Uh, I mean *we're* right," I amended.

"Right. Right," Sophie said with a raised brow. "Let's just play it by ear, what do you say?"

I nodded. "You're playing my song now, girlfriend. My improvisation is a real crowd pleaser," I added with a wink.

"Great. You can be the opening act, then," Sophie said, stepping aside and motioning to the boutique door. "After you, Magoo," she said. I grimaced. I really needed to know when to muzzle myself.

"Roger that," I said, reaching out to open the door. "Cadence? Hello? Miss Spiritual Adviser? Yoo-hoo! Anyone here?"

"Yoo hoo? Do people in Iowa still say 'yoo-hoo'?" Sophie asked as we stepped into the boutique.

"Affirmative. We're also partial to 'yippee,' 'yahoo,' 'woo-hoo' and 'yee haw' when the occasions call for it," I said. "Helloo! Anybody here?"

"That's strange," Taylor said. "I wonder where she is. It's not smart to go off and leave your business unlocked, especially with so many out-of-towners."

"Cadence?" I said, and made my way over to the

beaded doorway Gram and I had gone through the last time we were here. "Hello? Anybody in there?" I said, sticking out a hand to pull the beads aside.

"Come out, come out wherever you are," Sophie said, and I turned to give her a dark look and she shrugged.

"The occasion called for it," she said.

I moved through the beaded door and toward the room where Gram never got her spiritual checkup. Thank God.

"Cadence, are you in here?" I said, pushing the door open. I could feel warm breath on the back of my neck and could only pray it was Sophie's or Taylor's. "Hello?"

The room was illuminated by the tiny flames of more than a dozen candles, creating an eerie glow like a hundred tiny fireflies.

"Cadence?" I said, squinting in the dark to see. I took a step and my foot slipped out from under me, and I found myself sliding across the floor like a Disney Goofy on Ice move. I attempted to gain traction and frowned. What the devil?

The light suddenly came on.

"The better to see with, my dear," Sophie said, and I could sense skittishness in her voice.

"Thanks," I said, taking the opportunity to look down to see what I'd stepped in.

"Oh my god, would you look at that!" I heard Sophie's strangled cry before I could focus my line of sight downwards.

"It . . . it . . . it looks like . . . blood!" Taylor said, and I forced myself to look down at my defiled Skechers. The tan leather shoes were surrounded by a dark red pool. I began to shake.

"That's a lot of blood," Sophie said. "Do you think it

could be from a nosebleed?" she asked, wishful thinking pathetically evident in her voice.

"Only if she had a schnozz the size of a pachyderm,"
I said.

"Maybe she cut herself. You know. Accidentally,"
Taylor said, "and she had to leave in a hurry to get
stitched up."

I shook my head. "I don't think so."

"How come?" Taylor and Sophie asked.

"Well, for one thing, because of the crystal ball on
the floor over there. The one that looks like it might
have bits of hair, scalp, and, if I'm not mistaken, some
brain matter stuck to it," I said. "That's kind of how
come."

Dead silence followed for several long, heavy heart-
beats.

"Oh," Taylor and Sophie said.

"Oh, holy-let's-get-the-hell-out-of-here, you mean," I
said, backing out of the room, leaving footprints in
blood that could lead a blind tracker to my door. Taylor and Sophie slowly backed out behind me. Down
the hallway and back toward the beaded curtain and
the storefront we trekked bass-ackwards. I'd just
pushed my butt through the beads when I heard a
sound at the back door of the boutique. I looked up,
startled, my heart pounding in my chest so hard I was
lucky it didn't impale itself on a rib. A face stared at
me though the glass of the door. The face of death.

"Aaaagh!" I screamed, and pivoted and barreled
toward the front door with the force of a stampede of
spooked beef sensing a slaughterhouse ahead. "Run!"
I yelled. "Run!"

That was all the prompting required. My comrades
hit the front door like Hannibal Lecter had just announced dinner was served. A short struggle in the

doorway ensued when Taylor and Sophie tried to ne-
gotiate who would exit first, resulting in a temporary
logjam—for only as long as it took me to get to the
door and break it (the logjam, not the door) with a
red rover move I'm notorious for. I shoved Taylor and
Sophie aside and barreled through the exit and down
the steps. After a few frenzied, frustrating, terror-filled
seconds waiting for Sophie to beep the blankety-blank
car doors open, we piled in and locked the doors. Sophie started the car, slammed the vehicle in reverse,
hit the accelerator and drove away.

We sat inside the dark interior listening to the
sounds of our labored breathing.

Taylor, the two-year psych student, finally broke the
silence: "Okay, let's assess the situation, make some
observations about what just happened and where we
stand," she said, sounding way too calm, cool, and collected for what we'd just experienced.

"Well, I learned one thing for sure," I said. "Cadence the spiritual seer is piss-poor at predicting the
future."

"How do you know that?" Sophie asked, finding her
voice.

"She never saw that crystal ball coming," I said, "or
she sure as hell would've ducked."

We discussed several options for how to proceed,
and decided we had no choice but to call 911 and report the missing spiritualist and the evidence of foul
play.

"You can use a pay phone, Tressa," Sophie said, and
I stared at her.

"*I* can use a pay phone? Me? Why me? Why should I
be the one to call?" I asked.

"You've already left bloody footprints all over the
scene," Sophie pointed out, "so you're already impli-
cated. Besides, you were the only one to see the dude

in the mask at the door," she added. "And don't forget, I have to—"

"Live here," I finished. "I know."

We drove to a restaurant and I made the call from the lobby, reporting a prowler in a Hopi death mask behind The Spiritual Boutique and a possible burglary at that location; then I ran back to Sophie's car.

"We'll have to wait for the police, you know," I told my two deputies. "And give them the information we have. The artifacts and the clues. We might as well go back to The Boutique and get it over with." In a way I was glad to be able to hand over the quest to the professionals. Besides, it looked like we were at the end of the trail, anyway, as far as clues went.

Sophie's cell phone began to ring and she answered.

"Hello? No. No, he's not with us. No. I haven't seen him. Just a minute." Sophie put the phone down and turned to Taylor and me. "Did either of you happen to speak to Nick Townsend at the IMAX earlier? Did he say anything about his plans for later in the day? What he might be doing?" she asked. We both shook our heads.

"No, but I generally try to avoid the varmint," I said. "Why?"

"Apparently, they can't find the little guy. They thought maybe he'd tricked his way into coming along with us." She put the phone back to her ear. "No. No one here has had contact with him since the IMAX. How long has he been missing?" Sophie asked. "That long, huh? You know kids, maybe he's out on the grounds or exploring some of the hiking trails and lost track of time. Okay. Sure. We'll be right there. Yep. Bye." Sophie hung up the phone. "Mom wants us back at The Titan ASAP to help search for Nick."

"How long has he been missing?" I asked, thinking there was a chance the little buzzard had pulled this disappearing act to gain attention.

"They saw him at dinner, and afterwards he said he was going to check out the visitors center, but he hadn't returned to the hotel. They've alerted the hotel security to assist in locating him. So far, nothing," Sophie said with a worried wrinkle creasing her brow.

"I think, under the circumstances, we'd better get back to The Titan," I said. "I can always turn myself in once we find the kid," I added. Comforting thought.

I found myself praying that Nick Townsend *had* pulled one of his asinine, adolescent, attention-seeking stunts, and that he was sitting somewhere eating a candy bar and star-gazing. But like it or not, there was a possibility that, as a result of our Snowbowl partnership, I'd placed the boy in the middle of a high-stakes survivor scavenger hunt where to outlast, outplay, and outthink your competitor might be the only thing between you and the Happy Hunting Grounds.

We made it back to the park and The Titan in less than two hours thanks to Sophie's NASCAR predilections. She and Taylor hurried up to the rooms to see if anyone was about, and I hurried to the registration desk.

"Has there been any word on Nick Townsend, the ten-year-old who is missing?" I asked. The clerk shook his head.

"I don't think there's been any change," he said. "Are you with that party?" he asked. I nodded.

"I'm registered at your hotel," I said.

"Would your name be Tressa?" he asked.

"It would be," I said. "Why?"

"I have a message for you," he said. "Someone dropped it off several hours ago and asked me to hand-deliver it to you and you alone."

"Was it a guy or a gal?" I asked.

"That I can't tell you," he answered. "I wasn't on

duty when they left it. I only arrived at four." He handed me the note. I walked over to the fireplace and opened and read it. My legs went all linguine with clam sauce on me. I dropped onto a bright red leather sofa and read the note once more, wondering what the hell I was going to do next. I read the note again.

> *The child is alive and safe. As long as you follow these instructions to the letter, he will not be harmed. Take the Grandview Trail at nine P.M. Bring the artifacts and clues. Come alone. Tell no one. You will be met along the trail. If these terms are not strictly complied with, the child will meet with an unfortunate accident.*

I checked my watch. Not much time to gather the items—not to mention my wits. I clicked off in my head the things I'd need. The clues and artifacts. Flashlight. Water and candy bars in case the kid was dehydrated or hungry. Shoes minus the blood scent so I wouldn't scream "Prey! Get your prey here!" as I traversed the dark canyon trail. An extra sweatshirt for Nick.

But most of all I'd need the mother of all spirit guides, the one, the only, the alpha and omega spirit in the sky watching my back.

I sat a moment longer collecting my thoughts and locating my backbone. I wondered what sage words of advice Duke would have for me now. I suddenly remembered a favorite quote of Wayne's that appeared on a collectible coffee mug I'd gotten several Christmases back.

"Courage is being scared to death, but saddling up anyway," he had supposedly observed.

That just about said it all.

I stood, strapped on my make-believe holster and

drew my pretend six-shooters and twirled them several times.

Do you know a gal by the name of Calamity Jayne hereabouts? I hear she's got grit.

I holstered my finger revolvers with a flourish. Showdown time.

I managed to evade Taylor, Sophie and Gram, figuring the Big Guy above the clouds was working overtime to assist me in my quest to bring Nick home safe and sound. I'd visited the gift shop again and purchased candy and water, a flashlight—a glow-in-the-dark number the clerk swore any child would have hours of fun with—a Grand Canyon Park canvas bag to place the clues and artifacts in. I also picked up park information on the various south rim trails. I slipped up to the room and changed into boots and black jeans and sweatshirt, and gathered the rest of the items I needed.

I checked my watch again, noted it was nearing nine, and I hurried out of the room, taking care to avoid the lobby area as I made my way out of the hotel and in the direction of the Grandview Trail.

My hand shook as I double-checked the location of the trail. I pulled the new glow-in-the-dark flashlight out and turned it on. Then turned it back off. The damned thing didn't glow at all. When this was over, I was so gonna get my money back.

I made my way along the steep trail, using the flashlight to illuminate my way. The literature put the trail end at 3.2 miles, at which time you reached a plateau of sorts. I picked my way along, wishing I had thought to buy one of those geeky pedometer thingies you wear to measure how much you walk—or, I suppose, run, if you have the inclination. That way I'd know how far I'd come and how far it was back to the hotel.

I huffed and puffed and wondered how Rick Townsend was going to react when he found out his nephew had been kidnapped because I'd caved to the mini-manipulator's coercion and taken him with me to retrieve that first clue. Or how Townsend would feel when he learned I'd kept my discoveries from him to give my credibility another shot in the arm. Or if he'd ever speak to me again if something happened to his nephew.

My eyes got blurry at this point, my nose a little drippy, my steps a little loopy, so I stopped to snuffle the snot back up and dab at my eyes with my sleeve. It was then I caught the sound of rustling in the underbrush ahead. I flipped off my light to cloak myself in the night until I noticed my hands were glowing green. For a moment, stories of little green men, alien abductions and top-secret military experiments flashed through my head like a bad B-movie reel, until I traced the source of the unearthly glow to the damned glow-in-the-dark flashlight that had decided to start glowing for all it was worth.

"Son of a sagebrush!" I said, sticking the flashlight in the waistband of my pants. "Figures. Piece of crap'd start working now," I muttered.

I took a few steps forward, stopped and listened. More steps. Stop and listen. Step. Listen. Step. Listen. Talk about she'll be coming round the mountain when she comes. At this rate, I'd be lucky if I made it round the next bend before dawn. Inspiring display of true grit.

I ventured forward a good fifty steps, slow and steady, the darkness of the June night settling around me like a heavy velvet curtain.

"That's good right there."

I heard the command up ahead and off to my right, and I grabbed my glow light, switched it on, and turned it in that direction, the beam shooting straight into the frightening yet oddly compelling features of the kachina mask. My knees began to knock together. Give me a set of spoons, stick a harmonica in my mouth, strap a couple cymbals to my knees and you'd have a freakin' one-woman Ms. Bojangles band.

"Do you have the items?" the masked man asked, and I finally found the neurological function to nod.

"Do you have the kid?" I said, amazed that my voice hadn't permanently amscrayed.

The figure shined a bright spotlight up and to my left. I tracked the beam with nervous dread. The beam stopped, resting on two figures on a steep, rocky cliff. My blood cooled in my veins and my body began to shake. Nick Townsend stood on the narrow edge of rock. Beside him, with an arm tucked around Nick's chest, the other covering his mouth, was a second masked figure, his face eerily similar to his partner's.

"How do I know the kid's all right?" I asked. "I can hardly see him from here."

The masked man calling the shots nodded at his associate. "Let him speak," he instructed, and Maniac Mask number two removed his hand from Nick's mouth.

"Nick! Are you all right?" I shouted to him. He hesitated for a second and then nodded.

"I'm okay," he said. "I want to go home now, though," he added, and I felt my control begin to slip. I bit my lip.

"I'll get you there," I said. "I promise."

"Enough talk!" Maniac Mask number one interjected. "Now let's get down to business so the boy can return to hearth and home healthy and unharmed."

"How is this going to work?" I said. "How do I know I can trust you?" I added.

"You don't," he said.

"Doesn't that pose a particular problem then?" I asked. "Because I'm not going to hand over the goods until you let the kid go and he's safely on his way," I said.

"In case you hadn't noticed, you're outnumbered," the Masked Menace pointed out. "So, I think I'll call the shots if you don't mind."

"Would it matter if I did?" I asked.

"Here's how it's going to go down," Mr. Death Mask said. "There's a dead tree about fifty feet directly in front of you. On the ground in front of that tree is a bag. You're going to place the artifacts and those ridiculous clues into the bag and zip it up. Then you're going to start walking backwards. You'll keep walking backwards until the boy joins you on the trail. Then you turn around and keep walking toward the hotel and you don't look back. Not ever. Got it?"

I went over the instructions in my head.

"Why do I have to walk backwards?" I asked. "How am I supposed to see where I'm going? What if I trip over something and fall? What if—"

"Just do it!" Mr. Mask yelled. I nodded.

"Okay. I'll do it," I said, "but I'll warn you right now the pace will be slower than a javelina on stilts because I'm wearing my Dingo slouch boots and while they're great for a spirited two-step, they aren't the best for backing up. You see, they're just a tad too large—they didn't have a half size smaller and I so didn't want to squeeze the tootsies in where they wasn't room and end up with bunions like my gammy, and, as a result, they slip off from time to time and my heels get caught up—"

"Silence!" the Masked One said, and I cursed the nervous blathering babble that tends to erupt from my oral cavity during stressful situations. Or when I've had one too many beers.

"Shutting up," I said, and walked in the direction the masked man's light pointed.

I stopped at the base of the dead tree, located the tan canvas zipper bag, and pulled my javelina backpack off my shoulders, unzipped it and drew out the smaller bag with the fruits of my treasure hunt inside. I placed the small bag in the larger one and zipped it up, and began to take baby steps backwards.

"That's it. Nice and easy. No tricks now."

I'd just come abreast of the rock formation where Nick and the second bad guy waited when I heard Nick yell.

"Let me go! Let me go! Stop!" I turned to see him scuffling with the figure beside him, attempting to kick him.

"Nick! No!" I screamed. "Don't!"

Nick suddenly broke free and disappeared, and the masked figure disappeared after him.

"Nick!" I screamed, and grabbed my flashlight and turned it on, running in the direction Nick had taken. "Nick! Hide!" I yelled. "Run and hide!"

I remembered the bag and turned in time to see the first masked man grab it and take off. I didn't consider going after the man with the bag. Nick was my only concern. I took off in the direction I'd last seen him, climbing up and over rocks and bushes. I stopped. It was so quiet. Too quiet.

I turned my glow light off and pocketed it.

"Nick?" I whispered. "Nick?"

A millisecond later, out of the underbrush I saw Nick run past, just below me. A tenth of a second after that I saw the masked man appear right behind him.

Taking no time to consider the consequences, I leaped down on top of the masked man, clinging to his neck with a death grip, gripping his midsection with thighs that were saddle-tested and bareback tough. I reached into my pocket and pulled out the glow light and started smacking him on his head, hard, squeezing his innards with my legs like a Siamese python.

"Dammit! Shit! Stop! Son of a bitch! Ow!"

The masked man tripped and we both hit the rocks hard, Mr. Mask II getting the worse end of the deal since I was on top. I didn't miss a drumbeat as I continued whacking the dude with my light. His mask came off. Long, black, shiny hair—that also smelled heavenly, by the way, but that's beside the point—spilled out of a ponytail holder and over his shoulders.

"Raphael!" I hissed. "I knew it!"

Boom! I whacked him one for scaring the flip-flops off Kelsey.

Boom! I whacked him one for stealing Sophie's designer bag.

Boom! Boom! I whacked him twice for making off with my chocolate cake.

"Stop! Tressa, stop! Stop!"

The high-pitched, boyish screams finally penetrated the haze of battle and I looked up.

"Nick?" I said, keeping my leglock and headlock in place.

"You've got to stop!" Nick said, and I noticed tears glistening in his eyes.

"Nick? Nick, what is it?" I asked, hoping to God he hadn't been standing there injured while I was whooping the tar out of Raphael. He shook his head and tears slipped down his cheeks.

"Stop! You've got the wrong guy," he said, and I stared up at him.

"Huh?" I asked.

"You've got the wrong guy," he said, wiping the tears from his face. "He's one of the good guys," he said, and pointed to the man I had in a death squeeze under me. "You let the bad guy get away."

Several seconds passed while I replayed Nick's words

in a head that badly needed a strawberry daiquiri with lots of rum and a long, lazy afternoon in a hammock on the beach. I turned the glow light on and illuminated the chiseled features (okay, some new chisel marks, thanks to me) of the man beneath me.

"Damn. You really wanted that chocolate badly, didn't you?" he said with a crooked—and bloody—grin. "Raphael Calderas, Special Agent, Law Enforcement and Investigations, National Forest Service," he said. "At your service. Or maybe I should say, 'at your mercy.'"

I shook my head. I betcha a bunch of shiny beads Little Hiawatha never had a day like this.

CHAPTER TWENTY

It took at least twenty questions and answers before I felt comfortable loosening up my hold on Special Agent Calderas. Admittedly it was hard for him to respond with my arm around his neck, but he managed to get his story across just the same.

And his story was as hard to swallow as most of mine.

Raphael, a.k.a. Special Agent Calderas, had been working undercover infiltrating a smuggling ring dealing in the theft and sale of Native American artifacts for more than a year. His informant, the man who had left the trail of breadcrumb clues, had been about to hand over conclusive evidence to S. A. Calderas that would expose the key players in the international trafficking of the historic artifacts but suspected the traffickers had become suspicious of him. To convince himself Agent Calderas was also on the up-and-up, he had devised his own vision quest to not only test the agent but safeguard the evidence as best he could with time running out.

"Arturo loved history," Raphael said. "He felt a deep

connection to this land and its people, and it physically hurt him to see it stripped of its riches and treasures and sold to the highest bidder. At the end, I could see him losing his grip on reality and I tried to pull him out, but he wouldn't listen. It was then he went off the deep end and decided to turn his obsession into a mixed-up scavenger hunt."

"What happened to Arturo?" I asked, wondering about the man who'd taken the time to write the clues and leave them behind.

Raphael looked over at Nick and then shook his head at me. I winced, getting the grim message.

"Arturo . . . disappeared," Raphael said. "But not before they found out he'd placed that first clue in the figurine you purchased. I was supposed to pick it up the day before you got to it, but I was working on the inside then and I couldn't break away until it was too late. By that time, they were also on the trail of the clues. Since I was working with them, I had to attempt to retrieve the item from you, as well. Which turned out to be harder than I expected."

"If you'd been successful, would this have been over way before now?" I asked.

He shrugged. "Either that or I'd be dead, too," he said. I winced again.

"Whitehead thinks you're one of the bad guys," I told him, and it was his turn to wince.

"The only way I could protect her was to lie to her. These people play for keeps," he said.

"And The Spiritual Boutique?"

"Most likely a front."

I told him about our visit to the boutique and our grisly discovery.

"Who are these people?" I asked, and he shook his head.

"We've identified a few but not the major players. Tonight was the first time they've let me into the inner circle. When I learned they wanted to snatch the kid here to use as leverage, I volunteered to do it, figuring I could make certain the boy would not come to any harm. There wasn't a long line of other volunteers stepping forward to put their heads on the block for a kidnapping charge, so I was given the job. Communication is done by an untraceable cell phone. I am told where to go and what to do when I get there. Up until now I have been pretty much an errand boy. Arturo was the one in the thick of the business. Names, dates, places, artifacts, amounts—he had access to it all. I had hoped his little quest would lead us to the indisputable evidence he promised before more treasures disappear, but it has been a wash so far. And without those artifacts and clues, we're back to square one," he said. "At least my cover is still solid, thanks to the young one's great acting and the protective instincts of a mother grizzly you demonstrated on my skull a few moments ago," Raphael said, rubbing his head. "I had to find a way to let the boy escape without attracting suspicion, so I coached him on how to get the better of me." Raphael winced. "He was an apt pupil. I am hoping my battle scars will gain me an insider's role now. I can go back all bruised and battered and that should solidify my bona fides with my compatriots."

"Bone of what?" Nick said, and I caught him rubbing at his eyes.

"Oh my gosh! I need to get the kid back!" I jumped to my feet. "His parents are probably apoplectic. His uncle has probably secured one of those sightseeing choppers by now to search for him. Dude, we've got to go," I told Nick, hauling him to his feet.

"Now remember, you two. Not a word about what

happened out here or what you have just heard, all right? We'll have you covered until you leave the area, so no need to worry about further problems," Raphael said, and bent down to shake Nick's hand. "I am really proud of you. You followed my instructions to the letter and you did an awesome job of kicking my ass," he said. "Well, you and your friend, here."

"But we lost the clues and artifacts for you," Nick said.

"It will be okay. We will still build a case," he promised and stood.

"You'll be careful, won't you?" I said. "Don't let what happened to Arturo happen to you. Okay?"

He nodded. "I shall be careful. You two better go."

I nodded. "Whitehead still loves you," I told him.

"I know," he said.

I reached down to take Nick's hand and turned to say one final goodbye to Raphael, but he was gone. I shook my head.

"People come and go so quickly here," I said, pulling Nick down the trail.

He giggled. "Oh, really, Dorothy?" he said. "I hadn't noticed."

A few seconds passed and his grip on my hand tightened. "I was really, really scared there for a while," he said, and I looked down at him.

"I thought you felt safe with Agent Calderas," I told him.

"It wasn't that. When the guy called Raphael and told him that they wanted *you* to make the trade, that's when I got scared."

I felt a tug at the old heartstrings. "Oh, Nick, that's so sweet!" I said, squeezing his hand back. "But you didn't need to worry about me. I'm pretty good at taking care of myself," I said, "despite what you may hear from your Uncle Rick."

Nick shook his head. "No, that's not what I mean," he said. "What I mean is when I found out they wanted *you* to do the trade, I was scared because I didn't think you would come," he said. I stopped.

"You what?" I said.

"I didn't think you would give up those artifacts to get me back," he said, looking at his feet. I stared down at him.

"Why would you even think such a thing?" I asked.

"Because you don't like me!" he said, looking back up. "You can't stand to be around me. You think I'm a hairy little troll with Frodo feet and an Orc personality," he accused.

"Hey, don't flatter yourself, munchkin. I think all kids are little trolls with hairy feet and nasty tempers," I said. "Not just you."

"You don't think Kelsey's a troll," he said. "Kelsey wouldn't have had to worry that you'd come for her."

I hesitated, and then knelt down and took both of Nick's hands in my own. "I came for you, Nick," I told him. "Nobody else. Just you."

His eyes began to fill with tears and I felt the sting of a similar emotion in my own peepers. I stood and cleared my throat in an *it's-cool* way. He did the same.

"So, are you going to have any trouble keeping Raphael's secret from your folks?" I asked Nick. He grinned.

"Are you kidding? I'm a kid. That's what I do," he said. "What about you?" he asked.

"I may need your help," I admitted. "I've got a genetic predisposition that results in the stretching of certain mouth ligaments, resulting in loose-lip syndrome," I told him.

"Huh?"

"I'm a big blabbermouth. I get it from my gammy.

As a result, I may require some help keeping my lips zipped. At least until we're safely on a plane. Then I'm bound for the high seas, matey!"

"I wish I could go on the cruise, too," Nick said. "But Kelsey and I have to stay with my Grandma and Grandpa Corbett. Mom and Dad said they needed a second honeymoon. They started kissing and hugging. Ugh. Gross."

I nodded. "I hear you," I said.

"What are we going to tell my folks about where I've been?" he asked.

"We'll just say you lost track of time and got tired and fell asleep along one of the trails, and you woke up and were making your way back to the hotel when I met you on the path," I said.

"Do you think they'll yell at me?"

I shook my head. "Probably not for a day or two, and by that time, they'll know the real story. They'll just be glad to have you back safe and sound, Nick," I told him. "But be prepared for a lot of hugging and kissing and slobbering all over you, okay? It'll be gross, I know, but bear with them. They've been scared, too."

He nodded. "Will Uncle Rick be happy you found me? Will he hug you and kiss you and slobber all over you, too?"

I looked down at the runt. Hmmm. I hadn't thought of that. Would he?

I reached in my bag and pulled out my Binaca and gave my mouth a couple blasts, and handed it to the kid.

"First rule of Indian scouting. Be prepared, kid," I told him. "Be prepared."

My gammy's wedding day dawned—way too early.

My predictions regarding Nick's reception when we returned had been, for the most part, accurate. The entire lobby exploded into cries of joy, howls of happiness, and hugs of hallelujah resulting in buckets of tears and a short, but stern, lecture on not going off half-cocked all by oneself.

Okay, so this lecture happened to be delivered to me by Ranger Rick Townsend with a lot of head rubbing, jaw-jumping, finger-pointing and very little of the hugging, kissing and slobbering Nick had suggested might await me, as well. Uh, except from his parents and my parents and my gammy and Joe and Taylor and Sophie. Even Gloria Grant, still around for the next morning's nuptials, joined in the upbeat mood of our party, giving me a tight hug and tipping a glass of bubbly in celebration. Both Nick and I had called it a night way before the party wound down.

I climbed out of bed, realized Taylor, Sophie and Gram had already gone down to breakfast, and went to shower, then realized I still had nothing to wear to the wedding and the ceremony was in three hours.

I padded to the bathroom and stopped. On the door was a simple but exquisite turquoise and white dress with nary a bow or ruffle to be found. There was a note attached.

> *T: Didn't think you'd remember to get a dress. Saw this and thought it might work. Hope it fits. I had Pops help me with the size. Can't wait to see you in it. And out of it.*
> *As always,*
> *Rick.*

I sat on the pot and proceeded to get my bawling out of the way. Hormones.

The wedding was set to take place in forty-five minutes. In a small but cozy private dining room, a sit-down meal had been set up. A table at the far end of the room had been set up to accommodate gifts at one end and the cake at the other. I gently placed the gift-wrapped Kookamunga on the table, hardly able to contain my anticipation at the upcoming unveiling. We'd be lucky if Joe didn't stroke out when he got a look at the frisky fellow who would be sharing digs with him and his lady love ''til death did they part.'

I patted the package.

"You deserve a rest, Kooky, ol' chap," I said, finding myself suddenly sentimentally attached to the dubious work of art. Or 'work of fart' as Nick Townsend referred to it.

At precisely ten we gathered in front of the impressive fireplace in the lobby of The Titan Hotel where Hellion Hannah and Joltin' Joe Townsend exchanged their written vows. There was an added sense of celebration and joy over the festivities due to Nick's safe return. Following the brief ceremony, champagne flowed and giddy laughter rang out as we gathered together in the private dining hall. My new step-grandpappy winked at me as I found my dinner spot and discovered Rick Townsend already seated to my left.

"Nice dress," Rick said. "Someone has excellent taste. Fits like a dream, too," he added, lifting a glass of champagne to me in a toast.

I raised my own glass. "To a man who isn't afraid to venture into the ladies' department on his own," I said. "Cheers!"

"Hear hear!" Townsend said, and we sipped our bubbly.

"They look happy, don't they?" he said, tipping his glass at our grandparents.

"They do," I agreed. "It's funny how after all this time and after each of them went down their own paths, they ended up back where they started. Back at the beginning," I said. "Where it once began." I sat for a moment, pondering my words. They seemed vaguely familiar.

Where it once began. Your quest ends where it once began.

"Your quest ends where it once began," I repeated.

The meaning of this final piece of the puzzle fell into place like the final section of a wigwam.

"Oh . . . my . . . spirit . . . guide! Kookamunga!" I screamed and jumped from my seat, the tablecloth catching in my belt and shifting everyone's dinner setting one place over.

"Tressa, what on earth are you doing? You're wearing the tablecloth!" my gammy yelled. "Stop!"

I yanked the cloth out of my belt and ran to the gift table at the other end of the room. I rummaged through the packages.

"He's gone!" I yelled. "Kookamunga's gone!"

"Oh, shit."

I attributed that observation to Rick Townsend.

"Okay? Where is he?" I said, checking behind the cake and on the floor and under the table. "He was here before the wedding, I saw him!"

"What are you looking for, Tressa?" my mother asked, coming to stand beside me.

"My wedding gift for Gram and Joe," I said. "It's gone!"

A sudden suspicion came over me, and I turned to confront Nick Townsend but Rick beat me to it.

"You didn't do something with Tressa's gift, did you, Nick?" he asked, joining me. "Because I remember you didn't particularly care for Kookamunga," Rick added. "So, how about it, Nick? Care to own up to anything?"

But Nick shook his head. "I didn't take it. I swear," he said. He looked over at me. "I wouldn't do that. Not after . . ." he stopped. "Well, you know."

I looked at him for a moment and nodded. "I know you didn't take it, runt," I said. "But who else besides invited guests and hotel staff were in here, and why would they take that particular item? Unless . . ." I stopped. "Unless they knew Kookamunga was more than just another phallic-friendly fellow," I said. "Which would mean one wedding guest had more on their mind than felicitations," I said.

"Who's this Kookymunga and who got solicited?" Gram demanded. "And where's this friendly phallus you're talking about?"

"Mother!" Aunt Kay said. "There are children present!"

"Gramma, where is Gloria Grant?" I said, stepping over to the empty place-setting that held her name card. "Wasn't she also invited to dinner?"

"Ain't she here?" Gram asked, and I shook my head. "Well, don't that beat all? She was at the wedding. Wasn't she?" Gram asked. "I confess. I had my eye on a certain handsome feller and didn't notice," she added.

"Oh, Hannah, that's nice of you to say," Joe said, blushing.

"I was talking about that tight-bunned bellhop," Gram said, sending me a gotta-keep-'em-on-their toes wink.

"So, who last saw Gloria Grant?" I asked.

"I visited with her before the wedding," Joe said.

"You did?" Gram asked, giving her new groom a sharp look.

"While I was waiting for my beautiful bride to come downstairs," Joe added. Gram nodded. "She got a phone call and stepped outside. I never saw her after that," Joe said. "Honest!" he added, looking at my gammy.

"You think Gloria Grant took that fertility god?" Gram asked.

I stopped and turned to look at her. "Gram? How did *you* know I got you a fertility god as a gift?" I asked, and her eyes darted back and forth. I took a step in her direction. "Did you open that gift early?" Another step. Still no eye contact. "You did, didn't you?" I accused.

"I figured what could it hurt?" Gram said. "It was for me anyway. And it was a good thing I did open it, 'cause the derned thing was broken," she said.

I frowned. "The bottom came off again?" I asked. "That's weird. I was pretty sure I'd fixed that," I told her.

She shook her head. "Naw. It wasn't the bottom. It was the winkie," she said. "I gave it a twist and the damned thing came right off in my hand," she said.

At hearing Gram's description of her erectile encounter, Joe Townsend's eyes began to glimmer. Whether out of fear or excitement, I was not about to speculate. I shook my head.

"So, you broke my gift to you and just wrapped it back up?" I asked. "And then what? When you opened it up in front of everyone, I would look like a dope for giving you a fertility god with a missing johnson?" I asked.

"What's a johnson, Aunt Taylor?" Kelsey asked.

"Ask your mother," Taylor said, putting a glass of champagne to her lips.

"Of course not, dear!" Gram said. "I wouldn't do that to you!"

"Okay, so what *did* you do?" I asked, totally confused.

"I went out and bought a boney-fide, Native American fertility fella. Saw it in a first-rate shop while I was dress hunting, with Kay. Wrapped that up instead," she said. "This one was a beaut, too. Sleek lines," she added. "Nice package, and I ain't talkin' 'bout the gift-wrappin' either."

I stared at her.

"You . . . bought . . . a different one?" I asked. "And you wrapped that one up? *That* was the one sitting on the table earlier today?" I asked.

Gram nodded.

"That bee-atch, Gloria Grant. I knew she wasn't any better than she ought to be," Gram said. "She was all over Joe here like an Indian blanket on a paint pony," she added.

"Listen, Gram," I said, walking up to her and taking each side of her face in each hand, smooshing her cheeks together. "This is very important. What did you do with the gift I bought you? The one you broke," I added.

"You're not going to try to glue it back together like you did the one you broke from my collection, are you?" she asked. ' "Cause he never was the same after that. You got his willie glued on cockeyed."

I shook my head. "I'm not going to try to correct any inadequacies, Gram," I said. "I just need to know where you put it. So. Where is it, ol' woman?" I said, pasting a strained smile on my face.

"I stuck it in the bottom of Craig's suitcase," she said, and I stared at her. "Kimmie wants a baby," she went on, "and I want a great-grandbaby while I'm still young enough to dandle it on my knee, so I figured what could it hurt? Maybe it could still do its thing even though its thing was detached."

I took a step back and dropped my hands from her face. I turned to my brother Craig.

"Quick! Craig! Your key card!"

"What the—?" Craig said.

"Give it to her!" Taylor screamed and jumped to her feet, finally figuring out where I was headed with this.

"Would someone please tell me—"

"Now!" Sophie roared, and Craig furiously fumbled for the key.

"For God's sake, here!" he said, holding it up. "Hell, did you tell everyone you wanted a kid?" he asked

Kimmie. "Might as well have Tressa put it in the *Gazette*."

I snatched the card from Craig's fingers, kicked off my heels, and ran barefoot out of the room, heading for the stairs at a high lope, Taylor and Sophie on my tail.

"Was it the champagne?" I heard Gram inquire as we ran.

We rushed to Craig and Kimmie's room and entered. I ran over to Craig's suitcase—the much smaller one, naturally—and started tossing his clothes on the bed. Near the bottom I discovered Kookamunga. It took several additional minutes to locate his winkie.

I sat on the bed, Taylor on one side and Sophie on the other.

I picked the winkie up and looked at it.

"Ugh. That is downright disgusting," Sophie said as we looked at it.

"Gramma said she twisted it and it came off," I said. "I wonder . . ." I reinserted Kooky's manhood in the opening and twisted one way and then the other. We heard a click and one side of the base cracked open.

"Would you look at that?" Sophie said. "I thought you said the base had fallen off. Wouldn't that mean you've seen inside the statue's base already?" she asked.

I examined the bottom of the statue. "I don't know. There's something weird about it. The dimensions don't add up," I said.

"You think?" Sophie quipped.

"Give me that," Taylor ordered, and took the statue. "You're right. There's a small space along the side here that isn't covered by that same base section," she said, hading it back to me. "A tiny, secret compartment."

We looked at each other. I took a deep breath and gently maneuvered the end piece so I could check in-

side. I reached my fingertips in and pulled out a tiny
object.

"Is that a flash drive?" Taylor asked.

I nodded and held it up, remembering Arturo's
words from the first clue: *He whose eye misses nothing is
aware of all that has gone on before and has made a record.*

"What do you suppose is on it?" Taylor asked.

I put it to my forehead in a Karnack the Magnificent, I'm-picking-up-vibrations gesture from the classic *Tonight Show* DVDs my dad still chuckled at. I
closed my eyes.

"I see one washed-up actress who is about to have
her greatest wish granted," I said. "I see this star . . . in
pictures once again," I predicted.

"Who? Gloria Grant?" Taylor asked.

I nodded and concentrated for a few seconds
longer. "Yes!" I said. "Yes! I see her! I see her! I see her
in . . . mugshots!"

That evening we sat in the gardens of The Titan as
Special Agent Calderas walked us through what had
transpired since we handed over the flash drive to
him. The files on the drive revealed not only a paper
trail that would lead investigators to the ring of artifact
thieves/smugglers and their network and customers,
but also provided actual video of the pillaging and
plundering of the historic sites in progress.

"Arturo used hidden cameras to capture the crimes
in progress," Raphael explained. "The ring of procur-
ers and purchasers is rather extensive, but we've got
some of the key players already in custody or under
surveillance.

"Gloria Grant?" I asked, and Raphael nodded.

"She had to find some way to support herself once
her career dried up," he said. "I feel her son most

likely talked her into starting a family smuggling business," he added.

I frowned. "Her son? I didn't even know she had a son. She never mentioned him," I said.

Raphael handed me a picture. "That's him," he said, and I stared at the photo.

"Son of a Skecher! That's Ozzy! My shoe fetish speed-dater from Numbers!" I yelled. "He admired my leather black half Calfy with the zippered sides and two and a half inch heels." I looked at Gram. "You know the ones. You borrowed them for the senior center New Year's Eve party," I added. "This guy lifted Sophie's designer bag?" I shook my head. "And I was certain you were the culprit."

"Not I," Raphael said. "It was Fabian."

I raised an eyebrow. Fabian, not Fabio?

"That's Fabian Carroll," he said, motioning to the printed photo. "Apparently Grant starred in a beach movie or two with an actor so-named a long time ago," he added. "Fabian here is your basic mooch, but not without intelligence. He organized the smuggling network and got the distribution setup. I imagine he also talked his mother into getting her spiritual adviser involved."

"Cadence? Have you found her yet?" I asked, and Raphael shook his head.

"No. Not yet. We found no body at The Spiritual Boutique, but I am fairly certain she is deceased. I suspect Fabio Carroll realized her allegiance to the ring of smugglers was ending and he had to kill her. It is my belief we will shortly discover her body buried at one of the illegal excavation sites," he said.

"Among the very artifacts and ancient relics she valued so much," I observed sadly.

He nodded. "From what we have learned so far, it

appears Cadence was pulled in initially because she desired the artifacts. In fact, we have discovered quite an extensive collection at her home. I think, however, when she began to realize how many of the artifacts were being sold and even leaving the country, Cadence had a change of heart and started to see this was not spiritually a good thing or the right thing for her, her business, or those who had left these gifts from the ages behind. However, backing out of a business this lucrative is clearly not without its own risk." He sighed. "Anyway, with the evidence we have and the cooperation we're receiving from Gloria Grant, I feel confident we have enough leverage to obtain a confession from Fabian Carroll. Ms. Grant seemed shocked to hear that her spiritual adviser had apparently met with foul play. Since she'll be looking for a deal, I think it's only a matter of time before we discover the truth."

"Poor Cadence," I said. "She should have seen it coming."

Raphael nodded.

"I'm still a little fuzzy on why Arturo chose Kookamunga to place the clues and the Flash drive in," I said.

Raphael looked uncomfortable. "I imagine he it was as safe a place as any to facilitate such an exchange," he said. "That no one would pay good money for such an . . . unappealing slice of Native Americana."

I winced. "Uh, could we keep that little observation between the two of us?" I asked.

He smiled. "Of course."

"So. You really are one of the good guys," I said. "Does Whitehead know?" I asked.

"She does now!" I heard, and looked up to discover Carena Whitehead had joined our little post-wedding party. "I can't believe you hid this from me all this time," she said to Raphael. "How could you?" she asked.

His gaze locked on the fetching Carena like mine does on a Meat Lover's pizza from Thunder Rolls Bowling Alley and a frothy mug of brewsky.

"How could I not?" he said. "You mean the world to me."

I watched the romantic interlude with alternating emotions. Fascination, envy, curiosity, and yes, a wee bit of voyeurism thrown in just to be naughty.

A heavy arm settled on my shoulders. "Looks like you scared one more man into the arms of another woman, eh, Calamity?" Ranger Rick observed, his breath warm on my cheek.

I watched the couple embrace. "I'll start to worry when I scare one into the arms of another man," I responded.

"I guess I owe you an apology, don't I?" Ranger Rick said, gaining my undivided attention.

"Just one?" I asked. "I could've sworn we were into triple digits by now."

He tucked a lock of hair that had escaped my tightly braided crown behind my ear. "You were right about Kookamunga," he said.

"Which means?"

Townsend smiled. "I was wrong," he admitted. "There. Happy? I guess it's still hard for me to reconcile the girl who stuffed my gym locker full of horse shit in high school with the ace cub reporter who keeps stepping in that same horse shit now but manages to somehow come out smelling like a rose. I'm sure you understand my difficulty."

I looked into his firewater-colored eyes. "I'm sorry. I missed that last part. I got stuck back on 'I was wrong,'" I said. "Frankly, I wasn't sure I heard you right."

"How about this? I learned a valuable lesson from you and Kookamunga, Calamity. One I hope will stay with me forever," Ranger Rick stated.

I licked my desert-dry lips. "Lesson? What lesson?"

His arms went around my waist and he drew me to him. "Never judge a book by its cover, of course," he said. "That there's more to a person than meets the eye."

I poked him in the chest. "Isn't that what I've been trying to teach you all these years about a certain blonde, Mr. Ranger, sir? That looks can be deceiving?" I said. "And you're just now learning that?" I shook my head. "And people think *I'm* developmentally delayed."

My recent exposure to a ten-year-old who initially had me rethinking the merits of aunthood, and to a Dances with Poles cousin comfortable enough in her own skin to shed her apparel and any shame associated with not being a single-digit dress size, had reminded me we were all works in progress.

"There's a lesson here for you, too, you know," Townsend said, gripping my arms.

I looked up at him. "Oh? And what might that be?" I asked.

He put a hand to my face and stroked my cheek with his thumb. "That beauty is in the eye of the beholder, of course," he said, looking into my wide-open eyes. "And right now? In the *arms* of the beholder, as well."

I stared at Townsend, replaying his words. If he was the beholder, that would make me . . .

I put a hand to his forehead. "Is the altitude getting to you? Or have you been hitting the peace pipe again?" I asked. "Because you're sure seein' things that aren't there, pilgrim."

Townsend grinned. "Maybe you're right," he said. "Maybe what I need is a long vacation at sea and someone to nurse me back to proper mental health." He put his hand on top of mine and pressed it against his forehead. "You know anyone willing to keep a lonely, ailing sailor company?" he asked.

"I suppose that depends on the compensation," I said with a teasing taunt.

"I've never had any complaints about my benefit package," he said, and I felt my cheeks grow warm. "And I guarantee you'll love the sign-on bonus," he added with a wicked wink.

"Guess what! Guess what!"

I was saved a hasty response by the excited arrival of Townsend's niece and nephew.

"Guess what, Tressa! We're going to Disney World!" Kelsey said, and I looked at her and her brother.

"Disney World? I thought the two of you were spending the week with your mother's folks while your parents were on the cruise," I said.

"We were," Nick said. "But after everything that happened, Mom and Dad decided that we needed to go on a family vacation instead. So, we're going to go to Disney World together! Yippee!"

"But won't your parents lose all their money?" I asked. "These cruise package deals are usually non-refundable."

"Grandpa Joe and Gramma Hannah found another couple to take Mom and Dad's place, and Raphael is helping to get all the paperwork through so it's like almost a done deal," Nick said.

I frowned. The only *couple* Joe and Hannah knew back home was Devlin and Kurt from the Uptown Florist and Gift Shoppe.

I looked at Townsend. He just shrugged.

I felt eyes on me—other than Ranger Rick's, that is—and I glanced over to find Joe Townsend looking at me and grinning from ear to ear like a demented witch doctor. I gave him my version of the evil eye in return, thinking he'd been uncharacteristically silent about my wedding gift.

When Joe started to hum the song about love being a ship on the ocean and not rocking the boat or tipping it over, I started to get a queasy, uneasy sensation in my stomach. What was the old fart up to, anyway?

Icy knuckles made their way up and down my backbone, reminding me that paybacks could very well be hazardous to one's health.

I took a long, shaky breath and watched as Joltin' Joe performed a snappy sailor's salute for my benefit.

Bring it on, old man, I mouthed. Bring it on.

Shiver me timbers, mates! Batten down the hatches! Looks like choppy waters ahead!

Anchors away!